T0129287

THE RAPTOR

"In every generation there are aberrations which are so horrible people can't bring themselves to think about them let alone speak of them. The result is that when they reoccur no one remembers, and they become new problems to be solved all over again."

JOHN MCWRAY

THE RAPTOR

Copyright © 2019 John McWray.

All rights reserved. No part of this book may be used or reproduced by any means, graphic, electronic, or mechanical, including photocopying, recording, taping or by any information storage retrieval system without the written permission of the author except in the case of brief quotations embodied in critical articles and reviews.

This is a work of fiction. All of the characters, names, incidents, organizations, and dialogue in this novel are either the products of the author's imagination or are used fictitiously.

Author Credits: J. Jefferey Phillips

iUniverse books may be ordered through booksellers or by contacting:

iUniverse
1663 Liberty Drive
Bloomington, IN 47403
www.iuniverse.com
1-800-Authors (1-800-288-4677)

Because of the dynamic nature of the Internet, any web addresses or links contained in this book may have changed since publication and may no longer be valid. The views expressed in this work are solely those of the author and do not necessarily reflect the views of the publisher, and the publisher hereby disclaims any responsibility for them.

Any people depicted in stock imagery provided by Getty Images are models, and such images are being used for illustrative purposes only. Certain stock imagery © Getty Images.

ISBN: 978-1-5320-7822-4 (sc)
ISBN: 978-1-5320-7870-5 (e)

Library of Congress Control Number: 2019909834

Print information available on the last page.

iUniverse rev. date: 07/20/2019

ACKNOWLEDGEMENTS

I must first extend thanks to the US Coast Guard for sending me to Portsmouth, Virginia. The people of Portsmouth made me feel welcome and "at home". It's a great place to live or visit, and you can actually go aboard the Lightship *Portsmouth*.

Heartfelt thanks go out to my wife, family, and friends who have put up with my revisions and waited for this story for so long.

Further thanks go out to my editor Krista Hill of L Talbott Editorial, who believed in my characters and my writing.

Finally, thanks to Philip Jefferson and Almyra Defrange until we meet again. Perhaps we'll catch up in Milwaukee…

John McWray

PROLOGUE

The phone rang, and Deward Dumont rolled over to look at the clock: 2:40 A.M.

"Damn it!" he grumbled. "It's my birthday. Can't they leave me alone?"

He thought about not answering but reconsidered—people would panic if they couldn't readily get in contact with the only mortician within a hundred miles of Morning Glory, Mississippi. He'd learned that when people are confronted with death, by God, they want it taken care of immediately.

Deward never really believed that he'd get through his birthday without a call, but did today of all days have to begin before 3:00 A.M.? A fellow doesn't turn eighty every day, but death is never convenient, unless possibly for the deceased.

"Dumont here," he growled into the receiver.

He listened to the long monologue and almost dozed off while the nurse was talking. No one ever offered a pleasant greeting, or asked him how he was doing, or ever had anything new to say. It was like an impersonal call to the trash man who is responsible for picking up human "uh-ohs" who have finally crumpled into a lifeless heap.

Person died of…(drone, drone)…at Morning Glory Community Hospital… (drone, drone)…see you in a little while….

After Deward hung up, he couldn't remember the name of the deceased, or if the nurse had even told him.

Oh well, it doesn't matter. I'm sure there's only one body, and since I'm the only undertaker....

He slowly and stiffly rolled to the other side of the bed and lowered his feet toward the floor before he tried to sit up.

"Ooh," he moaned as he raised up and let his lumbar spine catch up with his pelvis. He sat for a moment until his head cleared before turning on the bedside lamp and heading for the bathroom.

Glad I brought the hearse home—that'll save me thirty minutes.

Experience had taught Deward that driving the hearse home was a good policy, especially on days he was trying to lay low. Today, anything that saved him time left him a few more minutes to celebrate his eighty-year-survival. He needed some variety in an otherwise lonely job that provided a good living but also left him alone at times when a little company might have been nice.

The town of Morning Glory was also dead at 3:00 A.M., and as he showered, Deward considered how he might break the monotony of the trip to the hospital.

I'll run the light at the four-way—that'll show 'em.

A little civil disobedience is always fun at three in the morning, but the local police wouldn't care if he ran a red light. After all, he was the Angel of Death, sweeping souls into eternity, and the local law always gave him wide-berth.

He wet his face and lathered to shave, observing in the mirror the telltale signs of eighty long years: the deep wrinkles had been forged by times of want, war, living and dying, and the loss of his wife and most of his family. Deward had outlived them all. He had been born during the Spanish flu epidemic of 1879, and he'd always figured that survival at such an early age had made him resistant to a premature demise.

He got dressed and stiffly buttoned his starched, white shirt, and his arthritic fingers created a perfect Windsor knot in his tie.

I need some help...an apprentice. Gotta remember to call that school in Vicksburg....

He smiled—he'd be thinking the same thing a week from now when he still hadn't made the call.

His coat was last in his ensemble, but he opted to wait until he got to the hospital to put it on. It was Mississippi, after all: hot and humid.

Deward walked out to the new Cadillac hearse. The sight of it gave him a sense of pride and accomplishment. It was the only new asset he'd purchased in years, and he spoke to it as though it was a living companion.

"Morning, you black goddess. We have to go to the hospital to pick up a body."

He coaxed the vehicle to life: among the many features and extras of the sleek machine, the air conditioner was the most important this morning.

"Ah," he said as the cool air filtered through the vents. "That's it, baby. Keep us cool, 'cause we're rollin'."

Deward launched off into the Mississippi morning, and in less that two miles, after running the red light at the four-way, he turned onto his favorite short cut around the formidable Delta Land Swamp. It was a place where one would not want to stop in the darkness—untamed and untouched—but it saved him even more time.

The road itself was an engineering marvel, built around the intricacies of the swamp with the idea of disturbing as little as possible. It had been a success, but the black top had more curves than a king snake chasing a chicken.

"C'mon girl," he urged, "we're not afraid, are we? We've seen this swamp before."

He was watching the road as well as the edge of the water when, in his headlights, he saw a huge gator slide onto the shore.

"Look girl," he whispered. "That old gator's hungry, but he won't get us now, will he? No, he will not!"

After the short trek through the swamp, the bright, electric-blue letters appeared in the distance: "Morning Glory Community Hospital".

Deward slowly pulled the hearse around the semi-circular drive in front of the emergency room, looking to see if anyone was waiting for him. It was just past 3:30, and the old man didn't want to waste time going into the hospital to look for a delinquent morgue attendant. There was no one out front, and no one was waiting in the sally port leading into the ER.

"Damn it! They knew I was on the way," he groused.

The staccato of light in the rear-view mirror caught his attention: a large black man in disposable white coveralls was motioning with a flashlight for him to back into the alcove beside the emergency room.

Thank God. Deward slowly backed the long vehicle into the tight space that ended at a loading ramp. The only hint as to the purpose of this short alley was a steel door at the top of the ramp marked with the letter "M".

He got out and moved toward the rear of the vehicle, putting on his coat as he walked. Being well-dressed was a sign of respect for the person who had lived in the body he was coming to claim, and whose demise provided him a comfortable living.

"Morning, Larry," he mumbled as he opened both rear doors at the back of the hearse. "I thought that was you with the flashlight."

"Mornin' Mr. Dumont. Here let me help you."

Each man took a side of the collapsible gurney, slid it from the hearse and, as if rehearsed, snapped downward on his respective side allowing gravity to pull down the folded wheels. Each chose an end as they ascended the ramp, and Larry unlocked the heavy door. In a moment, they were inside.

The small room they entered served as the office for the morgue, and though it was a bleak area with brick walls, overhead pipes, and multiple unknown sounds and smells, it was immaculate. The furnishings included a small desk and chair, a second chair for a visitor, and a trash can. Larry kept the area in perfect order as evidenced by the neat arrangement of the various papers and forms on the desk.

Deward looked about…looked at these surroundings.

In all these years, I've never noticed how this is such a perfect, non-judgmental setting for the debarkation of the deceased from one existence to another. From life to death, from now to forever.

He snapped back into the moment and addressed his helper.

"How you been?" Deward inquired with as much cheer as he could muster at that time of day.

"Not too bad, sir. Been a good summer for the garden. Latisha's been pretty busy with the cannin' and all of that."

Deward nodded. "Great. If I had known I was coming over here tonight, I would have called ahead to ask you to bring some of your beans. That is, if you have some to spare, and you're selling them."

"Always got plenty for you, Mr. Dumont. Let me know early one afternoon, and I'll bring some with me. You can pick them up here, or I'll leave home early enough to bring them by your house."

"I wouldn't expect you to do that," Dumont answered. "I can just pick them up here."

"Sounds good," Larry agreed. "Just lemme know."

"By the way," Deward said with a chuckle, "I was so groggy when they called, I forgot to ask. Who is the deceased?"

Larry's expression darkened. "You really don't know?"

Deward shook his head and eyed the younger man warily. "No. I don't know. All I could remember was that I needed to pick up a deceased person here. I was still nearly asleep while I was listening."

Larry looked down at the floor.

"The deceased is Marguerite La Truse," he confessed.

Deward caught his breath. He felt like he had been hit with a sledge hammer. "What happened?" he asked when he recovered. "Did somebody kill her?"

"No sir, nothing like that," Larry replied. "She came into the emergency room this evening complaining of chest pain. I think Doc Ballard thought she had indigestion or heartburn, but while he was examining her, she just closed her eyes and died. Just that quick. Massive heart attack, Doc said."

"I'll be damned," Deward replied. "I guess we never know, huh?"

"Guess not," Larry agreed. "I would have thought she would live a long time. She's only forty-five, according to her papers."

"Quite young," Deward said. He secretly laughed at himself for thinking someone had murdered Marguerite La Truse, although, upon reflection, he could think of a dozen women who would have murdered her if they'd thought they could get away with it. They were jealous of her slender figure, ample bust, flawlessly tanned skin, perfect blonde hair—and the fact that she liked to share it all.

"She is a slut!" Deward would hear women say. "Whore" was another favorite.

Marguerite often entertained some of the local men at her home, and the rumor was the she was exceptionally gifted at entertaining. Several wives publicly called her a whore, but that wasn't technically true, according to strict definition. Marguerite never charged for her entertaining— but, she never seemed to want for anything either.

From groceries to her utility bills being mysteriously paid every month, she always seemed to have whatever it was she needed or wanted. Over time, it became a subject people just didn't talk about, and the women only hoped that their husbands weren't contributing to Marguerite's welfare on a weekly or monthly basis.

"Mr. Dumont," Larry interrupted as he extended a sheaf of papers, "are you alright?"

The old man glanced down. "Oh, yes. Sorry! The never ending paper work."

He sat down in the chair beside the desk and studied the papers for a few minutes. Everything was in order, and he signed the document that made it legal in the state of Mississippi to take possession of Marguerite La Truse's body.

"There," he said finally, "we've complied with the law. "I noticed there is no next of kin noted. I guess she'll be another charity case."

"I guess so," Larry agreed, "but you always said you'd take anybody regardless. You are gonna take her, ain't you?"

"Of course, I'm gonna take her. After all, she is one of Morning Glory's more prominent citizens. As such, I owe it to her to do the best I can, and besides, she will be worth a fortune in goodwill and reputation."

"Hmm," Larry agreed as he pushed the button on the wall. Two large stainless-steel doors swung open, and they rolled the gurney into the morgue.

There were two autopsy tables on the right in front of deep stainless-steel sinks replete with hoses and high back walls to catch whatever got out of control. Four overhead lights illuminated the room, and above them was a large exhaust fan which ran constantly. This helped control the room temperature as well as unwanted smells. A simple railing at the back of the room cordoned off the holding area from the rest of the morgue. On the left was the large freezer unit with separate drawers for bodies awaiting transfer to other places. Larry opened the proper drawer, and Deward thought he detected a slight gasp from his companion.

Marguerite was nude, and the old man quickly covered her with the sheet and blanket from the gurney.

"I guess they can't afford to lose gowns," he complained, "but it's damned disrespectful to have folks in here like this."

"Yes sir," Larry said, "I've complained to the administrator, but he aint done nothin'."

"Well, maybe he will," Deward threatened, "if I report this to the State Board. This isn't actually illegal, it's just damned disrespectful."

They lifted Marguerite over to the gurney, and Larry lovingly tucked the blanket up under her chin. He seemed pensive.

"Lord 'a mercy," he sighed, "she is one beautiful woman. A lot of us is gonna miss her. Mr. Dumont, I gets off in about an hour. I'll come over to your place, I mean, if you need help unloading her."

"Thanks, Larry, but that's not necessary. The loading ramp over there is level with the back of the hearse so all I have to do is roll her out and roll her in."

Deward sensed that Larry didn't want to let her go, but he really didn't need help at the funeral parlor. Besides, Larry's motives might be leaning toward the kinky side of morbid, and that was the sort of thing Deward did not tolerate.

They rolled her out of the morgue, down the ramp, and into the hearse.

"Thanks, Larry," the old man offered. "I swear, you're the only one who ever has the papers in order. I'm always relieved to see you on duty. I'll call about those beans."

"Yes, sir, thank you Mr. Dumont. That'll be good. Anytime."

Deward got into the hearse and started around the semi-circular drive toward the main road. As he pulled away, he caught a glimpse in the rearview of Larry standing on the ramp in front of the door marked only with the letter "M". He had to concur with his helper's observations.

She was one beautiful woman, and a lot of us will miss her.

By 4:35 A.M., Marguerite La Truse lay on the stainless-steel table in the embalming room of Dumont's Funeral Parlor. She couldn't hear the ticking of the large grandfather clock in the foyer, or the incessant *drip, drip, drip* of the faucet in the restroom across the hall. She couldn't hear the low-pitched hum of the freezer, which sat in the utility room just beside the back door, nor could she hear the padding of footsteps that was growing louder.

She couldn't hear, and neither could she see. She couldn't see the dim glow of the light that filtered in from the family room adjacent to her suite, and she couldn't see the large sarcophagus fly which, after sneaking into Dumont's on a spray of flowers, now rested on the tip of her nose. Marguerite La Truse could not see, hear nor feel. Marguerite La Truse was dead.

He stared at her form for several minutes, excited by the sculpture of her contours that hinted at her nudity as she lay beneath the white sheet. He had seen her without clothes before—when she invited him in to "play" with her, as she called it—but somehow the throbbing he felt now was much more intense. There was also a pressure in his head, mostly behind his right eye, that he had never felt before, and though it was slightly painful, it was also delicious.

With a shaking hand, he pulled down the sheet and gazed into her opaque blue eyes. He pressed his cheek to her cold face and kissed her, groping her as he stared into the lifeless orbs.

This was a strange final chapter for a woman who had spent her entire life entertaining men in every sensual way imaginable. Marguerite had claimed to be from France, and many of the things she did for the local men were touted as being French in origin. But, in 1959 Morning Glory, Mississippi she could have convinced most of the local gentry that President Eisenhower had been born on the banks of the Seine.

Somehow, he didn't give a damn about any of that. He loved Marguerite—and now, here she was, like this. It wasn't fair: he was beside himself with feelings he had never had before.

He explored her body from lips to toes, finding her coldness much more exciting than her former warmth. He turned her body over and examined it for several minutes before turning it back.

Grammy would not like this: if she were to catch him, the punishment would be beyond endurance. She was snoring when he crept down the back stairs to the funeral parlor, so he felt reasonably safe. This was not the first visit he had made in the wee hours, but until tonight it had been a simple matter of self-preservation. He had some understanding that his actions weren't normal, but when your Grammy locks you in a closet for several days with no food, you learn to forage for whatever is available. Besides, he had never taken more than he could eat from the basins in the embalming room, and certainly no one ever missed what he took. It was all going to the incinerator, anyway.

He peered lovingly into Marguerite's eyes as he felt a strange and overwhelming sensation wash over him. It had something to do with the pressure in his head, and the feeling that yet another person he loved had left him. He likely could never have described the feelings he had on that August morning: anger, lust, nausea…arousal.

He raked through the items on the stand beside the table until he found just the right thing: the razor-sharp blade whispered to him. He slashed again and again until he felt the warm, sticky fluid fill the crotch of his jeans. He was ten years old.

At 9:00 A.M., when Deward Dumont walked into the embalming room, he wished he had never gotten up that morning. Any dreams of a birthday celebration evaporated like frost in the Mississippi sunshine.

"Holy God!" he breathed into the phone as he listened to the pulsating ring to the sheriff's department. When they finally answered, they told him they had never heard of such a thing, and they referred him to the State troopers. The troopers referred him to the State Bureau of Investigation, and the agents arrived from Jackson in record time. They got to work immediately.

"Mr. Dumont," began the older of the two men, I'm Special Agent Cleveland, and this is Agent Bartel. We're here to investigate the happenings in your funeral parlor."

Deward shook their hands in succession. The men were well conditioned, and they had the spit-and-polish look of professionals.

"Damnedest thing I've ever seen," Deward commented as he motioned toward two chairs while he took a seat on the couch.

"Mr. Dumont," Cleveland began, "let's see if can get through this with you before we do an inspection of the crime scene."

Deward looked into the agent's steely eyes and was suddenly struck with the realization that his funeral parlor was indeed a crime scene.

"Relax," Cleveland offered, and Deward tentatively leaned back against the soft sofa cushions. "I'm looking at the report you called in," Cleveland went on, "and I was wondering if the mutilated corpse is a local person?"

Deward blinked as he tried to refocus on the task at hand. "Yes," he replied. "She had been in Morning Glory for a few years, uh, since right before the Korean War."

Agent Bartel began jotting notes in a small, loose-leaf binder, and it occurred to Deward that anything he said might be repeated back to him sometime—maybe in a court of law—so he decided to speak cautiously.

"Well, this is such a small town," Cleveland continued, "how well did you know the deceased?"

"Hardly knew her at all," the old man lied. "She was what one might call 'local color'. You know, the type of character you don't really know, but you feel as if you do."

"*Oh*," Cleveland responded with too much emphasis for Deward's liking. "And what does that mean?"

Deward scratched the back of his head and looked at the floor. "Well, ah, she was what, ah, well...some of the locals referred to her as a loose woman. I knew her well enough to speak to her in public, and she was always very pleasant and charming." He shrugged, "She was respectable enough, I suppose."

Cleveland nodded. "Uh huh—a loose woman, you say? Would you elaborate on that a little?"

Deward began to wish that he had just kept this whole thing quiet, and let it go at that. This interview was cutting into his work time. He had already lost the morning, and Marguerite would take longer than usual to prepare. Also, there was a new intake that would require priority as there would be immediate funeral arrangements to be made. The old man decided to confess almost all he knew in an attempt to end this intrusion into his work day.

"Officers," he began, "Ms. La Truse entertained some of the local men at her home on a regular basis, but frankly it had become an accepted practice, overall."

"I see," Cleveland replied with a blank expression. He leaned in. "Are you saying, sir, that she had sex with some of the local men on a regular basis?"

Deward gulped. "Yes, sir, that was the rumor."

"Then you don't have any personal knowledge of that practice?"

Deward was mortified as he silently prayed that Marguerite's infamous diary was just a myth.

"Goodness no!" he replied with a half-hearted chuckle. "At my age, I couldn't have sex with any woman, even if I wanted to. Gentlemen, I am a respected businessman, and I am a deacon in the Baptist Church. It would not be fruitful for my business or my soul to have a carnal relationship with such a woman."

Both agents nodded.

"Do you know if Ms. La Truse had any relatives?" Cleveland asked.

"Not that I'm aware of. She always said that she was born in France, but some of the folks around here said that they'd known her family in Louisiana years ago. Said she was nothing but a coon-ass Cajun from Baton Rouge. There was no next of kin listed on her hospital records."

"Then who is paying for your funeral services?"

"Wha...who?" Deward stuttered. "Well, eh, it hasn't been determined that anyone is paying. Gentlemen, this is a small town where people care for each other, and I do a great deal of charity work. It's the Christian thing to do."

Bartel nodded as he wrote in his notebook.

Deward noticed that Cleveland's attention had drifted, and he followed his gaze toward the court-yard next to the office.

"Who is that?" he demanded.

Deward leaned so that he could see out of the window.

"Oh, he lives with his grandmother in the apartment over the funeral home. That's where I lived when I first came to town, until I got established, anyway. It's not very big, and most people don't want to live over a funeral home. I let Mrs. Cassidy have it for nearly nothing since her daughter, the boy's mother, committed suicide, and his dead-beat dad took off. I better shoo him away. His grandmother is very strict on him."

"Hold on," Cleveland demanded. "Bartel, ask that little fellow to come in here for a minute."

Bartel was back momentarily with a bashful little boy.

Deward stood and motioned for the boy to sit beside him.

"Tad," he explained, "these men are policemen. They just want to talk."

Deward turned to Cleveland.

"Is this legal?" he asked. "I'm not his guardian or anything like that."

"It's ok," Cleveland assured him, "we're just talking here, no big deal."

"Well," Deward countered, "I'm going to sit here with him. Just in case there are any questions later."

The boy sat at the end of the couch, and Cleveland studied him for a moment.

"Son," he began, "how's your summer been?"

"Good," the boy replied. "I've been fishing a lot, and Grammy let me go to the carnival with some older kids."

"Did you like the carnival?"

"Yes, sir. I really liked it."

"What did you like most about it?"

"Well, I liked the animals and rides, but I really liked the House of Horrors."

"Oh, I think that would scare me too much," Cleveland chuckled. "Weren't you afraid?"

"Sort of, but it's always important to remember what is real and what isn't. When I do that, I'm not scared at all."

"I guess," the agent replied with a grin. "Say, were you and your grandmother home last night?"

"Yes, sir."

"Yeah, and did you see or hear anything out of the ordinary?"

"No, sir. Grammy makes me go to bed at eight, and I don't remember anything until I woke up this morning."

Cleveland smiled and tousled the boy's sandy hair. "Ok, pal. We were just wondering if you heard or saw anything."

Bartel had been writing as fast as the boy had been talking.

The boy looked back and forth between Deward and the two agents. "May I go?" he asked.

"Sure, you can, son. Run along and play."

Cleveland eyed the boy as he ran out the door. "Great kid," he said when the outer door slammed. "Of course, we'll have to speak to the grandmother as well."

"Of course," Deward agreed.

"Mr. Dumont," Cleveland said finally, "do you know of anyone who would want to do this? I mean, did Ms. La Truse have any real enemies that you know about?"

Deward shook his head. He thought for a moment about Larry's strange reaction to Marguerite's death but decided he was not capable of doing anything of that nature—especially to Marguerite. He answered the agent with cautious amusement.

"Maybe half the wives in town, but I can't think of anyone in particular."

The agent was thoughtful for a moment. "Did you ever hear of anyone threatening to harm her, or even any rumors of anything like that?"

"No, but as I have pointed out, I'm a church official, and folks don't usually engage in that sort of conversation with me."

There were more questions for which there didn't seem to be any answers, and then the officers asked to see the crime scene. They told Deward to carry on his usual routine, but since they were in his workshop, he couldn't do that. Instead, he went to the kitchen and put on a pot of coffee. He had just finished a cup when Cleveland and Bartel entered. It had been less that twenty minutes.

"Mr. Dumont," Cleveland said, "a word if you please."

Deward followed the men back into his office an took a seat behind his desk. The agents remained standing. Deward wondered what they had planned after viewing the horror scene in the embalming room.

Cleveland quickly put his mind at ease.

"We've seen all we need to see," the agent began. "Obviously, a crime has been committed, but under the circumstances we're going to soft-pedal this. What I mean is that, while Ms. La Truse might have had some enemies, I don't think they were killers or anything of that sort. I mean, this appears to be a person who would take the opportunity to get even if they thought they wouldn't get caught. Our feeling is that it was probably one of the local women taking out her jealousy on the deceased, and since the victim was already dead—and there are no known relatives, it seems the events are moot. It's a victimless crime. Although, I can't imagine someone doing something like this out of a jealous rage, it's the only logical explanation. We've seen enough, and of course we'll speak to the lady upstairs—what's her name, the grandmother?"

"Oh, Mrs. Cassidy," Deward replied, "but listen, please don't tell her that the boy was down here."

"Don't worry," Cleveland assured him. "We won't rat on the kid. He's be the last person we'd want to be involved in any of this. We'll speak to the grandmother, and we'll ask the sheriff to collect anything you may discover regarding the body. In a nut-shell, we're going to close this thing before it even gets opened. This sort of event doesn't need to be publicized—a full investigation would be a waste of the taxpayers' money, considering the lack of evidence and no witnesses. Of course, we'll write it all up, so if anything like this ever happens again, we'll have a foundation for a full investigation."

Cleveland extended his hand, and Deward shook it.

"A pleasure to meet you, sir," Bartel added as he also offered his hand. "Sorry about all the disruption."

"Not at all," Deward lied.

The agents went upstairs, and Deward saw them depart a few minutes later.

It took all of two days and Deward's best efforts to make Marguerite La Truse look like the vixen she had been in life. He had to do considerable reconstruction of her face, and he used a lot of make-up; but, since she had always worn a lot of make-up, no one was surprised when they saw her in the chapel on Friday.

Deward chose a casket that opened only enough to allow mourners to see her head and upper body. That way, he managed to avoid having to remove all the various foreign objects that had been shoved into her vagina and rectum, some forced all the way into the abdominal cavity. He figured it was easier to take the loss on a few instruments than to have a closed casket service-which would have started a riot in Morning Glory.

Surprisingly, there were a lot of women present at the viewing and, not so surprisingly, so were a lot of men. Marguerite La Truse was the center of attention and no one, including Deward, noticed the little boy standing just behind the choir loft during the service….

He looked at Marguerite and felt the little twinges behind his right eye. His gaze swept from her waxen face to the drapes hanging in the windows. They were not hung evenly. For the first time, he noticed how dingy and decrepit the chapel was. The carpet was stained with grime, and there were cobwebs in the little shelf under the pulpit. The chairs in their straight rows did nothing to restore order. The place was a sham.

His friend Marguerite was gone. Mr. Dumont, the preacher, the organist, the singer, the florist—all were profiting from her death. He consoled himself that he and he alone was the only one who knew Marguerite: inside and out.

This had been his proving ground, and he had passed. He knew who he was, and he knew where he was going. He even knew how he would get there: by choosing a profession that would allow him many hours with the Marguerites of the world. His attention was drawn back to the service by the drone of the organ. *Amazing Grace how sweet the sound....*

Grammy's favorite tune, the one she hummed whenever she hurt him—but he no longer had to succumb. He had already devised a plan to kill her. He smiled and reached into the pocket of his jeans to finger the small leather pouch where, nestled in soft, cottony darkness, were the opaque blue windows to Marguerite La Truse's soul.

CHAPTER 1

GERRARD JOHNSON WAS the supervisor of the grounds crew at the Portsmouth, Virginia Memorial Cemetery. He was an average-size man, with strawberry blond hair, faded, poorly done tattoos, and a nasty scar that ran down the left side of his face. It went from just below the hairline on that side all the way across his nose down to the angle of his jaw on the right. It bespoke a man with a short temper and about an average IQ on a good day. At the moment, he was watching in amazement the spectacle going on just down the way from his warm hideout in the maintenance shed.

There was no lamb-like gentleness on this first day of March, 1997, and the graveside service he was observing was miserable. The wind was driving the rain sideways and had snapped the tarpaulin erected to shelter the grieving family. The priest's words were drowned out by the storm's ferocity, and when the ceremony concluded, the majority of mourners made a hasty exit, hunkering down under their umbrellas. A few friends lingered, however, for reasons God only knew. *Dumb bastards!*

"Maybe I can get one of them to drive this backhoe for me, and I'll go get a drink and get warm," Gerrard grumbled to no one.

Almost as if they had heard his words, the remaining faithful began to disperse toward shelter of their vehicles – everyone except for one gentleman who had been standing back from the others. The wind's force intensified ripping and tearing the flags on their poles, yet the man who had pulled up the hood on his slicker, did not retreat.

1

Johnson had noticed him earlier and thought he looked familiar, like someone he had seen on TV. *Maybe he knows the deceased.*

The deceased was Susan Brownley, and her family had already erected her grave marker, which lacked only the date of her death. She had died slowly over the past couple of years with ovarian cancer, and her demise was a relief to all who knew and loved her. Being relieved led to pointless guilt over being relieved—hence the hangers-on at the graveside.

Johnson drove the backhoe over to the sight and reversed the noisy machine. He lowered the scoop and pulled forward until he could see it was full of mud. He then raised the scoop and pulled forward until the load was directly over the mouth of the grave where he dumped it. Since the family hadn't been able to afford a vault the wet earth fell onto the casket with an ominous thud.

Four more of these, and I'm outta here. He smiled as he thought about warm, dry clothes, a stiff drink, and a hot woman.

The wind had increased to just under gale force, but the mystery man, who had moved up the road away from the grave, had not abandoned his vigil.

"Fuckin' idiot," Johnson grumbled, but then he reconsidered. *I'd better be careful. The bastard might be moonlighting for the Commonwealth. Probably some sort of inspector.*

After the fifth pass with the backhoe, Johnson jumped to the ground and made a great production of placing the drenched flowers and wreathes around the grave in what he considered to be an aesthetic arrangement. He sloshed over the remnants of the torn tarp as he shouted orders to his crew who had appeared like hermit crabs on some deserted shore. He directed them to do everything in accordance with the cemetery's license, and when they had performed to his satisfaction, he shivered as he looked toward the stranger.

Take that, you bastard! Report this to the Commonwealth!

As if he had read Johnson's thoughts, the man turned and started walking toward the back gate of the cemetery. Johnson watched closely until he vanished among the trees and tombstones, and his shoulders sagged with relief when the stranger finally disappeared.

He looked around at his scraggly, rain-soaked crew, hoping that, despite the inclement circumstances, they looked neat enough for an official inspection.

"Ok, boys!" Johnson yelled over the subsiding gale. "That's it for today, but tomorrow's going to be a long one too. We have five funerals that I know about, which means five grave openings, and if this weather doesn't break, you may have to dig a sixth one for me."

"Well, boss. You lush!" someone called out. "At least we won't have to bother getting you embalmed."

"Fuck you!" Johnson shot back. "If you had any brains, you'd be driving this backhoe instead of using a shovel."

The men laughed and joked among themselves as they wandered away.

"Jerk-offs," Johnson complained as he pulled the machine into the combination garage-storage shed. He turned the key to the "Off" position, and the tired engine sputtered intermittently before it died with a loud backfire.

"I gotta get this thing tuned up," he griped as he climbed down. He wiped the water from his eyes and popped the hood so he could check the ever-low dip stick.

"Bastards!" he cursed under his breath. "I've told them to have this thing looked at by a real mechanic. How the hell do they expect me to keep it running?"

Johnson stalked toward the back to see if he could locate just one more quart of oil. He had just turned on the light over the supply locker when he heard the door of the shed open and immediately slam closed.

He turned to face the front of the building. "Ben?" he called out. "I'm back here at the locker."

He expected to hear the slightly shrill voice of the cemetery manager, but instead there was silence.

Johnson called out again, only louder. "Ben? I'm back at the supply locker!"

Still no reply.

That snotty son-of-a-bitch, checkin' up on me, and now he wants me to come up front. God forbid he should have to walk back here and get his nice suit dirty.

Johnson snatched the last can of oil from the locker and walked to the front of the shed. When he came out into the garage area, he stopped short. The mystery man from the graveside stood before him.

"Oh, hey," Johnson greeted the man, his eyes wide with recognition. "I thought I knew you, but I wasn't sure until now. Why the hell were you standing in that downpour? I would have gladly let you observe from here in the shed."

The man did not reply.

Johnson chuckled. "Ok, ok. Old Gerrard's figured this out. You're working for the Commonwealth of Virginia, aren't you?"

The man remained standing where he was, saying nothing. Johnson became irritated beyond his shallow limits.

"Look, what the hell do you want? he demanded. "I've got Molly and a drink waiting for me, plus I've got to work on the damned equipment before I can leave. I don't have time to stand here fuckin' around with you, State Inspector or not!"

The man reached slowly into his inside coat pocket and retrieved a folded piece of paper. He extended it toward Johnson, who moved a step closer and sneered.

"Oh, I see. You gotta have me sign some form or other to show that you were here, and that we talked. Well ok, then. Anything for the good old Commonwealth. You scratch my back, and I scratch yours, right?"

The man smiled and nodded as he lay the paper on the oily work counter.

Johnson stepped up to retrieve it as there was a blur of movement and a stabbing pressure in his chest. He looked down in horror at the fourteen-inch bayonet as it was slowly twisted and withdrawn from his punctured heart.

"You bastard!" he gasped. "You've killed me!" Johnson fell back panting into the muddy scoop of the backhoe. *"Why?"*

"Because you know who I am," came the reply, "and because you don't matter."

Johnson, with blood-tinged mucus oozing from his mouth managed to struggle to his knees. He reached toward his attacker.

"Go to hell!" he gurgled.

"Oh, my stupid, stupid friend," the man replied, "we already live there, didn't you know?"

Gerrard Johnson fell face-first onto the concrete floor. He was still there hours later, unaware that the cemetery was under siege.

The rubber boots made a thumping sound as a dark figure moved over the same path he had walked earlier in the day. Black clouds raced across the moon like crows evacuating a cornfield at the sound of a shotgun blast. It had turned colder, and the phantom pulled the knit watch cap down over his ears as he approached Susan Brownley's grave.

"Here we are," a child-like voice echoed off the mausoleums.

The collapsible shovel came out of the back pack, and the sound of digging in soaked earth filled the darkness. It was a twenty-five-minute concert which ended in a dull thump.

"Yes! Here we are my dear," the excited voice whispered.

With his head ducking below ground-level, he switched on the spelunker's lantern and adjusted the strap so that the light was perfectly positioned. He used the shovel to break the seal on the casket lid. Clods of mud slid off the sides as he raised it to reveal the body of Susan Brownley.

"Hello, sweetie. Sorry to drop in unannounced, but I didn't think that you would mind. Anyway, I saw your obituary with your religious affiliation, and I know they didn't embalm you. You understand I needed to get here before our creepy-crawly friends got you first. It's also nice they didn't have to put you in a vault."

The scalpel blade reflected the moonlight as it went to the cadaver's eyes. They came out easily.

"There, there," he whispered, "I'll enjoy these now, much more than you will."

Susan's eyes joined Gerrard Johnson's in the leather pouch.

"Self-abuse, self-abuse," an old woman's voice cackled, "that will make you feeble-minded."

She giggled as the trembling hand unzipped his pants and stroked him slowly.

After a few moments, the same hand took on a practiced steadiness as it picked up the scalpel and made an incision from the top of Susan's breastbone all the way to her pubic bone.

"I'm glad they didn't ruin you with embalming fluid," he whispered.

The rib spreaders came out and were placed so as to force the body open. He carefully scanned the body down to the pelvis, which he opened further with the sharp blade. With a little probing, a large ovarian tumor appeared like a rabid bulldog from under a hedge.

"Oh, Susan!" he said apologetically. "You were a sick one."

He excised the tumor and examined it closely.

"I don't think I'll keep this," he whispered, tossing it into the mud beside the casket.

"As a matter-of-fact," he continued, "I don't think I want anything from in here."

He gathered his instruments and shovel, turned off the lantern, and scrambled out of the grave, leaving it, the casket and the body open for the world to see.

"Goodnight, Susan," he whispered as he jogged off down the path to the warmth of his car.

CHAPTER 2

THE PHONE WOKE him up. "Palachi here," he groggily answered.

"*Dr. Palachi,*" came the all-too-familiar voice, "*this is Pherson, down at the Precinct. We just got a call from a patrol car out at Memorial Cemetery, and it appears they have a murder victim and a mutilated corpse—and, they're not the same person.*"

By this time, Martin Palachi had gotten his six-foot frame out of bed and pushed his brown hair out of his eyes. His football player physique had begun to slip with age, but he was still an imposing, muscular man.

"Oh, God!" he groaned. "Ok, Pherson. I'm on it."

The medical examiner hung up and immediately set in motion the round-robin call system he used in just such emergencies.

"*Hello,*" came the sleepy voice.

"Dixon, this is Dr. Palachi."

"*Yes, sir,*" the voice replied, more alert this time.

"We have a situation out at Memorial Cemetery, and we need to roll now. I'll fill you in when you get here."

"*Right, Doc. I'm on the way.*"

Dixon would call the next man on the list, who would call the next man, and so forth until all six investigative techs had been contacted. Then Dixon would pick them up in the mobile crime van, with Dr. Palachi being the last stop. It worked well—there were never any excuses.

Forty minutes later, when the team rolled into Memorial Cemetery, they were greeted on the porch of the office by the grounds crew and a distraught manager who was not happy about being called in at such an hour. Palachi raised his hands in an attempt to stop everyone from talking at once, but he went unheeded until a voice broke in from behind him.

"You people shut the hell up," the voice demanded, "or I'm gonna run you all in—even the dead ones!"

Palachi laughed as he turned to greet his old friend. "What's the matter, Jeff? Miss your coffee on the way?"

"No, I just miss my sleep," Detective Jefferson replied as he walked up. "What are you thinking here, Palachi? I assume out of this chaos there's a murder victim somewhere?"

"Yeah, Jeff. I think from what I've heard so far there's a murder victim in that shed over there, and a grave that's been opened. The grounds crew discovered the murder, and the patrolmen found the grave and a mutilated body."

"Got it," Jefferson replied. "I'll work with the group that found the murder victim, and you can chase whatever happened to that corpse."

Palachi nodded. "Perfect."

Jefferson turned back to the group huddled on the porch, and Palachi watched in his usual amazement as his long-time friend took charge. Jeff was not a large man, but his countenance demanded respect; his carriage suggested years of martial experience. His thinning hair was neatly combed back, and his beard was sculptured to the angle of his face.

"Listen up! I'm Lieutenant Philip Jefferson, Homicide, and I want to talk to each of you about your involvement in finding the body in the shed. I don't wanna hear about the body at the grave, your grandmother's cat, or your hemorrhoids. Let's just concentrate on the body that's in the shed, shall we?"

Several hands went up, along with a generalized murmur.

"Hold it!" Jefferson demanded. "I don't want to hear anyone talking except the individual I'm speaking to directly. Got it?"

There was again silence as Jefferson patted the bulge protruding from under his left arm.

While Jefferson was arranging his witnesses, Palachi headed out to find the grave and the corpse. Dixon, his lead tech, was standing in the middle of the cemetery talking to several police officers.

"Mason!" Palachi called. "Do you know yet who found the grave?"

Mason Dixon was Dr. Palachi's right-hand in the field. He was quick-witted, intelligent, and always alert to detail. He often quipped that his iconic name sprang from his parents' sense of humor, and he good-naturedly took the inevitable guff.

"Yeah, he's right here boss," Dixon answered. A tall police officer stepped away from the group and approached Palachi.

"Morning, Officer," Palachi greeted the man. "I just need to hear about what you saw. Maybe you can show me?"

"Sure will, Doc. My name's Martinez."

"Good to meet you, Martinez. What you got?"

"Well," he began," my partner Albertson and I were called out here to investigate a suspicious death, and when we got here there were several employees on the porch, pretty much like they are now. They were all talking, but one fellow seemed to know what was going on so I singled him out. His name is Borland, and he was actually the one who found the body. The deceased is their supervisor…," he glanced at his notebook, "Gerrard Johnson. Borland is the one who called it in."

"Right," Palachi agreed. "Go on."

"So, I left Albertson to start getting statements, and I went out to look for anyone who might be skulking around. You know, like the perpetrator."

Palachi stopped an amused grin from taking over his face. "Yeah, good thinking."

"Well, I walked about fifty yards toward the back gate, and I was sweeping the headstones with my flashlight when I got a glimpse of something that just didn't look right. I went over, and sure enough, what had caught my eye was dirt piled up beside a grave. I looked into the hole, and I saw a young woman's body: she was slashed from stem to stern, you might say. I never have seen anything like it, and you can bet I got back to the office quicker than it took me to get over there to the grave. That's when I called the Precinct."

Palachi nodded. "Good job. Will you show me?"

"Sure," Martinez replied. "Right this way."

Palachi followed him toward the back gate, and after a moment as the man got his bearings, they turned to the left.

"Right over there," the officer said, pointing with his flashlight.

Palachi took out his light and walked over to the open grave. The body—a woman who looked to be in her early twenties—had been excised from the sternal notch to the symphysis pubis. She had obviously been moved from her original position in the casket. A sense of horror washed over him as he stared into her empty eye sockets.

"Officer Martinez," the ME said in a low voice, "will you please go bring my crew down here?"

"Sure will, Doc," the officer replied as he headed back in the opposite direction.

Palachi knelt so that he could see better. There were footprints around the body, so possibly, he thought, there might be fingerprints on the casket where the lock was broken.

Damn. We've been tromping all around here and may have ruined some footprints. I'll have to tell Jefferson.

His thoughts were interrupted by the sound of his crew approaching. Martinez led them up to the grave.

"What you got, boss?" Dixon asked.

Palachi directed his flashlight. "Take a look. I want all of you to look at this carefully. I don't think any of you have ever seen this sort of thing before."

"Damn!" Dixon said. "This is interesting, to say the least. I've read about this sort of weirdo, but I've never run into it personally. What's your plan?"

Palachi looked back toward the office.

"When Jefferson gets done," he said, "I'm going to ask him to expedite the police search for evidence in this immediate area, then I'm going to try to get permission from the family to allow us to examine this woman's body."

Dixon nodded. "Ok. What do you need from us?"

"Oh, you guys might as well crash in the van if you want. Maybe we can move the bodies before too long."

By the time Palachi got back to the office, Jefferson had finished his interrogations.

"Looks like only one man actually found the body," he told Palachi, "the rest of them only think they did."

"Yeah," Palachi agreed. "One of the officers said there was only one man who actually found the body."

"Ok then, Mr. Medical Examiner. If you will please follow me to the shed, we can turn this man over, and you can pronounce him dead. Then, maybe we can go home and get some sleep."

"Can do," Palachi agreed as they strolled off toward the shed.

"Not much to see evidence-wise," Jeff confessed. "Maybe your techs got something with all of their hocus-pocus. We can hope, anyway."

Palachi grunted in agreement as he considered his friend.

He had met Philip Jefferson professionally twenty-three years earlier, and they became friends. Their wives became friends as well, but when Jeff's wife died suddenly, they had drifted apart. Palachi thought Jeff avoided him and his wife Annie's company because he didn't want to be a third wheel. Nowadays, he saw Jeff at crime scenes mostly, except for the rare lunch they managed from time to time.

The squeaking door of the shed brought Palachi back to the business at hand. He performed his medical examiner's duty and pronounced the man dead. They turned him onto his back.

"Large blade," Palachi observed as he leaned down to examine the chest wound. "Looks like he bled out pretty quickly. Just from external examination, I'd say he clipped the aorta and the heart, and maybe a lung. We'll see at autopsy."

He directed his attention to the man's face.

"His eye sockets look similar to the woman in the grave. He used a much smaller blade for that work. Maybe a scalpel."

Palachi stood and wiped his hands on his pants. "My God," he said. "I don't know what we're dealing with here, but it's clearly some sort of psychopath. I think he's a necrophile with sadistic tendencies, but I wonder why he killed this man?"

Jeff pulled at his chin. "I think this guy got in his way somehow, but I don't know. This thing is bizarre, no matter how you look at it."

Palachi nodded. "That's for sure. Look, Jeff," he continued, "if you could expedite your fellows' investigation of the grave, I would appreciate it. I need to examine that girl's body to determine if I can tell anything about who did this."

"Gotcha. I'll go look around the grave, and your techs can check for prints. We'll take care of that right now."

"Thanks, buddy."

The sun was coming up as they left the shed. The new day was building to be as beautiful as the previous day had been stormy. Everyone finished their assignments. When the cops and support crew were gone, Jefferson cleared the grave, and Palachi called the girl's parents, requesting permission to examine the body. They took her to the main morgue, where upon completion of their examination they had learned nothing further.

More grave robbing occurred over the next eight months, until November, when it came to an abrupt halt. On the second of December, Palachi commented to Jeff, "We haven't had an incident in four weeks. I don't know if this guy died or just moved on, but he seems to have disappeared."

CHAPTER 3

PORTSMOUTH, VIRGINIA SIZZLED like a griddle in June, and the heat and humidity spread over Jefferson like a sticky coat of oil-based paint. It was just a prelude to the heat that was coming later.

Jefferson stepped into the coolness of his front foyer. He felt his body begin to cool down and relax as he slipped out of his jacket, loosened his tie, and removed his shoulder holster. He sighed a farewell to another twelve-hour day.

Portsmouth was home to Jefferson, and weather aside, June was more oppressive than usual. For the last six months he had been plagued with the phantasm of a serial killer who had murdered nine women, all without a single clue to his identity. The fact that he was still out there had become personal, and Jeff was devoting both personal and professional time to find him. The afternoon newspaper had put a new twist on the story, beginning with the front-page headline: "Portsmouth Police Impotent to Stop Raptor Rampage".

Jeff scanned the lead article: most of the story was hype. He noted particularly the phrases containing words like "ghost", "phantom", "woman killer", even "Jack the Ripper," as well as "police have no clue".

Raptor. Now he has a name, a persona. That should frighten people enough to sell thousands of extra newspapers.

He took a dictionary from the bookcase. "Raptor, raptor," he repeated as he scanned the pages to make sure he had the exact meaning.

"Ah, here we go," he said, and he read aloud.

"Latin raptor<pp rapere-to snatch, (see rape). (1) predator specif. belonging to a group of birds of prey with a strong beak and sharp talons. (2) adapted for seizing and killing prey. (3) one of a family of carnivorous dinosaurs with tearing claws standing on hind legs."

Not a bad analogy he thought as he reflected on the nine murder scenes he had investigated in recent months. At the same time, he was becoming more aware of his resentment of the press. It was bad enough to have such a killer in their midst, but to have him elevated to the status of a super-human character or some indestructible mythic creature was outrageous.

Jeff knew all too well how rumors of defenseless women being ravaged sold papers. The alarm spread and false information became fact, creating a hellish labyrinth for anyone seeking the truth.

He stretched and yawned as he thought about trying to get some sleep. That luxury had been elusive for weeks, and tonight was no exception. He laid the dictionary on the coffee table just as the phone rang. He glanced at his watch: 1:18 A.M. *This can only be bad news.*

"Jefferson."

"*Lieutenant Jefferson, this is Pherson, down at the Precinct. There's been another murder, and it looks like the work of your favorite quarry. You know the papers are calling him the Raptor?*"

Jeff sighed and walked to the kitchen to splash cold water on his face.

"Yeah, Pherson. I heard all about our killer's christening. Where did this one go down?"

"*At the Ravenscroft Apartments, across from the navy shipyard, corner of Dogwood and Jackson.*"

"Yeah, I know the building," Jeff replied. "Anything on the victim?"

The detective could hear papers being shuffled and the incessant chatter of police radios in the background while Pherson referred to his notes.

"*Here we are,*" Pherson continued. "*The body of a young woman was found in apartment 3-C. She was discovered by the patrolman who walks that beat at about 12:30 A.M. Evidently she's hacked up pretty bad.*"

…sharp beak and strong talons, adapted for seizing and killing prey…

"Do we have any idea who she is?" Jefferson queried.

"*The apartment is leased to a Ms. Wanda Marchant, and the assumption is that she's the victim. The manager told the officer that she's a twenty-four-year-old*" *white female, but there was no contact information on her application for lease. I guess Dr. Palachi will have to identify her—I mean, if he can."*

"Right. Speaking of which, have you called Palachi?"

"Yes sir, first thing. I'm sure he's probably on-scene by now."

"Good," Jefferson replied. "I'll need some men to search the building, and I want the apartment shut down until Palachi and his team release it. Anyway, people don't need to be wandering in and out to see what this bastard's done."

"No prob, Lieutenant. The beat cop secured the apartment, wouldn't even let the manager go in, and I put out a Code One alert for every available officer. There's probably a small army there by now."

"Great job, Sergeant," Jeff said. "It looks like I'm the only one not at the ball, and I'm rolling as soon as I can pack up."

"Thanks, and oh, Lieutenant. May I ask you something, I mean, just between two old cops?"

"Sure, Pherson, shoot."

There was a long pause, and if not for the background noise, Jeff would have thought they had been disconnected.

"Pherson? Hello?"

Finally, the sergeant found his voice. *"Well,"* he began slowly, *"I was wondering if it's true. Is she really coming to Portsmouth?"*

Damn it! How could anyone have known that he and Captain Chambers, at the advice of Dr. Winetraub and the SBI, were soliciting help to find this psycho.

"Is *who* really coming to Portsmouth?" Jeff asked.

"Almyra Defrange!" Pherson replied with a bit of reverence. *"You know, the famous detective from Milwaukee. Is she really coming?"*

Jefferson found himself dealing with some of the tactics used by the reporters he had been cursing earlier, but this was from inside his own department. It was unnerving.

"Why on earth would you think she's coming here, Sergeant?"

There was an audible sigh.

"It's just a rumor around the Precinct," he confessed, *"and I was just wondering if it's true. She's the best cop in the world, and she's a looker to boot. I've read all her books, and I was just wondering, uh, well, if you think it would be appropriate, would introduce me to her?"*

Jeff decided to use an old military diversion: neither confirm nor deny.

"Sergeant Pherson, if Almyra Defrange shows up in Portsmouth, and if *I* even get to meet her, I'll see that you have an introduction too."

"I hear you, Lieutenant," Pherson replied. Jeff visualized his goofy, pleased smile.

"In the meantime," Jeff went on, "I need to get over to the Ravenscroft because, as far as I know, there aren't any super-detectives around to help me right now."

"You know, Lieutenant, when I said she's the best cop in the world, I meant besides you."

"I understand, Sergeant. She is certainly prettier than I. I'm leaving now. Goodbye."

"Be careful, Lieutenant."

"Thanks, Pherson. I will."

Jeff pressed the disconnect with his thumb and sat down on his leather couch for a moment. He closed his eyes as the faces of the last nine victims raced across his mind. They begged for a justice he had yet to deliver. Now, he was going to meet one of their sisters in death, and she would be begging for her justice as well.

I don't know if I've seen too much life or too much death, but whichever it is, it's killing me.

Jeff checked his weapon before he slipped back into his shoulder holster and jacket. He didn't know how long he would be gone, so he double-checked the alarm system on the door as he stepped into the balmy morning. The air was heavy, and the aroma of honeysuckle filled his nostrils as he walked toward his car. His thoughts were of Wanda Marchant, and how she might have gotten involved with this killer he was chasing. Without warning or provocation, a ghost reappeared: one that he had often thought about, though not too much lately.

The flashback was like being in a hologram. In his mind it seemed quite real, as if it were happening all over again in that very moment.

He was looking at a young woman lying beside the road in the Mekong Delta. Her abdomen was ripped open, and her fetus, still attached to the umbilical cord, was lying pitifully beside her.

"Please kill me, Joe," she begged.

"Don't ask me to do that. You'll be fine," he lied.

"My—my baby?" she gasped as blood oozed from her mouth.

"He's alright," he lied again.

"Give me your pistol!" she begged. "Please!"

"Who did this to you?"

"Viet Cong," she answered between shallow breaths. "They raided the village and killed everyone suspected of associating with Americans."

"And have you been associating with Americans?"

She smiled weakly.

"My baby's father is American, but I know I will never see him again, so please, either kill me or give me your pistol. Please, Joe, I know you Mac Sog—so is my husband."

"Mac Sog", or correctly MAC V SOG, was a term she would not have known unless her husband told her. It was a ghost outfit whose existence wouldn't even be acknowledged until many, many years after the war.

"Kill me, Joe," she begged again.

Even if this poor woman were in the best ICU in the world, she would not survive. If he broke radio silence, no one could arrive in time, and they could do nothing for her anyway. It was one of the longest moments he would ever know, and it was filled with indecision.

"Please, Joe!" she gasped.

He turned as if to walk away…she never saw it coming. Afterward, he buried her and the baby in the jungle beside the road and said a prayer. He felt guilty, not for the deed, but because the only words he could remember to say were the Christian words from the Twenty-third Psalm. He finally found peace in the idea that whatever God she believed in would forgive him, at least for the words.

Reality flooded back as he put the blue light on the dash. He drove down Leckie Street before turning onto Crawford Parkway, reflecting as he drove on all the things he had done as a soldier and as a policeman

A murderer chasing a murderer—but at least I've never killed for the sheer pleasure of killing. I wonder if that matters?

CHAPTER 4

I *HAVEN'T BEEN HERE in years,* Jeff thought as he drove into the neighborhood known as the Yards.

He dodged a wino who appeared from nowhere and disappeared just as quickly.

"Poor old bastard," Jeff muttered as he checked the rearview to make sure the old man wasn't lying in the street.

The area had not changed for the better: broken windows, faded paint, and a general look of desperation that accompanied years of neglect. It wasn't the old Yards he remembered.

The name Yards came from the old Navy shipyard that stood between the residential area and the Elizabeth River. The homes were for the Navy's civilian ship builders, and each house had been the epitome of neatness and pride. The paint was always fresh, the windows spotless, and the small lawns immaculately manicured. That was before the government cutbacks closed the shipyard, and the Navy went elsewhere. The civilian workers moved away and left the area to be what it had become: low rent for anyone unfortunate enough to have to live there.

The Ravenscroft loomed on the corner at the end of a row of potentially condemnable buildings. Its look was formidable: six floors of cracked windows in cracked casings surrounded by runaway ivy over faded, peeling paint. Combine that with poor lighting and shadows, and the whole place took on the look of a B movie haunted house.

"I can't imagine living here," Jeff said to himself as he made a quick right and then a left into the parking lot in back.

Two patrolmen greeted him as he got out of the car. They had been stationed there in case someone flushed a suspect from the premises. They likely showed themselves only after they recognized him and waved approval as he walked around to the front of the building.

"Damn!" he said to himself. "Look at this."

There were at least a half-a-dozen patrol cars and emergency vehicles, along with a hearse and the mobile crime van scattered down both sides of the street in front of the Ravenscroft. *Everyone was in a hurry, so they parked piecemeal, like pine straws.*

The only person out front was an officer Jeff didn't know, so he looked at his name tag.

"Morning, Roth."

"Morning, Lieutenant," he replied as he opened the door into a dirty foyer.

"What we got here this morning?" Jeff asked.

When Roth didn't answer right away, Jefferson turned to look at him. The man had gone ashen, and he was gagging. It took a moment for him to regain his composure.

"Sorry, Lieutenant," he said finally. "I was the first one here. I found her body."

Jeff looked at the surroundings.

"Why were you here at all?" he asked.

"This is on my usual beat," Roth replied, "and I had gotten a call from the Precinct to check a disturbance in this building. When I got here, everything was quiet, but I did a floor-by-floor look around to see if anything was going on that wasn't obvious from down here. Everything seemed to be in order, until I got to the third flood and noticed that the door was ajar and the lights were on in apartment 3-C. I thought whoever lived there might have called in the disturbance, so I knocked and announced that I was the police. When no one responded, I went in to see what was going on. That's when I found her."

Jeff nodded. "Where is she?"

"She's in the bathtub, Lieutenant, and I swear to God it's like a pack of wild animals went after her. Her chest and belly are ripped open, and I could see the organs in her body. There's guts and blood all over the place, and I'm not sure if I ever saw her head. At that point, I sealed the apartment and called for help."

"You did the right thing. Look, this is tough, even for veterans like us. You ok now?"

Roth nodded. "Thanks, Lieutenant. I'm alright. This one just caught me off guard."

"Understood. I'm going up now. See you later."

Jeff walked across the foyer to the elevator only to discover a hand-made cardboard sign declaring that it was out of order. *Oh, well. I need the exercise anyway.*

The stairwell was cluttered with beer cans, empty wine bottles, and several varieties of flammable trash that would have sent the fire marshal into a citation-writing frenzy. The obvious feature, aside from the clutter and the odor, was the graffiti, and Jeff glanced at it while he climbed the stairs two at a time.

"Call me, or just come by apt 1-E. Booger."

"Like boys? Me too. Bring one to 2-G anytime. Willie Blue."

"Jesus loves you, and I could too. Meeting every Weds nite 7:30 until. 321 Harris Street. Bring your own communion wine. The Right REV LONGFELLOW."

As Jeff turned the corner on the landing heading for the third floor, one message stopped him cold. It looked like the red paint was still wet, and he put on his reading glasses to make sure it said what he thought it said.

> *"wanda was fonda me,*
> *so now she's totally free, but*
> *at least I didn't cut her*
> *out in some gutter*
> *so that's one extra point for me.*
> *xoxo raptor."*

The Lieutenant ran the rest of the way to the third floor and quickly located 3-C. The door was open, and the lab techs were working in the small living room. Jeff stayed in the hall so as not to introduce any extraneous, false clues.

"Gentlemen," he called from the doorway, "is Norris Quigley in here somewhere?"

"Mornin' Lieutenant," someone answered. "Yeah, Quigley's in the bathroom taking pictures."

"Would you ask him to come out here for a minute?"

"Sure," the tech answered, and he disappeared toward the back of the apartment.

In a moment, Quigley entered the living room with both hands and a backpack full of equipment. He came directly to the door. His disheveled blond hair and the twinkle in his blue eyes alerted everyone to his penchant for being light-hearted and mischievous.

Quigley broke into a wide grin when he saw Jefferson. "What's up L T?" he jived. "Heard you're looking for me."

Jeff motioned him into the hall.

"Look, Quig," he began in little more than a whisper, "I want you to go down in the stairwell, because just before you reach the second landing there's a message on the wall from our killer. It's written in fresh, red paint so you can't miss it. We need some good pictures of it."

"I'm on it, Jeff," Quigley replied, his smile fading. "I'm done up here anyway."

"Thanks Quigley. And please keep this quiet when the reporters show up. Hell, they'll find out soon enough without us pointing it out for them."

"Gotcha' Jefferson," Quigley said, and he headed for the stairwell.

"Excuse us, Lieutenant," came a voice from behind him. Jeff stepped aside as the forensic techs exited with all their hair and blood samples, their fibers, dust, prints, and all the other scientific evidence routinely collected from a crime scene.

"You done Dixon?"

"Yes, sir. It's a small place, and I believe we've sampled everything. The bathroom's a mess, but the rest of the place is fairly clean. Anyway, we'll see what we got."

"Right. We will see—oh, is Palachi still in there?"

Dixon looked puzzled. "No. He went down a few minutes ago, but I know he was waiting for you so you could go over evidence from the body with him."

Jeff chuckled. "How thoughtful. Knowing Palachi, he's probably up on the roof studying the moons of Jupiter or something. If you run into him, tell him to get his big ass up here. I'd like to have a few minutes of sleep time when we get done."

Dixon laughed. "I'll tell him Jefferson, but only if I can say that I'm quoting you."

"By all means…be my guest."

Jefferson entered the apartment to see if he could get a feel for the person who had lived and died there. With the overpowering lack of air conditioning it only took moments to detect the odor of blood. The living room furniture—a couch and two chairs—was dilapidated, and there was no radio or TV. An open pizza box on the floor revealed one remaining slice, and next to the box an empty diet cola can lay on its side.

The only other hint about Wanda Marchant's life was an ashtray full of cigarette butts, a matchbook from the Lone Pine Pizzeria in Norfolk, and a Polar Bar ice cream wrapper. There were no signs of a struggle and no evidence of a forced entry. Jeff retrieved a pair of latex gloves from his pocket and checked the telephone. He heard the hum of the dial tone, and it triggered a thought. *I wonder who called this in?* He dialed the Precinct.

"*Portsmouth Police Communications Center, this is Sergeant Pherson.*"

"Pherson, this is Jefferson. Look, I'm at the Ravenscroft, and I need some help."

"*Sure thing, Lieutenant.*"

"Did the original call about the disturbance here come directly to the Precinct, or did it come through the 911 emergency service?"

"*The 911 operator called it in,*" Pherson replied. "*I took the call.*"

"Ok, Sarge. Would you check with them and find out where the call originated, and if, by chance, the caller identified him or herself."

"*Can do, but it'll take a little while.*"

"That's ok, Pherson. I'm going to be here for a while. Just call me back here."

Jeff hung up and walked down the short hallway to where he knew he would find a kitchenette and the bathroom. The kitchen held no obvious clues. He took a deep breath to prepare himself for what was coming and moved toward the bathroom.

"Jesus, Mary, and Joseph," he prayed when he rounded the door frame.

The antique, clawfoot tub was filled with a bloody froth and human remains. The torso would have been described as face-up—if there had been a head attached. There were deep incisions beneath each breast, as if the killer had started to remove them. The longer incision, from the neck to the pelvis, revealed the ribs, under which the heart, lungs, and liver were visible. There was a large cavity in the abdomen left by the removal of the intestines: they were now draped around the edge of the bathtub like garland on a Christmas tree.

Jeff was magnetized in horror, but when he sensed a presence behind him, he spun, pulled his weapon and dropped to one knee.

"Good morning, Lieutenant!" Palachi greeted him, seemingly unfazed by the gun aimed at his chest.

Jeff exhaled and lowered his pistol.

"Medical Examiner Palachi, you almost got shot."

"Yeah, I noticed. How you been Jefferson?" Palachi extended his gloved hand, which looked clean, but Jeff wasn't taking any chances.

"Don't hand me that, Palachi," he warned.

The ME chuckled. "Why not? You police types are usually more than willing to accept a helping hand."

Jeff laughed. "Yeah, but I've gotten particular since I've seen all of your tricks, and I don't take help from just anybody. As far as how I'm doing, it's about the same as usual. No sleep, and an eighteen-hour work day—but the benefits are great."

"Ain't it the truth."

Jeff holstered his pistol.

"Where were you hiding just before I almost shot you?"

Palachi glanced away for a second. "I uh, had to go downstairs."

Jeff wondered about his friend's vague answer, but ignored it for the moment. "Did you run into Quigley? What do you think?"

"Yeah," Palachi replied. "He showed me the message in the stairwell. It looks like our killer is starting to communicate."

"Do you think his message has been garbled?" Jeff asked with feigned incredulity.

Palachi shook his head. "No—at least his actions haven't been. Dr. Stross from the Psych Unit at the State Medical Examiner's Office reviewed the other murders, and he felt that our killer would try to contact us in some bizarre way. He also thought we might attract copycats."

"It's bizarre all right," Jeff agreed. "But our killer's no poet. Look, Palachi, do you believe all this stuff about predicting his behavior and all of that? I think he's jerking us around—he only gives us what he wants us to have."

"You're probably right, but since this scrawling on the wall is the only physical clue we've ever gotten, I'll take it."

Jeff frowned. "C'mon, scrawl or not, do you really believe that he's just trying to get out attention? Do you think someone else did this murder and then decided to change from a copycat killer to a poet laureate?"

Palachi removed his safety goggles and wiped them on his coat. "I doubt it. I suppose anyone could hack up a body, but look at the Y incision he uses. It makes one consider a mortician or a professional butcher might have done this. Hell, that's the way I start every autopsy I do. Whoever he is, he knows his way around the inside of a human body. It took skill to remove the intestines as cleanly as he did."

It was time to get to the task at hand: Jefferson spent the next thirty-eight minutes taking notes. Palachi was thorough, and Jeff noted everything that might lead him to other clues. Finally, Palachi stood up from beside the bathtub, taking on the thousand-yard-stare.

"No doubt Jeff. This was our boy."

"Where's the head?" Jeff asked.

Palachi, who had done a preliminary walk-through with the lab techs nodded toward the commode.

Jeff turned, lifted the lid, and found himself staring into the eyeless face of Wanda Marchant. Her blond hair had been washed, and the commode had been flushed several times to get rid of the excess blood.

"And the eyes?" Jeff asked, although he knew the answer.

"Same as usual. You know, the sick son-of-a-bitch took them with him."

Jeff looked at Wanda's face, then to the bathtub, and finally the blood on Palahci's apron. The whole scene wrapped around him like a spider's web. He was the moth: the more he struggled, the tighter the web.

"Doc, can we continue our discussion in the living room?"

Without comment, Palachi removed his goggles, apron, mask, and gloves and dropped them in a pile on the floor. He nodded to the door.

"I work with death every day," he said, "but I've never gotten used to this."

They walked down the short hall and Palachi lit a cigarette. He looked tired as he leaned against the back of one of the soiled living room chairs.

"I don't know, Jeff," he began, "I think we're chasing a real phantom. Think about it. He's killed ten women now, and we've never gotten a clue until tonight—that is, if you consider his writing as a clue. I've done this new DNA test, but so what? We don't have anything to compare the results to. It shows that the same man committed all of our murders up to now, and we can scientifically prove that we have the right man when we catch him. But even that will depend of whether or not we can find a judge who will go along with the new science."

"You're right. We have yet to get a real clue like a footprint or a fingerprint," Jeff said, "but I agree about the DNA. It seems useless, but I've read that one day, when we've built up a database of known offenders and we have their profiles for comparison, we'll have a real tool."

"No doubt you're right," Palachi responded. "Maybe the handwriting experts can figure out something about him."

"Maybe, but I'm not counting on it."

The shrill ring of Wanda's phone caused both of them to jump.

"That's probably for me," Jeff said. He walked over and grabbed the receiver. "Jefferson."

"*Lieutenant Jefferson, this is Pherson, down at the Precinct.*"

Jeff rolled his eyes at Pherson's signature greeting. "Yes, Pherson. Got anything on the 911 call?"

"*Yes, sir. I talked to the operator who took it, and she even played the tape for me.*"

"And?"

The sergeant cleared his throat. "*Lieutenant, the call originated from the phone on which you're speaking now, and the caller sounded like a child.*"

Jeff thought he had misunderstood. "Repeat that last part, Pherson. A child? Are you sure?"

"*Yes, sir. Absolutely sure. I thought the same thing, and I had the operator check and re-check. I am positive that the call came from that phone, and it was a child. It sounded more like a boy than a girl. They're sending us a copy of the tape.*"

"Ok, Pherson. Good job. I just have to figure out what to do with this alarming bit of information." Jeff hung up the phone.

Palachi had overheard. "A child? How is that possible?"

"I tell you he's jerking us around," Jeff said. "Unless you think a child did this?"

"No." Palachi replied with a dismissive laugh. "Definitely not a child."

Jeff had a sudden thought. "You know, this gives me a different starting point, maybe. Isn't it just possible that the caller wasn't the Raptor at all? I mean, God forbid, what if a child really found this murder and called it in to 911?"

Palachi blinked. "God, I hope not. If a kid did find this, he or she will need therapy for the rest of their life."

"No doubt," Jeff agreed. He took his walkie-talkie from his belt.

"This is Lieutenant Jefferson," he announced to every officer in the building. "Meet me in the foyer in five minutes."

Palachi lit another cigarette.

"You better quit that," Jeff admonished. "Those things will kill you."

Palachi snapped out of deep thought. "What? I'm sorry. What did you say?"

"I was saying that those cigarettes will kill you. What's the matter, buddy? You seem a little off this morning."

Palachi shook his head. "If we don't get a handle on this killer pretty soon, Annie's gonna' kill me. I was downstairs on the phone with her when you first got here."

"Are you two having trouble?"

"Not really yet, I suppose, but these weird murders and these hours are taking a toll on us."

Jeff nodded with compassion for his friend. "I understand, but I know you two well enough to know that if you're alright, she's alright, and vice versa."

Palachi blew streams of smoke from his nostrils. "Yeah, I guess so. Thanks, Jeff. I just needed to tell somebody."

"If things get too bad, and you need to talk, c'mon over. You know where I live. Hell, bring Annie with you. You guys have too much history to throw it away because of something like this."

"You're right, Jeff. I guess I'm just a little insecure with all the time we've been putting into this investigation. It's all resulted in zip, and if you combine that with an unhappy wife, things aren't as rosy as one might like."

"Yeah, I suppose so—but we will catch this bastard, and you will feel better at home."

The walkie-talkie beeped, and Jeff opened the frequency.

"Go," he said.

"Lieutenant, this is Galloway. The men are assembled in the foyer."

"Thanks, I'll be right down."

Palachi had resumed his faraway look.

"Dr. Palachi," Jeff said, "Paging Dr. Palachi."

Palachi shook his head. "Huh? Oh sorry. Just thinking about Annie."

"I understand. Listen, I'm going back downstairs. Do you want your crew back up here to remove the remains?"

Palachi stubbed out his cigarette in the overflowing ashtray. "Yeah, yeah, that would be good. Tell them I'm done up here, and if you want, come by the morgue later today. Maybe this guy left something behind this time."

Jeff offered a hopeful smile. "Yeah, maybe he did. I know they dusted the phone, but if you could, give that priority when you start looking at prints and so forth. Goodnight, or good morning to you."

Palachi nodded absently and lit another cigarette. Jeff wasn't even sure the ME had heard him.

When he got down to the foyer, Jefferson told Dixon they were cleared to move the body. He then began to address the nine officers who had assembled at his request.

"Has anyone found out anything?"

No response.

"That's what I expected," Jeff went on, "and while you were knocking on doors, did anyone see any children?"

Again, no response.

Jeff shoved his hands in his pockets. "Gentlemen, we've learned that the call reporting this murder came from the apartment where the murder occurred, and that the caller, as far as we can determine, was a child."

Some of the men shifted positions while others began whispering among themselves. Jeff raised his hand.

"Hang on a second," he said. "As hard as it is to believe this thing about a child, I need a couple of volunteers to stay and see if they can locate any children in this building."

Several men raised their hand.

"Ok, Miller and Roberson, you can go ahead and get started, but if you locate a child, don't push it. Just get the vital information and contact me. I'll have Juvie get parental permission and be present during interrogation."

"Right L T," Miller answered, and he and Roberson disappeared into the stairwell.

"Roth!" Jeff called. "Where are you?"

"Here!" came the answer from the front door.

"If you would, stay here until the ME and his crew have left and then seal the apartment. After that, you might as well go back to your regular beat."

"Will do, Lieutenant," Roth replied.

"Everybody else might as well go too," Jeff added. "And thanks to all of you for your help."

The officers exchanged a few words before they dispersed.

Jefferson walked back to his car with the feeling he had been here before. As he headed back around Crawford Parkway, he had a feeling of déjà vu. *Of course, I've been here before! Ten times, now!*

He drove to 1500 Leckie Street and forced himself to think about sleep rather than murder. He had to be at the Precinct in three hours, and he hoped that at least two of them could be spent in his bed.

CHAPTER 5

I N THE EARLY morning hours of Friday, June 13, 1998 Almyra
Defrange slid out of a taxi in front of the Police Precinct Building in
Portsmouth. Her back hurt, and she was in no mood to put up with
the gawkers who stared at her legs as she exited the vehicle.

Goddamned rubes. She snatched her small suitcase and tote from the
backseat, and she paid the driver.

Almyra and her Italian temperament had no patience for pretense, and
this morning, she didn't have much patience for anything. She'd been called
off a case in Milwaukee unexpectedly the night before, with just enough
time to pack a few things and get to the airport in time for her flight.
When she arrived in D.C., she discovered that the airline had screwed up
her ticket, thus causing a delay of several hours. When she finally got to
Norfolk, her taxi had broken down in the Downtown Tunnel en route to
Portsmouth, and she had to sit in a snarl of traffic and gasoline fumes until
another cab was dispatched. Her mood was as volatile as a thunderstorm
over the Chesapeake Bay.

She stalked up the steps of the Precinct Building and strutted into the
main lobby. Her gaze locked onto that of the duty officer, and she charged
toward him like someone would approach a bar tender after finding a
cockroach in their whiskey sour. He stood up when she stopped in front
of the desk.

"You, I-I mean, that is, you're Detective Almyra Defrange," he
stammered. The blushing man extended his hand.

She dropped her bag and tote to the floor, leaned across the desk, and she winked.

"I know I am," she replied in a lower than alto voice as she squeezed the startled officer's hand.

"Detective Defrange, I'm Officer Rex Daniels. It is my distinct pleasure to meet you. You're the first legend I've ever met in person."

"Thank you," she replied, trying to look flattered. "Now, will you please direct me to Captain Chambers. He's expecting me."

"One moment," Daniels replied. "I'll ring up and see where you're to go. Would you like to sit down, have some coffee?"

"No thanks. I hope I won't be here that long."

Daniels dialed the phone but didn't avert his gaze. Defrange smiled. It was something she'd learned to tolerate.

Almyra had heard her eyes described as jade, and that her high cheek bones and coal-black hair drove men crazy. Of course, her rich, masculine, honey-coated voice only added to her mystique. She exercised regularly to keep her body well-toned—she moved with control from her core. It was effortless motion with a rhythmic flow like molten lava. She slipped out of one of her designer pumps and placed one hand on her cocked hip.

"Marsha," Daniels whispered into the receiver, "Detective Almyra Defrange is standing in front of my desk, and she says that Captain Chambers is expecting her…Oh really! I see, yeah. I'd heard that, but I thought it was a rumor…Right! Yes, I will tell her."

He hung up the phone.

"Well?" Defrange asked as she looked down to replace her shoe.

"The Captain *is* expecting you," Daniels beamed with what he considered an epiphany.

Derange felt the frayed cord of her patience stretch to just short of the breaking point.

"I told you he's *expecting* me," she growled. "I just need to know *where to find him*!"

A startled Daniels looked up and saw his paladin.

"Doc!" he called out. "Doc Winetraub, would you help me please?"

A distinguished man, about fifty, with salt-and-pepper hair diverted his path toward the elevator and headed for the desk. As he approached, he broke into a wide smile and offered his hand.

"Dr. Defrange," he greeted her. "It's such a pleasure to finally meet you."

Defrange offered a curt smile as she took his hand. "I'm afraid you have me at a disadvantage, sir. I don't believe I know you."

"Not at all," the doctor confessed. "We've never met, but I've followed your career with great interest. I'm Milton Winetraub, the resident sawbones around here."

"A pleasure, Dr. Winetraub. Officer Daniels was about to direct me to Captain Chambers' office. Could you help me?"

"Of course. I was just on the way up there. C'mon, we'll grab the elevator."

Winetraub scooped up her suitcase and tote and trotted to the elevator just in time to catch the closing door.

Defrange smiled as she stepped onto the elevator. "Thank you," she said as the doctor pushed the button for the fourth floor.

"Chad Chambers is expecting you, and I can assure you that he'll be ecstatic that you've finally made it."

He sat her bags down and looked at her. Defrange sensed that he wanted to say more but was hesitant.

"So," she said, trying to make elevator conversation, "you're the medical officer for the Precinct?"

"Yes," he replied. "I've been here for years. I love the atmosphere and excitement, and if you promise not to tell, I'll let you in on a secret."

The doctor's eyes twinkled, and Defrange found him charming in a paternal sort of way.

"Your secret is safe with me, Doctor. My lips are sealed."

Winetraub blushed. "Well," he said, lowering his voice, "as I said, I've followed your career for years, and aside from all of your accolades, teaching, writing, profiling, lecturing, all of that and more, you're a damned good cop. I envy that. I've always wanted to be a detective, but I just don't have the nerve to do it."

Defrange gave him her best sympathetic pout.

"You're too kind, Doctor, but don't be silly. I'm sure you'd be a fine detective."

Winetraub chuckled. "Well, maybe I would, until somebody shot at me, or I had to go to one of our serial killer's crime scenes. I'm afraid I'd lose it in a situation like that. I am devoted to the profession of healing, and I guess being a cop is completely antithetical to what I'm trained to do. Oh, here we are."

The elevator stopped, and the door opened.

The doctor ushered her off the elevator with a wave of his arm. "This is four, and if you turn to the right, Chad's office is at the far end of the hall. I'm afraid I have to get back downstairs."

Defrange gave him a knowing grin. "You weren't coming up here this morning, were you?"

"I'm afraid you've found me out," the doctor confessed. "My office is on the basement level, but I couldn't let a distinguished visitor such as yourself wander around lost, now could I?"

She picked up her bags and stepped into the hallway. The door started to close, but Winetraub caught it with his foot.

"Thanks, Doctor," Defrange said. "I hope to see you again while I'm here."

He had already released his foot, and the door closed over his reply.

Defrange walked down the hall to a door marked "Captain" and entered a small, comfortable reception room where a slender, fortyish-looking woman looked up from her desk. Her short hair, with bangs, and large blue eyes gave her a pixie-like air. When she spoke in sudden animation, Almyra jumped.

"Oh, Detective Defrange!" the woman squealed, popping up from her desk, "or would you prefer to be called Dr. Defrange? Or, should I call you Miss Defrange? I'm Marsha Smathers, the Captain's receptionist and secretary."

"You may call me Almyra if you like, but should I call you Miss, Ms., Mrs. or what?"

The woman's face turned scarlet as she giggled. "Call me Marsha."

Defrange, amused, liked the woman immediately. She made it a point to always treat other women in her profession with respect. There was a shared, unspoken camaraderie in a world dominated by men.

"I love your name. Almyra is so pretty," Marsha offered.

"Thank you. I like yours too. I was actually named for an aunt who killed several Nazis and blew up their tank, but that's a story for another time." Defrange's bad mood was slowly dissipating.

Marsha started to reply when the door to the inner office opened, and a dapper man appeared. His hair was snow-white as was his impeccably trimmed mustache. His tie perfectly matched his charcoal, three-piece suit, and his shoes were shined.

"Detective Almyra Defrange, I presume. I'm Chadwick Chambers, and I'm so glad you're here. Please, come in."

Almyra beamed as she looked at this man and thought of her late grandfather.

"Thank you," she said, as he stepped aside to let her pass.

"Marsha, please hold my calls while I'm in with Detective Defrange."

He closed the door quietly behind her as she surveyed the captain's office. The far wall, which was all plate-glass windows, offered a panoramic view of the Elizabeth River and the city of Norfolk beyond.

"Captain," she began, "this is so beautiful, but how on earth do you ever get anything done with that distracting view? All those ships gliding by… it's hypnotic!"

Captain Chambers smiled. "Well," he replied, "sometimes I feel a little guilty about looking out as often as I do, but at my age I suppose a little quiet conceptualizing is permitted from time to time."

"I would certainly think so," she agreed.

She walked to the windows to get a better look. The captain stood behind her as she drank in the view.

Almyra sighed. "This is intoxicating. Just look at all those ships—and, especially that small, odd one over there. What sort of ship is that?"

"Which one do you mean?" Chambers asked as he leaned forward.

"The red one at the pier," she said. "See it? It's right across from the parking lot. *Portsmouth* is written on the side of it."

"Oh, yes," he replied. "That's the *Portsmouth* lightship."

"Lightship?" Almyra echoed. "Sounds like something from a sci-fi movie!"

The captain chuckled. "Not quite. The *Portsmouth*—and the whole fleet she belonged to—have generally been out of service since the turn of the twentieth century. They were hard working vessels."

"Really?" Almyra asked with genuine interest. "What was their function?"

"Do you see the large light on the mainmast?" he asked. "That was the beacon for incoming ships so they could safely find the harbor. Our city is at the ports mouth, hence the name Portsmouth."

Almyra was intrigued.

"Did this ship move around, or was it in the same place all the time?"

"She stayed at anchor in a fixed position so that incoming ships would know generally where to look for her," he explained. "The U.S. Lighthouse Service, and later the Coast Guard manned her. Those fellows stayed out there, on station, twenty-four hours a day no matter what the weather."

Almyra was impressed. "What a duty station! That's all so incredible."

"Yes," the Captain agreed. "And when she was decommissioned, the citizens of Portsmouth decided to buy her to make a permanent museum to memorialize that mission and those men. While you're here, you can go aboard if you like."

"I'll make a point of it," she promised.

"Would you like a cup of coffee?" he asked her.

"That would be wonderful!"

She looked around for a coffeemaker, but the Captain was way ahead of her.

"No, no Detective DeFrange," he said, reading her mind, "please sit down and make yourself comfortable."

He gestured to the over-stuffed leather recliner in the corner where the wall met the long bank of windows. She sat down and tilted back. She was not accustomed to being pampered. The captain went to the coffee service and got out two cups.

"Cream, sugar, both?" he asked.

"No thanks—just black for me," she replied.

"Me too," Chambers chuckled. "I've always maintained that if you have to put something in your coffee, it should be good Irish whiskey."

He brought her coffee before taking a seat in his desk chair positioning it so that he was close without being intrusive.

"How was your trip?" he asked. "I apologize for the short notice, but as of today we have ten murder victims."

"No problem, sir," Almyra replied. "The pitfalls along the way got a little pesky, but I'm no worse for the wear."

For the next half hour, Chambers asked her questions about her career, her family, life in Milwaukee, and life in general. She noticed that he never mentioned her role in the apprehension of Jeffrey Dahmer, her mind walking abilities, her PhD in psychology, her work with INTERPOL, or the case that brought her to Portsmouth.

While they spoke, his brown eyes never lost contact with hers. His genteel manner, along with his soft Tidewater accent fascinated her, and she surmised that he was a man who rarely had to raise his voice. In short, she found Chadwick Chambers to be quite gallant. At some point in the conversation, Defrange realized that she was sitting in his chair.

The old sweetie. I bet he catnaps in this sometimes....

After two cups of coffee and a pleasant conversation, Chambers stood.

"Detective," he said, "please excuse me for just a moment."

He went to his desk and took two sets of keys, along with a large manila envelope, from the top drawer.

"These," he announced as he walked back over to her, "are for your rental car. We didn't want you to feel stranded while you're here."

He handed her the keys, and she dropped them into her purse.

"And these," he continued as he handed her the second set of keys, "are for the crow's nest."

"Excuse me?" she said. "Did you say 'crow's nest'? I'm almost afraid to ask."

Chambers laughed. "'Crow's nest' is how we refer to our luxury suite on the top floor of the Harbor Inn next door. It's isolated from the other rooms, and it has its own private entrance and elevator. It was created for us to house protected witnesses or special VIPs like you. It's quite nice, and you should be very comfortable. You'll have access to the pool, gym, and shops as well."

"Thank you, Almyra replied. "You'd better be careful. You'll never get rid of me."

"Detective Defrange, if I thought you really meant that, I'd call your Captain in Milwaukee and tell him you're never coming home."

Almyra laughed a low, dusky laugh. "Watch what you say, Captain. He might just take you up on it."

Finally, Chambers handed her the envelope.

"And this," he continued, "is the background on the case that you'll be working on. I'm going to assign you to work with Lieutenant Philp Jefferson, and this case, of course, will be your only focus. Jeff's been chasing this killer since the beginning, and he can give you more information. I'm sure your expertise and your unusual abilities will take some of the pressure off Jefferson and me. Folks are tired of this—but we just can't get a line on this guy."

Almyra had a feeling, but she wouldn't let herself go there. She started to open the envelope.

Chambers reached out and touched her hand. "No, no Detective. I don't expect you to travel all night and then go right to work. It's the weekend. I want you to go over to the Harbor Inn and rest. You can look this over at your leisure and start fresh on Monday."

Defrange opened her mouth to object when there was an abrupt but soft knock on the door.

"Yes!" Chambers called.

Marsha's head appeared around the side of the door.

"Yes, Marsha. Come in," the captain said. "We're almost done here."

"I'm sorry to disturb you," she said in a whisper, "but something has happened, and the watch commander thought you should know right away."

"By all means, Marsha. What's happened?"

Marsha shot a nervous glance in Almyra's direction as she stepped into the room. "A young woman has been found at the Tidewater Breeze Apartment Complex, and she's been mutilated."

Almyra was at once blinded by a vision. She shook her head. "The Raptor," she said.

"That's the odd thing," Marsha went on. "If it was the Raptor this is the only victim he's ever left alive."

Almyra shot up from the recliner and put her hand on the captain's arm. "I need to get to the crime scene."

"Dr. Defrange, you don't need to go to the crime scene. Just go on over to the hotel and get some rest. It's probably not even our killer since this woman's still alive."

"I appreciate that, Captain," she countered, "but with all due respect I'm not here on vacation. And," Almyra added, looking over at Marsha, "I can assure you that this woman's attacker was the Raptor."

Chambers stepped to his desk and picked up the phone. "Jakoby, send a driver to my office—and make it someone with savvy. He'll be driving Almyra Defrange to a crime scene."

He hung up the phone.

"Thank you, Captain," Defrange said.

"No, Detective. Thank *you*. If I've ever learned anything over the years it's that when someone in my charge wants to do something positive, I should just empower them and get out of the way. I'll contact Jefferson, and he can meet you at the scene."

A patrolman entered the outer office, and Marsha swung the door open.

"Almyra," she tweeted, "your escort is here."

An officer of about thirty-five years entered the office. His square jaw and military bearing certainly suggested that he was someone with savvy as Chambers had requested.

"Ferguson!" Chambers called. "Come in. This is Detective Almyra Defrange, and I want you to take her out to the Tidewater Breeze. She's in charge, so whatever she says goes. Please stay with her until Lieutenant Jefferson arrives on the scene."

"Yes, sir." Ferguson replied. He looked at Almyra. "It's a pleasure to meet you, Detective," he added, and he touched the bill of his cap.

"The pleasure is mine, Officer Ferguson. If you don't mind, I'd like to get rolling before the energy trail at the scene gets cold."

He stood aside, and Almyra started for the door.

"Detective!" Chambers called out behind her. "I'll have your things taken over to your suite, and the host on duty will know where your rental is parked. Most of all, I want you to be careful."

"Thank you, Captain Chambers, "and thanks for the hospitality," she called over her shoulder, "but I can take care of myself."

CHAPTER 6

ALMYRA MADE SMALL talk with Ferguson as they traveled the three miles from the Precinct to the Tidewater Breeze. When they arrived, several police cars and EMT vehicles were already on-scene. When they reached the main entrance, Defrange jumped out of the car before Ferguson came to a complete stop.

"Damn it, Detective," he growled after her. "I'm supposed to be taking care of you!"

Almyra swooped in on the startled uniformed policeman standing in front of the elevators and shoved her ID in his face.

"Where was the woman attacked?" she inquired with urgency in her voice.

The officer frowned. "Who are you?" he asked as Almyra shook her ID up and down until his eyes focused.

"Oh—sorry, Detective. Upstairs, apartment seven-eighty-six."

The door of one of the two elevators opened, and Almyra ran in. She had just pushed to button for the seventh floor when several people surged toward the open elevator door.

"Get the next one!" she demanded and waved her ID in their general direction.

"You heard her, folks!" boomed a male voice. The crowd moved away from the door and Ferguson joined Almyra in the elevator.

He looked at her with a stern expression. "Ma'am," he began, "Captain Chambers put me in charge of your safety. Please give me the courtesy of telling me when you're going to jump out of a moving car, or some such other dumb shit!"

Defrange blinked in surprise as she stifled a laugh.

"I'm sorry, Ferguson," she apologized. "It's just that during an investigation it's terribly important that I get on scene before it's cold—and when I say 'cold', it's totally different from the usual sense. You see, I use my psychic ability to solve crimes."

Ferguson nodded. "I know, Detective. I've read your books, and I've seen you on TV. All the more reason for me to want to protect you. I realize that you are one of a kind, and all I ask is a little courtesy, please."

Almyra knew that this was as close as a man like Ferguson would ever get to expressing his feelings. She offered a warm smile. "You got it," she said as the door opened.

She followed the sound of the clamor down the hallway to an apartment on the right. Almyra pushed past a policeman stationed outside. She knew that the medics would remove the victim as soon as possible.

"Who's in charge here," she asked the medics as they made their way toward what would logically be a bedroom.

A young man in scrubs stepped in front of her. "I am ma'am," he said. "I'm EMT Whiteside. Who are you?"

"I'm Doctor Defrange," she replied. Her medical ID might go farther in this situation than being just another cop.

Whiteside's eyes grew wide, and he stepped aside. "Doctor" was enough ID for him. Almyra walked into the bedroom.

A young woman was lying on the bed. She had a floral-pattern pillow case over her head with twine wrapped around her neck to hold it in place. There was a gaping wound at her left inner thigh, and her breast was bleeding where a nipple should have been.

Whiteside hurried over and pressed gauze on the leg wound as he instructed a female tech to hold pressure on the woman's breast.

"Any idea how long she's been here?" Almyra asked.

"The doors were locked when we arrived, and we had to wait for the manager to get up here. That was five minutes I guess, and it probably took us ten to get here. Before that, I haven't any idea. You probably know as much or more about this than we do, Doctor."

"Careful," Defrange warned. "Don't mess up those teeth marks."

She opened her tote and took out a pair of calipers and a small, Instamatic camera. She took pictures of the wound on the inner thigh, and then she had Whiteside dab the blood while she measured the bite marks. Anxious voices echoed from the hallway.

The young woman began to writhe and emit low moans.

"Do we know her name?" Defrange asked.

"Maureen Charbenau," the female tech replied.

"Maureen," Almyra said in a soothing tone. "You're hurt, but we're here to help you. You're gonna be alright."

"Grandma," Maureen whispered through the pillow case.

"No, it's not Grandma. I'm Dr. Defrange, and the voices you hear are people who are here to help you. Try to relax. There's a pillow case over your head, and I'm trying to untie it. Whiteside, give me your scissors!"

He handed over his bandage scissors, and Almyra cut the twine and removed the pillow case.

Maureen, looked just like her Irish name. Red hair, freckles, and large, frightened, blue eyes. "Why, you're not Grandma at all," she said. "You're an angel—an angel with green eyes."

Her head drooped to one side as she lost consciousness.

"That looks like semen on her breast," Almyra commented. "Please get a good sample for the lab."

She helped the paramedics gently lift Maureen to a stretcher. Once they were satisfied that their patient was as comfortable as possible, they rolled her slowly into the hallway.

Ferguson stuck his close-cropped head in the doorway.

"Coming, Detective?" he called.

"No," Almyra replied. "Please have your officers stay outside just for a few more minutes. I have to be in here alone."

"Yes, ma'am—Detective."

Ferguson spoke to the officers in the hallway, and in deference to their respect for him and Defrange's reputation, they opted to go to the far end of the hall and investigate the vending machines until Defrange was done.

"Ma'am?" Ferguson questioned from the doorway. "Where would you like for me to wait?"

"You can go on downstairs now," Almyra called to him. "I'll be fine. Tell Jefferson to wait in the lobby, and I'll be down in a few minutes."

"Jefferson?" the officer asked, "Jefferson's not here."

Almyra smiled. "Yes, he is—and be sure to tell him to stay down there. I don't need any distractions."

Ferguson shrugged and left.

Satisfied that she was alone, Almyra stood in the middle of Maureen's living room. She sensed an ominous presence. Closing her eyes, she let her mind slip into that inexplicable realm that she had tried to explain so many times. "ESP", "clairvoyance", "bugaboo", were some of the terms used by both fans and critics. The critics were often red-faced when she turned out to be correct. Duke University had determined that her accuracy rate was ninety-nine percent plus, which meant that she was seldom wrong, but there were always the die-hards who had to see for themselves.

She shifted her concentration, and her breathing deepened as she was aware of both everything and nothing. She stood as if frozen and allowed mental images to flow toward her like headlights approaching through a dark tunnel. Faster and faster they came until they were like a swarm of fireflies in a summer meadow, and then suddenly they focused and meshed together into one on-going scene. She began to speak aloud from her concentration as though her inner self were communicating with her conscious self.

"There is a man in coveralls," she began, "and he has dozens of keys. I can't see his face, but the emblem on the coveralls is 'Tidewater Breeze'. He's letting himself in with one of those keys."

As the image of the man moved down the hallway, she became a spiritual parasite locked into the energy of something that had occurred hours ago. She was tuned in to what she described in her writing as the energy fingerprint that is left by all events—and this one was the strongest she had ever experienced.

She was as one with Maureen's attacker, and with her eyes still closed she moved down the hallway from the living room to the bathroom. Locked in this blueprint, her hand reached for the louvered door of the linen closet, and she wedged herself into the narrow space which was left when the door was closed. She could hear the shower running, and she watched as Maureen emerged from the tub.

Defrange sensed male arousal when the attacker saw Maureen's nude, wet body, but she was also aware of two other strong psyches. Almyra sensed a hate and revulsion completely alien to her. The vision began to move.

Maureen opened the door to the linen closet, and while Almyra simultaneously watched and participated, she felt herself leap from the closet into the bathroom. Maureen braced herself to face her attacker—Almyra saw the fear in her eyes when the fist hit her forehead. It was at once savage and orgasmic.

Experience took over, and Almyra began to extricate herself from the event: even as she did, she realized that she was humming the old spiritual *Amazing Grace*. Torn between reality and her vision, she recalled a warning from one of her favorite professors at Duke.

Be careful, Almyra. We're dealing with a science that cannot be tested other than by our own psychic participation. Take care not to put yourself in a place from which you cannot return.

She was physically scouting in a very sick place and had begun to feel trapped.

"Return, return, return," echoed over and over again in her mind until her eyes popped open. She exhaled as if she had been punched in the stomach.

"The man works here," she said aloud, but then she was being drawn back into the scene. The reality of her own reflection in the mirror kept her from going too far.

"No, he doesn't work here," she whispered, "but where did he get the coveralls and keys?"

Her eyes closed, and she held on to her own being as the energy fingerprint began to race forward and backward like a video machine that had been struck with lightning. In a few seconds, she saw the whole scene that had played out earlier that morning. When her green eyes flashed open, they nearly glowed in the dimly-lit bathroom. The vision was over.

CHAPTER 7

J EFFERSON PARKED ACROSS from the exterior stairs which led to the basement at the Tidewater Breeze. On his way to the front entrance, he was greeted by Officer Alec Ferguson.

"I'm glad to see you, Lieutenant," he said.

Jefferson looked around. "Mornin' Ferguson. What's happened here?"

"Well, Lieutenant, I could tell you, but Detective Almyra Defrange is upstairs on the seventh floor. I think she wants to tell you herself. She told me to have you wait down here because she's up there doing her psychic investigation, and she doesn't want—what was it she said? 'Any distractions'."

Jeff was a little chagrined. He'd never considered himself a distraction, but he quickly decided that distraction was in the eye of the distracted.

"Wait a minute," Jeff said. "How did she know I was even down here?"

The officer shrugged. "Beats me," he smiled. "She's what we used to call a 'voodoo hoodoo' back when I was a kid in the Louisiana swamp."

In the face of all of this evidence, Jeff surrendered. "Ok," he said, "I'll wait down here."

"Right," Ferguson agreed. "The Captain told me to stay with her until you got here, so I'm going back to the Precinct unless you need me to stay for some reason,"

"No, I guess not," Jeff said, "I'll take the vigil from here. I'll watch over her for a while."

"Ok, Lieutenant," Ferguson smiled. "Good luck. It's not an easy job."

Jeff walked around to the front entrance and entered the cool lobby. His eyes had just become accustomed to the change from sunlight to artificial light when a woman bolted from the elevator like a refugee from a medieval insane asylum. He instinctively reached for his weapon.

"Jefferson!" the woman yelled. "I'm Defrange! Follow me!"

"What the hell?" he blustered.

He followed her around the building toward where he had parked across from the stairs leading to the basement. The door at the bottom of the steps was stenciled "Maintenance Shop", and the single bulb over the door was still on though it was well into the morning.

Defrange had drawn her pistol and was descending the steps as Jeff drew his .45 and cautiously followed her. She opened the door of the shop and visually swept the room before she turned to him.

"Jefferson," she said breathlessly as she gave him an unexpected hug.

"Yes, I'm Lieutenant Jefferson. Nice to meet you, too."

Detective Defrange stepped back. Her green eyes were looking through him.

"Let me look at you," she said as she brushed something off his lapel.

"I'm sorry, Dr. Defrange," he ventured, "but do I know you?"

She brushed that aside like she had brushed the lint off his jacket, and at once her tone sounded terse and professional.

"Lieutenant, we have a body in here. Do you want to investigate, or do you want to call the Medical Examiner first?"

It occurred to Jeff that, while this woman seemed in control, maybe he should confirm the body before calling Palachi out on a snipe hunt.

"Why don't we have a look first?" he said.

Defrange smirked. "I thought as much." She stepped back into the darkened basement as Jeff followed right behind her.

"Where's the body?" he whispered.

"I don't know exactly," she replied, "but it's in the shop somewhere."

"Wait a minute!" he said, keeping his voice low. "I thought you saw a body?"

"I did," she protested. "But I didn't see it when I looked in here a minute ago, I saw the evidence *before* I came down here."

Jefferson was incredulous for a moment until he remembered with whom he was working. Defrange acknowledged his hesitation.

"Trust me. There's a body in here. It just wasn't clear to me where. Sometimes a sense of urgency overwhelms the end of my visions, and I have to work on this plain like everyone else."

Jefferson stared into her electric emerald eyes. *Damn! It's really true what they say about her.*

Defrange smiled. "Trust me, Lieutenant. It's here. I'm just not sure if anyone else is. The energy from this killer is so overwhelming that I haven't been able to adjust to what is now and what was then."

"I don't understand," he said.

"You will," she replied, "and if you want to take the left perimeter, I'll take the right. We can meet at the back of the shop next to the door."

The area was dark except for the light from a small lamp on a workbench near the back.

"What door?" he asked.

"Just take the left side," she said impatiently, nodding in that direction. "You'll see when we get there."

They separated and fanned out so as not to be a clear target in case someone was hiding in the shadows. Defrange silently drifted around to the right side of the shop. It was a routine police sweep, and Jeff was impressed that she didn't need any reminders or have questions about how it was done.

He moved slowly, taking in every shape and shadow as he went. He was trying to keep Defrange in his sight as they played this potentially lethal game, but he knew that if he didn't focus on his sweep, he might get them both killed. He forced himself to stop watching her and concentrated on the task at hand.

Jeff worked his way around to a shower stall. The word "Decontamination" was stenciled on the side, and he recalled the OSHA regs that required the availability of a shower in areas where hazardous chemicals were routinely used. The stall was empty, but the odor of cleaning solvent brought tears to his eyes.

He returned to his slow, methodical orbit, and in three minutes he met Defrange at the back of the shop.

"Clear?" she asked.

"Clear," he said, "but I want to turn on the lights to get a better look at things – especially the shower."

Defrange tapped her gun against a fifty-gallon drum.

"We can look if you like," she said, "but the body is in here."

Jefferson's need for confirmation got the better of him, and he removed the lid of the oil barrel. The glow from the small lamp on the work bench made the scene appear even more macabre than it actually was.

"Oh, God," he exclaimed. "He's been hacked up all right. I wonder how he did this so fast?"

"Having doubts?" Defrange asked with pointed sarcasm, and she nodded toward the work bench with several types of power saws in plain view.

"Well, not really," Jeff hedged. "I guess I just had to see it before I called the M-E."

"Uh-huh." Defrange snorted as she threw a large switch by the back door, and lights came on all over the shop.

"Let's look at the shower," she suggested.

Again, the odor of solvent was overwhelming when they opened the curtain, but this time Jefferson saw something lying on the otherwise spotless tile floor. Closer inspection revealed that it was the first joint of a human finger with the nail still attached.

"This doesn't look good," he offered.

"No, it doesn't," Defrange agreed, "so let's look in here."

She used her ball-point pen to twist off the cover to the shower drain.

"Look," she said. "No doubt he did the dismemberment in here to contain the mess, and then he cleaned up to prevent exposing his presence."

Trapped in the drain was a mishmash of what appeared to be bloody hair and other unidentified tissue. Jeff was suddenly glad that the solvent odor was as strong as it was.

"Now you wanna call the ME?" she asked.

"Yeah," Jefferson replied, "and I'll be sure to mention this drain. I don't want Palachi to miss this."

They left the shop, and Defrange engaged the night latch on the door. "No sense in sharing this with anybody else," she offered.

"Right," he agreed. "I'm sure we can get a key to get back in."

Just as they got to the top of the steps Jeff had a feeling they were being watched.

"Me too," Defrange said.

"What?" Jeff asked. "You too, what?"

"I also feel that we're being watched."

Jeff's mind raced as they walked back around to the front of the complex. He had a million questions, but he would wait until he could speak to Defrange privately. He opened the door, and they entered the main lobby.

The housekeeping staff in their light blue polyester uniforms were gathered in the apse overlooking the pool. The group fell silent as the officers approached.

"I'm Lieutenant Jefferson," he said, flashing his badge, "and this is Detective Defrange. Could someone please direct us to the manager's office?"

"Sí," a young woman answered, "I will show you."

They followed her to a short, dead-end hallway beside the elevators and thanked her as she indicated the door at the end of the corridor. Jefferson knocked, but they entered without waiting for an invitation. A rotund, balding, red-faced man of about forty-five years was sitting at a desk. He stood when they entered.

"May I help you?"

The man was already nervous. Beads of perspiration glistened on his forehead. When Jefferson showed his badge, the man actually began to shake.

"I-I'm Thomas Whitaker," he said as he fell back into his chair.

"Yes, sir. I'm Lieutenant Jefferson and she's Inspector Defrange. We're Detectives. I'd like to use your phone, if you please."

"Of course, Detective. Help yourself. Do you need privacy?"

Jeff shook his head. "No, you need to hear this anyway."

Jeff called Palachi, and Whitaker's face went ashen as he listened to the conversation. By the time Jeff hung up, Whitaker's face had started to twitch.

"Lieutenant?" he began, "this is horrible. An attack on a tenant is bad enough, but if I understand what you said on the phone, I have a dead employee, too?"

"That's right," Defrange confirmed, "and we need to ask you some questions."

"By all means, Detectives. I will cooperate in any way I can."

"Who was your maintenance man last night?" Jeff asked.

Whitaker gasped. "Oh, no. George McGee. He's one of our best employees."

"I'm sorry, sir," Defrange said. "We presumably have found his remains it the maintenance shop."

Jefferson noted she didn't mention the condition of the remains. He sat down in a chair across from Whitaker, and Defrange deposited herself on a nearby loveseat.

"Due to the condition of the body," Jeff began, "I suggest that you wait for the ME to make a positive identification before you alarm the family. I suppose there's some possibility that the deceased is someone else."

Whitaker's face went whiter. "Not likely," he said. "McGee's wife has already called. He's late getting home, and he's always punctual."

"I see," Jeff replied with measured calmness. "Well, the police will hold off on informing the family until we have a positive ID."

"Now, sir," Defrange interrupted, "who found Maureen Charbenau?"

"Oh, one of the maids," Whitaker offered. "You see, we have a full service here, and unless a tenant instructs us to the contrary, we clean every day."

"Do you have her name?" Defrange asked.

Whitaker nodded. "Yes, it's Juanita Lopez. I talked to her just a few minutes ago. She's very upset."

"Understandably," Defrange agreed, "and where might we find Ms. Lopez?"

Whitaker sheepishly looked down as if to study some papers on his desk.

He can't look Defrange in the eye, Jeff thought.

I believe," Whitaker began slowly, "she may be up on the second floor. We have an employee lounge up there, and I suggested that she compose herself before she decided whether or not to go home for the day."

"Why wouldn't she go home?" Defrange pushed. "I imagine she is distraught."

"Well, if she goes home," Whitaker admitted, "she won't get paid."

"I see," Defrange replied. Jeff could feel the ice creeping in around her words.

"So," she continued, "if an employee has a traumatic event like, say, finding a mutilated woman with a pillow case over her head, or even possibly a death in their own family, they don't get a day off with pay?"

"That's strictly against policy," Whitaker said. "They're all part-time, and if they don't work, we can't pay them."

Defrange gave the man a look of derision. "Very humanitarian."

Jeff intervened. "Do you have a file on Maureen Charbenau?"

"Of course," Whitaker replied. "I have the usual tenant application, but we don't have anything personal other than that."

"Ever had any problems with her?" Jeff asked. "You know, loud parties, late rent, unwanted boyfriends hanging around, anything like that?"

Whitaker seemed to take the question personally.

"Oh, no," he replied. "Not Maureen. She's the ideal tenant. She works evenings at Portsmouth General— she's a nurse, you know—and yes, in that respect there is something unusual about her."

"What's that?" Jeff asked, leaning forward.

"She cares," Whitaker said. "I mean she cares about everybody. She's even taken her own time-off to tend to some of the elderly tenants who weren't feeling well. As far as I'm concerned, she's a beautiful, caring person, and I can't believe that someone attacked her like this."

Jeff looked at Defrange. He intuitively understood that she didn't think this man was a suspect. He also gathered that she was mentally contrasting his praise for Maureen with his lack of compassion for Juanita Lopez.

"Mr. Whitaker," Defrange said, "if you could spare the time, I would like for you to come upstairs with us to speak to Ms. Lopez. She'll probably feel more comfortable if you're with us."

"Of course," he agreed, and the two detectives followed him to the elevator.

CHAPTER 8

J UANITA LOPEZ WAS a small Mexican woman of about sixty. She was sitting alone at a table in the break room with a paper cup half-full of coffee in front of her. Whitaker introduced the detectives, and they all sat down. Juanita shifted nervously in her seat as she dabbed her dark eyes with a wadded-up tissue. Jeff sensed she wasn't comfortable with police.

"Senora Lopez," Defrange began calmly, "we know you're upset, and we don't mean to upset you further; but we need to ask you a few questions. Would that be all right?"

Juanita looked at Defrange in wide-eyed disbelief that this beautiful Anglo woman was speaking to her with such respectful politeness.

"*Sí,*" she said. "I will speak with you."

Her hands trembled and she spilled what was left of her coffee. Defrange ran and grabbed some paper towels from a dispenser on the wall.

"Mr. Whitaker," Jeff suggested, "let's you and I have a seat at that back table. We'll just let the girls speak privately."

The two men got up and seated themselves at a table farthest from the women. Whitaker began to prattle, but Jefferson kept one ear tuned in to the conversation across the room.

"Now, Juanita," Defrange began as she wiped up the spill, "may I call you Juanita?"

The woman smiled. "*Sí,*" *she* replied as she wiped a tear.

Defrange walked over and got the woman a fresh cup of coffee. "I know you've had a terrible morning, but I need for you to tell me what you saw in Ms. Charbenau's apartment this morning. Just take your time and don't worry. We know you haven't done anything wrong."

"Senora Defrange," Juanita addressed her, "it was horrible."

"Juanita," Defrange said, handing her the steaming Styrofoam cup, "I am a senorita, and you may call me Almyra."

Juanita smiled nervously. "Oh, *sí*," Almyra. I went into the apartment like I always do. I know that Senorita Charbenau sleeps during the day, so I was very quiet, but this morning her kitty was making so much noise I was afraid he would wake her up. I tiptoed to close the door to her room, and I saw blood all over the bed—and, she had something over her head. I was afraid that she was dead, and that maybe someone was still in the apartment."

She took a sip of coffee and took in a deep breath.

"Go ahead," Defrange urged.

"Well, I just ran," Juanita went on. "I closed the door and ran down to the far end of the hallway before I could gather my wits. When I stopped, I knew I had to do something, so I used an outside line from the house phone, and I dialed 911."

The detective nodded.

"Did you go back into the apartment?" Defrange asked. "I mean after you made the call?"

"Oh, no. I was too afraid. Senorita Charbenau has always been very kind to me, and I couldn't stand to see her hurt."

"I understand, but did you see anyone else?"

"No. By the time I got back downstairs to tell Mr. Whitaker what had happened, the police had begun to arrive. I came up here shortly after that. Is Ms. Charbenau…?

"No," Defrange patted the woman's hand. "She's at the hospital. She is hurt, but she should be alright."

"*Por Díos!*" the woman exclaimed. "I was so afraid she might be dead."

"Juanita, you are a hero, and if you hadn't found Ms. Charbenau when you did, and if you hadn't reacted so quickly, she might have bled to death." Defrange looked over at Whitaker and spoke in her best stage whisper. "I'm sure Mr. Whitaker will want you to take the rest of the day off with pay. It's a small enough reward for someone as courageous as you."

"W-why of course, Juanita," Whitaker stammered. "By all means, take the day off—er, with pay. The man glared at Defrange as Jeff stifled a laugh.

"*Oh, Bueno! Gracias, Señor Whitaker.*"

"No problem," he replied with a forced smile. "Now, if you officers don't need me anymore, I need to go back to work."

"Go right ahead, sir," Jeff smiled, "and thanks for all you help."

Whitaker stormed from the room.

Defrange got up from her chair. "Juanita, we have to go back to work now, too. Go home and get some rest. You've had a long day already."

"*Gracias,* Almyra, and you too, Senor Jefferson."

Juanita hugged them both.

"*Adiós,*" she said.

Moments later Jefferson and Defrange stepped off the elevator in the main lobby and came face to face with Martin Palachi.

"Good morning for the second time," he boomed. "Which way to the murder?"

"Yeah, good morning again," Jeff replied dryly. "The body is in the basement. C'mon, I'll show you."

"I don't know why we should bother," Palachi groused. "If it is the Raptor, there won't be anything but the body. There won't be any clues—"

"I know," Jeff replied. "Uh, Martin I'd like for you to meet—"

"I swear, Jeff," Palachi went on, unhindered, "this guy is driving me nuts. I mean is he changing his MO or what? Look, he kills nine women—nothing, then he kills the tenth one, and he leaves us a note for God's sake! Now, he's killed a man, but he left a woman alive. I can't even imagine what he's up to."

Defrange had been listening patiently.

"He's jerking you around," she said softly.

Palachi went off.

"Now, just a minute, lady! We're having enough problems with this killer without you people from the press and your amateurish speculations. It's irresponsible journalism! Why don't you just take care of whatever it is you do, and let us do the forensics and police work?"

"Martin," Jeff interrupted, taking hold of his colleague's arm. "I was trying to introduce you. This is my new partner on loan to us from—"

"Milwaukee," Palachi finished Jeff's sentence, recognition revealing itself in his now flushed face. He gulped as perspiration emerged on his forehead.

"Dr. Defrange," he apologized, "I am so sorry. I was so caught up in my own tirade I didn't recognize you. Can you ever forgive me?"

Defrange offered her hand with a reassuring smile. "I understand, Dr. Palachi. There's nothing to forgive, and it's a pleasure to meet you."

Jeff thought Palachi was about to hyperventilate, but the capable physician managed a fair recovery.

"Dr. Defrange," Palachi went on, "I've admired your work for years."

"I'm looking forward to working with you as well," Defrange replied.

"Thank you," Palachi said with a slight bow. "You're very gracious." Palachi glanced briefly at Jeff. "Have you seen the body?" he asked Defrange.

"Yes—twice," she answered. "Once in my mind and once in person. Neither time was very pleasant."

Palachi nodded sympathetically. "Yes, I understand. I better get down there and earn my pay. Do you wanna come along?"

"We'll pass," Jeff replied. "Unless Dr. Defrange needs to see more, we really need to get to the Precinct and let Captain Chambers know what's going on."

"I've seen enough," Defrange offered, "but, I would like to come to your office sometime, Dr. Palachi, to review anything you have on our psycho."

"By all means," Palachi replied. "Maybe you two could come by this afternoon. Oh, damn! It'll have to be later. I have to swing by Portsmouth General. I understand there were bite marks on the woman who was attacked here, and I want to get some pictures and measurements of the marks. I can compare them with evidence from the other attacks."

Defrange reached into tote and handed several pictures to Palachi.

"Here are pictures of the bites, and I have the measurements in my notebook."

Palachi grinned broadly.

"Dr. Defrange, you are a breath of fresh air!" He handed the pictures back to her. "Why don't you hold on to these, and we'll review them later."

Jefferson all at once felt a strange pang of something like jealousy—and he didn't like it.

Defrange nodded. "That will be fine. If you want to get a key from the Manager, Mr. Whitaker, there's an entrance to the maintenance shop just off the lobby. The door locks automatically to keep people from wandering down there."

"That must be how our killer got into the main part of the building," Palachi surmised. "He came in from downstairs."

"It is how he got in," Defrange replied, "and I think he picked his victim from the master list of tenants. I know he got the master keys from Mr. McGee. You'll find his remains in the oil drum beside the desk."

"I'll find it!" the ME said confidently as he started down the hallway.

"Last door on the end," Jeff called after him, "and the manager is in his office."

"Be sure to check the shower drain," Defrange called.

"Got it!" Palachi replied as he disappeared around the corner.

Jeff looked at Defrange. "Ready to go?"

"Yes," she said. "I think we've seen enough for one morning."

They left the building and walked around to the side where Jefferson had parked the car. Again, he had the sensation they were being watched.

"Me too," Defrange said once more.

She's been in my head again. Like his recent pang of jealousy, Jeff wasn't sure how he felt about *that*, either.

There was a nagging feeling that he'd met Almyra Defrange before. He opened his mouth to ask her, but he was cut off.

"Just think about it," she mysteriously grinned as they approached the car.

Jeff was thinking about it, but his thoughts were interrupted by Palachi, who came running upstairs from the maintenance shop, ducking under the yellow crime scene tape as he waved a piece of paper in his gloved hand.

"Jefferson! Defrange! Wait! He left another note!"

When he reached the Detectives, he held out the note so that both of them could see it.

> *"two heads are better than one*
> *so, I left an extra for jefferson…*
> *xoxo raptor"*

Jeff looked at Palachi. "Where did you find this?" he asked.

"It was lying on the desk. Just under the base of the lamp."

Jeff frowned and looked at Defrange. "It wasn't there earlier, was it, Almyra?"

"No, it wasn't," she replied as her eyes darkened by several shades. "He was either still in the basement while we were there, or…." She paused. "He still has the master keys! Wait until Whitaker finds out he's going to have to replace over a thousand locks!" She started walking toward the car.

"A thousand locks?" Palachi echoed.

"Yeah," Jeff said. "I hope that doesn't push our shaky manager right over the edge."

"Gentlemen!" Defrange called out, motioning for them to join her at Jeff's patrol car. "If you would be so kind…."

Jeff walked up and peered through the back window: George McGee's head, with its vacant, bloody eye sockets, was resting on the black leather seat."

"Jesus!" Jeff said under his breath. "I guess that's what the note meant." He sensed a storm in Defrange's head.

"Maybe our feelings about being watched weren't too far off," she commented as she stared at the macabre sight.

Jeff reached for his weapon.

Defrange touched his arm. "Never mind. He's gone."

"How do you know?" Jeff asked as he surveyed the perimeter.

"Because I *know*!" she snapped back.

Palachi took a small, plastic evidence bag from his lab coat pocket and carefully dropped the note into it.

"We'll need to keep your car, Lieutenant," he said, "so we can go over it for evidence."

"Yeah, sure," Jeff replied with impatience. "I'll borrow another car so we can get back to the Precinct. Damn it! He's killed two people in less than twenty-four hours, and we're no closer to catching him than we were six months ago."

"Three," Palachi added, "and we're still no closer."

Jeff took a step back. "*What?* What do you mean, 'three'?"

"Three," Palachi repeated. "One of the lab techs took a message while we were inside. Maureen Charbenau died a little while ago. Apparently, when the surgical team approached her with an anesthesia mask, she thought she was being attacked again. She went into cardiac arrest, and they couldn't get her back. We're gonna pick her up when we're done here. I'll have to do an autopsy."

Defrange's eyes blazed. "I've never felt a presence like this before. He's not going to stop. He enjoys this too much."

CHAPTER 9

JEFFERSON COMMANDEERED A squad car, and he and Defrange rode back to the Precinct with little conversation. They each had to decompress, and the conversation he so desired begged to wait until a more appropriate moment.

When they got to his office, Jeff offered Defrange the couch, and he sat behind the desk for what he thought would be a few minutes of relaxation. A knock on the door interrupted that plan, and before Jeff could say "Come in!" Dr. Winetraub was peering into the room.

"Dr. Winetraub!?" Jeff began. "What can we do for you?"

"Keep your seats," he insisted as he walked in. "I'm just here to get some information on our newest employee."

Jeff emitted a relenting sigh. "I see," he said. "Dr. Milton Winetraub, may I introduce you to—"

"Forget in Jefferson," Winetraub cut him off with a wink in Defrange's direction. "Dr. Defrange and I are old friends."

Jeff shot Defrange an inquisitive look. "Oh, really?"

"I helped her find the Captain's office early this morning," Winetraub said as he approached Defrange. He leaned down toward the sofa and took her hand.

"Really, Doctor," she said. "I'm only here temporarily. What could you possibly need from me?"

"Dr. Defrange, you should be more patient. Since you're here, and since this is such a risky job, I want to get some baseline medical information, just in case."

"*Just in case?*" she echoed and took her hand away from his.

"Well, yes." The doctor went on. "Just in case something happens, and I need to care for you in an emergency."

"I see," she replied, looking over at Jefferson, who was amused at seeing this woman finally caught off guard. "What sort of information do you need?"

"Well, for starters, do you have an immunization card?"

Defrange picked up her purse, pulled out a small yellow card from her wallet and handed it to him.

Winetraub nodded. "Good, very good," he said as he read over the card. "Everything seems to be up to date. Do you have any allergies.?"

"None," Defrange replied, replacing the card back in her wallet.

"Any physical impairments that would keep you from doing your duties?"

"None," she repeated. Jeff noticed her eyes getting darker.

You better be careful, old Doc. You're gonna go too far.

Winetraub went on blindly in his official tone. "Dr. Defrange, have you had a chest x-ray in the last six months?"

Defrange raised her hands in mock surrender, but her voice was icily stern. "Dr. Winetraub, I'm just passing through. Isn't this all just a little too much."

"Well, we've had a recent increase in TB cases in some of our homeless shelters. I just want to be safe and get a baseline."

Defrange looked to her new partner for guidance, but Jeff only offered a shrug even as his eyes twinkled in amusement. "It's up to you, partner. He'll probably hound you until you do it. I'll wait here if you wanna go. How long will it take, Doc?"

"Fifteen minutes at the outside," Winetraub replied, "I'll feel better to have a baseline on everything, just in case."

"There you go with that 'just in case' again,'" Defrange replied, emitting an exasperated sigh as she rose from the couch. "Lead the way!"

Winetraub held the door as Defrange stepped into the hallway. He closed the door behind them.

Jefferson sat at his desk, chuckling at Defrange's impatience with Dr. Winetraub. As he leaned back in his worn leather chair, he mused over Dr. Winetraub's history with the Portsmouth Police. The man had saved the department countless hours and dollars by triaging illnesses and injuries that weren't serious enough for the emergency room, and he voluntarily took call twenty-four-hours-a-day, though no one ever called him. Captain Chambers always discouraged it.

"He does enough around here during his usual ten-hour days without us bothering him at home," he would say.

Jeff had once asked the doctor why he wanted to help the police rather than be in private practice, and he'd confessed that he liked the excitement of the Precinct and had considered becoming a cop at one time in his life.

"I just don't have the nerve," he had confessed.

Jefferson's thoughts switched to his new partner. Why did he feel he had met her before? He couldn't imagine forgetting her, for one thing, but try as he might he couldn't shake out any memories. All at once his stomach growled. He was starving. Then he wondered when was the last time Defrange had eaten.

He picked up the phone and called the New Delhi Deli on High Street and ordered what he thought might be a familiar lunch for someone from an area primarily settled by Germans. He ordered Reuben sandwiches, German potato salad, pickles and soda.

He was right. Defrange hadn't eaten for almost fifteen hours, and she and the lunch order arrived at the same time. She was delighted.

"Hungry?" Jeff teased when she grabbed a pickle from the tray and bit into it with a loud crunch.

"Famished," she confessed as she polished off the pickle. "Just let me freshen up a bit."

"Of course."

He opened the door to his private bathroom.

"The throne room," he announced.

Defrange laughed. "Thank you. I just need to wash my face and hands."

She slipped out of her pumps and stood at the sink with the door open.

"Lieutenant Jefferson," she called out.

"Right here," he answered as he popped the tops on the sodas.

Jeff heard the water go off, and she emerged, standing in the door frame while she dried her hands on a paper towel.

"I've been observing you all morning," she said, "and, I believe that you are very good at what you do. I like your style."

Jefferson was a little shocked. After all, this was the South, and a woman didn't generally voice opinions like that, especially to a man she'd just met. He loved it.

"Thank you, Detective Defrange, "I want you to know that I have been likewise impressed by your performance. I have to admit that you're more than a little spooky, but I do appreciate the compliment."

"Lieutenant, I don't give compliments," she replied sternly. "I either say what I feel, or I just keep my mouth shut. By the way, have you known him long?"

"Whom do you mean?" Jeff asked.

Defrange walked over to him. "Winetraub. Dr. Winetraub!"

"Yeah," he replied. "I've known him for more than fifteen years or so. He's even patched me up a few times. Why do you ask?"

"Oh, I don't know. I met his nurse, and they are sort of, well, 'cute' together. Has she been with him a long time?"

"Oh, you mean Sally Brevet. Yeah, she was hired, I believe, about a week after he got here."

"Are they a couple after hours?" Defrange asked with a sly grin.

Jeff chuckled. "Honestly, I don't know. There have been rumors about them for years, well, since the Doc's wife passed away, but I've never given it much thought. Anyway, if two people can find happiness in this world, more power to them."

Jeff glanced at Defrange. She was sitting on the arm of the couch, barefoot, no make-up, and her eyes were mint green, not the usual darker, forest-green shade. She was the loveliest creature he'd ever seen, except possibly in his dreams, and at that moment he wasn't sure of that.

"Have you found any sort of happiness, Lieutenant?" she asked.

He panicked. What the hell did she mean asking him a question like that?

"Of course, I have," he lied. "What do you mean?"

In truth, he had probably never really been happy. He'd made himself conform to the role because he'd made a commitment, and because he thought it was the right thing to do. Defrange seemed to be looking right through him.

"Are you sure?" she smiled mysteriously.

He was trying to think of something to say, anything, as she walked over to the table. He was learning that her shifts in topics of conversation were neither accidental or flighty. She was always on top of whatever was going on around her, and she was always in control.

"Oh, Reubens!" she exclaimed as she removed the wax paper from a sandwich. "How did you know this is my favorite?"

"Oh, a lucky guess," he replied, relieved at the change of subject. "Or maybe your ESP is contagious."

All at once, something went off in his head, and his mind flashed back to Duke University and his experience in 1971.

He'd been injured in Nam, and he'd been sent to Duke to save his life. It was also a medical opportunity for testing not only himself but also Commander Robert Douglas. Douglas was the founder of MAC V SOG, and it had come to the attention of the upper echelon that he and Jefferson could communicate non-verbally—and, neither time nor distance had any bearing on their accuracy. They called it "jungle telepathy', and they were trying to determine if it was innate, or if it could be taught to others.

On the morning Jefferson was injured, Douglas communicated that he was in an area of danger, but the message came too late. Jeff stumbled into an ambush and somehow, he'd gotten a head injury that sent his mind somewhere other than where in usually lived. He'd been rescued, triaged, and sent to Duke. He was in a coma for four months.

Now, that memory, or lack of memory, was stirring something deep inside him. He'd lost his extrasensory abilities after the coma, and he had found that to be a mixed blessing. There was something now, though, that was pulling him back almost against his will, to those four months at Duke.

"Dr. Defrange," he whispered.

"Go ahead," she urged softly, placing her paper plate on the conference table. "It's time."

Jeff's consciousness was whirling around in a spiral, like a high-pressure front on the evening weather. He felt for a moment that he might black out until, suddenly, all of it stopped just as suddenly as it appeared. A clarity he hadn't experienced in nearly thirty years washed over him.

"Dr. Defrange," he whispered again, "you were with me at Duke!"

She broke out in laughter. "I sure was! I was at your bedside off and on for four months."

Jeff dropped into his chair. "But why didn't I recognize you or remember you right away? I still can't remember ever seeing you, but I can sense you now, in my head. My God!"

Defrange pulled up a chair and sat down in front of him.

"You don't remember me with any definition because you probably never looked at me with your eyes. I was doing post-grad research, and I'd already chosen you and Commander Douglas as my project. It wasn't in the plan that you'd arrive with head injuries, so I had to modify my approach. When you started waking up, I faded into the background and studied you from afar."

"Why'd you do that?" Jeff asked.

"Because," she explained, "I had been walking around in your mind, and while you were aware, I was there, you didn't understand who or what I was. You actually believed that I was a spirit, and that I was guiding you."

"Weren't you?" he asked as his feelings of recognition grew stronger.

"Of course, I was," Defrange confessed, "but I didn't want to affect your abilities when you woke up. I needed to get out of the way so that we could study you and Douglas without any distractions. You might not have tested as well if you'd known that your 'guardian angel' was standing there, in the flesh, looking at you. I had become an unwanted variable in my own experiment."

Jeff got up and paced the room. "Oh, my God! The spirit in my dreams. The beautiful, wispy, warm being that led me back to where it was light." He spun around to face Defrange. "Did I ever thank you?"

"Yes, you did thank me, but not as your spirit guide. You thanked me when you left Duke as one of the docs that saved your life, and you're thanking me now because you know what happened. I have never been able to determine why your sixth sense faded after the coma. In that respect, my experiment was a total failure."

Jeff smiled. "Well, maybe, maybe not. There have been times when I was glad I had lost the ability. In that respect you were a success." Jeff shook his head, and he threw up his hands. "Anyway, I can't think about this anymore right now. I'm starving."

They sat at the table and ate and talked about nothing in particular. As they chatted, Jeff reveled in the reunion, but he was also cautious. Defrange really did seem to understand him better than anyone ever had, and, for some reason, he felt closer to her than he'd ever felt with anyone. He needed time to decipher it all.

The phone rang, and they both jumped.

"Ok, Nostradamus," Jeff said as he walked toward the desk. "Who's calling us?"

"It's Palachi," she answered casually. "He's excited about us coming to the morgue."

Jeff grabbed the phone without looking at the ID and switched to speaker. "Palachi, this is Jefferson."

"Jeff!" the voice boomed across the room.

"Yeah, Martin, I know you're excited about us coming to see you at the morgue"

There was a brief silence.

"Right," Palachi said with an air of incredulity. *"Can you two come over this afternoon. We can go over what I've gotten so far, but it's not really that much unless you two can put something together that I can't see."*

"Yep, we'll be there shortly. I just have to report to Captain Chambers first."

"Perfect," Palachi agreed.

Jeff hung up and looked at Defrange. She looked smug and refreshed as he braced himself for the inevitable teasing over her accurately knowing who was on the phone. It never came.

"You're amazing," he confessed.

"No more than you," she replied.

Somehow, he pulled himself from the vacuum of her peridot eyes and finished his lunch.

"As soon as we're done," he said between bites, "we can go down and see the Captain. I know he's anxious to hear first-hand about our morning at the Tidewater Breeze."

Defrange stood up, stretched her arms and yawned.

"Ok, partner. I'll just stretch out on the couch until you're done."

She glided across the room to the sofa and lay down on her back. In another minute Jeff heard her rhythmic breathing, peppered by just the hint of a snore

He sat back and thought about his experiences with psychic phenomena and decided that he should just let it lie dormant and not pursue it. He'd never been—nor would he ever be—on Defrange's level.

He watched her sleep as he picked up the remnants of his lunch. The gentle rise and fall of her breasts was leading him somewhere he shouldn't go, but he couldn't resist watching her.

Get a grip, Jefferson! She's just another cop. Special, yes, but just another cop—and, I was her lab rat!

Before making his way to Chambers' office, he took his raincoat from the closet and covered Defrange. She smiled without opening her eyes.

CHAPTER 10

JEFFERSON WENT DOWN to the fourth floor and entered Marsha's domain.

"Hi, Lieutenant," she greeted.

"Hi, Marsha. Is the Captain in?"

"Yes. He'd just asked if I'd seen you. How were things at the Tidewater?"

"Quite interesting," Jeff replied, "but I don't have time to go into it now."

Marsh leaned across her desk; her eyes were filled with intrigue. "Did you meet Detective Defrange?"

Jeff grinned. "Ohh, yes. She is quite a cop. I left her taking a nap in my office. She was up all night you know."

"Oh, I know," Marsha replied. "She's such a lovely person—tell her that I asked about her. I enjoy talking with her, and I like her very much."

He tried to suppress another grin, but he couldn't.

"So do I, Marsha."

She announced Jefferson's arrival by intercom, and the Captain replied by opening his office door.

"Jefferson, come in!" he barked.

Jeff followed Chambers into the office and took a seat across from his desk.

The captain peered into the outer office. "Where's Dr. Defrange?"

"I left her taking a nap," Jeff replied. "She was coming down with me, but she nodded off. I thought it might help her to rest for a while."

"Good decision. She's been going since sometime yesterday. You know, I tried to send her to the Harbor View, but when the call came in about the Tidewater, she'd have no part of taking time to rest. She had to be where the action was."

Jeff nodded. "She is tenacious—she's a helluva cop and partner."

Chambers' expression became serious. "Then I take it you don't mind working with her?"

"Mind? No not at all," Jeff replied. "Why would you ask that?"

The older man's eyes regained their sparkle, and he leaned back in his chair.

"Well, frankly Lieutenant, I know how you like to work alone, and some men would resent being stuck with an out-of-town expert, especially if the expert was a woman." The Captain's curious eyes searched Jeff's for a reaction, but he was ready.

"No problem as far as I'm concerned," Jeff replied with as much nonchalance as he could muster. "You know, we discovered that we had met before, actually. She was at Duke when I was there. Hell, it's been a good while ago, but I'll tell you one thing: I've watched her all morning, and she's one of the best investigators I've ever seen. She is thorough and careful, and she's quick with good instincts. We worked together like partners who've been together for years. I'd trust her with my back anytime."

The captain leaned forward. "That's a stellar recommendation coming from you, Lieutenant, but I'm not surprised you feel that way. I've been perusing her service record from Milwaukee, and I'm sure she won't mention it; but she's gotten more commendations than anyone in the history of their department. Did you know the FBI *and* INTERPOL rely on her expertise, either in person or in the form of written recommendations, anytime they have a particularly elusive fugitive?"

"Yeah, I'd heard that," Jefferson replied.

"I have one request of you, Jefferson."

The detective leaned forward. "Yes sir, what is it?"

Chambers picked up his pen from the desk and rolled it between his thumb and index finger.

"She's proven that she's tough enough to make it in a man's professional world, but I want you to promise me that you'll take care of her. She's probably the greatest criminologist of this century, hell maybe ever, and while she's here we need to make sure that she doesn't get hurt—or worse."

"Got'cha, Cap. I'll do my best. She's pretty headstrong, but I'll do my damnedest to keep up with her."

"Good. I know you will. Look, why don't you suggest that she take the afternoon off so she can rest. I've already sent her things over to the crow's nest."

I'll suggest it, Captain, but I can tell you that she won't take off early for any reason. Maybe she'll agree after we go over the Tidewater evidence and some other things the ME wants to show her. That's our plan for the afternoon."

"All right," Chambers agreed. "I'll leave that to your judgement. Now, what happened over there this morning?"

Jeff spent the next half hour relating the events of the morning, and how he felt that it was a continuation of the situation at the Ravenscroft. He told the Captain about the unexpected death of Maureen Charbenau, and that he had a hunch about why the Raptor didn't kill her outright. The Captain took notes while Jefferson gave his report, but he seemed distracted. When Jeff finished, Chambers leaned back in his chair and sighed.

"Before I forget," he said, "I've called a press conference for nine o'clock Monday morning. I want the public to know that Defrange is here, and that we're doing everything possible to contain this killer. Any conflicts?"

"No, sir," Jeff replied. "We'll be there. Maybe her appearance will lessen the flack."

"Look, Jefferson," his boss assured him, "I know you've done everything possible to catch this butcher, and I know you take him personally. Flack is part of *my* job, and I didn't ask Defrange here to belittle you or our department. This killer is something unusual in this world, and we need extraordinary help to nail him."

Jeff raised his hands. "Oh no, Captain. I understand why you asked for help, and you're right about the Raptor—he is something different. I've often wondered how and why he ended up here.

Chambers was thoughtful.

"It's been my experience," he said finally, "that good things usually come from the most adverse of circumstances, if we're willing to look for them. I'm just waiting to see how the Raptor fits into the scheme of things."

It was Jeff's turn to be pensive.

"Cap," he began, "why did you pair her with me rather than a female officer, or even let her work as an entity unto herself. She's certainly capable."

The impish gleam returned to the Captain's eyes.

"I put her with you for two—no three—three reasons. First, I know that you're alleged to possess some of her same talents. I've never known you too use them on the force, but I'm well aware of your military record and the psychic abilities you used then. I also know that you seemed to lose that ability sometime before you were discharged from service, but I don't believe it. I don't think that something like that gets taken away from a person. Anyway, I've never understood all the psychic stuff, but hell, I know the theory of the internal combustion engine, and I've never understood how that works either. I just know that it does."

Jeff was a little intimidated by this revelation. He hoped the Captain wasn't expecting his abilities to return overnight.

"The second reason," Chambers continued, "is that you're both outstanding investigators, and since you know more about the case than anyone, I believe the pair of you can overcome whatever it takes to crack it."

Jefferson was a little embarrassed by the Captain's praise. His boss was up to something.

"Thank you," Jeff replied, "but, you mentioned three reasons. What's the third one?"

Chambers pushed back from his desk and swiveled his chair so that he could look out over the Elizabeth River.

"Let's just say," he said, "that you and Defrange aren't the only people with insight, and we'll talk about the third one over a beer when the Raptor's locked up—or dead."

He turned his chair back around: his eyes were dancing.

"Go get her, Jefferson, and you two get over to see Palachi."

Both men stood.

"Thanks, Captain. I'll do that." He headed for the door.

"See you, Marsha," he called as he made his exit.

"Have a good afternoon, Lieutenant," she replied in is wake. "Be sure to tell Almyra to come down and see me. I feel as though I've known her all my life."

"I know what you mean," Jeff replied with a smile as e headed for the elevator.

Jeff entered as quietly as he could, but Defrange woke up. She stretched and yawned as she focused her eyes on him.

"Partner," she said, smiling a sleepy smile, "you went to see the Captain without me."

"Yes," Jeff confessed. "I thought you might need a few minutes sleep. The Captain sends his best, and Marsha wants you to come see her."

Defrange got up and headed for the bathroom.

"I'll just make a quick pit stop before we go see Palachi," she said, closing the bathroom door.

"Ok. I'll go requisition a car and meet you at the front entrance in fifteen minutes."

Jeff picked up the car from the motor pool in the basement and drove around to the front entrance of the Precinct building. Defrange was standing on the sidewalk, waiting. He got out and opened her door, secretly hoping that a least a few people inside the building were looking out the windows.

They headed off for the morgue as Jeff filled her in on the press conference scheduled for Monday morning. She agreed that, while it might get some heat off the Captain, it might not be wise to let the Raptor know who she was and why she was in Portsmouth.

"I didn't think of that," Jefferson admitted. "I wonder if the Captain did?"

"He probably did," she replied. "I suppose a press conference is alright if Captain Chambers thinks so. We can just play it by ear."

Just as they turned onto Crawford Parkway, Dr. Winetraub stepped from the curb. Jefferson pulled over.

"Hey, Doc!" he called. "Where you going?"

The afternoon humidity had taken effect: the doctor's shirt collar was damp, and his gray hair was glued to his forehead.

"Nowhere really," he said through Defrange's open window. "I just finished mid-day sick call, and I came out for some air. I saw you two leaving, and I was wondering if I might tag along, just for a change of scenery. I promise to stay out of the way."

Jeff deferred to Defrange.

"Partner?" he asked.

"It's certainly alright with me, Lieutenant. I don't have any objections."

"Hop in, Doc. We're going over to see Palachi. You might even enjoy going over whatever evidence he's got"

Winetraub nodded and slipped into the backseat behind Defrange.

"Thanks, Detectives," he said, flashing a grin. "I hoped you might be going somewhere that involved the Raptor case."

Jeff was suddenly curious. "Is the Captain having you look in on this?"

"Well, he did mention that, as Medical Officer, I should be more involved that I have been. I thought I'd look into it, so long as it doesn't interfere with my other duties. I've never been much into this serial killer stuff, anyway. Psychopaths and sociopaths have never been my forte. I'd much rather deal with a gunshot wound or a broken finger than to try to deal with all the hypothetical stuff that that can't be seen."

Jeff chuckled. "I understand. I hope this won't be too boring for you."

"Oh, I don't think it will be," Winetraub replied. "I've never had a boring encounter with Martin Palachi."

Everyone laughed as they rolled through the traffic and the Virginia heat. Defrange's eyes had darkened like the sky before a thunderstorm.

"What'cha thinking, partner?" Jeff asked.

"Nothing much," she replied. "I just have a feeling that I can't explain, that's all."

"Maybe it was the Reuben," Jeff teased.

"Yes," Winetraub added, "not to mention being on your feet for a day-and-a-half."

"Probably so," Defrange agreed. "I suppose it's a combination of things."

Jefferson looked at his partner. Her stress was not physical.

"Here we are," he announced as they pulled into the main parking lot of the Medical Examiner's Office.

The only available space was between two hearses, and Jeff reluctantly parked as he wondered why he'd agreed to meet here. The morgue was not one of his favorite places. The smells, sights, and sounds came from a world he'd just as soon not think about.

They entered through a side door, and Jeff led the way down a long corridor that led to Palachi's office. The whining of an oscillating skull saw being wielded for the purpose of removing the top of someone's cranium reinforced Jeff's loathing for this place of death. He was relieved when they reached Palachi's door, and he knocked a little more loudly than necessary.

"Damn it! Come on in! It's not locked," thundered the familiar voice behind the door.

Jeff allowed Defrange and Winetraub to enter first into the usual chaos of Martin Palachi's world.

The office looked just the way one would expect if they really knew the Medical Examiner. Papers were scattered on the desk, boxes of books were stacked on the floor, and half-open file drawers greeted those who might think this was the office of a complete slob. However, those who knew and respected Martin Palachi understood that this office and his life were on-going dynamic processes, and that he could instantly lay his hands on anything he wanted from either.

"Detectives and Dr. Winetraub!" Palachi greeted them with enthusiasm.

He had obviously been looking at something under a microscope, and Jeff was in no way curious. Palachi quickly unloaded the only three chairs and motioned for everyone to sit while he leaned against the desk like a professor about to speak to his class.

"How's your afternoon?" he asked.

"Quieter and more pleasant than this morning," Jeff replied. "You got anything on our killer?"

"I'm not sure that we do," Martin said, "but I'm not sure that we don't. I've finished with Maureen Charbenau, and I can assure you that it was one senseless death. She was literally scared to death, and I don't know anything else I can say about it. I've sent samples of the semen to the State Lab for DNA, but I can tell you from the bite marks, in comparing them to others I've collected, Ms. Charbenau was bitten by the same person who has bitten all of our victims. We can confirm that with Dr. Defrange's pictures and measurements also."

"Then it was definitely the Raptor?" Jefferson asked.

"It seems so," Palachi replied. "If the DNA matches, we'll know for sure."

Jeff frowned. "Then why didn't he kill her?"

Palachi looked as though he were wrestling with something that had been bothering him.

"I can't imagine why," he said, "unless he was tired from the Ravenscroft, or maybe was pushed for time. Maybe it was the time of day when he should have been thinking about being somewhere else."

"I hadn't thought of that angle," Jeff mused, "because, you know we've been thinking it might be a vagrant, or some other displaced person. I hadn't given a lot of thought about his being someone who actually lives here. Someone with a stable life. Someone with a job, maybe?"

"No," Defrange interjected, "he's no vagrant. He's intelligent and could always have steady quarters just from living by his wits if nothing else."

Everyone became lost in their own thoughts for a moment.

"What about the handwriting?" Jeff asked. "Has anyone looked at that?"

"Yeah," Palachi said. "I faxed pictures of the Ravenscroft message to some friends at the University of Virginia, and at the Medical College of Virginia, and to one cryptology expert I know at the FBI. Here, I kept copies."

"The FBI guy emailed me a few preliminary thoughts without analyzing them closely," Palachi went on. "It's the usual: the killer writes in lower case because he feels inferior or inadequate, if you will."

Winetraub picked up one of the photos and inspected it. "Well, he began, "if I remember my psychology classes, that would go along with the usual profile of a killer of this sort."

Jeff looked to Palachi, who shrugged.

"What do you think?" the ME asked.

Jeff tilted his chair back. "Hell, don't ask me. I've never quite understood all this psycho hocus pocus anyway. If I get you drift, you're telling me that this guy feels less a person than the rest of us, so he mutilates and kills women?"

"Right," Palachi answered. "That's pretty much it, in an understated, over-simplified way. He writes that way because he feels inferior, sort of lower case and unimportant."

Winetraub put down the photo. "I've never understood, though, if he kills women *because* he feels inferior, or does he feel inferior *because* he kills women?"

Jeff glanced at Defrange: her eyes were ablaze.

"Bullshit, boys!" she calmly scoffed. "This killer doesn't feel inferior to anyone. He's playing a role to lead us away from the truth. He knows all the stereotypes, and he's using them as a smokescreen."

"So," Jeff ventured, "he's smart enough to know criminal psychology, and he's using it to throw us off?"

"Dr. Defrange," Winetraub interjected, "do you really believe that this killer is smart enough and deviant enough to use standard models and profiles of a serial killer to intentionally throw us off his trail?"

"That's exactly what I mean," Defrange replied.

Palachi sat down on the edge of the trash barrel behind his desk.

"I can't imagine that a person who'd done what we've seen from this killer would have a very high IQ," Winetraub added.

Defrange looked at him and shook her head. "He's even more intelligent than we've begun to discover. I think he only started leaving notes because that's what a killer of this ilk would ordinarily do. I've been inside his psyche, and he's not disturbed, as such—he's laughing the whole time we're running around in circles. He's doing what he's conditioned to do, for whatever reason that may be."

Dr. Winetraub stood up. "I need to get going," he said.

Jeff stood also. "Sure, Doc. We'll give you a ride back if you can stick around for a few more minutes."

"No that's ok. I'll catch the bus right out front. I just remembered I have a gunshot wound to check this afternoon, and I don't want to put it off on the nurse. It may be leading to gangrene, and if it is, I'll have to admit the officer to the hospital."

"Ok, sure Doc, but you can ride if you can wait."

"No, I'd better go."

Winetraub said his goodbyes and walked out. Jeff and Defrange looked at each other, and Palachi looked at them both.

"Look," he offered, "the handwriting experts won't have their official report ready until tomorrow, and I know it's Saturday, but, if you two are willing, you could meet me for breakfast. We could come over here afterwards to see what they say about our killer."

"Great!" Jeff replied. "Bring Annie with you, and we'll make it a double date for breakfast."

Palachi glanced at Defrange. "Sure. Sounds good," he said with a huge smile.

Jeff nudged his new partner. "How about it? Would you do me the honor of escorting me to breakfast with the Palachis?"

She gave him one of her sternest looks.

"Only if it's not before eight," she warned.

They agreed to meet at nine at the Merrimack Restaurant on the corner of High Street and Crawford Parkway. Jeff glanced at his watch. "It's getting late. Let's call it a day—what do you say, Partner?"

To his surprise, Defrange agreed and they said goodbye to the ME and headed for the car.

"I'll take you over to the crow's nest," Jeff said as he pulled onto the main road. "I'm sure you'd like to get settled in."

"Fine," Defrange replied as she removed a lipstick from her purse and used the sun visor mirror to see to apply it. "How's the restaurant?" she asked as she pressed her full lips together.

"Great," Jeff replied. "You up for dinner company later?"

Defrange smiled and touched his arm. "I thought you'd never ask."

"Perfect. We can eat on the terrace, if you like. The breeze out there usually cools things off pretty quickly."

"Whatever you say, Lieutenant. This is your town, and I'm at your disposal—at least for the time I'm here."

Jefferson slowed in the bumper to bumper traffic just as the police radio crackled to life.

"*Virginia Creeper, this is Precinct Communications Center. Do you copy?*"

Jeff picked up the microphone.

"PreCom dispatch this is Virginia Creeper, go ahead."

"*Lieutenant Jefferson,*" the voice began, "*Captain Chambers is requesting that you call him on a land line ASAP.*"

"I copy, PreCom," Jefferson answered, "I will comply immediately."

"*Roger Virginia Creeper, PreCom clear.*"

Jeff returned the microphone to the clip on the side of the radio.

"What's that all about?" Defrange asked.

"Beats me," Jeff replied, "but if he wants me to specifically use a land line, he doesn't want to chance anyone hearing the conversation on the radio or the mobile phone. Help me look for a phone booth."

"There's one coming up on the right," Defrange said. "See it. In the corner of that service station lot."

"I see it," Jeff replied, whipping the car into the gas station parking lot. He pulled up next to the phone booth.

Jeff dialed the Captain's private number, and Chambers answered on the first ring.

"Is that you, Jefferson?"

"Yes, sir. What's going on?"

"Is Defrange still with you?" the Captain asked, his gruff voice full of urgency.

"Yes, sir. She's in the car."

"Thank God!" Chambers replied, *"I was afraid she might have actually taken the afternoon off."*

"What is it, Captain?"

"Lieutenant, listen carefully," Chambers implored. *"I got a note in the afternoon mail. It was in a manila envelope, but it wasn't stamped or postmarked. It was obviously planted in my mailbox."*

Jeff covered his exposed ear to dull some of the traffic noise.

"Go ahead, Captain."

"The address was a composite made from letters cut from magazines," the Captain continued, *and the note inside was an unidentifiable scrawl similar to the Ravenscroft message. Also, there was an article about Defrange cut from the Baltimore Sun. There's a full-face photo of her, but the eyes have been cut out of the picture."*

Jeff turned around and looked at Defrange, locking in to her penetrating gaze. "Captain," he said, "since we've kept his note from the Ravenscroft secret, it has to be the Raptor."

"No doubt," Chambers agreed, *"I sent it all to the lab in case there happens to be a fingerprint or DNA, and I copied the message. Listen:*

> *"things would be calmer were i Jeffrey Dahmer*
> *now its disaster playing the master…*
> *can you play without doubt, or sit this one out*
> *secure in those lies in defrange's eyes…*
> *let this be the sign they'll soon be mine…*
> *xoxo raptor"*

"It's him," Jeff said. "What do you want me to do?"

"Here's my plan. And, please, if you have any questions or suggestions speak up. Take Defrange to the Harbor Inn as planned. The only thing different is that, when she's going back to the suite anytime while she's here, she needs to call PreCom and let them know her expected time of arrival. I'm having a SWAT sniper stationed on the roof of the Precinct building anytime she's at the hotel. Also, I have an extra man assigned to go over to the Harbor Inn anytime she's there. The two-man guard detail for the suite itself will stay the same."

Jeff nodded, still staring at Defrange. "Yes, sir. I understand."

"Look, Jefferson, I don't want her to feel like she's being used for bait, so if she has the slightest qualms about any of this, call me back immediately.

"Yes sir, I will," Jefferson replied.

"Ok, Lieutenant. If I don't hear from you, I'll know that our guest is staying next door."

"Yes, sir," Jeff said, and he hung up.

Defrange was smiling when he got back in the car.

"What's the new game plan?" she asked.

"What are you talking about?"

"C'mon, Jefferson! This is me. What's happened?"

He related all that the Captain had told him, fully anticipating that she would demand a ride to the airport, and a ticket back to Milwaukee. Instead, she agreed with the plan.

"Let's go check in," she said.

"You got it."

CHAPTER 11

THE AC REINVIGORATED them as they braved the afternoon sun and crawling traffic back toward the center of town. The Harbor View Resort Hotel loomed on the horizon as they approached the Elizabeth River and the City County Plaza. The resort was just two stories shy of being as tall as the Police Precinct Building, and many visitors got confused as they thought that the hotel was part of the city government complex.

Jefferson pulled around to the back of the hotel and pointed out the unmarked door that Defrange would use to get to her suite. Once inside there was an elevator to the fifteenth floor, and the luxury suite that overlooked the Elizabeth River with a panoramic view of Norfolk on the other side.

"We'll park back here," Jeff said, and he pulled into a parking space just across from the visitors' back entrance.

When they got out of the car, the heat hit them as if they were looking down into a volcano, but the air in the long hallway that transited the building to the front desk was refreshingly cool.

"Whew! Quite a contrast," Defrange remarked.

Their trip took them through several doors until they arrived in the main lobby. There were two clerks behind the desk, and Jeff motioned to the one who wasn't busy. He spoke in a quiet tone so that the clerk had to lean over the desk to hear him.

"I'm Lieutenant Jefferson, and this is Detective Almyra Defrange from Milwaukee. I believe you're expecting her."

"Of course," the young man said. "Let me get a key card for you, Detective."

He disappeared into the office with a flare and returned momentarily with the card.

"Here you are, Detective." He smiled and handed the card to Defrange. "Did Lieutenant Jefferson show you the door and the activation box for your key card?"

"He can show me when we go up, thank you." Defrange replied.

The clerk suddenly came around the desk and put out his hand in a rather feminine manner.

"Detective Defrange," he began with a slight lisp, "I'm Willie, and if you need anything, I'm here from noon until midnight every day but Sunday. Honey, anything you want or need, just call down and ask for Willie."

"Thanks, Willie. I'll keep that in mind."

"Now, let me show you something over here."

Willie, obviously feeling a sense of camaraderie with sister Almyra, strutted over to a door with no markings.

"You can use your card to get in here. "Lemme see you card."

Defrange gave it to him, and he slid it through the slot on the reader. A loud click told them that the attempt was successful.

Willie opened the door and invited Defrange to look down the long hallway which ran all the way to the back of the building. At the end was an elevator, and he explained that it went only to her suite. There were no other doors along this corridor.

"Got it," Defrange assured him, and they stepped back into the lobby proper.

"All of the shops, the indoor-outdoor pool, and the restaurant are through the doors on the far side of the lobby," Willie added with the sweeping arm motion of a game show hostess. "Uh, let me see—oh yes, I almost forgot. You can get room service or anything else you might need twenty-four seven. That's just for the crow's nest," he whispered behind his hand. "That's not for the general population."

Jefferson was amazed at this elaborate presentation, and he felt it was because of Defrange's magnetic pull for anyone who needs a friend.

"Oh and," Willie continued, "I'm supposed to relay the message that your police guards will be here momentarily, and they might not be in uniform. Sometimes we don't even know who they are until they open the lobby door to go up. I think that's about it," he gasped with a theatrical collapse of his shoulders. "If you have any questions, lemme know."

Defrange glanced knowingly at Jefferson and smiled. "Thanks, Willie. You sure know how to treat a girl."

Willie giggled. "Thank you. I just treat people the way I would want to be treated."

"Yeah, thanks," Jeff echoed. "I'm sure we'll be seeing you around."

He and Defrange excused themselves and headed back down the corridor with doors to retrieve Defrange's tote from the car.

"Hey," she said. "I'm gonna try this card on the outside door. I sure hope it works so we don't have to go all the way back to the lobby."

Defrange slid the card into the reader, and the door clicked open. There were two uniformed officers sitting beside her elevator.

"Jefferson," one of them called as the door opened.

"Yeah, Tyler," Jeff replied. It's me. You guys got the duty, huh?"

"Yeah," Tyler said as he stood up.

"Gentlemen," Jefferson began, "this is Detective Almyra Defrange, and she's the reason you guys get this cushy job for a few days."

"Ma'am," Tyler replied with a nod, "it's a pleasure to meet you. He gestured toward his partner. "This is Officer Lowe."

"Nice to meet you, Detective," Lowe said."

"Ok," Jeff said, not wanting to be compelled to linger like they had been forced to do with Willie. "We're going up so the Detective can check out her new digs. Stay alert, guys."

Defrange wielded the card again, and the elevator door opened.

"You know we will, Lieutenant," Tyler assured them as the door closed. Jeff hit the "UP" button.

"What a great set-up," Defrange observed. "This is a perfect hiding place."

"Yeah," Jeff agreed. "We've never lost a single witness up here."

"That's reassuring," Defrange replied ominously, looking at Jeff from the corner of her eye.

The elevator came to a halt, and the doors opened into a small sitting room. There were two over-stuffed chairs, a love seat, and a recliner, along with a small coffee table. The room was softly lit with overhead can lighting and a couple of mid-century style floor lamps. Directly across from the elevator was the main door to the crow's nest.

"That door," Jeff explained, "opens with your card, or if the guards are up here—and, you don't want to fool with the card, there's an override switch for the door. Here, I'll show you."

Defrange buzzed them in, and Jefferson showed her the toggle switch just inside the door. He flipped it and a loud click alerted them that the door was unlocked. He flipped it again, and a softer click told them that the door was locked again.

"Wow!" Defrange exclaimed as she looked from the foyer into the large living room. It was all done in white, with royal blue accents. The furniture was either white or blue with a large circular, royal blue rug in the middle of the white carpet. The bank of windows overlooked the river.

"Very much like cruise ship décor," she observed, "and those windows remind me of the view from the Captain's office."

"So, you approve?"

"Absolutely," she said, gesturing toward a white pocket door. "What's in here?"

"The bathroom," Jeff replied.

This room was also in white and blue with a garden tub and a shower stall. There was a telephone and an obvious alarm button which Jeff explained went to the outer sitting room and the area by the downstairs elevator.

"Not taking any chances, are you?" Defrange teased.

Jeff shook his head. "Not with you, we aren't."

Defrange opened the door which led from the bathroom into the master bedroom. It was as white and plush as everything else. There was a queen-size bed, a dresser, side tables with phones and blue lamps, the beautiful view—and another alarm button on the wall beside the bed.

The kitchen and dining area were also magnificent, and while there was no food stocked, there was a wine rack with several choices.

"Wine?" Defrange asked.

"Sure, why not? Jeff said. "I'll get it if you wanna freshen up, take a shower maybe."

"Deal," Defrange said over her shoulder as she headed for the bathroom. "I did have time to pack some clean underwear—which will feel good after all this heat."

"No doubt," Jeff called after her, trying to ignore the visual that arose from Defrange's wry comment.

He searched the kitchen until he located a corkscrew, and then he selected a nice rose.

He opened the bottle and let the wine breathe while, having a sudden pang of domesticity, he checked the cabinets for food. A trip to the grocery store was in order – Jeff couldn't remember the last time he'd done that. He ate out most of the time, especially the last five years since his wife had passed.

He had bought his condo at 1500 Leckie Street and had the upstairs converted into an apartment for visitors. The problem was there had never been any visitors, so he mainly stayed downstairs. He had his laundry done, his food prepared, and all of his other needs taken care of by strangers.

Sadly, he didn't miss his wife, as they hadn't been in love for years. She had confessed to him that she was having an affair with the Presbyterian minister while she was dying of breast cancer. She had also told him that he had ruined her life by being a cop....

"Partner!" Defrange called from the bathroom. "Where's that wine?"

He poured two glasses and walked to the bathroom door.

"Here you are," he said.

The door opened suddenly: Defrange stood before him, wrapped in a fluffy white bath sheet.

"Thank you," she said, taking the stemmed glass. "What a treat."

Jeff took in her wet hair and green eyes. He pursed his lips before he replied, "I'll say."

Her green eyes flashed gentle admonishment. "Be out in a minute," she said as she closed the door. A second later she called out, "This sure is a great place."

"Thanks," Jeff hollered from the living room. "I'll let the management know you like it."

Defrange emerged from the bathroom a minute or two later dressed in cream-colored silk drawstring pants, with a matching silk jacket draped over a white t-shirt. They sat on the sofa, enjoying the view while they chatted and polished of the bottle of rose.

Eventually, they drifted down to dinner, which turned into a lovely evening with good food, more wine, and even a dance or two. Defrange suffered him to go to one of the shops where she bought a two-piece bathing suit and some clothes for her stay in Portsmouth. Around 10:30, Jeff escorted her upstairs.

He went into the outer sitting room with her and waited until he was sure the door had opened into the main suite.

"Goodnight, Partner," he said, resisting an urge to kiss her.

"Goodnight," Defrange replied, leaning in and kissing him lightly on the lips. "I'm glad we found each other again."

"Me too," Jeff confessed. With that, she was gone.

Tyler and Lowe were at their posts when Jeff exited the elevator.

"All squared away, Lieutenant?" Tyler asked.

"Yeah," Jeff replied, "but be careful. She got the equivalent of a death threat this afternoon. Pass the word that if anything should happen, I'm to be called immediately."

"Right, Lieutenant," Tyler replied. "We heard about the note the Captain got and that extra men are on tonight, but we haven't seen any of them."

Jeff nodded. "You likely won't see them unless something goes wrong. You two here all night?"

"No, sir. We're on until midnight, and then I'm not sure who relieves us."

"Ok, fellas. I'm sure I'll be seeing you over the next few days."

"Right, Lieutenant. Goodnight."

Jeff stepped outside and looked up to the top of the Precinct building next door. He saw the sniper at his post. He waved, and the man waved back. He got into his car and headed around Crawford Parkway. As he sped through the night, he couldn't shake the disturbing sense that someone, somewhere, was watching his every move.

CHAPTER 12

DEFRANGE'S GREEN EYES flashed open and she stared at the clock glowing in the darkness: 3:38. She held her breath and listened. Someone was in the crow's nest besides her.

She eased her Glock from under the pillow, keeping her ears tuned to the slightest sound. There it was: the soft padding of measured footsteps in the living room. She eased from the bed and slipped down to the floor opposite the door to the living room.

The thick chintz drapes in the windows were open, and the lights of the city bathed the room in twilight. Something in her peripheral vision moved: in the mirror over the dresser was the reflection of a man. His white dress shirt made him easy to spot in the dim light.

The bed moved as the intruder fell onto it. Defrange reached up slowly and turned on the bedside lamp before leaping to her feet.

"Freeze!" she ordered as the young man blinked and raised his hands.

"Don't move!" she warned.

In an instant she caught the odor of stale beer. The petrified man's mouth gaped as he held his hands in the air.

"Don't you dare move," she ordered as she pushed the alarm button.

In less than ten seconds the room was full of officers. Some were in uniform, others in plain clothes. The man was handcuffed and dragged to the outer sitting area. Defrange followed the officers into the outer room where Sergeant O'Keeffe was in charge.

"Who are you?" the officer demanded.

The man's speech was slurred, and he was having trouble focusing his eyes.

"I'm Jerry Friedman," he answered. "I'm in the Navy."

"The Navy? What the hell are you doing in this suite, and how the hell did you get in here?"

"I'm third-class petty office Friedman 222 46 8834 721, and I'm in the United States Navy.

"Look, Friedman," O'Keeffe barked, "you're in some deep shit. The Geneva Convention rules don't apply here."

"Friedman, Jerry, third class, 222 46 8834 721, United States Navy."

"God damn it, Friedman! Changing the order of the words doesn't make any difference. Do you even know how you got in here?"

Friedman blinked as he tried to focus on O'Keeffe's face.

"Okay, lemme up," he slurred.

Defrange threw on her robe and followed the officers as they dragged her intruder onto the elevator. She was still holding her Glock. When they got to the ground level, Friedman staggered down the long corridor toward the office. He stopped at the end and caught his breath.

"Ya see that door?" he said after a moment, "That's how I got in!"

"How'd you get the door opened?" O'Keeffe demanded

Defrange folded her arms cradling her Glock as she leaned against the wall. *He didn't open it.*

Friedman blinked and weaved for a moment. "Oh," he said in a flash of sudden memory. "I didn't. I followed this guy in—he opened the door."

"What guy?"

"I don't know," Friedman whined, waving his hand. "A guy."

"Was he a cop?"

Friedman shook his head. "He didn't look like one. His clothes were all black, and he was wearing a hoodie."

O'Keeffe cursed under his breath and searched the officers. "Who has a walkie-talkie?"

"I do, Sarge," somebody answered.

"Call upstairs and make sure everything is alright. Tell them to look around carefully. We may have a bogey in here besides this guy."

O'Keeffe turned his attention back to the sailor.

"Look, where did the man go that let you in?"

Friedman pointed and hiccupped. "I followed him down the hall to that elevator we just came out of. If you haven't noticed, it's the only way to go."

"How'd you get in the elevator?" the cop pushed.

"I saw the man get in and go up, and then the elevator came back down and the door stayed open. I got in and I went up too. I just wanted to go to sleep. I didn't know that lady was in there. I swear!" He nodded in Defrange's direction. She smiled curtly.

"What happened to the man?" O'Keeffe demanded.

Friedman winced. "I dunno. I never saw him again after he got on the elevator."

O'Keeffe growled. "Son-of-a-bitch! There is a bogey in here. Everybody get back upstairs and find that intruder. Except two of you need to escort this guy outta here and call the shore patrol."

Within ten minutes there were cops on every floor of the Harbor Inn. Defrange returned to the crow's nest and waited.

Jeff arrived at the Harbor View, blue light, siren and all. He hadn't gotten below 80 mph between Leckie Street and the Harbor View. He left his car our front and immediately found O'Keeffe.

"What the hell happened, Sergeant?" he growled as he stepped off the elevator.

"Hang on, Lieutenant! We're still trying to sort it all out."

Jefferson listened to the story of the drunk sailor, the phantom he'd followed into the inner sanctum, and the daunting possibility that he was still in the building and no one could find him.

"Who was on the back door?" Jeff asked.

"Apparently no one," O'Keeffe replied.

"How the hell could that happen?"

"Tyler and Lowe were on until midnight. They hadn't been relieved by 2:15, so they called the Watch Commander. He told them to stand down because everything had been called off."

Jeff shook his head in bewilderment. "*What?* Called off? Where the hell did that come from?"

"That's what I'm trying to find out now," O'Keeffe said.

"By God I'll find out!" Jefferson declared. He sprinted out the back door and headed for the Precinct. After taking the elevator to the third floor, he unceremoniously entered the door marked "Watch Commander", causing Al Tompkins to jump from his chair behind his desk. He snatched his reading glasses from his nose.

"Jefferson! What the hell?"

"Who called off the watch at the Harbor View?" Jeff demanded to know.

"I have no clue what you're talking about!" Tompkins answered.

"Well, the officers who were on until midnight said that they were told by the Watch Commander to stand down."

"Jefferson, have you been drinking?"

"Hell, no!"

Tompkins teeth were clenched as he spoke. "You have to believe that I never talked to anyone on watch at the Harbor View, and I certainly never told them to stand down!"

Jeff waved his arms. "Are you serious? Why would those men lie?"

"Yes, I'm serious," Tompkins assured him. "I've been here all night, and there's been no conversation like that from this office."

Jeff inhaled deeply and let it out. "Ok, Al. Look, I'm sorry. I'm just trying to figure out what happened."

Tompkins took a cleansing breath as well. "It's ok, Lieutenant. Let me know what you do find out. I'm equally as concerned."

Jeff nodded and retreated back down the hall. As he eyed the elevator button, a thought occurred: *the roof!* He pushed the button for the sixteenth floor, and when he arrived, he opened the utility door with his pass key. Jeff took the stairs to the roof two at a time.

He spotted the sniper on the east side of the roof, and he quietly announced his presence.

"Lieutenant!" the sniper called out as he turned around. "What on earth are you doing up here?"

"Just trying to find out what the hell's going on," Jeff said breathlessly as he approached the man. "Look, did you see anything out of the ordinary going on over at the Harbor View between two and three this morning?"

The man thought for a minute.

"The only thing I saw, not necessarily out of the ordinary, was a phone company truck over at the big phone exchange box between the Precinct and the Harbor View."

"Was there someone working?" Jeff asked.

"I assume so. The guy kept getting in and out of the truck. He was wearing those headphones they wear."

"Ok, that helps. You didn't see anyone coming in or out of the Harbor View, did you? More specifically, someone dressed all in black?"

"Not from back here. Once in a while one of the guys on watch would come out back and get some air, but that was much earlier."

"Thanks," Jeff said as he turned to go. "Stay alert. There may be a bogey in the Harbor View who might try to get away."

When he got back to the hotel, he picked up the phone in the hall beside the elevator and dialed the Watch Commander's office. The line was busy. Jeff went to the phone exchange box in the parking lot. The door to the box was unlocked, and he opened it and peered inside, his eyes wandering over hundreds of connections.

He spied a piece of paper folded and stuck between two last rows of connections. Carefully, he pulled it out by one corner and unfolded it.

> "i tried to call, but couldn't get through
> so i left this note here for you
> did you really think i couldn't see
> the ploy you tried to play one me
> the phone man's in the swamp somewhere
> i'm sure he's dead if you care
> i just needed to borrow his truck
> which means that he's run outta luck
> she's right over there as it were
> and i'm gonna get my hands on her
> you really shouldn't screw around with me
> xoxo raptor"

Jeff ran back to the hotel and gathered all the officers. After informing them of his discovery, he called the phone company.

O'Keeffe walked up and shook hands with Jefferson. "I'm sure embarrassed about this, Lieutenant," he said. "I'm glad no one was hurt."

"Don't worry about it, Sarge," Jeff replied. "Who knew that we were dealing with someone with the brains to be this devious."

Jefferson went upstairs to get Defrange. By now, it was nearly seven, and the sun was just breaching the eastern horizon. When he got off at the crow's nest, she was in the outer room, lying on the sofa, fully dressed. Her Glock lay on the coffee table.

"Hey, partner," he greeted her. "I didn't know you were gonna be up all night or I'd have stayed. We could have played poker or something."

She laughed. "Well, you know I can't resist a handsome, albeit drunken sailor."

Jeff laughed as he picked up her suitcase. "Let's get outta here. Grab your tote and your toothbrush."

"Ok," she said as she sat up, "Just give me a minute."

As they drove over to the Precinct, Jeff spotted a phone repairman at the exchange box. He drove over and rolled down the window.

"Good morning," Jeff said as he extended his ID.

The man looked at the badge and picture. "Good morning, Lieutenant. I'm Ted. How can I help you?"

"Were the police lab guys out here when you came?" Jefferson asked.

"Oh, yeah, they're done, but I don't know if they found anything."

"That's ok," Jeff said. "I just wanted to pick your brain about this equipment."

Ted nodded. "Go ahead."

"Could someone tap into this box, send and receive calls, and disguise who they were and where they were?"

"Sure. Piece of cake really. The only complicated part would be finding the connector for the phone you were calling. Once you did that, you could connect one of our keyboards with a mic/headphone set, and anyone talking to you would think you were the number you were pretending to be."

Jeff glanced over at Defrange, whose eyebrows were arched. "I see," he said as he turned back to the repairman. So, it wouldn't take a rocket scientist to do this?"

"Oh, not at all," Ted replied. "Like I said, if someone had the keyboard and discriminator to attach to this box, the list of numbers would show up in order so all they'd have to do is hook up to the right connector. As a matter of fact, someone's left a clip on one of these connectors."

"What does that do?" Jeff asked.

"Nothing really," Ted replied. "Just if anyone calls this number, they'll get a busy signal until this clip is removed."

"Could you remove the clip and tell me the number?" Jeff asked.

"Sure. Just give me a second to hook up my discriminator." Ted removed the clip and hooked up his equipment.

"It's a Precinct number, Lieutenant," Ted said. "It says "Watch Commander, office."

Jeff smiled and nodded. "Thanks, Ted. You've been a bigger help than you know. Thank you, sincerely."

"No problem, Lieutenant. Glad I could help."

Jefferson moved his car out of earshot as he grabbed the microphone from the radio.

"Last night is starting to make sense," Defrange commented.

"Yep," Jeff replied before he spoke into the mic.

"PreCom dispatch, this is Virginia Creeper, copy?"

"This is PreCom, go ahead."

"I need for you to put out an APB on a missing telephone company repair truck. Sorry, I don't have the license number, but the driver is also missing—he may be deceased."

"Roger Virginia Creeper, and be advised a truck fitting your description has already been found."

"Roger, PreCom. All I have on the driver is that he may be in a marshy or swampy area. I don't even have his name."

"Roger, Virginia Creeper. We'll check with the phone company and see what they know, over?"

"Roger PreCom. This is Virginia Creeper, clear."

Defrange looked at him inquiringly. "Wow, Partner. It sounds like you've been busy all morning."

"Yes, I have," Jeff replied. "And we're supposed to meet the Palachis in less than two hours. Do you wanna cancel?"

"No," Defrange replied. "Let's have breakfast as planned."

"Ok," Jeff agreed. "But first we're going to see the Captain. I'm about to save the Precinct a whole lot of money."

Defrange leaned back in her seat with a sly grin. "Oh? How are you going to do that?"

"Well, for one thing, you're not staying at the Harbor View anymore."

Defrange nodded as if she already knew the answer she was about to pose. "So, where am I staying?"

Jeff looked into her emerald eyes: they were green mischief.

"I'm thinking," he said.

CHAPTER 13

MARSHA WAS OUT of her chair before they got through the door.

"Oh, Almyra!" she twittered. "I heard something horrible happened at the Harbor View, and I was afraid you'd been hurt. I'm glad you're alright."

Defrange hugged her lightly.

"Thank you, Marsha. It was nothing, though I almost shot a drunken sailor."

Marsha gasped. "Really?"

The inner office door opened, and Captain Chambers quickly ushered Defrange and Jefferson inside.

"Detective Defrange," he began, "I'm so sorry. Are you okay?"

"Sure, I am," she replied. She looked at Jefferson with mild accusation in her eyes. "But I wasn't there for all the excitement."

"Please, sit down," he offered. He walked around his desk and hit the intercom button. "Marsha, would you mind making coffee?"

"Cap," Jefferson began, "we can't leave Detective Defrange at the Harbor View. This crazy bastard knows she's there, and apparently he can come and go at will."

"I agree, Lieutenant, and here's what I've been thinking this morning. I want you to situate Dr. Defrange somewhere, anywhere, but I want the location to be secret. I don't even want to know where she is. No one will officially know except the two of you. Money is no object, wherever she wants to stay, so long as you deem it safe."

"Agreed," Jeff said. He looked at Defrange. "Partner?"

"That's fine by me," she replied, "but if I may add one thing."

"Yes, Dr. Defrange," the Captain said with eagerness.

"Why don't you leave the appearance of all the security and hullaballoo next door. That might accomplish one or two things."

The Captain nodded slowly. "Yes, go on."

"Well, for one, it's a smoke screen, and two, it might be a way to catch him if he thinks I'm still there."

"Perfect," Chambers agreed. "Consider it done."

Jefferson got up from his chair. "Let's go, we're supposed to meet the Palachis in about twenty minutes."

The Captain chuckled. "You're making the ME work on Saturday?"

"Well, I have to feed him breakfast, first," Jeff said with a smirk.

Chambers laughed. "I see. Well don't keep him waiting – enjoy your breakfast."

Marsha came in with the coffee.

"Sorry, Marsha," Defrange apologized. "We'll take a raincheck on the coffee. We have to meet Dr. Palachi."

Marsha offered a shrug. "That's perfectly fine. It won't go to waste around here!" She looked at the Captain, who smiled sheepishly.

When they got in the car, Jefferson paused before he started the engine.

Defrange looked at him. "Partner, what gives? We aren't supposed to meet the Palachis for another hour and a half."

"I know," he admitted, "but I needed some time out of pocket for us to talk."

"Oh? What's going on?"

"I don't know how to ask this exactly, and you certainly don't have to agree…." His voice trailed off. He was searching for the right words.

"Yes?" she said, her voice a gentle nudge.

Jeff sighed. "Ok, here it is. I have a two-story condo, and the top floor is a finished apartment, fully furnished with a private entrance. It's very comfortable, and you'll be safe there. If the killer can break through all the defenses, we had at the Harbor View it's really the only place I can guarantee your safety."

Jefferson held his breath. He didn't know if she would take him up on his offer, or maybe just slap him and demand to go back to Milwaukee.

Defrange let him squirm for a moment before she replied. "Ok, let's do it."

Jeff exhaled and started the car. "I'm glad you're in agreement. I couldn't stand having you out there somewhere like a sitting duck."

"Quack!" Defrange replied as she strapped on her seat belt.

They drove around Crawford Parkway, past the Naval Hospital to Leckie Street. He opened the garage door with the automatic opener and whisked into the garage before anyone had time to see Defrange.

"Here we are," he said as the door closed behind them. "Home at last."

Defrange got out and Jeff handed her a key. "Here," he said. "Open the door, and I'll get your things."

Defrange took the key but stopped short at the door. He walked up behind her and looked over her shoulder.

"Oh," he said, "I forgot. The code is 11994466, and you have to punch it in before you put the key in the lock. It's part of the security system."

"Ok," she replied. What was the code again?"

"Let's make this easier," Jeff said, setting down her luggage. "What's your birth date?"

"Why, Lieutenant!" Defrange replied in mock surprise. "what a clever way to get a girl to tell you her age. It's June twentieth, nineteen forty-eight.

Jeff deactivated the alarm and reset the code to 62048.

"There you go," he said. "So long as you remember your birthday, you can open this door without setting off the alarm. I'll reset the front door too. It's the same key for both, so it'll be the same code."

"Thank you," she replied. "I feel like I'm moving into Fort Knox!"

"C'mon," Jeff said as they entered the kitchen, "the stairs are just around the corner, toward the living room."

She followed him across the foyer and up the stairs.

"Nice place," she said as she admired the upper level. "I think I'll be very comfortable here. Good vibes, too."

They were standing at the top of the stairs, and Jefferson took hold of Defrange's shoulders. He turned her so that they were face to face.

"Listen," he said, "if you feel the need to leave, to go somewhere else, for any reason that you don't want to discuss with me, it's ok. I'll understand."

She didn't reply, and Jeff released her shoulders.

There are towels in the linen closet, and there's a new toothbrush and tooth-paste in the bathroom, here."

He opened the door to the bathroom.

"And," he added, "there's shampoo and soap under this sink."

Defrange whistled. "Wow, you running a motel here Lieutenant?"

Jeff shook his head. "I never come up here, but I like to have everything ready for guests, just in case. So far, you're the only one."

Defrange smiled. "I'm honored. Really, very honored."

Jeff stared into her dark green pools. "I'm honored to have you here," he said, "and I'll really feel better knowing where you are when somebody's trying to kill you."

She laughed. "Thanks a lot!"

He looked at his watch.

"We have a little time before we have to leave."

"Good," Defrange replied. "What do we do next?"

"Well," Jeff said. "I don't have any food in the house, so we could go sit at the kitchen table and make a grocery list. I also need to call Marge and tell her not to come over."

"Marge?" Defrange asked. "Girlfriend?"

"No, no. She's my maid. She comes in three days a week, but she won't mind having a week or so off, so long as I pay her. The fewer people that know you're here, the better."

After making a grocery list, the two detectives headed for the Merrimack Restaurant. They arrived at the same time the Palachis pulled in. The meal was uneventful, with lots of talk about vacations and the best places to have them. Finally, Martin looked at his watch and became all business.

"Unfortunately," he said, "it's time for some of us to go to work."

"What a horrible thought!" Annie said. "Look, why don't you come home with me, Almyra? We can visit some more and certainly find something better to do than to talk about dead people."

Defrange smiled.

"I'm afraid I'm at work twenty-four hours a day while I'm here," she replied, "and if my partner's going to talk about dead people, well, I have to be with him."

"Well, thank God I don't have to do that," Annie replied. "But, if you get tired, come on over. Jefferson knows where we live, or I can come get you."

"Very tempting," Defrange replied. "If I can get away, I'll take you up on it."

The Palachis had arrived in separate cars since Martin was going to work. When they walked out to the parking lot, Annie got into her Volvo. "Martin," she called to her husband, "don't work too late. We're supposed to have dinner at the Porter's tonight. You need to get home early enough to get that morgue smell off you before we go."

She slammed the door and pulled out into traffic.

Martin looked lost.

"Morgue smell?" Palachi repeated. "What morgue smell? Jeff, do I smell like the morgue?"

Jefferson was a firm believer that evasion was the better part of valor. He took Defrange by the elbow and made a break for the car.

"See you over there!" he called to the ME.

"Coward!" Defrange chuckled as Jeff slid into the driver's seat.

By the time they got to the morgue, Palachi had already gotten the emails and other papers together.

"What we got?" Jeff asked.

"I'm afraid not much. It seems that all of our psycho boys pretty much think the same thing we heard yesterday. The handwriting guy didn't really say anything, since he's convinced that our perp is disguising the way he writes."

After a few more minutes of discussion that led to the same conclusion that they had nothing new it was time to go.

Jeff sighed. "Well, I have some errands, so if we don't have anything else."

"I'll just tag along with you, if you don't mind," Defrange said.

Jeff grinned. "Of course not. Maybe we could even shop at some of the same stores."

CHAPTER 14

CLIFTON DOTHAN WAS an embalmer—and funeral director at the Sterling Point Funeral Home. He'd been late for work, and his boss, Dan Hinson had chewed him out again. However, the menu he was presented with when he finally did get to work quickly diffused his anger, and he knew that Dan Hinson was always glad to see him, no matter what he did.

Clifton was forty-five, a little too pudgy, a little too flat-top, a little too mama's boy for most of the men he knew, but women, for whatever reason, seemed to love him. Maybe it was because he was meticulous, maybe it was because he was a good listener, maybe it was because they didn't see him as a threat.

Clifton Dothan, Master of Mortuary Sciences, was good at his profession. Families often requested that he take care of their loved ones. That was the case on Saturday, June fourteenth. Yesterday, it seemed four women who should never have gone sailing alone, especially with two quarts of gin, had gotten in the pathway of a Navy destroyer, and one of the husbands who was familiar with Dothan's work suggested Sterling Point. The other husbands were too numb to know the difference so they all agreed, and Dothan smiled at his own good fortune. The women had drowned, they were all in their thirties, and they were all his.

He loved touching them inside and out, and he delighted in watching the chicken fat clots spew from their arteries while he pumped in the embalming fluid. All the while, he reminded them that he would be the last secret they ever had, and that they were nothing be whores, anyway. Sometimes, if the opportunity presented itself, maybe alone on call, he would make love to them. Then, as a final touch, he would make them look better in death than they had ever looked in life. That was Dothan's calling card, and it was well-known throughout the Tidewater area that if a body was prepared by Clifton Dothan, the deceased would look totally natural and life-like.

"Son-of-a-bitch," he mumbled as Hinson's reprimand crept back into his thoughts. *I can get a job anywhere.*

He had just finished enjoying the third drowning victim when the voice from the intercom beckoned him to Hinson's office.

If that bastard starts giving me grief again….

He slipped out of his apron, removed his gloves, and he washed his hands. The voice over the intercom had killed his erection. He put on his blazer, and he walked down the hall to what he thought would be his last confrontation with Dan Hinson.

He entered the boss's office without knocking, hoping that his defiance would irritate him more than ever, but Hinson stood up and smiled when Dothan barged in.

"Clifton Dothan," he began, nodding toward a chair behind the door. "Meet Erica Merriweather. She's an intern from the Medical College of Virginia, and she'll be doing a rotation with us for a couple of months. Please try to help her all you can."

Dothan turned his gaze upon Erica Merriweather, and his mind shifted gears. She was young and beautiful – he had a momentary vision of her lying nude in a casket.

Shaking off his fantasy, he gushed, "How do you do Miss Merriweather?" He looked deep into her blue eyes, and his erection signaled a recovery.

"Of course, Dan," he said, briefly looking over at Hinson. "I'll help Miss Merriweather any way I can. I remember what it's like to be student."

"Fine, that's fine Clifton," Dan replied. "Then you won't mind if Erica looks over you shoulder for the rest of the afternoon?"

"Not at all," Dothan replied as he bowed at the waist to Erica. "You must be very dedicated to come in on a Saturday. Are you ready to go to work? I've finished three of the four bodies I've been preparing, and, if you like, you may help me with the fourth."

Erica stood. She fidgeted nervously. She was afraid: it was just the kind of demeanor that excited Clifton.

Like someone who is about to die….

"Yes, Mr. Dothan," Erica replied barely above a whisper. "It would be an honor to assist you."

What Clifton didn't know was that Erica was as much a phony as he was. The difference being: she was benign. She'd learned in high school that using her five-foot-six body in certain ways could get her most anything she wanted from the male population. Her bust was quite ample, and her body supple and inviting. Her early encounter with sex had been a fumbling first fiasco, and while it had excited her, she'd learned that the perceived promise of it could get her as far at the actual act. Now she was in the real world, and she hadn't tried too much to impress the men. She was just not sure.

"Let's go," he said as he opened the door. They proceeded down the hall, and Clifton gave her a gentle admonishment.

"Let's get started on the right foot," he said. "First, don't call me 'sir' or 'mister'. My name is Clifton, and that will suffice."

"Yes, sir—I mean, Clifton."

Erica was at least twenty-five years his junior. Clifton liked that. He kept up his dignified, professional demeanor so as to build up her confidence in him. Charm was the key: he wanted her eating out of his hand.

The next two hours were spent in the preparation of the fourth drowning victim. Of course, Clifton had to modify his usual behavior, and he did things strictly by the book. He didn't mind, though. He was enjoying Erica's company. He found himself staring at her for an unusually long interval.

"Is something wrong?" she asked.

"Oh, no," Clifton replied, shaking his head. "I was just admiring your build. You look quite athletic. Are you a runner?"

Erica blushed.

Maybe the same tricks will work here….

This was more of an instinct than a developed thought.

"Not anymore. I used to be, but my schedule keeps me from running regularly."

"Well, that's too bad, he said, "but regardless, you look very healthy— and you're quite attractive."

Erica blushed again.

"Why, thank you Mr.—oh, I mean, Clifton"

He leaned in behind her as she unsteadily wielded a scalpel, intent on opening the femoral artery for insertion of the embalming catheter. He lay his strong and steady hand over hers and guided it to the proper area for the incision.

"Just here," he said in a low voice in her ear. "It's right here. Don't be nervous or afraid. I'll show you exactly what to do."

Clifton pressed his erection against her firm buttocks, and the girl flinched as a drop of blood appeared at the incision sight.

"That's normal," he assured her. "Just put your hand on the artery above the incision until you have inserted the catheter. There's no heartbeat, so there's no blood pressure or pulsing blood to contend with."

She followed his instructions.

"Good, good," he encouraged her. "Just hold that for a moment."

He passed the catheter around in front of her and showed her how to slide it into the artery.

"A trick I've learned," he explained as he pulled a curved suture needle through the flesh and tied the thread around the tubing, "is to secure the catheter with one stitch so that pressure from the pump won't dislodge it from the artery. That could allow embalming fluid to extravasate into the body, and that can get messy."

Erica turned to look at him. Her eyes were wide with amazement.

"Oh, Clifton," she said excitedly. "I've read about this a hundred times, but I never knew it would be like this. It's very simple, isn't it?"

"Yes, it is," he replied. "Now, it's just a matter of turning on the pump to evacuate the blood, and when that's complete, we'll turn off the valve from the container. Next, we turn on the valve from the embalming fluid, and we reverse the pressure. *Voilà!*"

Erica watched him in fascination as the blood drained into the cannister and then the clear fluid started making its way up toward the body.

"It's always important to note the amount of blood that was evacuated," Clifton added, "so we can replace it with an equal amount of embalming fluid. That gets tricky if the subject has had a lot of bleeding before you get them, but that's a problem we'll work on some other time. For now, we'll just replace an equal amount to what we've removed. You must be careful at this point that the body doesn't take on a bloated or swollen appearance from adding too much fluid."

Erica emitted a nervous giggle. "Clifton, this is wonderful! "I thought I could do this, but I was never sure until now."

"Good," he replied in his pedantic tone, "but remember, this is the easy part. Don't forget that we're creating a product, and the final judgement of our skill comes from how the body looks. No one gives a damn about how much embalming fluid you put in Grandma—it's how she looks when they see her. Speaking of looks," he said, turning to her, "I find you extremely attractive, and I honestly believe that I could get lost in those beautiful blue eyes. Would you even consider having dinner with me tomorrow night?"

Erica's eyelids fluttered, and her cheeks were ablaze.

"Yes, of course!" she replied. "I'd love to have dinner with you. I'm living at 221 Glasgow Street in the Celtic Apartments. Do you know where that is?"

Clifton smiled at his good fortune. "I know *exactly* where that is."

Oddly, their two games were meshing, but Erica had no idea that the outcome wasn't even close to her fantasies.

"Great!" she added. "I'm in apartment 14-A on the ground level. You can't miss it."

"Is six good for you?"

Erica raised up on her tiptoes excitedly. "Perfect! I'll be ready then."

The pump made a loud hissing sound as the last drop of embalming fluid ran into the body.

"All right," he said, becoming all business again, "now, watch this carefully. I just slip out the catheter, and then I take the needle and slip it through the other side of the incision, pull gently, and it's closed."

He tied a surgeon's knot and pulled it tight.

"That's it," he announced. "Now, we'll work on the makeup, and I'll show you some tricks that will help you as long as you're in this profession…."

CHAPTER 15

ERICA WAS BEYOND elation by the time she got home later Saturday afternoon. She felt as though she'd learned more in a few hours than she'd learned in the last two years at school—and, Clifton had asked her to go out with him. She could hardly believe that this polished professional would even waste his time talking to her, let alone ask her out.

"Rica," her mother said on the phone, "he's an older man, and he may have some ideas that you aren't prepared to handle. What was his name? Dothan?"

"Yes, Mother," she replied impatiently. "He's quite well-known in our profession. I don't understand why you have such a problem with him."

Her father broke in on the extension.

"Erica, sweetie," he began, "there's not a problem. Your mother and I just want to make sure that you're safe. I know Mr. Dothan by reputation, and I think he's alright."

"Alright?" her mother broke in. "Joel, how can you say he's alright. What do you know about him?"

"Honey," her father said reassuringly, "I've seen him at annual meetings, and I've heard him speak on several occasions. He's received the National Funeral Directors Reconstruction Award for five years in a row. He's a professional and an artist, for God's sake!"

"Well, I don't like it!" her mother snapped. "He's so much older than she is, and I just think he should be interested in older women."

Erica listened while the argument between her parents accelerated.

"Mom…Dad? I love you both," she said as she hung up the phone.

Erica loved her parents, especially her father. She had chosen to attend the medical college with the plan of taking over his successful funeral business when he decided to retire. She also secretly hoped that it would make up for the son he'd never had but often had mentioned.

Clifton said that he would show her an evening that she would never forget; she couldn't imagine what that meant, coming from such a fastidious and reserved man. She found herself attracted to him, and the age difference was especially intriguing. There was definitely sexual tension between them, but it was different than the bumbling attraction she'd had to her paramour in the ninth grade. The idea of being with an older man with experience thrilled her, but she immediately felt guilty for having such thoughts. Still, she felt dampness and an urging that left her pleasantly uncomfortable.

Sunday dragged on, and she was on edge by the time the doorbell rang at exactly six. She checked herself in the hall mirror before opening the door.

"Hi, Clifton," she twittered.

"Hi yourself. Are you ready for our evening?"

"Yes! I'm starving. I haven't eaten all day. Why don't you come in while I get my purse?"

Clifton smiled. "I'd like that," he said. "This heat is a little much. Could I trouble you for something cold to drink?"

"Of course," she said as she pushed open the storm door. "Come in. Let's see. I have cold beer, some lemonade, or ice water. What's your pleasure?"

"I'd like a beer," he replied as he stepped into the small living room.

"Coming right up," she called as she disappeared toward the kitchen. "Have a seat. I'll just be a minute."

While Erica was getting the beer from the fridge, she strained to catch anything he might be saying to her.

He's not really handsome, she thought as she poured the beer into a frosted mug, her father's favorite treat, *but somehow, he's really quite attractive.*

She had noticed his muscular arms protruding from his seersucker shirt, and she thought he was quite sexy in his white duck pants and deck shoes.

He's not wearing socks.

Erica startled him as she returned with the beer.

"Here we are!" she announced as she joined him on the couch. "Don't look at this messy apartment. I just can't get enthused about doing housework, and I'm usually too tired to care. I hope you like the frosted mug."

"Well," he said, "for future reference, I don't, but that's ok. Thank you. Aren't you having something?"

"No," she replied. "I don't drink much, especially on an empty stomach, and I'm afraid with this heat I would get quite ill."

Clifton nodded and licked foam from his upper lip. "I know what you mean. Alcohol affects me that way when I'm tired, and I haven't eaten. So, tell me about yourself. Do you have relatives in the Portsmouth area?"

"No," she replied "All of my immediate family lives near Danville. I'm afraid that this part of the state is quite alien to someone who's used to the mountains."

"Nonsense, Erica," he said plying his charm. "Don't sell yourself short. With your poise, charm, and ambition you should feel at home anywhere."

"Why, thank you Clifton. That's very sweet of you to say."

He slammed the beer mug firmly on the table, and Erica jumped. He didn't appear to notice that beer had sloshed out onto the doily her grandmother had made. The noise startled her, but she liked his forward manner.

"Don't be coy, Erica," he said.

"Rica," she interrupted. "Call me Rica, please."

"Very well," he continued, "*Rica*, let's not be coy. I like your company, and you're *soooo* attractive. You also seem to have a natural talent for what we do. I noticed as much yesterday, and I admire that."

Erica felt herself flush with the same unfamiliar urging.

She put her hand on his knee. "Clifton, you are too kind."

"I hope you won't mind," he said, pausing to sip his beer, "and I hope you won't find me presumptuous, but I've prepared a special meal at my place. Of course, if you're uncomfortable with that we—"

"I'm not uncomfortable with that at all!" Erica replied enthusiastically. "What are we having?"

He smiled an sat up proudly. "We're having my special steak and kidney pie, branch lettuce salad, home-made bread, and I've made a very special dessert. Just wait until you taste it."

"That's so romantic, Clifton, but I hope you don't think that I make it a habit to run off to a stranger's home on the first date."

Clifton reared back in his seat. "Rica, you're being coy again. I don't make judgements about my friends, and anyway," he said with a shrug, "your dating habits are your business. You're an adult, and what you do is up to you."

Rica felt like the Princess of Wales. This man, unlike her parents, was treating her like the grown-up woman she knew herself to be.

"Well, Mr. Dothan, I can't wait. If you're finished with your drink, I'm ready to go"

He answered by chugging the last half of the beer before he headed for the door.

He opened it wide for her and then checked the lock.

"Got your keys?" he asked.

Erica thrilled at his protectiveness, "Yes," she replied. "Thank you for reminding me."

She held his arm as they meandered around the series of shaded walkways that led to the parking lot. Clifton's car turned out to be a 1971 Corvette Convertible. This had to be a project of which he was very proud, so she made a great to-do of being impressed.

"Wow!" Would you look at this! What a gorgeous car! You don't drive this every day, do you?"

Clifton shook his head. "Oh no. I just drive it on special occasions. I have an old clunker that I drive the rest of the time. Would you like the top down?"

"I'd love it, if it's not too much trouble. That will be a lot cooler in more ways than one."

"Consider it done, my dear," he replied as he opened her door. "Your chariot awaits."

Erica giggled as she slid into the passenger's seat, and Clifton ogled her cleavage as she bent over to get in. Her shapely legs didn't go without notice either. He was initially disappointed that she didn't wear shorts, but now, as she swiveled around to put her legs into the Vette, he was glad she didn't. After all, a secret peek at her panties was more of a turn on than shorts, anytime.

Erica admired the beautiful interior of the masterfully restored car while he put the top down—that's when she noticed the deep scratch marks in the finish on the passenger door. They glared against the background of the otherwise pristine interior. She ran her fingers across them.

"What happened to this door?" she asked as Clifton lowered into the driver's seat.

He leaned toward her, and opened his eyes in a wide, mad-man stare. He snarled and curled his upper lip to expose his teeth.

"Oh, those scratches," he lisped in his best Lon Chaney voice. "My latest victim did that when she was trying to escape. You see, my dear, I'm a serial killer."

For a long moment Erica's blue eyes froze in a wide-open stare, with her mouth agape, and her breath seeming more difficult to draw, she couldn't speak. Neither of them blinked, and he didn't smile. Finally, as her air began to flow easier, she burst out laughing.

"Oh, Clifton! What a wicked sense of humor. Seriously, what happened to the door."

He grinned and shrugged. "Ok, if you don't believe that I'm a serial killer, would you believe that my dog is the culprit?"

"Your dog?" she echoed.

"Yes. She got terribly sick, and I had to rush her to the vet. She was thrashing around, and she scratched the door."

Erica exhaled. "I do like the dog story better—you know, serial killer jokes aren't too funny around Portsmouth these days."

Clifton smiled and looked down. "I know. You are right. But on that note, would you like to see where the Raptor killed Wanda Marchant?"

Erica turned in her seat and leaned back against the scratched door panel. "You mean the girl from the other night. Oh, I don't know. It's all so scary—but intriguing."

"That's the spirit! It's just a few blocks out of the way, and you know we have the remains at Sterling Point? Remind me tomorrow, and I'll show you what the Raptor does to little girls."

They backed out of the parking space. Clifton couldn't resist putting the Vette through it paces by playing slalom around the speed breakers and making the tires yelp every time he changed gears.

He laughed into the wind. "The old girl still has it!"

Erica laughed as she hung on lightly to his right shoulder with her left hand. "She sure does. This is heavenly!"

Clifton turned off High Street and crossed Washington to intersect with Jackson, just in front of the Tidewater Breeze.

He pointed toward the building. "That's where he got Maureen Charbenau. She was the last one, so far. We'll have her as soon as the medical examiner sends her over. She was scared to death, you know?"

He continued down Jackson before he slowed and pointed to the Ravenscroft. He turned onto Dogwood and stopped right in front of the building. He proceeded to tell her about Wanda Marchant's death, even adding some gruesome details as he watched her squirm.

Erica reached over and gripped Clifton's let, digging her nails into his flesh. He pulled up the parking brake and yanked her to him, kissing her deeply as he drew her hand to his crotch. Erica tried to pull away, but he kissed her harder, grinding her lips against her teeth. She backed away in pain, but he continued to force his mouth on hers. She stroked him clumsily until she managed to push him away. She was breathless.

"Let's slow down," she said as she gasped. "Let's take this slowly. Maybe we can explore this later."

Clifton relaxed against the seat. "Ok, Rica. You're so desirable I couldn't help myself. I didn't mean to make you uncomfortable."

"Oh, no Clifton, It's alright. I just prefer a more private setting, rather than sharing our intimate moments with downtown Portsmouth."

Clifton smiled. "I agree," as he pulled away from the curb. "We'll be alone soon, and we can make some real intimate moments."

"Maybe," she smiled teasingly.

CHAPTER 16

THE RIDE TOWARD Newport News was breathtaking as Erica drank in glimpses of inlets, bridges, piers, and sailboats as the appeared through the summer foliage. It was like riding through a kaleidoscope as they took the scenic route along Highway 164 W and crossed the James River Bridge into Isle of Wight County. The warm sun, along with the purr of the Vette's engine, lulled her into a dream state as the scenery rushed by. She opened and closed her eyes frequently, pretending that she was changing scenes at will.

In thirty minutes, they pulled onto a rural road, and then into a driveway in a secluded settlement that bordered the river. The homes were on large, wooded lots separated by enough land to afford complete privacy. Erica roused with a yawn when the Vette slowed.

"Oh, Clifton," she said as she gazed over the sloping lawn that rolled gently down to the riverbank. "This is lovely."

A gazebo, covered in hundreds of tiny white lights, sat in the shade of the weeping willows near the water. She looked beyond to a small pier where a modest cabin cruiser was tied.

"Oh! You have a boat! May we go for a ride sometime?"

"Of course—I was planning on later the evening, if you like."

Erica turned her attention to the two-story Colonial house with a walkway leading from the circular drive to the front door. Immaculately trimmed boxwoods lined the walkway, and behind those, in perfect alignment, were red rose bushes in full bloom. Their fragrance was intoxicating.

She giggled. "Why, you old sneak! Who would ever believe that you live in such a beautiful place!"

"Probably nobody who didn't really know me," he said as he got out of the car. "I keep my personal life to myself, and I only invite special friends to visit. Just one thing, though. My dotty old Aunt Ashley lives with me. I have an apartment for her in the basement, and she may cackle, or howl, or any number of other strange things that might upset you if you're not prepared. Don't worry though—she's quite harmless."

How sweet! Erica thought. *He cares for an elderly relative!*

"I wanna meet her," she said.

Clifton's eyes locked onto hers. He was quiet for a moment until he said, "I don't know if you should meet her on your first visit. Maybe some other time, when I've had a chance to prepare her for company. Mostly, she's just noisy, and if she weren't my mother's older sister, I'd put her in a home."

"You're so sweet, Clifton. It doesn't surprise me that you provide for her. May I walk down to the gazebo? It looks so peaceful down there."

"Of course," he said. "I'll just check on dinner, and then I'll join you momentarily."

He walked on toward the house as she got out of the car and headed down the grassy slope toward the gazebo. She was taken by the soft scenery, and she broke into a child-like running skip.

Instead of checking on dinner, Clifton went straight to the basement. Aunt Ashley was taking a nap in her recliner, which made it easier to inject her. The needle penetrated her skin, and she stirred.

"Clifton, what are you doing?" she slurred. "You have one of them here, don't you? I've warned you about that. Those trollops are nothing but trouble."

The injection worked quickly, and the old woman's eyes rolled back in her head.

"Nothing but trouble," she repeated as her body went limp.

Clifton chuckled. "Yes, ma'am. I hope she is exactly that."

He laughed as he went upstairs to the kitchen. Dinner was ready a little sooner than he expected, so he served the plates and put them into the warmer in the dining room. He got salads from the refrigerator and put the bread in the oven before he exited the screened-in side porch. Erica waved to him from the gazebo.

"Dinner is served," he called.

"Coming!" she replied as she headed in his direction.

He watched her intently as she approached the house. Her young, supple body aroused him as he watched her breasts bounce under her white blouse.

She bounded up the three steps onto the stoop and, to his delight, she gave him a little peck on the cheek.

"Thank you," she said as she panted, "for bringing me here—and for thinking I'm someone special."

Clifton took her hand and covered it with his own, sweaty palm. "Believe me, it's my pleasure."

He opened the screen door and motioned for her to enter. As Erica gazed around the kitchen, it put Clifton in mind of a child at an Easter egg hunt.

"What a great space!" she marveled. "Everything looks antique."

"Most everything is," he replied. "If you'd like to freshen up a bit, there's a bathroom on the left, just down the hall."

"Perfect! I'll just be a minute."

When she returned, she joined him in the dining room. He pulled out her chair.

"Ooooh, what a wonderful aroma" she said as she smelled the food on the steaming plate in front of her. "I'm famished!"

"*Bon appétit!*" Clifton said as he sat down across from her.

She ate like a she-wolf, and Clifton though it interesting that she never inquired about the recipe.

"I'm stuffed," she confessed after several minutes of gorging. "I'll never eat again!"

Clifton held up a hand. "Hold on, Rica. Don't be too hasty. We're not done yet."

He got up and went into the kitchen to retrieve dessert.

"Ta-da!" he exclaimed as he presented the platter of lemon pound cake smothered in strawberries.

"I've whipped some fresh cream too, if you like, and I've brewed some fresh coffee."

"Whipped cream? For me?" Erica gushed. "No coffee, though. Maybe another glass of the lovely wine. It's *soooo* good!"

Clifton executed a curt bow. "Of course. I'll just be a minute."

He went to the kitchen, grumbling under his breath at her simpering, subtle demands. *A small price to pay…*he reassured himself as he took the whipped cream from the fridge. When he re-entered the dining room, Erica was nodding off in her seat.

He sat the crystal bowl of cream on the sideboard. "Why don't we go out on the veranda and relax a bit?" he asked. Erica blinked a few times before she responded.

"Of course," she agreed.

He ushered her out onto the screen porch as he removed a cigar from his shirt pocket.

"Do you mind?" he asked.

"Of course not," she replied with a dreamy glaze over her eyes.

They sat down on a wicker loveseat with overstuffed, paisley cushions, and she snuggled against him. Clifton leaned back and puffed on his Montecristo. He blew a couple of smoke rings and she voice slurred words of amusement. *She's becoming more pliant by the moment….*

"Clifton," she said as she suddenly sat up and looked at him with renewed awareness, "where's your puppy dog?"

He looked away and forced tears into his eyes.

"She never made it home from the vet," he replied with a sniff. "She was just too old and sick. They had to put her down."

Erica put her hand to her chest. "Oh, I'm so sorry!"

"Thank you," he said, "but it's alright. I have another pet."

"Really, what do you have? A cat? I haven't heard any barking since we arrived."

"Let me just fetch her," Clifton said. He gingerly lay his cigar aside in an ashtray on the wicker table next to the loveseat, stood up and went inside.

Against the far wall of his bedroom was a large terrarium. He removed the perforated metal cover and gently lifted the six-foot python out of the enclosure.

"Come, Cleo. We have a guest," he said as he draped the reptile around his shoulders and kissed its head.

When he walked back out onto the porch, Erica leapt to her feet and shrieked.

'God Almighty! What is that?"

Clifton grinned. "This is Cleo," he said. "She's a reticulated python."

"Keep it away from me!" she pleaded as she covered her face with her hands and took several steps back.

Clifton leered at her. "Why, Rica, I thought you liked animals."

"I do!" she replied. "The warm, fuzzy kind! Not snakes! Please, Clifton, take it away!"

Clifton put the python down on the floor with its head resting on Erica's foot. The snake sensed warmth—and *fear*. Clifton reveled as it wrapped itself around her bare leg and began to glide up inside her skirt.

She screamed, "Get it away! Please, God! Please get it off me!"

Her nipples hardened through her blouse, and Clifton's erection began to pulse.

"Alright!" he barked impatiently. 'I'll take her away. Perhaps," he said as he yanked down his zipper, "you might like this better!" He approached her and, taking care not to step on Cleo, forced his turgid penis into her right hand.

Erica began to sob. "Clifton, please. I'll do anything. Just take that snake away—please! I'm begging you!" She began to cry uncontrollably. Clifton nearly had an orgasm in her hand.

He lifted her skirt and gently disentangled the creature from around her leg before placing it on the floor.

"Good Cleo," he whispered softly as he slowly pulled down Erica's silk panties.

"Clifton, I-I can't have that thing near us when we make love! Please!" she pleaded once more.

Clifton looked into her tear-filled eyes. She was petrified, and her fear was electrifying—only, she didn't want him. She wanted to run away, the first chance she got. He could sense it with every measured breath she took.

Something snapped. His erection fell like the half-masted flag at a veteran's funeral. He became frustrated and angry.

He raised his arms over his head and sliced down through the air violently. "All right! I'll get rid of the snake."

He picked up the python and threw against the wall….

It was useless. His erection had disappeared as though he'd been dipped in a tub of ice water, and no fantasy he could recall would revive it.

"God damn it!" he roared. "You're just like the rest of them! I wish you were dead!"

Erica's look of terror instantly flashed to an angry glare.

"You son of a bitch!" she spat. "Take me home right now, or I'll start screaming."

He fumed but made no comment as he picked up the snake. He thought for a moment as he stared at the defiant young woman.

"Rica," he cooed, "I'm sorry. I was teasing, and I didn't suspect you'd take it so seriously. Please, sit down. Let me get you some more wine."

She glared at him. "You slimy bastard! You can call me a taxi, or I swear, I'll start screaming."

Clifton reeled from the onslaught as he fought to regain control. He put up both hands.

"Alright," he said calmly. "I'll call a taxi, but I've never seen someone act so childish. Such immaturity will have to be considered in any reports I give to Hinson about your performance!"

She flashed a look of panic, and her shoulders sagged. "Clifton, I'm sorry," she said in a lowered, significantly calmer tone. "I know I over-reacted, but that snake scares the pee out of me! Can we just sit down and start over?"

Clifton pouted a moment for effect until he finally relented. "Of course," he said. "I didn't intend to frighten you. I had no idea you'd react the way you did. As one who works with the dead, I didn't think you'd think twice about a simple snake. Look, since we're starting over, would you still like that boat ride?"

Erica retrieved her panties and stepped into them.

"I don't know, Clifton."

"Ok, then," he said with a tone of slight warning, hoping she was still thinking about that professional reference. "Your decision…"

Erica sighed. "All right, Clifton. I'll go for a boat ride. I'm sorry I spoiled the moment."

He feigned protest, "Oh, no, sweetheart! It was all my fault—poor judgment on my part. I'm sincerely sorry. Are you alright now?"

"Yes, I'm fine," she replied.

Her tone did little to convince him, but it was no matter. She was his regardless.

"I'll just go in and fetch the life jackets," he said.

Clifton grabbed Cleo and, after putting her back in her cage, hurried to the large pantry off the kitchen and grabbed two life jackets and two bottles of red wine. As he headed back, he pictured Erica making a mad dash for the road, but in that event, he had another plan. He was surprised when he found her still waiting patiently on the porch.

"Ready?" he asked as he handed her a jacket. "The river is quite nice tonight."

Erica teetered slightly. "Yes, I'm ready. I'm feeling a little light-headed though."

"Don't worry," he assured her as he helped her with the life jacket. "I'll take good care of you…."

At 4:23 A.M. the following morning, the lookout on the Coast Guard Cutter *Avenger* spotted a body floating face-down in the James River. He pulled the night-vision binoculars from his eyes and hit the intercom button on the wall behind him.

"Bridge! This is aloftcon. I've spotted a body at zero-four-zero degrees."

"*Roger!*" came the reply from the darkened bridge. The Cutter, which had been cruising with just her running lights, suddenly roared to life. Commander Barry Pitillo began to bark orders.

"Helmsman! Come zero-three-five degrees, Quartermaster, sound general quarters, and messenger alert the diver and the Chief Bos'n to stand by on the fantail."

"Aye, Sir!" resounded as the men moved to their tasks.

In less the fifteen seconds the Cutter had altered course and Pitillo was standing on the starboard wing of the bridge.

"Helmsman!" he shouted through the open door. "Steady as you go!"

"Aye sir," the sailor replied as he took the wheel in both hands.

The engines were idled, and the ship slowed as the swimmer went overboard; and, the Chief directed the lowering of the dive platform behind him. Pitillo looked on as the man swam furiously toward the victim.

"Ma'am!" Pitillo heard the diver call out as he reached the body. "I'm a Coast Guard rescue swimmer. Hold on! I'm here to help you!"

A second later, the diver spun around and called out toward the ship. "Good God in Heaven! Her eyes are gone!" He began to wretch and vomit into the river.

CHAPTER 17

S UNDAY AFTERNOON WITH Almyra Defrange was the best time Jefferson ever had with another human being. They talked, laughed, napped, ate, drank wine and genuinely enjoyed each other's company.

After dinner, they drove down to the pier behind the Naval Hospital to admire the lights from Norfolk. They walked along the beach, and watched the boats moving silently up and down the river. They talked about the time at Duke—it turned out that it had been even more amazing than Jeff imagined.

While he had been in the safe cocoon of his coma, Defrange sat with him day and night. She held his hand, and though he never saw her, he was acutely aware of her presence. When he awakened, he had decided it was all a dream.

He learned that she was the one who devised the tests for him and Commander Douglas, and that she had written her thesis on what she had discovered from the results of her altered experiment. The only unexplained point was why Jefferson had lost his ESP after the coma.

She knew his thoughts, but Jeff didn't mind. If she was in his head today, then she would know how much it meant to him.

They got home about 11:00 that evening, and Jeff let her open the door to be sure that she was comfortable with it. After discussing the pros and cons of a nightcap, he walked her to the foot of the stairs.

"Goodnight, Partner," he whispered. "Thanks for a wonderful day."

Defrange smiled. "No, thank you."

"Sleep tight," he offered.

"Oh, I will. I'm totally exhausted."

She kissed him lightly on the cheek and disappeared up the stairs.

Jefferson checked the doors and made sure the alarm was set before he turned in for the night. He was tired, but he forced his eyes to stay open until he was sure by the sounds above that Defrange was settled in upstairs.

She is beautiful…inside and out. I'm glad she's here.

He drifted off and dreamed of sailing the Chesapeake with his rediscovered angel. They were sailing a forty-footer, they were tan, and they were holding hands. He was just about to kiss her when a loud crash shattered his lovely dream. He instinctively rolled off the bed, and as he did, he pulled his pistol from under the pillow. He'd slipped his .45 off safety just as a light came on in the foyer.

"Defrange!" he called. "Is that you, Partner?"

"Yes," she answered through the door. "Don't shoot! I'm sorry about the noise."

Jeff laid his pistol on the bed and pulled on a robe before walking into the hallway.

Defrange was fully and furtively trying to pick up the pieces of an umbrella stand she had knocked over in the darkness.

"I'm sorry about this," she apologized. "I should have turned on a light, but I was in a hurry. I'll be glad to replace it."

Jeff laughed. "It's ok," he assured her. "I never liked the damned thing, anyway."

Defrange faced him in the low light. Her eyes were dark, forest green. "I was coming to wake you. You need to get dressed. The Raptor has just killed a young woman."

Jefferson wondered for a moment if he was still dreaming.

"What?" he asked. "Did the Precinct call or something?"

"No, not yet," she replied. "But hurry up. We need to get rolling."

"Rolling?" he repeated. "Rolling where?"

She started to answer, but the ringing phone cut her off. Jeff glanced at his watch: 5:12. He reached for the phone.

"This is Jefferson."

"*Lieutenant Jefferson,*" the familiar voice began, "*this is Pherson, down at the Precinct.*"

"Good God, Pherson!" Jeff half-seriously growled. "Don't you ever call anyone at a decent hour?"

"*No, sir,*" he replied. "*I work third shift.*"

Jefferson rolled his eyes at the man's obvious reply. "What's up, Sergeant?" he asked.

"*We just got a call from the Coast Guard, and they've found a body floating in the James. The eyes have been removed, and Captain Chambers wanted me to call you. He thinks it's the Raptor.*"

"Damn! Are they sure about the eyes? Maybe little sea creatures got them?"

"*Maybe so,*" Pherson replied, "*but the corpsman on the Cutter didn't think she'd been in the water long enough for that to happen.*"

"Where's the body now?"

"*The Avenger is bringing her in. ETA Base Portsmouth is about thirty minutes.*"

"Where was she found?"

"*Up north of the bridge,*" Pherson replied.

"Ok, Sarge. Let the Captain know I'm rolling on it."

"*Will do, L T, and oh, he told me to remind you not to forget to pick up Detective Defrange.*"

Jeff looked over at her svelte figure in her khaki pants and white, short-sleeve pullover. Her .9-millimeter Glock was tucked neatly in a fanny pack holster. He emitted a low chuckle.

"Don't worry, Pherson. You tell the Cap I couldn't forget her if I tried."

Jeff hung up. Defrange began to pace anxiously. He leaned against the newel post and waited.

"You wanna tell me?" he asked finally.

Defrange was in the midst of whatever she saw. She closed her eyes and put her hands to her temples.

"It was horrible," she rasped. "I saw a man killing a young woman…it was near the water. He mutilated her, and then he strangled her before he had sex with her."

Jeff went into the bedroom and she followed him.

"You saw all of this?" he asked. "Who is he?"

"I don't know, yet," she said. "These things take time, and so far, I haven't seen a face—but, just like the Tidewater, the victim is very clear to me."

"Do you have any feel for who the victim is?"

"No," Defrange replied, "but she's young and she's athletic. He strangled her to the brink of losing consciousness, and then he took her eyes with a scalpel. That's definite. It was a scalpel. She was aware when he mutilated her—I saw her eyes. They were strikingly blue."

Jeff turned his back and pulled on his shorts and pants under the cover of his robe. When he turned around, Defrange was staring at him with a curious look.

"Then what happened?" he asked as he pulled on a shirt and his shoulder holster.

She waved him off. "We can talk more on the way to the Coast Guard Base. Just hurry!"

Jeff stopped.

"How did you know that we're on the way to the Coast Guard Base? I didn't tell you that?"

Defrange slumped against the door jamb as though she was exhausted.

"Because," she said, "because, Jefferson I *saw it*! I saw it all, and it's horrible. Can we just go?"

Jeff holstered his .45, put on his ankle holster, and threw on his jacket.

"Absolutely. We can be there in twenty minutes."

He paused at the mirror to comb the few strands of hair he had left, and when he turned back to Defrange her eyes were blazing.

"Dr. Defrange," he offered, "you scare the hell outta me. You really do!"

"Ditto," she replied dryly.

They drove around Crawford Parkway without speaking. The river and the night were two of his favorite things, and she was enjoying them with him. She seemed to understand his mood, but more importantly, she was content with it. Jefferson finally broke the silence.

"You wanna talk some more about your vision?"

"No," she admitted, "but, I'd like to share the profile I've formulated on this killer."

"Please do."

She stared ahead in deep concentration, and he imagined that she was cataloging each bit of information in the order of presentation.

"The Raptor," she began softly, "is a middle-aged white male, and he lives with a doting, mousy, overly protective female who will do anything he asks. She protects him in his crimes."

Jeff thought for a moment.

"You say a doting female?" he asked. "You mean like, his mommy?"

"It's even deeper than that," Defrange replied. "In his sub-conscious, this woman represents the weak side of a domineering female somewhere in his past, and it's the dormant side of this memory that's controlling his behavior."

"Wait," he interrupted, "you mean he lives with a weak woman who he dominates, but *he's* really controlled by some woman who ran over him a long time ago?"

Defrange sighed. "Sort of."

"I'm sorry," he said. "Go on. I'll try to hold my comments."

She seemed to go into a trance-like state as she continued.

"The dominant female personality is so entwined with his own that, at times, he can't separate her, and she takes over entirely."

"You mean," he interjected again, "the Raptor is some sort of dual personality or something like that?"

"Exactly," Defrange answered and sank back to her trance. "But it's more than a dual personality. There seems to be a least three personalities struggling for control. The host—the Raptor—has become a personality unto himself, but it's controlled by the dominant woman. But, there's also a child in there. I sensed him at the Tidewater Breeze, and I believe he only emerged for the purpose of calling in the murder at the Ravenscroft— but, only because that's what the dominant woman wanted. He was the instrument for the call that led to the discovery of Wanda Marchant."

Jefferson was totally confused and at sea. Defrange gave him a sympathetic look.

"Let me try to clear this up," she said. "The Raptor is a highly intelligent and educated man, but he's controlled by horrible memories of some woman who dominated him in the past – probably during his childhood. She suffocated him beyond endurance. He was once frustrated by her domination, but now he's into it. He allows—no, *welcomes* it. The child personality is the only balance left, an innocent conscience, but he's no match for her.

Jeff was trying to keep up.

"As for the woman he lives with," Defrange went on, "she represents yet someone else. She's someone he loved, someone who left him, or died, and now his dominance over her is the only control he has over anything in his psyche. The dominant woman is the personality that kills, and he has a love-hate relationship with her. He's probably been in a constant state of flight of fight since early childhood."

Jeff nodded.

"Your turn," Defrange said.

"What about his father?"

"That was part of the problem too, as I see it. I don't think he ever had any sort of male role model, and I don't believe that this dominant personality is his mother. She was a foster figure, like a grandmother or aunt maybe."

Jeff had more questions, but he didn't know where to start or how to ask them.

"So," he ventured slowly, "the Raptor actually becomes someone else when he kills people—I mean, psychologically?"

"Yes and no," Defrange replied. "He uses her personality because she's so strong and he's so weak. He and the child blame her for what he does—but, and this is an important point that you should not forget for a moment—he's gone so far into this that his own personality, whatever is left, is only a shadow. He's actually become what has controlled him for so long, and no matter how horrible his acts may be, he enjoys them."

"So, you're saying…what the hell are you saying?"

"Bottom line, the Raptor has a very high IQ, has some sort of medical training, and he can't help what he does anymore than the tides can help what they do."

Jeff shrugged. "Ok, but what do we have to do to stop him?"

"Wait," she said, "before we get to that, there's one more important thing you need to know."

"What's that?"

"Along with the other abhorrent characteristics we see manifested in this killer, he's also a cannibal."

Jeff let his head spin around that for a moment.

"Oh, God, Defrange! You are kidding, aren't you? Do you mean he eats the eyes he takes away with him?"

"That's my assessment, Partner."

Jeff fought off both revulsion and fascination. "Why the eyes?"

Defrange leaned against the passenger door and put her foot on the seat.

"Best guess?" she said. "He may tell himself that it keeps the victims from seeing him, but I believe it's really a simple fetish."

"This is too bizarre," Jeff said. "It seems that a person like him would stand out in any crowd."

"That's part of it, too," Defrange replied. "For all outward appearance, he fits right in with everyone around him. It's part of his defense mechanism, and he maintains his façade very well. He's also able to mask his psyche by denying his own reality and pretending he's part of actual reality. If I were in a room with him, I wouldn't feel his presence."

Jeff marveled at his new partner.

"How can you know all of this?" he asked. "You haven't even been here for forty-eight hours!"

"Experience, and—" She stopped suddenly, as if a new thought came to her.

"Defrange, are you alright?"

She put her foot back down on the floor and faced forward again. Her hand was against Jefferson's knee— he could feel her trembling.

"Yes, I'm fine," she replied." What I was going to say is that I'm inside his head, and please don't' ask me to explain that. Just try to understand that it's ugly in there, and the force of his psyche is stronger than I've ever experienced from another human."

Jeff put his hand on hers.

"*Is* he human?" he asked.

"Yes. Quite. But there is a side that is human to the lowest predator level. He's a killer, and though he tries to inwardly deny it, he loves being a killer."

The sign for the Coast Guard Base appeared on the left.

"Here we are, Partner," Jeff said softly." Are you ready for this?"

"Lieutenant, I'm readier than you are. Remember, I've already seen it."

CHAPTER 18

THE DETECTIVES WERE detained at the gate of the Coast Guard Base by a first-class petty officer who gave new perspective to the term "spit and polish". Jeff recognized the insignia of a gunner's mate on his crisp, white sleeve.

"Gun morning, Guns," Jeff greeted him.

"Good morning, sir," the guard replied. "May I help you?"

"Yes. I'm Lieutenant Jefferson, and this is Detective Almyra Defrange. We're here on police business."

"Yes, sir. The Officer of the Day told me to expect you on my watch. May I see some ID?"

"Yes, of course," Jefferson replied as he handed him his photo ID and shield.

The guard studied them until he was satisfied and handed them back.

"And the Detective?" he asked politely.

Jefferson handed over Defrange's credentials, and the gate guard peered over them as closely as he had Jefferson's.

"Milwaukee!" the guard observed. "You're a long way from home. Welcome to Portsmouth."

He smiled at her as he returned her ID to Jefferson.

"Lieutenant," he began, "as you may know, per government regulations, I have to ask you to lock all of your weapons in the trunk of your car while you are on the government reservation."

"Yes," Jeff agreed. "I am familiar with that regulation."

Defrange handed over her Glock, and Jeff removed the riot gun from the door mount and the .45 from his holster before dutifully exiting the car and walking to the rear of the vehicle. He placed the weapons inside and started to close the lid.

"*All* weapons, sir," the guard respectfully reminded him.

Jeff grinned sheepishly. "Oh, yeah." He bent over and removed the .44 Derringer from his ankle holster and placed it in the trunk as well. He started once more to close the lid.

"Lieutenant Jefferson!" the guard barked. "I don't think you're playing games, but all weapons, means *all weapons*."

Jefferson had to think for a second before he removed the knife from a sheath sewn into the nape of his jacket. A trick he had learned in Viet Nam had saved his life more than once.

"Sorry, Guns," he apologized. "These things become such a part of my routine that I forget about them. How did you know I had them?"

"Lieutenant Jefferson, your police and military records are a benchmark for some of us in law enforcement. Your tactics, martial arts expertise, and your choice of weapons are well known to those who follow your career. I knew who you were when you arrived, and I've also followed Dr. Defrange's career. I started to pass you through without even stopping you, but I knew you wouldn't want me to do that."

Jefferson blushed and nodded his understanding.

"You're cleared to pass, sir," the guard announced as he handed Jefferson a laminated sign with the single word "Visitor".

"Please place this pass on your dash," he continued, "so that roving security will know that you're legally here. You may park in any space designated for visitors. You're to meet the *Avenger*—she'll be tying up in the berth just behind the guard house here."

"Thank you," Jefferson said as he got back in the car. Defrange snickered, and he rolled his eyes.

They pulled into the designated parking space just as the *Avenger* was making the final turn into the slip. Two seamen jumped over the side and in less than a minute they secured the one-hundred-and-ten-footer to the dock.

Jeff got out and got Defrange's door. He looked up toward the main gate and saw Palachi standing beside his car, waving in animated fashion as he spoke with the guard. He thought about going back to vouch for him but then checked himself. Why should he and Defrange have all the fun?

Clifton Dothan had gone to work early at Sterling Point Funeral Home. He was angry over wasting a whole Sunday evening with Erica. She had excited him, but he wasn't quite satisfied.

"Silly little bitch," he grumbled.

He had come to work early because he had an uncontrollable desire to fondle a dead body, and he hoped one in particular was available.

"What's this?" he whispered over the log-in sheet. "I'm so sorry I wasn't here to greet you."

Name: Maureen Rosalyn Charbenau; Sex: female; Age: 30; Cause of death: Myocardial infarction due to physical trauma and shock; Autopsy: Dr. Martin Palachi, ME.

"Damn!" he complained to no one, "That nosy Palachi has already been at her, but I'll salvage everything. I'll fix her right."

The door to the embalming suite banged loudly against the wall as he entered.

"Maureen?" he called in a stage whisper. "I hope I didn't startle you. Don't worry. I'm here to set you free."

Clifton located the correct drawer, pulled it out slowly and drew a breath as he feasted his eyes on Maureen Charbenau. He studied the neat incision down her chest. The ME had incorporated the incision made by the thoracic surgeon so there was only one.

Palachi is good—I'll give him that much.

He pulled the wheeled drawer from the refrigeration unit and rolled Maureen to an embalming table. He gently slid her over and began to caress her breasts as he reached up and opened an eyelid.

"Oh, baby!" he whispered. "Are we gonna have fun!"

He suddenly thought of Aunt Ashley: she would be upset that he hadn't been home last night—and then he grinned as he envisioned her torment.

He kissed Maureen and whispered in her ear.

"You know, my dear, if Aunt Ashley weren't so crazy, I'd let her out sometimes."

CHAPTER 19

JEFFERSON AND DEFRANGE were welcomed aboard the *Avenger*. They were led directly to the fantail where the ship's corpsman Bill Morris had set up a make-shift examination area for Palachi. The purpose of an on-site exam was to find any clues that might be lost in moving the body to the morgue or other area before the ME's examination. The body was covered and lying on a gurney, which had been placed under powerful lights that Morris had positioned to aid in the examination. Jefferson was impressed that Morris had taken time to lash up canvas tarps to ward off prying eyes.

"Jefferson," Palachi called out as he approached the waiting cadaver. "You wanna give me a hand?"

"Sure. What do you want me to do?"

"We handle this like the others," the ME said as he adjusted the headband on his microphone. "Just jot down anything you notice that you don't hear me say into the tape recorder."

The recorder was attached to his belt, and he turned it on. He pulled the blanket from the body and paused. His expression was solemn as he took in the sight of Erica's remains.

"The victim is a Caucasian female," he began, "estimate her to be five feet six inches tall, weight, one-ten to one-twenty pounds."

He looked briefly at her fingernails before scanning the body from head to toe.

"The victim is clothed," he continued, "except that her shoes are missing."

He pulled he blanket up for privacy.

"Her panties are missing," he said finally before he switched off the recorder.

"You might want to note that, Jefferson. Her killer might have taken them for a trophy."

Jeff nodded, and Palachi turned on the recorder once more.

"There are ligature marks around her throat," he said as he turned her head from side to side, "and the eyes appear to have been surgically removed."

Palachi looked up for a moment and closed his eyes before going on.

"The victim has good muscle tone, and she appears to have been in good health. I estimate her age to be mid-to-late twenties, and judging from the motility of the body, the color of the nail beds, and allowance for time in the water, death occurred between one-thirty and three-thirty a.m."

Palachi glanced at his watch.

"The time now is six seventeen a.m."

Palachi's hand shook as he paused the recorder.

Corpsman Morris stepped respectfully toward the gurney.

"Dr. Palachi," he said, "she was holding this in a death grip when the rescue swimmer brought her aboard."

He handed a small leather purse to the ME before stepping back out of the light. Palachi opened it, pouring out the water and other contents onto the edge of the stretcher. He turned on the recorder once more.

"When recovered from the James River, the victim was clutching a small brown purse. It contains: one lipstick, a comb, chewing gum, seven dollars and change, and a Virginia driver's license number 3008762631. The victim is Erica Lynn Merriweather, Route Four, box five-zero-zero-four, Danville, Virginia."

Palachi's thumb fumbled on the recorder switch as he reeled backward from the gurney. He tore the mic from his head and threw it on to the deck. Jefferson rushed to him.

"Easy, Martin! What's wrong?"

"Damn it all to hell!" he cursed. "I know this girl's father. He's a funeral director in Danville."

Defrange come forward and lightly took hold of Martin's arm.

"Easy," she whispered.

Palachi jerked his arm from her grasp, and she stepped back.

"Morris! Is your commanding officer available?"

"Yes, sir, Doctor Palachi. Would you like me to request his presence?"

Palachi took a deep breath. "Please, if you would be so kind."

Morris exited through a slit in the canvas and headed for the bridge.

"Where's Dixon?" Palachi asked.

"Here Doc!" came the reply as the chief lab tech pushed his way forward and stood patiently at the edge of the exam area.

Palachi held up his hand to signal that he should stand by. He picked up the microphone and plugged it back into the tape recorder.

"Gross examination aboard the CGC *Avenger* is complete. This dictation will be continued at full autopsy back at the City-County Morgue."

Palachi walked over and leaned against the deck rail, and he stared at the water for a long moment.

"Dixon!" he called finally. "Please get our stretcher. We'll be transporting Miss Merriweather as soon as I've spoken with the CO."

Dixon exited through the same flap Morris used. The oppressive silence that lingered was broken by a young, second-class petty officer.

"Dr. Palachi," he said softly, "I'm in charge of the six-man work party, and we will be happy to assist you if you would like us the carry the deceased to the hearse."

Palachi's shoulders seemed to relax a bit when he noticed the young man and the six other seamen were in dress uniforms, in honor of the deceased.

"I'm touched," Palachi confessed, wiping the corner of his eye, "but, we'll take it from here. You men have done enough."

The petty officer saluted Palachi, who returned the gesture rather clumsily.

"Honor Guard," the second-class snapped. "About face! Forward, march." The men filed reverently from the fantail.

Jeff looked at Defrange.

"Partner?" he asked without asking.

"She's the girl I saw, no doubt about it," she replied.

The tarp snapped open and Commander Pitillo entered the area.

"Who is Dr. Palachi?" he asked.

"I'm Palachi," the ME answered.

"Doctor, I'm Mark Pitillo. I'm the Commanding Officer, and my corpsman informed me that you wish to speak to me."

"Yes, Mr. Pitillo. With your permission I'd like to remove the deceased to the morgue so that a proper post mortem may be performed."

"Permission granted, Doctor. I'll just need for you to sign the release forms. If you'll accompany me to the bridge, the duty yeoman will fix them up for you. It'll take five minutes."

Dixon had returned with the stretcher.

"Are we cleared to move her, Doc?"

"By all means," Pitillo answered. "You may remove her while the doctor signs the release."

Dixon moved the stretcher into position and Jefferson helped him slide Erica Merriweather on to it. Dixon covered her, secured her with straps, and headed for the gangway.

"I'm going to do the post immediately," he said to Jefferson. "I need to contact her father as soon as possible, but I want to have as much information as I can before I call him. He put an arm on Jeff's shoulder and the other around Defrange. "Listen, I'm sorry about my behavior. It was just such a shock when I realized who this child is."

"It's ok, pal," Jeff replied. "We understand perfectly."

Defrange squeezed his hand but didn't speak. The look in her green eyes spoke volumes.

Palachi exited the area with Commander Pitillo.

"I sure hope he's alright," Jeff said.

"He will be, in time," Defrange replied.

The detectives went ashore and retrieved their car. Defrange didn't say much, but Jefferson was beginning to learn that this wasn't necessarily a bad thing. They stopped by the gate to return their visitor's pass and to retrieve their weapons from the trunk. They waved to Dixon, who was waiting for Palachi, as they exited the gate.

"You know," Jeff said, "we're supposed to be at a press conference in less than three hours."

At Sterling Point, Clifton Dothan was enjoying himself with Maureen far more than he had with Erica. He found their conversation stimulating. He was combing her hair and softly laughing when he heard a faint noise in the hallway outside the embalming suite.

"Maureen," he whispered, "you naughty girl! Did you invite someone over without telling me?"

He lay the comb aside and listened, recognizing the distinct creak of the hardwood floor. He waited until he heard it once more.

"Excuse me, my dear," he whispered. "But I think I should check to see if we have company."

Dothan stood up just as the door to the suite swung slowly open, making a dull thump when it hit the wall.

"Who's there?" he called out, taking a large scalpel from the table and slipping it up his sleeve. There was a silhouette in the doorway.

"Who's there?" he demanded again as he backed away.

"Dothan!" came a voice like a search beacon cutting through the darkness. "What the hell do you think you're doing?"

Dothan relaxed.

"Boss? I'm glad that's you. I couldn't sleep so I came in early."

"That's commendable, Clifton," came Dan Hinson's icy reply, "but you're lying. I've been watching you. I've also been filming you for several minutes from the observation room. I want you to step forward—and keep your hands where I can see them!"

Dothan slowly raised his hands, feeling the cold comfort of the scalpel as it slid down to the level of his armpit.

"Wh-what do you mean?" he stammered as he stepped into the circle of light coming from the fixture above the embalming table. Hinson had a pistol leveled at him.

"What do I mean? You ghoulish bastard! I've been watching you with that corpse, and revulsion doesn't even come close to describing the emotions I'm having right now."

Dothan looked down his nose, indignant. "I don't know what you're talking about! Just what are you insinuating? I would never do such a thing! Are you out of your mind?"

"No, Clifton! I'm not, but you are!" Hinson replied as he switched on the overhead lights. "How long have you been doing this? You son of a bitch! To think I've trusted you, believed in you—hell! You've been in my home, around my wife and children. How long Clifton? How long have you been a necrophiliac?"

"Dan, no!" Clifton whined. "This was the first time! What difference does it make, anyway? They're all whores!"

Hinson stepped menacingly toward him.

"I'll tell you what difference it makes," he growled. "You have been given a talent that entrusts you with one of the most honorable things that one human being can do for another, and you've violated that trust. You've reduced the dignity of this woman to a level as low as yours, and you don't have that right!"

Dothan's mind was spinning.

"Dan, please!" he begged. "This was the only time. She is just so beautiful and helpless. I couldn't help myself. You know how it is!"

"No, Clifton! I don't know. Now, you step away from the table, and you keep your hands where I can see them. Remember, I have the tape of what you were doing, and no jury in the world would convict me if I killed you in cold blood right now. Move!"

Dothan's fear gave way to panic.

Hinson circled until he had placed himself between Dothan and Maureen's body.

"What I am going to do is call the police, and I'm going to press charges against you. I hope they lock you up for a long time, because you need help."

Hinson motioned with the pistol.

"Move slowly into the hallway," he ordered, "and slowly walk toward the office."

Dothan complied, and they moved in a macabre ballet down the darkened corridor.

When they reached the office, Hinson turned on the lights, and he had Dothan stand in front of the desk while he used the phone.

Suddenly Dothan clasped his left chest and contorted his face in mock agony.

"Oh, God!" he wheezed. "Dan, help me! I'm having a heart attack!"

Clifton lowered his right arm, allowing the scalpel to slide down to his waiting grip. Hinson slammed down the phone and ran to his aid. As soon as he was close enough, Clifton lunged, driving the scalpel into Hinson's larynx and ripping the blade to the right. The pistol tumbled to the floor as blood from Hinson's carotid spurted across the room. The man fell to the floor, gurgling as the life drained from his body.

Clifton smiled down at his boss. "Sorry Dan," he said.

He watched Hinson die and then went to the observation room and retrieved the damning tape. Before he departed, he went and bade Maureen a fond good night: it took all of thirty minutes.

It was first light when Clifton got into the Corvette, placing the tape and scalpel under the driver's seat. He headed for home, taking a brief detour to a secluded, one-lane bridge. He threw the tape into the middle of the channel, but elected to keep the scalpel.

As he watched the tape sink into the murk, and large water snake stuck its head above the surface, clutching a frog in its mouth.

Predators and prey....

CHAPTER 20

T HE TRIP FROM the base to the morgue was a solemn one. Jefferson and Defrange both worried about Palachi, and the Merriweather family.

"Depressing part of the job," Jeff said.

"Yeah, the part I hate," Defrange replied.

The radio squawked.

"Virginia Creeper this is PreCom dispatch, do you copy?"

Jefferson picked up the mic.

"This is Virginia Creeper, go ahead PreCom."

"Be advised that Captain Chambers has postponed the press conference from this morning until Tuesday morning at the same time, over."

"Roger, PreCom, understood. Virginia Creeper out."

"Roger Virginia Creeper, PreCom out."

"Good," Jeff said. "I guess the Captain figured we might still be busy from last night's activities. What a thoughtful guy."

"Yes," Defrange agreed. "Insightful too."

They parked at the morgue and went to Palachi's office to wait for him to finish the autopsy on Erica Merriweather. *Unusually quiet* was Jeff's last thought as he dozed off in Palachi's desk chair. He awoke to the sun blazing through the blinds. Disoriented and groggy, he looked up at Defrange, who appeared not to have slept at all; her eyes were puffy and glazed over.

"Good morning, Partner," she said.

Her warm gingerbread, alto voice could have melted the polar ice cap.

"Hi," Jeff offered as he tried to stretch fatigue out of his back. "Any word yet?"

"Not yet. Martin is taking his time."

"Uhmm," Jeff replied mid-stretch. "Makes sense. He wants to give her father as much info as he can."

Someone had a pot of coffee going, and Defrange followed the aroma down the hall until she found it. She was back in two minutes with two steaming mugs full of the life reviving liquid.

"Coffee?" she handed him a cup.

Jeff took a sip just as the door opened and Palachi entered. He looked haggard and distraught as he fell into a chair, his shoulders slumped.

"Martin?" Defrange inquired gently.

He put his hands over his eyes, his elbows on the desk, and he began to sob.

"That bastard! He strangled her just to the point of death, and then he cut out her eyes. Then, when her oxygen level was *almost* depleted, he raped her vaginally and anally. Then, he just dumped her in the river!"

Defrange moved behind the desk and began to massage the ME's shoulders.

"It's alright," she whispered.

Palachi looked up, and his face softened for a moment.

"No, Dr. Defrange, it's not alright. The son of a bitch is mutilating and murdering people, and we can't stop him!"

"C'mon, Palachi," Jeff said reassuringly. "You of all people should know better than to let this get personal."

Martin glared at him through red eyes—for a moment Jeff thought he was going to hit him.

Then, without warning, in a flare of rage, Palachi swept all the items from his desk onto the floor and stood up. He tore the desk lamp from the receptacle and threw it against the back of the door, sending shards of glass cascading to the floor.

"Goddamn it, Jefferson!" he screamed. "Don't lecture me. I know all that bullshit we learn in psychology class, but this *has* become personal. While I was in there cutting on this beautiful girl, while I was taking samples from her pelvic cavity, and while I was weighing her organs, something came loose in my head. It all caved in on me, and, now, I have to call her parents and tell them that their child has been killed by a psychopathic, asshole, screw-loose, motherfucker because we're too stupid to stop him!"

Defrange stepped back, and Jeff sat down in a chair against the far wall.

Martin fell back into his chair. After a few moments, he craned around to look back at Defrange. She smiled and took a seat beside Jeff.

"Sorry, my friends," Palachi mumbled. "I had to vent— I'm sorry you saw me do it."

They both assured him that they understood.

"Look," he offered as the spark returned to his eyes, "we're all off duty, aren't we?"

He directed his question to Defrange, but she deferred to Jefferson.

Jeff nodded. "Of course—since Friday afternoon. I guess we're technically off until 8:30—a few more minutes."

"All right, then," Palachi said as he opened a side drawer in his desk and removed a fifth of Wild Turkey. "Let's have a drink!"

He poured two fingers each in their coffee mugs.

"Whoa! Hold on, Doc," Jeff said. "I still have to drive home, or work depending on how we feel later!"

"Go ahead, pal," he urged with a wink. "Have a drink or two, or three. We can always find someplace around here for you to sleep it off."

"No damn way!" Jeff replied. "Hell, a fellow could wake up around here with his skull sawed open!"

"That's the least of your worries, Lieutenant," Palachi retorted. "Your skull's too damned hard for any saw we've got."

The phone on Palachi's desk rang. The ME let it ring three of four times before he finally reached over and picked up the receiver. He handed the phone to Jefferson.

"It's for you."

Jeff reluctantly took the phone.

"This is Jefferson."

"Lieutenant Jefferson, this is Pherson, down at the Precinct."

"Yes, good morning again, Sergeant Pherson."

"Lieutenant, there's been a homicide over at the Sterling Point Funeral Home, and a body has been violated. Captain Chambers wants you and Detective Defrange to check on it."

Jeff looked over at Defrange, whose green orbs were glowing. "Sure, Pherson. We can roll right now. I'll advise the ME. By the way," Jeff said, glancing at his watch, "aren't you supposed to be off work?"

"I've been off for a few minutes. Just wanted to make sure you got the Cap's message. Give my best to Detective Defrange."

"You bet," Jeff said and hung up. He looked at Palachi.

"There's been a murder and a violation of a corpse at Sterling Point Funeral Home. You ready to roll?"

Palachi leaned against his desk.

"Gimme a few minutes. I have to call Joel Merriweather."

"Martin, do you want me to call him?" Defrange volunteered.

"No, Dr. Defrange, but thanks for offering. This is going to be devastating for him and his wife. Maybe it will be a little easier coming from someone they sort of know."

Up on the James River, Clifton Dothan was laughing at his livid Aunt Ashley.

"Clifton!" she shrieked. "How could you accidentally over-medicate me? You're a medical person, for God's sake! Plus, you put me in the basement without even introducing me to your guest. It's not proper, and then you stayed out all night with the little tramp!"

Clifton snickered. "Oh, dear Auntie, why would you even imagine I would want my friends to meet the likes of you—but you're right, she's not a very nice young lady. She didn't even like Cleo. Don't you worry though. I taught her a lesson!"

CHAPTER 21

JEFFERSON AND DEFRANGE rode with Palachi. They arrived at Sterling Point just before nine. The officers from that patrol area were already on-scene, and they were questioning the custodian. An officer came over to greet them.

"Good morning, Detectives, Dr. Palachi," he said. "We've got a real mess in there."

"What you got?" Jefferson asked.

"Someone apparently stabbed the funeral director and left him to bleed to death. His body's in the office. The custodian found him, but he also discovered a corpse that's not, uh, exactly what one would expect to find at the funeral home."

"Ok," Jeff replied. "We'll start with the custodian. What's his name?"

The officer checked his notebook. "Uh, it's Bradley. Tom Bradley."

As the detectives and the ME mounted the steps, Bradley rose from the porch swing of the ornate, Southern Colonial-style funeral home. Jefferson sensed the man's uneasiness as he extended his hand.

"Mr. Bradley? I'm Lieutenant Jefferson, and this is Detective Defrange, and Medical Examiner Palachi."

Bradley's hand trembled as he lightly shook Jefferson's. Defrange took over before Jeff could say anything else. She walked over and sat down on the swing.

She patted the seat next to her. "Mr. Bradley, would you join me here for a few minutes?"

The man sat down, slowly; his gaze locked onto Defrange's the whole time. Palachi and Jefferson stepped down to the sidewalk while she worked her magic, taking care to remain within earshot.

No one's ever asked his opinion about anything, and certainly no one like Almyra Defrange.

Defrange stared down the tree-lined drive that led to the main road as she began to pump the swing.

"Do you mind?" she asked.

"No ma'am," he replied in a hushed tone. "I kind of like it."

"I like it too," she confessed. "When I was a little girl growing up in Milwaukee, we had a swing just like this one on our front porch, and I'd spend hours there swinging and daydreaming."

"You did?" he asked as though it was impossible that this lovely woman had ever sat in a swing. His shoulders relaxed, and he ventured to lean back just a little.

Jefferson watched in amazement. A moment of silence followed as they all listened to the *whirr* of insects in the trees.

"Tom," Defrange began, "is it proper for me to call you Tom? I can use Mr. Bradly, if that's better. I don't want to be improper, but it just feels better to call you Tom. You may call me Almyra if you like."

He gazed out at the highway.

"Yes ma'am—Almyra," he replied, "that's shore a purty name. I've never heard it before."

Defrange smiled. "Thank you. It's a family name. Look, Tom, I want to assure you that we don't think you've done anything wrong. I just need for you to tell me what you found this morning—I mean, if you feel like it."

He began to pump the swing. "Are you really from Milwaukee, Wisconsin?" he asked finally. "I've never been there before. Is it true they make all that beer up there?"

Defrange laughed softly. "It sure is. Millions of gallons a year. You should come up sometime and visit the breweries. They even give you samples, if you like."

The man guffawed. "Dang-a rang-jingo! I can hardly imagine traveling all the way to Milwaukee, much less all that beer."

Defrange gave the man time between questions and responses. Jeff and she both knew that not talking can be just as beneficial in an interrogation.

"Almyra?" he addressed her in the middle of their exchange.

"Yes, Tom."

"I come in the back door this mornin', like I always do, and I turned on the lights. The first thing I seen that won't right was the door to the embalmin' suite had been left a'standin' wide open."

It was Defrange who pumped the swing this time.

"Oh," she replied as though they were talking about something as mundane as the weather, "is that unusual?"

"Yes, ma'am. It's a strict rule around here that them doors is to stay closed unless there's somebody in there a'workin'."

"I see. What did you do, then?"

Bradley looked down at the woven mat that covered the floor of the porch. "I, uh, went into the suite to see if anyone was workin' earlier than usual, and that's when I found that woman in there. Whoever done it was trying to be funny, I guess, but it damned near scared the hell outta me. Oh, sorry, Almyra—I didn't mean to cuss."

She reached over and gently patted his arm.

"It's ok, Tom. I've been a police officer for a long time, and you can believe that I've heard a lot worse."

Her touch was the catalyst that let him know that she was truly a friend, and he leaned all the way back in the swing. There was relief in his eyes.

"Well, Detective, uh, I mean Almyra, like I said, I reckon somebody thought it'd be funny, but when I seen that woman a'sittin' there, God Amighty, I hollered right out loud. I run outta there as fast as I could, and I beat it straight up to the office. I was gonna call somebody, but then I found poor Mr. Hinson."

Bradley was perspiring at recalling what he had seen. The swing made a few more passes.

"Go ahead, Tom," Defrange said. "We're almost done."

Jeff watched Bradley gaze into her green eyes. The guy would have followed her off a cliff.

"Well," he continued, "I really got scared when I saw Mr. Hinson. He was a'layin' there like something out of a horror movie."

"Did you go all the way into the office," she asked, "did you touch anything in there?"

"Hell, no! Why, I run outta there as quick as I could, and I called the cops from the pay phone down near the road."

"Let's back up a little, Tom," she suggested. "What was it about the woman that scared you? You must be accustomed to seeing corpses from time to time."

He nodded. "Yes ma'am, I am, but she was a'sittin up in a chair instead of lyin' down like she was supposed to be—and, she was naked! Now, I've seen that before too, but her face was what bothered me. I swear, she was made up, excuse me, like a whore. Red lips and everything. I aint used to seeing no corpses like that."

Jefferson looked at Palachi, and they started for the front door at the same time. When they got to the front office, they stopped short in the hallway. Hinson lay on his back in a four-foot pool of blood. His skin tone matched the gray carpet. Palachi began taking notes.

"It looks like his attacker got his right carotid," he observed. "It's relatively painless, but it's certain death."

Jeff looked out the window and saw the mobile crime van pull into the parking lot.

"Your boys ae here," he said.

"Good," Palachi acknowledged. "They can start in here while we check the embalming suite."

Jeff went to the porch and waited while Palachi explained the scenario to Dixon and the others. Tom Bradley was now quite at ease with Defrange.

"Tom," she said, "you will be around if we need to ask you anything else? I mean, about what you saw?"

"Oh, sure. I'll be right here at work if you need me, or anybody at my house can tell you where I'm at. I'll tell them that you're somebody important, and that you might need me."

Defrange stood. "Well, Tom, it's been my pleasure to meet you, and it's been a real pleasure to share this swing with you. If you ever get to Milwaukee, give me a call. I'm not in the book, but you can call the main police number. Tell them you're a friend of mine, and they'll patch you right through to me."

"Alright, Almyra. I might just surprise you one of these days. You aint like them other police I talked to. I like you."

He smiled at Jefferson as he went down the steps.

"Nice fellow," Defrange observed as he disappeared around the building.

"Not a suspect, then?" Jeff teased.

Defrange waved him off. "Oh, no. I don't think he'd step on a bug. It would take a mean kind of spirit that I just don't see in him."

Palachi, who was all business by now, stuck his head out the front door.

"I'm going to the embalming suites now," he called, "if you two want to join me."

The sky had darkened, and there was the rumble of thunder. By the time they reached the far end of the building it had begun to pour. The odor of ozone was heavy in the air.

Palachi pushed open the door of the suite where they were greeted by Maureen Charbenau. Her body was propped up in a chair, her make up giving her the appearance of a street walker. Palachi knelt to examine her, reminding them not to touch her without gloves. He pointed to a creamy, white liquid on her thighs, and Jeff shook his head in revulsion.

Palachi checked the incision he'd made at autopsy. He slipped on a pair of gloves and examined the body more closely. After studying one of Maureen's hands, he gently laid it back on her lap. When he forced one of her eyes open, Jefferson was shocked to see that it was intact.

"Does anyone think the Raptor is playing a joke on us?" Jeff asked.

"Don't know," Palachi mumbled, "but if the Raptor is responsible for this, he's let this victim off twice."

Defrange offered no input. She watched and listened.

"Jefferson," the ME directed, "would you put on a pair of gloves and help me lift her onto the table?"

Jeff complied, and as they lifted her there was a rush of air and a low moan. The ME laughed at Jeff's discomfort.

"Quite normal, Lieutenant," he explained. "But if we lived in the Middle Ages, the aristocracy of our fair city would have insisted that we burn this body as being possessed. The living dead, you know?"

"Thank God it's not the Middle Ages," Jefferson replied. "Burning a body would be all we need to complete this morning."

Defrange, either from clinical experience, or from just walking around in Palachi's head—Jeff wasn't certain— slipped on a pair of gloves and started looking through the drawers of a supply cabinet.

"Ah-ha! Here we go!"

She was holding a large syringe on to which she twisted a needle that looked like a ten-penny nail. She handed it to Palachi.

Jeff gasped. "What the hell is that for?"

"You'll see," she said. "Is a twelve-gauge needle large enough, Dr. Palachi?"

"Perfect, Dr. Defrange," he replied. Without ceremony, he stuck the needle into Maureen's neck. As he slowly withdrew the plunger, he extracted several milliliters of clear liquid.

"Just as I suspected," he announced. "She's been embalmed!"

"How do you know that?" Jeff asked.

"It was the color of her nail beds and her skin that tipped me off," Palachi explained. "I'm positive that the fluid I just took from her jugular is embalming fluid."

He carefully capped the needle and put it into his bag.

"Oh, my God! What's happened here?"

The three of them spun to face the doorway.

"Clifton Dothan," Palachi snapped. "I haven't seen you for a while. What's happened here is a murder, and a violation of this corpse."

He motioned for the man to step closer. Dothan hesitated, swallowing hard before he approached.

"Oh, this lovely girl," he said with a piteous look. "I prepared her this morning. I simply cannot believe this."

Jeff looked at Defrange. Her eyes were the color of pool table felt. "So, you were here this morning, Mr. Dothan?" she asked.

"Why, yes," he replied. "I often come in early and do some work when I can't sleep. It helps get a head start on the day."

Defrange started to say more, but Palachi cut her off.

"Clifton," he began, "do you know a funeral director from Danville named Joel Merriweather?"

"No," he answered. "I've never had the pleasure, but I know Erica, his daughter. She's here in Portsmouth doing her student rotation from MCV. Why do you ask?"

Palachi snapped off his gloves and threw them into the receptacle at the end of the table.

"Erica Merriweather is dead, and when I spoke to her father about an hour ago, he indicated that you might have seen her socially last night. *Did you see her?*"

Dothan slumped onto a lab stool as tears welled up in the corners of his eyes.

"This is almost too much to comprehend," he blubbered. "First, they called me to tell me that poor Dan had been murdered, and that a body had been desecrated. Now, you're telling me that Erica Merriweather is dead."

Defrange and Palachi had the appearance of a pair of jackals as Jeff stepped forward and gently placed his hand on Dothan's shoulder.

"Did you go out with Miss Merriweather last night?" he asked.

"Yes," Dothan replied between sniffles.

"Ok. I need for you to tell me about it. Don't leave anything out!"

"There's nothing much to tell. I picked her up at her apartment at six, and we went to my home for dinner. We ate, and then I took her for a short boat ride. After that, I took her home."

Defrange started to speak, but Jeff raised his hand and nodded "no".

"Clifton," he said, "you need to be aware that we are conducting a murder investigation, and I want to remind you that you don't have to talk to us without an attorney if you don't want to."

The color drained from Dothan's face.

"Lieutenant Jefferson," he said, as the timbre of his voice began to rise, "you don't think I had anything to do with Erica's death, do you? Is that what you're suggesting?"

"Not at all, sir," Jeff replied. "But I have to make sure that you understand your legal rights. This is a murder investigation."

Defrange took Jefferson's comment as a cue.

"Let's just say," she added, "we know that you're one of the last people to see Erica alive. What we need to prove to our satisfaction is that you weren't *absolutely* the last person to see her alive. What time did you take her home?"

Dothan's face went from ashen to flushed.

"About one-thirty this morning."

"And, did you see her to the door?" she pressed.

"Of course," he replied as if insulted. "I'd never abandon a lady in the parking lot. It's idiotic to even suggest such a thing."

"I wouldn't have expected anything less of you, Clifton," Jeff interrupted. "But, did you possibly notice anything out of the ordinary in the area around her apartment? Maybe a suspicious person or car that looked out of place? Anything at all?"

"No, it was very quiet and normal. I even waited on the stoop until I heard Erica lock the door behind her."

"So, you wouldn't know how Erica got from her apartment here in Portsmouth all the way back up the James River to where she was found?"

"No!" Dothan snapped. "I told you. She went inside, and I heard her lock the door!"

Palachi broke in.

"What did you serve for dinner last night?"

Dothan cleared his throat. "Steak and kidney pie, eh, home-made bread, strawberry-lemon shortcake, and some wine."

Palachi narrowed his gaze. "How much wine did the Merriweather girl have?"

"I don't know," Dothan replied. "Maybe a coupla glasses at dinner—and she had a nightcap when we got back from our boat ride."

"Clifton," Palachi said calmly, "Joel Merriweather has requested that Erica be brought here to Sterling Point, and that you prepare her body for her trip home and the funeral. Are you up to that?"

Dothan swallowed hard and blew his nose.

"Y-yes," he replied. "It would be my honor to do so."

Palachi stepped closer to Dothan. "Alright," he said, "the Merriweathers will be arriving by plane this evening, and we've arranged for them to leave on a flight tomorrow at four. Can you have her ready by tomorrow morning? Her folks will want to see her before they leave."

"Of course," Dothan agreed. "I'll make it my priority, although I've been asked by the owners to take over as interim director until they can find someone."

"I see. I'll get her over here before two, if I can. You know, Clifton, these questions are just routine. It's by your own admission that you were around during some very strange occurrences last night and this morning."

"I understand, Martin," Dothan replied. "And I don't take it personally."

"Good!" Palachi said as he shook Dothan's hand and then looked at Jeff.

"I need to get over to the morgue to arrange to have Erica brought over. See you two, later!"

Without further discussion, Palachi turned on his heel and was gone.

Jeff looked at Defrange, and she raised one eyebrow. He sensed that the screws were about to get tighter than he or Palachi could ever turn them.

"Mr. Dothan," Defrange purred, "what time did you arrive, and what time did you leave here this morning?"

Dothan stiffened as the green vacuum of her eyes closed in around him.

"Eh, well, eh let me see…what time?" he repeated. "I got here about one-fifty I think, right after I took Erica home, and I guess it was about three forty-five when I left."

"And, Defrange continued, "I don't suppose you saw any strangers around here, either?"

"No," he answered," I didn't see anyone at all."

The detective walked over to the table and looked down at Maureen. She stared silently for a full minute.

"What a lovely woman," Defrange observed before spinning around to meet Dothan's surprised expression. "Did you have sex with her?"

Dothan writhed. "God, no! What the hell do you mean asking me a question like that?"

Defrange let him stew for a moment before she walked up to within inches of his face and looked directly into his eyes. He had to look away.

"And did you have sex with Erica Merriweather?" she asked in a raspy whisper.

"Absolutely not!" he snarled. "She was just a child."

The rain had stopped, and the heavy, post-storm atmosphere was stirred by a knock on the door. It was Mason Dixon.

"Lieutenant," he called through the door, "be much longer? We need to get to work in there as soon as possible."

Jeff gave Defrange a look of inquiry.

"I don't have anything else right now," she hissed, and she moved away from Dothan.

"We'll be outta your way momentarily, Mason," Jeff answered. He walked up to Dothan.

"You're not planning a vacation any time soon, are you?" he asked.

"No," Dothan replied. "As a matter of fact, I'll be lucky to be off Christmas Day." He forced a polite smile.

"Well," Jeff went on, "we're not suggesting that you can't go anywhere, but if you do, please leave your itinerary, just in case we need to talk to you. It's just routine."

Jefferson handed him his business card. Dothan took it without comment.

Jeff shot a look at Defrange. "We'll be getting out of your way, now, Mr. Dothan. Thanks for your cooperation."

Defrange slowly pulled her eye daggers out of Dothan, and they left him sitting on the lab stool, looking at Maureen Charbenau, a drained look on his face.

"Ok, Mason," Jeff said as they left the room, "it's all yours."

When they got to the parking lot, Jeff looked around until he realized they were stranded.

"Damn!" Palachi ran of and left us. He must have forgotten that we rode with him. I'll get one of the officers to take us back downtown."

"Fine," Defrange replied and waved her hand to indicate it wasn't a priority at the moment.

"I couldn't quite get what came over him," she said, "but his rush to get back to the morgue had nothing to do with getting Erica over here."

"I don't know," Jeff replied. "I do think he needs some time off. Anyway, whatcha think? Is Dothan telling the truth?"

She was thoughtful for a moment.

"Yes and no," she said finally. "I'm not sure if he killed Erica or not, but he was not truthful about their evening. I think they had some weird moments together, and I feel that he had sex with her. He also knows more about what happened here earlier this morning than he would like us to believe."

"Is he the Raptor?"

When he got no answer to that question, he knew that she was not ready to talk about that subject. He stopped one of the patrol cars, and the officer dropped them off at the morgue. They opted for a day-off and headed back to 1500 Leckie Street to get some much-needed rest.

"Damn it!" Palachi roared. "What the hell have you done with the contents of Erica Merriweather's stomach?"

Kay Driver, RN, MS Forensics, and Palachi's right hand in the morgue like Mason Dixon is in the field, stood her ground.

Kay was a vivacious, energetic, ambitious, and knowledgeable spitfire without whose expertise Palachi would be lost, as he often was.

"Dr. Palachi, I'm telling you for the fourth and last time. You were the only one in here during the autopsy. You salvaged the specimens and put them somewhere, and I still haven't seen them since the last time you asked."

Palachi rubbed his temples. "I'm sorry," he apologized. "And, you're right. I just need to stop and remember where I put those containers. I was upset this morning during all of that, but it's not your fault."

Kay smiled knowingly and put her hand on Palachi's shoulder.

"It's okay, Dr. Palachi," she soothed. "Let me help you look again."

CHAPTER 22

SOMETIME MONDAY AFTERNOON, Jefferson was awakened by a knock on the front door. It was Palachi.

"Martin," he welcomed him groggily, "come on in."

"No," he said sheepishly. "I just came by to apologize for skipping out on you this morning. Anyway, Annie's just gone down to turn around, so I'll let you get back to sleep."

"What's with you?" Jeff asked. "You sure blew outta there this morning."

"I don't want to tell you, yet," Palachi replied with an air of mystery, "but I'm working on something that may hand us the Raptor."

"Oh, really?" Jeff was incredulous.

"If I'm right, I believe his identity will be obvious."

Now he had Jefferson's attention.

Palachi looked from side to side as if he thought someone was listening.

"I don't want to say until I'm sure, but I'll know something by tomorrow morning. I'm processing some specimens. At least we'll know something more that we do now."

Annie pulled up to the curb and waved.

"Gotta go, pal," Palachi said. "Things are still a little tense right now."

"I understand," Jeff responded sympathetically. "Are you two ok?"

"Yeah, we are. I'll see you tomorrow morning sometime."

The ME jumped down all three steps at once, and as he got into the car, Annie began to talk in an animated manner. Jeff watched them drive away and then went back to bed.

The Tuesday morning press conference was held in the auditorium of the Communications Center with all the local and state media in attendance. Captain Chambers did well as far as crucifixions go: he was smart enough to introduce Defrange early on—and she took over.

Her striking appearance, charm, and charisma silenced the dubious crowd who had come for immediate answers. Jeff smiled to himself as the crowd looked on in fascination as she began to speak.

"Ladies and gentlemen, in every generation there are aberrations which are so horrible people can't make themselves think about them, let alone speak of them, and when the recur, no one remembers—they become new problems to be solved all over again."

It was a treat to watch her surreptitiously lead them away from the Raptor case and get them interested in Jeffrey Dahmer. She talked for forty-five minutes, and, in the end, she had turned the group from a lynch mob into a cautiously reserved, pro-police audience.

"In conclusion, she said finally, "in the end, the Raptor is no different in many ways from Dahmer. He's human, and he will make a mistake. When he does, he will be apprehended because he is being pursued by one of the finest, and most capable, police departments I have ever seen!"

After Defrange's standing ovation subsided, Police Commissioner Arthur R. Donaldson was quick to take full credit for her presence in Portsmouth. At that point, Defrange left the stage and took her seat beside Jefferson.

"Let's go over to the main Precinct Building," Jeff whispered. "We can take the elevator here to the top and go across the breezeway. This will be over as soon as Donaldson assures everyone that he's going to get the Raptor all by himself."

Defrange emitted a sigh of relief and gratitude. "Lead the way."

They were almost to the elevator in the back hall when Captain Chambers caught up to them.

"Lieutenant Jefferson, Detective Defrange!" he called as he jogged toward them, loose change jangling in his pockets. "Wait up! I need a word with you."

The Captain extended his arms as he approached—Jeff thought he was going to hug them.

"Dr. Defrange," he said as he took her hand. "Thank you. You're a genius!"

"Not really," she smiled, "but maybe they'll let up for a while."

"Yes, I think they will," he agreed. "Thanks to you. Listen, I don't know what's on your schedule this morning, but I have a priority assignment for you."

The elevator opened, but they ignored it and stepped away from the door. The Captain paused before he spoke.

"I want the two of you to pick up the Merriweathers at the airport in Norfolk," he said in a hushed tone. "Console them if you can, but also see if you can ferret out anything unusual about their daughter's stay in Portsmouth. They were originally supposed to fly in last night, but they couldn't pick up their daughter's dress from the storage facility until this morning. It was her graduation and prom dress, and evidently it means a great deal to them that she be buried in it."

"Will do, Cap," Jefferson responded. "What time is their flight?"

"It's scheduled to land at one-thirty. I have the info in my office."

"We can find out when we get to the airport. They're coming from Danville, right?"

"That's correct," the Captain confirmed, "and you know what I want?"

"Yes, sir," Jefferson answered. "We'll treat them like VIPS, but we'll find out all we can about Erica Merriweather's stay here."

Chambers turned to Defrange.

"Thank you again, Dr. Defrange. Your lecture was perfect."

"My pleasure, Captain," she replied with a gracious nod, "but remember—it's just Almyra."

The twinkle in his eyes seemed a little brighter than usual.

"All right, *Almyra*."

At that moment, Donaldson appeared at the far end of the corridor. The elevator doors opened and Chambers shoved them aboard.

"No point in all of us having a wasted morning," he said with a wink as the doors closed.

"What's with Donaldson?" Defrange asked.

Jeff thought for a moment, prioritizing a list of sins.

"The bottom line," he said, "is that he's a politician, but Captain Chambers understands his game—and he plays so that we all can survive."

They crossed the breezeway and caught the elevator down to the garage level of the main Precinct Building.

"How about some breakfast?" Defrange suggested.

"Good idea," Jeff agreed. "We have some time to kill before we need to be at the airport."

At Sterling Point, Clifton Dothan was busy. He had spent hours working on Erica to make her look perfect for her viewing. He was nervous: he needed another pill. That sanctimonious Palachi had worried him enough, not to mention Jefferson, but they were amateurs. It was Defrange with her green eyes that haunted him. Those eyes, both scary and exciting at the same time. They penetrated his soul. He pulled the sheet over Erica's face – but it was Defrange's face that he saw.

The Merriweathers were due to arrive soon, and he needed some time to prepare himself. After he was satisfied that Erica was as perfect as he could make her, he went to his newly-inherited office to shower and dress. He stepped gingerly around the bloodstain on the carpet and stopped abruptly.

"Sherry!" he growled into the intercom.

"Yes, Mr. Dothan."

"Please call some carpet places and arrange for someone to come out and give me an estimate. I can't stand this mess—it gives me the creeps!"

"Right away, Mr. Dothan."

He shaved, showered, and dressed. His performance this afternoon would have to be flawless if he was going to survive. He was, after all, about to meet the parents of a young woman with whom he'd had sex less than twenty-four hours ago, who had been murdered, and now he would be presenting her as an example of his skill and expertise."

He put on his patent leather shoes and brushed his coat. Satisfied that his look was impeccable, he took another pill and sat down to collect his thoughts. He wondered if Aunt Ashley had figured out the slip knots he had used to tie her in her chair. He laughed aloud at the thought of that scene.

"That silly old dolt," he said as he closed his eyes.

CHAPTER 23

BREAKFAST WAS MORE of a brunch because the morning had been spent at the press conference. Jefferson and Defrange got to the airport just in time to get the flight number and meet the Merriweathers at the gate. Although the bereaved parents were mobile, they were still in shock; but they seemed to find comfort in Defrange's presence. Jeff left the three of them at the terminal and went to claim their luggage, which was only one hanger box containing Erica's dress. He took it to the car before he went back to fetch his passengers.

Defrange consoled the bereft parents as they proceeded into the Virginia Beach Parkway traffic en route to the Down-Town Tunnel.

"Are the arrangements made for us to take Rica home?" Dorothy Merriweather sobbed.

"Yes," Almyra replied. "Mr. Dothan saw to her care just as you requested."

"I'm so anxious to meet him," Dorothy snuffled, "I know our little girl was fond of him, and when I think of the way I spoke to her about him…." She broke down.

Defrange reached over the seat and took her hand.

"Almyra," Dorothy went on when she had regained her composure, "it's so nice of Mr. Dothan to do this for us. I realize that it must be difficult for him too."

"Yes, it has been difficult for him," was her icy reply. "Had Erica known him for a long time?"

Joel Merriweather cleared his throat and broke in.

"I was the only one who had seen Mr. Dothan until Erica met him last Saturday. He was her mentor at Sterling Point, and he has a stellar reputation in our wider professional community. I've seen him at seminars and exchanged pleasantries with him, but I really don't know him. I regret now not getting to know him under these circumstances. I need to assure him that, if he did see Erica on Sunday night, we certainly don't hold him responsible for this horrible event."

Defrange zeroed in on his words like a Plott hound on a scent.

"What do you mean 'if he saw her on Sunday'?" she asked.

Joel took a handkerchief from his jacket pocket and dabbed his eyes.

"Frankly, Detective," he said, "we had a little family spat on the phone on Saturday, and though we know it was Rica's intention to go out with Mr. Dothan, we don't know for sure that she went. I'm afraid our overly protective attitude on the phone made her angry, and she hung up. It was our fault!"

Dorothy wailed aloud. "I just knew something wasn't right!"

"Oh, Dorothy, not now," Joel grumbled. "We can't martyr ourselves!"

Dorothy glared at him wildly. "God damn you, Joel Merriweather! You and your self-righteous professionals. The only solace I have is that Rica sounded happy for the first time since we sent her off to that school full of dead people. She did it just to please you anyway!"

Joel sobbed as he turned and stared out the window.

"Folks, please," Defrange said calmly, "this is not the time for this sort of discussion. You need each other right now more than you ever have."

"Virginia Creeper, this is Digger One, do you copy?"

Jefferson hit the silent mode on the radio and slipped on the headset.

"This is Virginia Creeper."

"Jefferson, Palachi here. I can barely hear you."

"Environment," Jeff replied as loudly as he dared.

"Oh, is the family with you?"

"That's affirmative."

"Roger, I understand. Call me on a land line as soon as you can. I'll be at the morgue."

"Will do," Jeff replied. "Virginia Creeper, clear."

Jefferson took of the headset. Palachi had always been the king of poor timing.

The Merriweathers, who hadn't seemed to notice the radio conversation, were now talking quietly with Defrange.

They exited the tunnel and proceeded to the Harbor View. The crow's nest was now reserved for the Merriweathers, just in case they needed to stay over or a place to freshen up and relax. It was a little more than an hour before they were expected at Sterling Point, and Jefferson needed to call Palachi without an audience.

Defrange sensed the situation and gently urged that they go to the Harbor View to decompress before going to the funeral home. The Merriweathers were reluctant, but those green orbs urged them into submission.

Defrange went into the hotel with the couple to get them settled while Jeff used the phone in the lobby. She wasn't gone long.

"What's going on?" she asked when he hung up.

"Palachi's finished with the extra lab tests he was doing," Jeff replied. "It seems that the steak and kidney pie Dothan served to Erica was human viscera."

"Is he sure about that?" Defrange asked without blinking.

"Yes. He said that he cross-referenced everything he ran, and that Erica's stomach contained bits of undigested tissue. He's sure that it's not fish, pork, beef, or fowl. It's definitely human DNA. That differentiation is one thing that's quick with that test. He finally found a use for this new science."

"Well, that certainly adds a new dimension to Dothan," she said. "So, what do you want to do now?"

Jefferson hadn't had time to consider it, but he knew that he had to decide quickly.

"The Precinct is just next door," he reminded her, "so I'll walk over there. I can get a warrant for Dothan on suspicion of murder. Can you make excuses for me and get the Merriweathers to Sterling Point?"

"Of course! But when will you arrest him? Certainly not now!"

"No. I'll wait until the Merriweathers are gone. There's no need to upset them more until we're sure about Dothan."

Defrange's eyes glowed.

"You mean you're *not* sure about Dothan?"

He searched the green for help.

"I'd be sure without a doubt," Jeff confessed, "but something tells me that you aren't sure. So, until I get into your head, I will proceed with caution about what I'm not sure of. I think he killed Erica, and I think he's the Raptor; but I have this nagging feeling that you don't share my opinion."

She smiled.

"Partner, you're getting better already," she said. "Go ahead to the Precinct. I'll take care of the Merriweathers."

"Thanks," he said. "I'll be out to Sterling Point as soon as I can secure a warrant and requisition a new car."

"Ok," she said. "But be careful."

Jefferson jogged across the parking lot to the Precinct Building and went straight to Captain Chambers' office. Their conversation was short.

"All right, Lieutenant," Chambers said after Jeff filled him in, "here's what I'll do. Judge Griffin is on our side, and I'll get a warrant from him. You go on out to Sterling Point, and I'll send the warrant by a patrolman. There are two reasons why I want you to move cautiously. One, I don't want anyone to get hurt, and two, when you arrest this bastard, I don't want him to be able to walk on a technicality. You with me?"

Jeff stood and moved to the door.

"Yes, sir!" he replied.

Dothan was pacing again. The pills hadn't carried him to the level he had expected, so he took another one.

"Sherry!" he barked into the intercom. "Have you called those carpet people yet? This damned blood is driving me crazy!"

"*Yes sir,*" came the sugary reply. "*They'll be here by the time you get back from the airport. They can put down new carpet this evening if you're willing to close the area for tonight's visitations.*"

"Yes, by all means! We'll close it off. I'm tired of walking around this blood stain."

He snapped off the intercom and fell into the chair behind the desk. He thought about what he was risking, about how Defrange had made him whimper and crawl. The pills began to take effect, and he began to fantasize.

"Oh, wouldn't I love to look into those lifeless, green eyes while I took control. I'd make her up so that her own mother wouldn't recognize her!"

He visualized Defrange lying on a cold steel table with her feet up in stirrups, and he became aroused.

He emitted a long, low giggle. "She thinks she knows so much, but I'll show Ms. Mind Reader the time of her life!"

The phone crashed into his reverie.

"Clifton Dothan," he answered as smooth as oil.

"Clifton! When are you coming home?"

"Aunty, I told you to never call me here. Did you feed Percy?"

"No, and it's not like him to wander away at meal time. I don't know where he can be."

The spin of the pills had him now, and he chuckled.

"Well, I have a cat in a jar in the lab," he offered. "He looks like Percy. Should I bring him home to you?"

The scream hurt his ears, and he slammed down the receiver.

"I suppose I should tell her that I locked Percy in the cabin of the boat, but hell, what fun would that be?"

His frivolous demeanor gave way to thoughts of Defrange, and then he remembered the scene he was about to play in just a short while. He started to take another pill but decided against it. He tossed the bottle onto the desk.

"The whole world is insane," he muttered. He removed the scalpel from the desk drawer and slipped it into his inside coat pocket.

"Defrange is waiting to declare her love for me," he chortled, "but I might need the scalpel to make her prove it."

He sat down and programmed his office phone to constantly ring the phone in his study at home. The door was locked—it would drive his aunt to distraction.

"I think I'll serve that damned cat to her for dinner— when she's had her fill, I'll let her in on the recipe!"

CHAPTER 24

JEFFERSON WAS HEADED to requisition another car when Palachi appeared at the end of the hall.

"Jefferson!" he called. "Wait!"

"Palachi! What are you doing here?"

"Defrange called and said you need a ride, and since I stranded you yesterday, I thought it was the least I could do."

Jeff laughed. *She's always one step ahead.*

"Or," Palachi held up a finger, "at least she's taking care of you. To be honest, I also want to see how Dothan reacts to the Merriweathers. Can you believe he fed that poor girl human flesh?"

"I'd rather not think about it," Jeff replied, "But the more we find out about Mr. Dothan, the more nothing would surprise me. What I want to know is, why you were checking the girl's stomach contents?"

Palachi stopped just as they got to the door that led to the parking lot. "Jefferson, when we talked to Dothan at Sterling Point on Monday, he said that Erica hadn't had more than three glasses of wine over an evening, but I know from her blood alcohol that's she'd had more than that. From there, I started wondering about the texture of some of the solid contents I'd found in her stomach and intestine. It was obviously meat, and I decided to determine what species she'd eaten. That's when I tried the new DNA test for that determination, and I found that she'd been eating people or parts of people. I can't believe that she did it willingly, but willingly or not, I think we've found the Raptor. I think he fed her, gave he too much wine, attacked her, and then threw her in the river. I don't think he thought she'd be found so soon."

Jefferson, acutely aware of the time, motioned for the ME to follow him to the parking lot.

"Let's talk more in the car," he suggested. "Where did you park?"

"I parked in Winetraub's designated spot. He's not here, and I didn't think he'd mind."

When they got in the SUV, Palachi cranked the air conditioning. "It's damned hot," he grumbled as he looked for an opening in the Crawford Parkway traffic.

"Yeah," Jefferson agreed, "and it's gonna get hotter over at the airport."

"Why? What's happening?"

Jeff told him about the warrant and that he planned to arrest Dothan at the airport as soon as the Merriweathers were gone.

Palachi's jaw dropped. "That's great. Then you think he's the Raptor too?"

"It seems he should be," Jeff confessed, "but I don't know. Defrange has some reservations about that, and she has something in mind that she hasn't shared. Maybe it's not clear to her yet, or maybe she just wants to be sure. You know, like you wanted to be sure of your tests before you said anything."

"Yeah, for damned sure."

When they got to Sterling Point, Defrange and the Merriweathers had just gotten out of the car. Palachi rushed over to them.

"Dorothy and Joel Merriweather," Defrange said, "this is Dr. Martin Palachi."

Joel recognized Palachi and shook his hand tightly.

"Dorothy," Joel said, "this is the gentleman who called yesterday to tell us about Rica."

Dorothy graciously extended her had.

"Then you…you're the medical examiner?" she said as she choked back her tears.

"Yes," Palachi replied, "and I'm so sorry about Erica. Joel used to share stories about you, and Rica, when she was a little girl. It's been too many years since he and I have seen each other."

"Thank you, Doctor," she replied, releasing his hand.

Joel put his arm around Dorothy's waist. "Shall we go in?"

Dorothy took in a deep breath and removed a fresh tissue from her purse.

"Martin," Jefferson said, "why don't you show them in, and Defrange and I will join you in a few minutes."

"Of course."

Palachi escorted the Merriweathers toward the front entrance while Defrange and Jefferson lagged behind to get Erica's dress from the trunk. They took it around to a back door and passed it to an associate who was standing by in the hallway.

"Mr. Dothan has been waiting for this. I'll get it to him, and he'll get Erica ready for viewing."

The detectives walked back around to the front of the building and joined the Merriweathers and Palachi in one of the large family rooms. They all sat and waited quietly for a few minutes until a young man in an impeccable black suit entered.

"Mr. and Mrs. Merriweather," he said in a hushed voice, "I'm Jason Albright, and Mr. Dothan asked me to see to your comfort. He'll be out momentarily, but in the meantime, do you require anything?"

"No, thank you," Joel replied. "We're holding our own for the moment."

"Very well, but I'll be right over here if you need or want anything."

"Thank you," Dorothy added, "but the only thing we need is to see our little girl."

She put her face against Joel's shoulder and began to sob softly.

"I understand," Albright replied. "Mr. Dothan will have her ready in just a few minutes."

At that moment, the doors to the viewing room parted, and Clifton Dothan stepped in. He quickly shut the doors so that the Merriweathers couldn't see what was behind him. He glided across the short space between himself and the bereaved parents.

"Mr. and Mrs. Merriweather," he said softly, "I'm Clifton Dothan."

The couple stood, and Dorothy melted into his arms.

"Oh, Mr. Dothan!" she managed between sobs. "Thank you for taking care of Rica. I admit I had reservations about you at first, but she was very fond of you. I know now how wrong I was."

The irony of the whole scene flooded into Jefferson's consciousness like a November nor'easter rip tide across the Eastern Shore.

Dothan comforted Dorothy as he led both parents into the viewing room. He slid the doors back as though he was proud of what he was about to present, and then helped them look at the reality of their daughter's death. Defrange got up and silently closed the doors behind them.

"Whew!" Palachi exhaled. "I never get used to this part of the business."

"If you ever got used to it, it would be time to quit." Defrange whispered.

The three of them sat in the family room until the doors reopened and Dothan emerged with the Merriweathers. Their composure was surprisingly calm, and Dothan actually slipped his arm through Dorothy's as they walked toward the lobby together.

Defrange overhead part of Dothan's invitation as they passed.

"If you feel up to it," he schmoozed, "we can go down to the casket display room so that you may select one for Erica. Please, select any one that you like as there will be no charge to you."

Joel began to sob unashamedly.

"I couldn't do that, Mr. Dothan," he said as he regained his composure. "You've done too much already."

"Nonsense," Dothan countered. "Erica was a member of our family too, and she was an asset to our profession. Please accept this as a token of our affection for Erica."

Joel nodded, and the little group walked out of the family room.

Jefferson looked at his comrades.

"Damn! He is smooth!"

Palachi nodded agreement.

The three of them waited on the porch until the family was ready to go. A hearse was standing by to transport Erica while a limo was waiting to transport her parents.

"I'm not sure if we've solved the Raptor case," Defrange said as if thinking aloud.

Palachi was incredulous and began to pace back and forth across the porch.

"Jesus, Defrange! Do you not think our case is in there with the Merriweathers?"

Jeff watched her eyes turn moss green. She wasn't about to be baited.

"I'm not ready to discuss that yet," she replied, "and, I'm *not sure* that Dothan killed Erica—but I do think we should arrest him for murder."

The ME knew that he'd received his signal to drop the subject. He tried to cover his confusion and frustration and threw up his hands.

"Well, as much as I'd love to go to the airport with you two, I've got to get back to the morgue."

He fled the porch, and Jefferson followed him to the car.

"Look," Martin he said, "Defrange didn't mean anything personal. She's onto something, and I guess the rest of us will just have to wait and see what it is."

Palachi opened the door of his vehicle and got in.

"I know she didn't mean it personally," he said. "It's just this whole damned thing has gotten to all of us, and you know how I am. Sometimes, hell, *most* of the time, I speak without thinking. I just really need to get back to work. I haven't been there too much lately, and I think Kay Driver is getting tired of picking up the slack for me."

"Yeah, you are lucky to have her. Ok, Martin. Thanks for picking me up at the Precinct, I think they're getting tired of furnishing cars for me, sort of like Kay's getting tired of you. See you later?"

"No, problem, Hey, maybe Annie and I can get together with you two later." Palachi drove out of the parking lot.

Just then, the Merriweathers appeared in the doorway of the funeral home. Albright escorted them to their limo and then walked over to let the detectives know that they would be leaving momentarily. The parents opted not to watch Erica being sealed in her casket, and they didn't even want to watch her being placed in the hearse.

Everyone waited until the hearse emerged from the rear of the building. Dothan got out of the vehicle with just a little too much flair, it seemed to Jeff. He began issuing instructions and explaining the obvious.

"Detective Defrange," he cooed, "if you would like to ride with the family and me there is ample room in the limo."

Her cold, green eyes nailed him to the spot where he stood.

"No, thank you, Mr. Dothan. Since this is an official police escort, I'll ride with my partner."

Dothan stared at her blankly for a long moment – so long that Jeff wondered if the guy was narcoleptic.

"Very well," he finally snapped before he spun on one heel and stalked back to the limo.

Jefferson opened the door for Defrange, and they drove into position bringing up the rear of the small procession.

"I think you insulted Mr. Dothan," Jeff ventured.

Defrange snapped her seat belt.

"Oh, I don't think Mr. Dothan is exactly insulted," she replied. "He's just jealous."

"Jealous of whom?"

"You and me," she replied. "He was testing me."

"Testing you about what?"

Defrange turned up the AC one click.

"You see," she explained, "he may not admit it to himself, but he's playing a game of sorts. He wanted me to leave you to ride with him."

Jefferson was puzzled. Defrange didn't say anything for a few seconds. It was as if she was waiting for his mind to get up to speed.

"Because," she said finally, "he's a manipulator, and he finds me to be a challenge—but, he's also petrified of me."

"I certainly understand that," Jeff parried.

Defrange turned in the seat to face him. "Oh, so now you're afraid of me?"

"Yeah, I am," Jefferson confessed. "But not for the same reason as Dothan."

She didn't say anything, and that was more unnerving to Jefferson than if she'd answered.

The patrol car edged down the drive, and the officer pulled across Highway 17 in order to stop traffic. They were on the way, but the trip seemed shorter than usual. Jefferson was preoccupied with planning to arrest Dothan, but most importantly, he was thinking about the effect Defrange had on him.

After they took the airport exit, they were shunted through a special gate that led to a private boarding area. From there, the Merriweathers could be boarded and the casket loaded without other passengers knowing it was happening. Jeff was sorry that he hadn't had time to tell the Merriweathers goodbye, but he was fairly certain he would be seeing them again soon. He drove around to the passenger discharge area in front of the main terminal and stopped.

"What's this?" Defrange demanded.

"I was gonna let you out while I parked the car," he said.

Her green eyes flashed, "No you won't. I'll just be going with you, if you don't mind."

"Oh, what the hell!" Jefferson relented. "I'll just park right here. Official police business!"

As he walked around to open Defrange's door, Jeff noticed several reporters and a mobile broadcast truck from a local TV station.

"Uh-oh, Partner," he said, nodding toward the TV truck. "I wonder who tipped them off?"

"I wonder *what* they were tipped off about?" she replied.

"About Erica Merriweather, of course. What else could it be?"

Defrange didn't reply, but her eyes told him that she had moved to the realm where he couldn't go. He was quiet as they walked toward the observation deck, and a uniformed officer approached them.

"Lieutenant Jefferson?"

"Yes."

"The officer handed him a yellow envelope. "This is the warrant you requested. I just missed you at Sterling Point."

"Thank you," Jeff replied. "I'm glad you found us. Can you please wait for one moment?"

The officer nodded.

Defrange looked over Jeff's shoulder as he read the writ.

"That should do it," she said.

"Right," Jeff replied. He glanced at the officer's name tag.

"Officer Lane," he began, "we're going to make an arrest here in a few minutes. Could you stand by my car at the main entrance in case we run into problems?"

"Yes sir, Lieutenant," Lane replied. He headed for his position.

"Let's go, Partner," Jeff said, and they proceeded to the observation deck.

Jefferson assumed that Dothan would come to this area as part of the impression he was trying so hard to create, but he had also instructed the officer in the escort patrol car to detain Dothan if he tried to leave from the boarding area. Jeff's assumption was correct: Dothan appeared one minute before the Merriweathers' plane was to take off. He was all business.

"Detectives," he greeted them, "it's commendable that the city has provided the two of you to escort this bereaved family. This has been a trying time for us all."

Everyone watched as the 737 taxied into position, and then, in a surge of power, roared down the runway until it was airborne. They all stood there until the last hint of fire disappeared and the vapor trail had melded into the atmosphere. After a momentary sense of relief, Dothan turned to go back down to the loading area. Defrange promptly stepped in front of him, pulling her jacket back to reveal her Glock. Jefferson moved in behind him.

"Clifton Dothan," he said.

Dothan turned around. His expression was still one of superiority.

"Yes," he replied, looking down his nose. "What is it, Lieutenant? I'm a busy man!"

Jeff took the warrant from his pocket.

"Clifton Dothan," he continued, "you're under arrest on suspicion of the murder of Erica Merriweather."

"What?" Dothan shrieked. The sound of his voice echoed across the terminal.

Jeff read him his Miranda rights as Dothan's face became ashen, and he began to shake.

"What the hell do you mean, Jefferson!" he spat. "I'm a respected member of the community—you can't treat me like this!"

While Dothan ranted, Jeff removed the handcuffs from his belt, and the would-be prisoner suddenly clutched his chest and began to gasp for air. At the same time, a swarm of reporters and cameramen surrounded them.

"It's my heart!" Dothan gasped.

Jeff froze, and Defrange stepped back.

"I've got to have my nitro glycerin! My pills!" Dothan gasped as he slid his hand inside his coat.

In the time it took Jefferson to draw his gun, Dothan had produced a large, stainless-steel scalpel. He whirled around, grabbed Defrange and placed the blade at her throat. His eyes were ablaze, but they paled in comparison to hers. It was a signal to Jeff that she was alright – for the moment.

"Get back, Jefferson and drop that gun!" Dothan ordered. "I'm not fooling around. I swear to God, I'll cut her head off her shoulders!"

The crowd had moved dangerously close, and Jefferson was momentarily blinded by the TV spot lights. He closed his eyes and took in a long, deep breath. The soldier turned cop widened his stance and aimed his .45 point-blank at Dothan's head.

"Go ahead," Jeff said calmly. "Go ahead and cut her!"

Dothan blinked.

"What?" he screamed. "Do you mean you'd kill her?"

"Nope," Jeff said just above a whisper. "*You'll* kill *her*, and then *I'll* kill *you*. The only way you're coming out of this alive is to let her go. Now!"

In situations where one is forced to concentrate on center stage, peripheral activities become blurred, and Jeff sensed a blur coming toward Dothan. As it entered his field of vision, Jeff saw the form of a man, an arm, and a pistol being brought smartly to Dothan's temple.

"Drop it!" a booming voice demanded. "This is a .357 Magnum pressing into the side of your head, and if you don't release the detective immediately, I'll blow your fucking head off!"

It was a millisecond, but it seemed like an eon. Jefferson watched as the scalpel tumbled to the floor. The clatter was deafening as Dothan crumpled to his knees. Defrange kicked the blade out of reach, cuffing Dothan where he knelt. In a moment, it was over. Jeff looked to their rescuer.

"Doc Winetraub!" Jeff exclaimed, lowering his gun.

The doctor holstered his pistol. "I was just over here checking on some equipment that came in, and it appeared that your hands were full. I thought you might need some help, so I gave it a try without even thinking."

Jefferson was incredulous, and he began to laugh. "Doc," he said, letting the air return to his lungs, "as hard as it might be for you to believe, I'm glad that in this case you didn't think. Thanks for your help."

The Doc's look was one of self-satisfaction. "My pleasure, Lieutenant."

Applause erupted from the crowd that had surrounded them. Dothan was still on his knees, and Defrange, Glock in hand, was standing over him. Jeff walked over and whispered in her ear.

"Let's get him outta here, Partner."

"I was just waiting for you to say that," she replied, heaving Dothan to his feet.

The crowd of reporters parted as they started to move toward the entrance. Jefferson was disturbed by the questions he heard.

"Is that the Raptor?"

"Does he really have sex with his victims?"

"Does he really eat his victims' eyes?"

"Damn!" Jeff cursed as he raised a hand to wave them off.

It was futile: the reporters, jostling their notebooks and cameras, pushed their way toward the exit. When they got outside, Jeff was glad to see Officer Lane made his way around to help them, and between the two of them, and Defrange, they were able to get their prisoner safely into the car. Winetraub was with them every step, performing like a veteran policeman.

"Good luck, Lieutenant!" he hollered over the din. "I'm going back to see if my microscope has arrived."

"Thanks again, Doc," Jefferson yelled. "We appreciate your help."

Winetraub disappeared into the terminal, and Defrange got into the backseat with Dothan.

"You set, Partner?" Jefferson called over his shoulder as he started the car.

"I'm fine," she barked. "Let's get the hell outta here!"

Jeff hit the blue light, and they sped off toward the Virginia Beach Expressway.

He looked at Defrange's eyes in the rear-view-mirror: their color showed her agitation. Dothan was looking away from her, saying nothing as they headed toward the Downtown Tunnel.

CHAPTER 25

B
Y THE TIME Defrange and Jefferson got to the Precinct, there was already a lynch mob of reporters out front. Though the car windows were rolled up, Jeff heard the same barrage of questions he had heard at the airport.

"Would you really have shot him, Lieutenant?"

"Tell us about murder and cannibalism!"

"This isn't gonna work, Partner," Jeff called over his shoulder. He gunned the car back toward Crawford Parkway and circled two blocks out of the way before returning to the rear entrance of the Precinct.

"Looks like we've avoided them back here," Jefferson observed, "but it won't take long for them to catch on."

He drove to a seldom-used side entrance and alerted Defrange to get ready.

"This door is the closest one to booking. I'll let you and Dothan out, and I'll be in shortly."

Defrange smiled. "Gotcha, Partner," she replied, pulling her Glock. "But I may have to shoot somebody!"

"Go ahead," Jefferson teased. "I'll back you up if you do."

Jeff stopped, and Defrange fairly dragged Dothan from the backseat. Two officers appeared at the side door, and Jefferson was satisfied that they would help Defrange get her prisoner to booking, He parked and entered through the same door.

Defrange was half-way down the hall, but she was stalled in a tidal wave of media personnel who had managed to work their way from the front entrance. Jeff caught her attention and motioned for her to bring Dothan back toward him. Jeff placed himself between them and the mob.

"Hit the 'up' button on the elevator!" Jeff yelled. When the door opened, he shoved Defrange and Dothan inside and then jumped in. He pushed the button for the sixth floor.

"Where are we going?" Defrange asked.

"Interrogation," Jeff replied. "We'll get our prisoner settled, and then we'll go back down to booking."

Dothan had remained silent since they left the airport. When he finally spoke, his voice trembled. "Why are they calling me the Raptor?" he asked.

"I honestly don't know," Jeff answered. "*Are* you the Raptor?"

Dothan leered, but he didn't answer.

The doors opened on the sixth floor, and Jefferson led the way to the interrogation suite. They entered one of the rooms, and he indicated that Dothan should sit down. Dothan obeyed, but he raised his handcuffed wrists in a questioning gesture.

"No, Mr. Dothan, we're not taking those off yet." Jeff said. "We'll be locking you in here for a few minutes, but we'll be back to talk to you. You might want to think carefully about what you're gonna say to us, and remember, we already know some interesting things about you."

With that, he and Defrange left Dothan in the room and headed back toward the elevator. They rode down in silence, but by the time they got down to booking there was total chaos. The questions continued.

"*Does the Raptor work at Sterling Point?*"

"*Do you think he can get a fair trial anywhere in the Tidewater area?*"

Jeff was grateful when he heard the Captain's voice boom over the din.

"Ladies and gentlemen," he yelled, "Please, if you please, BE QUIET!"

The roar subsided into paper rattling as the Captain's presence was recognized.

"If you will please file down to the Communications Center, a statement will be forthcoming. Just cooperate and let us do our jobs. We are required to follow proper procedures, and you *must* follow them also. If not, I will have you all removed from this Precinct building."

There were a couple of muffled carps, but then, like a herd of lemmings the crowd headed for the Com Center auditorium. The Captain was right on their heels, and while there was relative calm, Jefferson booked Dothan on suspicion of murder.

The two detectives went back up to the interrogation suite, and Defrange seemed distracted as they stood behind the one-mirror, looking at their prisoner.

"What is it?" Jeff asked.

"I want to talk to him alone," Defrange replied.

"You know better than that! There's no way you can talk to him about this case if his lawyer's not present – that is if you want to use anything he tells you in court."

"You've heard of a waiver, haven't you?"

"Get real, Partner—he'd never sign it."

"Will you get the form for me?" she insisted. "Let me worry about getting him to sign it. I'll get it myself if you'll direct me to Legal."

Jefferson had learned over the past couple of days that it was useless to argue with Almyra Defrange when she had something in her head.

"Ok," he surrendered. "I'll get it."

He left her staring at Dothan while he ran up two flights of stairs to Legal, grabbed a form from a bewildered clerk and ran back downstairs.

He got a curt smile on his return. "Thank you," Defrange said.

"You're welcome," Jeff said, "but he won't sign it unless he's even crazier than I think he is."

She didn't say anything as she exited to the hall and jerked open the door to the interrogation room. Jeff left his .45 in the holster, but he reached up and slid off the safety.

Dothan had his head down on the table when Defrange entered.

"Mr. Dothan," she said softly.

His shoulders tensed at the sound of her alto voice, and he sat up.

"Yes?" he replied.

"Do you remember me from the funeral home? Do you know who I am?"

He scowled. "Of course! You're Almyra Defrange. You're a famous person. A famous detective from Milwaukee, and I also know that you hold a Ph.D. in psychology."

"Thank you, Clifton. May I call you Clifton?"

He paused to look at her for a moment before he smiled. "Of course," he replied. "May I call you Almyra? It gives me the feeling that I have some dignity left, and it makes me feel that we're friends—although, I suppose we're not, really."

Jefferson didn't like the way that sounded, and he didn't like the sneer on Dothan's face when he said it. Defrange was unphased.

"Well, Clifton," she continued, "I want to help you. Do you believe me?"

"Yes, on some level I do because I know I need help."

Defrange sat her things down on the table, out of Dothan's reach.

"If we're going to talk like this, sort of like doctor to patient, I'll need for you to sign a form that states you're speaking to me of your own free will, and that no one is forcing you to talk to me. Otherwise, we'll have to phone your lawyer, and then we'll have to wait for him to get here. As you may understand, I might talk to you about some things you wouldn't want your lawyer to hear. So, the choice is yours."

Defrange walked half the length of the long table and slid the form the rest of the way to Dothan. He picked it up and studied it for a few moments.

"I understand," he nodded, "and I'm willing to talk to you like this privately. After all, you *are* a doctor."

She slid a ball point pen toward him, and Dothan signed the document. He pushed the pen and the form back to her.

Defrange smiled congenially. "Ok, Clifton, now that we have that formality out of the way, let's get rid of those handcuffs."

Dothan looked at her in amazement. Jefferson took his gun from the holster, poised for any hostile movement on Dothan's part.

She slid a handcuff key down the table and Dothan unlocked the cuffs. He slid the cuffs and the key back to her, and she dropped them into her tote.

"Clifton," she said as she sat down, "I need to ask you some pretty tough questions, and even under these circumstances you know you don't have to give an answer. I'll know if you're lying, so don't bother. If you feel the need to lie about something, just tell me you'd rather not answer, and I'll understand. Remember, there is nothing you can't say to me, but it's entirely up to you what you do say."

"I understand," he replied. "What do you want to know?"

"I want to know what happened between you and Erica on Sunday."

Dothan shifted in his chair and looked down at the table.

"What do you mean?" he said in barely a whisper.

"C'mon, Clifton," Defrange challenged, her voice elevated. "If you're going to talk to me, *talk to me*, because I have better things to do than play word games. What happened with Erica?"

Dothan pouted. "She didn't like Cleo," he said softly.

"Who is Cleo?"

"My pet python. Erica was terrified of snakes, and she went berserk."

"So," Defrange pushed, "she didn't like your snake. So what?"

"So, I thought it was rude of her. After all, I brought her to my home as a guest, and I'd prepared a wonderful meal for her. I was just trying to share myself, and she didn't respond properly."

Defrange took a legal pad from her tote and studied her notes for a moment.

"Ok. So, you thought she didn't react properly. Did you really take her for a boat ride?"

"Yes," Dothan admitted. "She…I mean…."

"What?" Defrange insisted.

Dothan looked into her eyes and abruptly averted his gaze.

"What I mean is," he went on, "she and I made up about Cleo, and I took her for a boat ride. Then, the ungrateful little bitch passed out on me."

"Passed out?" Defrange echoed. "Why did she pass out?"

"We tied up on the far side of the river, kind of a romantic spot away from the main channel, and we shared two bottles of wine. She passed out on me—by that, I mean she went to sleep."

The timbre of Dothan's voice had risen, and Defrange let it echo around the room before she said anything.

"So, she passed out, went to sleep, and then what happened?"

"I splashed water on her to wake her up, "he said, "but she wouldn't come around, so after a few minutes I got impatient."

"You got impatient, and you killed her!" Defrange slammed her fist on the table. "You got impatient, and you killed her!" she repeated.

"No! No, I didn't," Dothan shouted, and then his voice trailed off again. "I got impatient, and I took her clothes off and…I had sex with her, but I didn't kill her."

Defrange let him think for a minute or two.

"C'mon, Clifton! Don't tease me. I mean, that must have been a real feat. Having sex with somebody who's not conscious would be like trying to have sex with a dead person."

Dothan's head snapped up so fast that Jefferson aimed his pistol at him through the glass. The man's face was distorted—he looked like a different person.

"Oh, no!" he hissed through clenched teeth. "The dead ones are much easier—and better!"

Defrange didn't flinch as Dothan's face revealed his realization of what he'd just said. His entire body began to shake.

"We can talk about that aspect of your life some other time," Defrange said, barely hiding her disgust. "What happened to Erica after you had sex with her?"

His voice dropped to a whisper once more. "I kept throwing water on her, and she finally woke up. She said that she didn't feel well, and she wanted to go home."

Defrange sat back in her chair. "Be honest with me, Clifton. You didn't really want her to wake up for sex did you. That's why you poured so much wine down her. You wanted her lifeless, didn't you?"

"Yes!" he said, and then he screamed, "YES!"

"And, you never took her home, did you?" Defrange pressed him.

"Yes, I mean, no, not really. I took the ungrateful little whore about two miles down the river, and I put her out on somebody's private dock. I told her to call a cab and told her if she squealed on me I'd fail her for her entire three-month rotation at Sterling Point."

"That wasn't very nice, Clifton," Defrange said, "and since you've lied to me before, how do I know you didn't kill her before you had sex with her?"

Dothan's look was one of disgust.

"God, Almyra! She made me mad," he said, "but I didn't kill her. I DID NOT KILL HER!"

"Are you sure?" Defrange urged. "Maybe you just went into a rage, and maybe you didn't mean to kill her; but maybe things just got out of control."

"No," he snapped. "I DID NOT KILL HER!"

Dothan stood suddenly, and Jefferson aimed his weapon directly at his head.

Easy, you sonofabitch!

Defrange had the situation under control.

"Sit down," she demanded, "or our talk is over, and you can believe that I'll have one hell of a time convincing them that you didn't kill Erica and some others too, maybe."

Dothan fell back into his chair.

"Wha...what do you mean, *others?*" he whispered.

"C'mon Clifton. You heard those reporters. You heard their comments and questions about you. They think you're the Raptor."

Dothan started to stand again, but he thought better of it.

"Oh, my god! How can they think that?"

"Because," she replied, "they don't know you as well as I do, but I need to know the truth. Did you do anything to hurt Erica other than what you've told me? You know, other than leaving her alone and drunk in a strange neighborhood in the middle of the night?"

"No, I did not. I swear!"

"Are you sure?" she grilled him. "I'm beginning to think you don't like women, especially women who don't respond the way you think they should. What a waste. Hell, maybe you are the Raptor!"

"No! No, Almyra! Please don't you think that of me too," he begged.

Jefferson had never seen anyone be both the good cop and the bad cop at the same time, but Defrange was the master.

"Oh, Clifton," she said softly, "settle down. I believe you."

Dothan put his head down on the table and began to sob.

"Thank you," he said between spasms. "Thank you for believing me, at least."

Jefferson didn't believe him, and he didn't think Defrange did either.

"One last question," Defrange said, "and then I'll leave you alone."

He raised his head and sniffed. "Yes? What is it?"

"Where did you get the contents of the steak and kidney pie that you served Erica for dinner?"

He wiped his face on his sleeve. "May I have some water?" he asked.

"In a minute," she said. "We're almost done."

"Almyra, I know where this is headed, and I'm not sure that I want to talk about it."

"Ok. That was my last question, anyway. We've gotten along so well; I just hope I have enough to give to the reporters to convince them that you didn't kill Erica."

Defrange was playing psychic blackmail, and from Dothan's reaction Jefferson couldn't tell if he knew it or not. His face turned red, and his eyes bulged as if he were about to vomit. Jeff thought he was going to get up again, but Defrange knew how to time her thrusts and jabs. She began to roar like a drill sergeant.

"Where did you get the ingredients?"

Her outburst startled Dothan, and he hit the table with both fists.

"From the funeral home!" he shrieked. "I got them from the fucking funeral home. There! Are you happy?"

"Most happy," she cooed. "But why would you do such an odd thing?"

"Because it's such a rare treat, and I wanted Erica to share it. That's all, really. I just wanted her to share and understand, and I wanted her to care about me."

"Thank you, Clifton," Defrange said. "That's all for now, and I will see what I can do on your behalf."

She glanced at the one-way as she cleared her things from the table. Jeff gave her a nod despite the fact she couldn't see him.

"Almyra," Dothan whispered.

She paused at the door. "Yes?"

"I want to thank you. I love your eyes."

"Thank you, Clifton," she replied coolly as she turned to leave.

Jefferson acted out of instinct. Defrange had her back to Dothan as he rose from the chair and moved toward her. Jefferson was in the room before he could grab her.

"Hit the deck!" Jeff yelled as he burst into the room.

Defrange dropped to the floor. Dothan's momentum carried him over her, and he ran face-first into Jefferson's fist. He was addled, and Jeff helped Defrange to her feet while making sure that Dothan saw his pistol.

"Are you alright?" Jeff asked.

"Yes," she said and moved toward the door.

When Dothan regained his orientation, he came up swinging even as Jeff deflected the blows.

"Jefferson, you son-of-a-bitch!" Dothan screamed. "My talk with Almyra was not private at all, and I want my attorney right now. Patient to doctor my ass! You tricked me! I demand to see my lawyer immediately! Do you hear? I said immediately!"

Jefferson heard the door close, and he knew that Almyra was clear.

"Calm down, Dothan," Jeff warned.

By now, Dothan was like some animal. His face was red as he grabbed Jefferson's lapel. Jeff paralyzed his arm with a wrist lock and threw him hard against the wall.

"Brutality!" Dothan screamed. "This is police brutality! I'll have your badge, Jefferson! You tricked me! I want to see my fucking lawyer! Right now! Do you understand?"

Jefferson kept his eye on him as he backed out of the room.

CHAPTER 26

DEFRANGE WAS LEANING against the wall in the corridor. Jeff couldn't tell if she was shaken, or tired, or both.

"That was unexpected," she said.

Jeff took in a deep breath before he replied.

"Detective Defrange," he began, "you never cease to amaze me. How the hell can you have so much insight into these people, and then be surprised when one of them attacks you?"

She stood up straight—her expression became what one could call impish.

"I mean," he went on, "this guy you've been talking to kills people, hacks them to pieces, eats parts of them, and you're surprised when he attacks you? What the hell am I missing here?"

Defrange's eyes turned to a mint green. He resisted an impulse to hug her as she kicked off her pumps.

"Oh, that's better," she sighed. "I've about had it with today, but yes, there's a lot you're not getting. And the story is that you're not ready for the story yet."

"What? What are you talking about?"

"You're not ready for the story yet," she repeated, "but let's get down to the Captain's office so we can get that over with."

"Get what over with?"

She didn't reply as they walked down the hall to toward the elevators. Jeff stopped to use an in-house phone to get someone the take Dothan and put him into a cell. While he was on the phone, she kept shaking her head and looking at him with that amused smile. He didn't dare ask.

When they got to the Captain's office, he welcomed them with elation.

"Congratulations, Detectives! You've done it!" Defrange gave him a dismissive look and assumed a lotus position on the sofa. The Captain looked at her and then turned to Jefferson.

"What's with you two? You should be thrilled!"

"What do you mean?" Jeff asked.

The Captain drew back his chin in consternation. "The Raptor—you got the Raptor! I knew you could do it!"

"Yeah, maybe," Jeff said. "But somehow it doesn't feel the way I thought it would."

"Oh, Lieutenant!" Chambers said, waving him off. "I understand. Sometimes when you finally solve a challenging case like this it just takes time to sink in. The bigger the case, the more normal it is to feel let down at the end."

"Captain Chambers," Defrange said softly.

"Why in no time," he went on, "you two will be on the cover of *Time* magazine. Lighten up! Don't be so glum."

"Captain," Defrange called again from behind closed eyes.

He turned to her as if she were a child tugging on his coattail. "Yes, Dr. Defrange?"

Defrange unfolded her legs and sat up. "Clifton Dothan is not the Raptor," she announced.

The silence in the room was painful as the three exchanged looks.

The Captain winced. "Excuse me, but what did you say?"

Defrange threw her shoulders back: she was all business.

"He's not the Raptor," she repeated.

"But, Detective," the Captain said, "he has to be. Look at all the evidence."

She raised her eyebrows. "What evidence?"

Chambers' head swiveled from Jefferson to Defrange in utter confusion.

"Well," he said, "obviously he killed the Merriweather girl. Look at it. The press didn't know the Raptor's MO before, so Dothan must be the Raptor. Just look at how he killed her. Who else could it be, unless Dothan is a copycat?"

"I don't know who it is *yet*," Defrange replied. "I'm just telling you that Clifton Dothan is not the Raptor."

The Cap rushed over and stood in front of her. "Please, Detective," he pleaded, "just tell me what the hell you're talking about?"

She assumed the look of someone who is used to dealing with critics and doubters.

"What I'm saying, gentlemen, is that Clifton Dothan is not the Raptor. I don't mean that he isn't a psychopath who needs to be hospitalized, probably for the rest of his life, I'm just asserting that he isn't the Raptor. I do, however, believe that the Raptor killed Erica Merriweather, but circumstantial as the evidence may be, I don't think it was Dothan."

Chambers pulled up a chair. "If things are as you say, you're telling me we have *two* psychopaths with unusual culinary preferences on our hands. Seriously?"

Defrange locked eyes with Chamber. "Who called the press and tipped them off that the Raptor was going to be arrested at the airport today?"

"It was an anonymous caller. Someone called in to WTID radio this morning, saying that the Portsmouth Police were going to arrest the Raptor this afternoon at the airport. The DJ taped the call—I haven't heard it yet, but I understand that it's rather comical."

Jeff frowned. "How so?"

"The caller told some screwy story about the Raptor being at the airport to see his last victim off in person."

"Do they know the origin of the call?"

"Yes," the Captain replied. "They had the usual traces on the WTID news lines, and the call came from a phone booth across the street from the main post office in Norfolk. The DJ thought it was some crank just taking advantage of a grave situation. He described it as 'hilarious.'"

"Hilarious?" Jeff questioned.

"It seems," Chambers continued, "that the caller was an old woman, and after she told him about the Raptor at the airport, she started singing 'Amazing Grace'. She was intermittently trying to quiet a child. That almost cinched it as a hoax, but the news editor took it seriously enough to send a crew out to the airport. Those guys called buddies at other stations until the entire Tidewater news media was involved."

Jeff looked at Defrange. "A child!"

"I think it was a call from the Raptor," Chambers said, "and I also think it was a call from Clifton Dothan."

Jefferson again looked to Defrange: she was tense.

"What time did the call come in to the radio station?" she asked.

"I'll have to check to be sure, but as I recall it was a couple of minutes after seven."

Jeff thought for a moment. "Dothan had time to place the call, but why would he tip us off if he's the Raptor?"

"It was a way to turn himself in," Chambers declared. "He wanted to give up in a public setting, drawing attention to himself, instead of walking in to the Precinct."

A couple of minutes passed as the three of them thought things over.

"Dr. Defrange—Almyra," the Captain said finally, "are you *sure* about what you're saying?"

Defrange avowed that she was *quite* sure.

Chambers looked at the floor and sighed. "Well, I'm not sure what we should do at this point, but I do know we need to keep this conversation under wraps for a few days. Almyra, I don't doubt you—your reputation is unquestionable. We may have trouble keeping Dothan from hanging in the press."

"I wish I could tell you that we have the Raptor," she replied, "but it's just not Dothan."

The Cap threw up his hands. "Ok, we'll just hold him on the other charges, and you two stay focused on the Raptor. I have to assume that he's still out there somewhere."

"We'll stay on him, Cap," Jeff replied. He wasn't completely in agreement with Defrange, but he didn't feel that this was the time or place to discuss it.

"If it's any consolation," Defrange added, "we got Dothan to admit some creepy things he did with Erica. That alone should be enough to get him admitted to a psychiatric hospital for the criminally insane."

The Captain didn't reply. He was awash in dejection. Jefferson searched for reassuring words but found none. Chambers walked out of the room, closing the door behind him.

Jeff stood there thinking that there must be a least a million better ways to make a living.

"Me too," Defrange agreed.

"Partner," he ventured, "I heard you earlier when you said you'd had it with today. Do you want to go home?"

To his surprise she slipped on her shoes, picked up her tote, and smiled. "Let's go," she said.

Dothan's attorney, David Saperstein, had been raising hell. He'd started with the desk sergeant and made his way to the Legal Department before heading to the Captain's office.

Jefferson found out later that there had been discussions about police brutality, doctor-patient confidentiality, and a lot of other legal bullshit that was beyond him. In the end, it was a call from Saperstein to Commissioner Donaldson that got Dothan released. It was the politics of politics in action.

CHAPTER 27

O N THE WAY to Leckie Street, Defrange suggested that they stop off for a bottle of wine. Jeff pulled into his usual convenience store.

"Chardonnay?" he asked.

She smiled. "You know it."

"Anything else?"

"No, just the wine."

Jefferson went in the store and quickly selected a bottle. He was standing in the check-out line when he glanced up at the TV behind the counter. What he heard almost caused him to drop the wine.

"In a late-breaking story, the Portsmouth Police have released Clifton Dothan, the only suspect ever arrested in the ongoing rampage of killings in our city. We are now going live to City/County Plaza where Jerry Coleman is standing by with Mr. Dothan's attorney. Jerry?"

The camera panned from the Lightship over to the steps of the Precinct Building, and Jeff recognized the on-scene announcer.

"I'm here with David Saperstein, attorney for the man arrested today at the Norfolk International Airport. Mr. Saperstein, your client is purportedly the prime suspect in the now famous Raptor case. Can you comment on that sir?"

"Yes Jerry. Thank you. My client has been wrongly accused in this case, and moreover has been mistreated by the Portsmouth Police. We're talking about a professional, upstanding member of the community who, through a number of extenuating circumstances, seems to have been at the wrong place at

the wrong time. He was questioned without benefit of legal counsel, and he has been brutalized and defamed by this department. I will be in conference with him this evening, and we may have no recourse other than filling a lawsuit against the City and certain members of the Police Department. I have no further comment at this time."

Saperstein walked off camera.

"There you have it, Don. It looks like someone may have egg on their face. Just a moment! Here comes Police Captain Chadwick Chambers. Just a word Captain, please! What is your Department's position on the apparent wrongful arrest and alleged mistreatment of Clifton Dothan?"

"Jerry, I don't want to get into a lengthy interview here, but I will tell you that there will be an investigation into the allegations. The two detectives involved will be held accountable for any wrong-doing. I have no further comment at this time."

"Was the famous Dr. Almyra Defrange involved?"

"No further comment!"

"There it is, Don. It sounds as though Captain Chambers doesn't want to say too much, and he seems to be aware of some misconduct by the arresting officers."

The coverage shifted back to the studio.

"Lieutenant Jefferson?"

Jeff looked up at Mike, the cashier. Everyone else in line had finished their transactions and left.

"Sorry, Lieutenant," Mike commiserated. "When this story broke earlier, I thought you had the bastard."

Jefferson sat the wine on the counter and shook his head.

"Yeah, me too Mike," he replied. "I guess we'll have to try harder."

He paid for the wine and walked out. When he got in and started the car without comment, Defrange stared at him.

"C'mon, Partner," she admonished, "you know better."

He looked at her as if for the first time, admitting to himself that he had feelings for Almyra Defrange that went far beyond being his work "partner".

She placed her hand on his arm. "Our bust went South, didn't it? You don't need to protect me—it's okay. It's okay they let Dothan go, too."

Defrange was deeper into his psyche than he was. Jeff killed the engine and slammed his hands on the steering wheel.

"Yes! Damn it to hell, yes. They let that bastard go, and the Captain sounded like he was blaming us for some sort of screw-up!"

He flashed back to Dothan holding the scalpel against Defrange's throat, and how he'd potentially jeopardized hundreds of people at the airport. Jefferson was rabid.

She put her hand on his thigh, and it sent electricity to places he had long since forgotten. After a few moments, he relaxed.

"I suppose it has to be alright," Jefferson opined, "but it looks like they could have held him on something!"

She was gently rubbing his thigh now.

"They could have," she replied. "We both know that. There's something afoot that we don't know about—at least not yet."

Suddenly there was no one else in the world. Her touch was like ionized velvet: it sent impulses across his synapses that caused chills and hot flashes at the same time. He shuddered, and she stopped. Gradually, he became aware of their surroundings once more…the street noise…the heat. She moved her hand.

"You're right," he said. "There is something going on that we don't understand. Thanks for helping me regain my grip."

Jeff re-started the car, and they drove home.

Dinner turned out to be frozen pizza, fresh salad, and the Chardonnay. It was cozy and comfortable, and Jeff could still feel Defrange's touch.

But he still couldn't shake the Captain's remarks. The man had always been supportive of his officers to a fault, and what he had said to the news anchor was not the Captain whom Jefferson knew. Defrange discounted it, suggesting the he not worry until he had a chance to talk with him.

"I think I'll go up and shower," Almyra announced. "Maybe it will help clear today out of my head."

"Sure, go ahead," Jeff replied. "I'll just clean up here, and maybe I'll grab a quick shower too."

Almyra glided across the floor and sprinted up the stairs.

As he cleared the dishes, Jeff's thoughts were on Defrange. Maybe he was totally confused, and he was misreading the energy between them. He stood over the sink and tried to send his mind someplace else.

"Lieutenant?"

"Yes?" Jeff spun around startled, knocking a plate to the floor with a loud clatter.

Defrange was standing on the third step, leaning against the bannister. Jeff's eyes swept over her body, clad only in green panties. Her perfectly shaped breasts nearly caused him to join the fallen plate.

"Why, Lieutenant Jefferson," she said. "I believe I've caught you off guard!"

Her eyes were the color of the tiny green mints that his Aunt Lily used to make when he was a child. He was totally stunned: he had to force his locked jaw muscles to form words.

"Detective," he said calmly, "how do you know that I wasn't playing possum, just to lure you in?"

She bit her lower lip and suppressed a laugh. "The plate? Or, was that part of your ruse?"

"No," he replied in feigned confession. "You got me."

Defrange smiled. "Good, because I really want you. I was wondering if you intend to be down here all night holding that dish cloth, or if possibly you'd rather hold me?"

In an instant he was clinging to her in a way he had never held anyone, as if she were life itself, kissing her with more passion than he had ever thought existed in his soul. Her devastating beauty was irresistible—he succumbed, losing himself in her presence. She lowered herself to the steps as he knelt over her.

"Almyra," he whispered, "what do you think you're doing?"

She looked unashamedly into his eyes.

"Something I wanted to do years ago."

He pulled back and looked at her. "Even then?"

"Yes, you idiot. I was in your head constantly, and I got to know you pretty well. As a matter of fact, I know you better than you know yourself."

He recalled the elusive angel in his dreams, the guardian who was always there when it was darkest.

"Oh, Partner," he said, "I knew you were there, always. I just never knew how to reach you." Jeff tapped his head. "But I always sensed you here."

"I know," she replied. "We've been together forever, and though I don't know who you have been, I know who you are now. I've been waiting for you."

"Are you sure?" he whispered.

"Ooh, yes," she replied as she lifted her hips.

Jeff kept his gaze locked on her green pools of desire as he slipped off her panties. He ripped off his shirt, popping a couple of buttons in the process, followed by his pants. Kneeling on the lower step, he lifted her knees over his shoulders and put his mouth over her, probing her with his tongue until she quivered and moaned.

"My God!" he panted. "You are delicious!"

Somehow in the erotic confusion of it all they traded places, and she took him into her mouth. After a few mind-blowing minutes Jeff could no longer contain himself.

"Jesus, Mary, and Joseph!" he cried as he exploded.

Defrange leaned back and brushed her lower lip with her thumb. "Let's take that shower," she invited.

"I don't think I can move," he replied, trying to catch his breath.

Following that beautiful derriere up the stairs was almost more that he could endure. He wanted her in ways he had never wanted anyone.

She turned on the shower and stepped in pulling him in after her.

The water was so hot that he considered for a brief moment that she might be a member of a criminal element sent to assassinate him by scalding. He gazed at her hair, all wet and down in her eyes. His eyes dropped to the alluring and mysterious, dripping triangle between her legs. At that moment, he didn't care if she were the Empress of the Underworld.

Jeff knelt in front of her while the water cascaded down on his balding head and spilled around the line of his gray beard into the tub. He was ageless and utterly carnal.

She moaned and trembled as his tongue probed deeper. He looked up at the water streaming over her breasts as she shuddered in release, emitting a low growl that excited him even more. Regaining her balance, she pulled him toward her.

They embraced, and he kissed her hard as she stroked him until he reached another climax. He writhed and perhaps even screamed—he wasn't sure. He didn't remember turning off the water, either, before she led him to the bedroom. With every step he wanted her, craved her, until she threw him onto his back and took a superior position. Her guttural sounds when she climaxed made him crazy, and he flipped her over and mounted her, driving himself into her, a rush of frenzied, longing thrusts until they collapsed, breathless and sated.

"Merciful Georgia! Are you trying to kill me?" he said finally.

"Yes," she replied breathlessly, "but I want to go with you. They'll rule it a murder suicide."

Jeff shook the bed with his laughter. "Always the cop," he said and pulled her to him.

CHAPTER 28

J
EFF OPENED HIS eyes to the clock on the nightstand: 10:22. He rolled over and looked at Defrange, and she smiled.

"Hi Partner," she said sleepily.

"Sorry, if I woke you," Jeff apologized. "I can't help looking at you."

Tears formed at the corners of her eyes. "I've waited a lifetime to be here."

She kissed him lightly on the lips – then harder. They made love again and fell asleep until they were both jolted out of their contented slumber.

"What was that?" she asked groggily.

"The doorbell," Jeff replied as he got up and grabbed a pair of jeans from the closet. "Damned unusual for my doorbell to be ringing at eleven-thirty on a Tuesday night. Wait here."

Jeff suddenly remembered his weapons were downstairs in the kitchen. Defrange was one step ahead of him, as usual.

"Here," she said as she handed him her Glock from the bedside table.

"Oh, now I see," he teased. "You were gonna force me if I wasn't willing."

Her eyes danced with her smile. "Well, a girl has to do whatever it takes."

Jeff laughed. "Right. You stay up here until I find out who this is."

She nodded and pulled the sheet up over her shoulders.

Jefferson cautiously made his way down the stairs in the dark, side-stepping the landing so he wouldn't be visible to whomever was at the door.

His visitor was now leaning on the bell, and Jeff could hear the muffled screaming of a male voice on the other side of the door.

"Damn it, Jefferson! I know you're in there! Open this frigging door!"

Jeff crossed the foyer and inched his way along to wall toward the door. He duck-walked the last few feet and from a kneeling position he slowly slid the dead bolt. With a swift movement he stood up, flipped on the porchlight as he turned the knob and opened the door, balancing the nine-mil with both hands as he aimed it toward his caller's head.

"Jesus! Jefferson! Don't shoot!"

"Palachi!" Jeff said, lowering the gun. "Are you out of your mind? I nearly shot you!"

He unlocked the storm door, and opened it for his friend. Palachi tripped as the stepped inside, and Jeff caught a whiff of booze as he grabbed his arm and steadied him.

"I'm sorry, Jeff," he apologized. Palachi steadied himself against a chair in the foyer. "You see, I just have to talk to you."

"Ok," Jeff said warily. "What's on your mind?"

Palachi walked into the kitchen and collapsed into a chair at the table. He was disheveled, his tie loosened and half of his shirt tail hanging over his pants.

"It's these damned murders," he slurred. "The Merriweather girl, and now they've cut Dothan loose. It's like *we* have to play by the fucking rules, but nobody else does."

Jeff stepped into the kitchen and looked at the ME sympathetically. He'd been feeling the same way himself.

"C'mon," Jeff said. "We just have to keep this in perspective. It's hard on all of us, but we can't just call it off."

"But why can't we catch this bastard?" Palachi complained, putting his elbows on the table and cradling his head. "No, that's not what I mean. What I really mean is why, after we catch him, do they turn him loose?"

"I don't know," Jeff replied. "For that matter, why do half the criminals we apprehend get turned loose? It's a tough business, and when it involves senseless carnage it's even tougher. I guess we just have to keep trying, and as far as Dothan goes, Defrange doesn't think he's the Raptor anyway."

Palachi bolted upright and tipped his chair forward. He caught himself on the edge of the table.

"What? How could that slime not be the Raptor? Is she serious?"

"She says Dothan doesn't fit her profile for the Raptor. Do you want a beer or something?"

"Yeah. I shouldn't, but I'll take a beer."

Jeff put the gun on the table and fetched a couple of beers from the fridge. Palachi grew more animated.

"You know," he said, "you scared the hell out of me when I knocked on the door, and I almost forgot."

"Forgot what?" Jeff asked.

Palachi weaved in his chair and tried to look serious.

"I almost forgot to tell you that the Corvette Dothan drives is parked just a couple of blocks down the street."

Jeff had just twisted the cap off a beer. He paused, holding the bottle and staring at Palachi.

"Where?" he asked as foam dripped over his hand and down onto the floor.

"Just two blocks down," Palachi replied. "Down toward the Naval Hospital. Easy! Don't spill my beer!"

Defrange, now fully dressed, came into the kitchen.

"Almyra!" Palachi exclaimed. "I didn't know you were here. No wonder Jefferson is being so protective and paranoid."

"Hi, Martin," she said, playfully punching him in the shoulder. "What are you doing out this time of night? Annie know you're out prowling?"

He belched. "I'm just down in the dumps," he said. "This Raptor mess is driving me to drink."

He gave her a goofy smile, and Defrange sat down across from him. She looked over at Jeff.

"How about a glass of wine?" she asked. "I hate for Palachi to drink alone."

"Coming up."

Her look told Jefferson that she was on to something.

"Dothan's very near," she said.

"Yes," Jeff acknowledged. "Palachi saw his car. I was about to go on a recon mission down toward the hospital. Do you know where he is?"

She took the wine and motioned for Jeff to follow her into the foyer. He grabbed the gun from the table and joined her.

"He's about two blocks down on this side of the street," she said in a low voice. "He has a weapon in the car, and it's loaded."

"Ok," Jeff replied. "Any suggestions?"

She thought for a moment.

"If you go through the back yards," she said, "until you come to Butler Street where it intersects Leckie, you can circle around the corner house, and you'll be behind him. He's looking in this direction, so he shouldn't notice you."

"Got it," Jefferson replied, and he started for the back door that exited the garage.

"Wait," she said. "One more thing, and it's confusing me."

"What?"

"I feel another strong presence. I felt it before at the Tidewater Breeze. The Raptor is nearby, too."

Jeff narrowed his eyes. "So," he said, "you really do finally see. Dothan *is* the Raptor. I can't even pretend to understand why you thought anything else. You do see now, don't you?"

She regarded him like a kindergarten teacher regards a little boy who has fibbed about how he tore his pants.

"Oh yes, Lieutenant," she replied, "I see quite clearly, and you'd better be careful out there. Dothan is *not* the Raptor."

"You know me," he smiled as he tucked the Glock into his waist band, "I'm nothing if not cautious."

Jeff headed through the garage and out the back door. The night was heavy with scents of honeysuckle and freshly mowed grass. The moon was high, and except for the distant barking of a dog and the occasional toot of a harbor tug, it was quiet. He turned right and jogged through the neighboring backyards until he reached the house on the corner of Leckie and Butler. He pulled the pistol from his waistband, hugging the porch until he could get a look around the corner.

Leckie Street was well-lighted, and it only took a moment to locate Dothan. He was thirty feet away, hiding in a grouping of forsythia, looking in the direction of 1500. Jefferson carefully moved toward him.

"Turn around—slowly."

Dothan turned around and raised his hands. He didn't seem too surprised.

"Tell me one good reason why I shouldn't shoot you right now?" Jeff asked.

"Because it's against the law," came the lisped reply.

Jeff glared at Dothan. "Let me get this straight: you don't think I'd be justified in shooting a murder suspect, who assaulted an officer earlier today, and who is watching my house in the middle of the night with a loaded gun in his car?"

Dothan's grin became even wider.

"Well, for your information, Lieutenant Know-It-All, allegations like that, coupled with the way you mistreated me today are the reasons I'm not in jail. It's also why my attorney is preparing a lawsuit against you and the city."

Jefferson motioned with his pistol. "Move over to your car and put your hands on top where I can see them," he ordered.

Dothan obeyed, and Jefferson cautiously leaned down and looked into the car from the passenger side.

A 30.06 rifle, equipped with a night vision scope lay between the seats. Jefferson stepped behind Dothan.

"Going hunting are you, Mr. Dothan?"

"*That*, Lieutenant, is none of your fucking business!"

Jefferson spun Dothan around and shoved his pistol hard against his soft abdomen. He grabbed the man's throat with the other hand, but stopped just short of crushing his larynx. Jeff smelled aftershave and the faint odor of gin.

"Mr. Dothan," he warned, "I'm going to release you in just a moment, and I want you to hand out that rifle. But, please don't do anything that I can even imagine might be an aggressive move."

He squeezed Dothan's throat until his head bobbed in surrender. Dothan leaned down and reached into the car. Jeff hoped that he might try something with the rifle, but he slid it quickly from the car and laid it on the sidewalk. Jeff kicked it into the grass.

"Sir, you may go now," Jeff said. "I don't know how you got out of jail this afternoon, but I'm sure that if we couldn't hold you on those charges, my running you in now for stalking would be a total waste of time."

Dothan laughed in Jeff's face.

"I'm an upright citizen, Lieutenant," he said, "and as soon as I can get to a phone, I'm going to call my lawyer. It'll be your badge and your career, you son of a bitch!"

Jeff grabbed his throat again.

"Listen, you sick bastard, you call whomever you like, but if I ever catch you lurking around my neighborhood again, or if you ever try to put your hands on Detective Defrange again, God help you, because no power on earth—no gun, no lawyer, anything, or anybody—will be able to help you."

Jeff shoved him hard against the car and released his throat.

"Oh, yes," Dothan hissed. "Your precious Defrange. Tell me, is she as good as she looks?"

Jeff's foot made contact with Dothan's left ear. He went down hard to his knees, but Jeff pulled him up by his necktie and shoved him backward over the hood. He held him so that his feet were barely touching the ground and shoved the Glock under his chin hard enough to force his head backward.

Jefferson growled, "Did that hurt as much as it looked like it did?"

"Lieutenant Jefferson, is that you?" came a shrill voice from the corner house.

Docia Treadway. She considered her title as the captain of the neighborhood watch a license to watch everybody and everything. Jefferson kept holding Dothan over the hood.

"Yes, Mrs. Treadway," Jeff called out. "Please go back inside and turn off your light."

"Do you want me to call for backup?" she persisted with jargon from her favorite police shows.

"No, ma'am," Jeff replied. "That won't be necessary. Everything is under control. Please get back inside."

"All right, Lieutenant, if you're sure," she replied. "By the way, that's a lovely woman staying at your house."

Damn it. She just blew Defrange's cover.

"Thank you. It's my sister from Abingdon. Maybe the two of you can have tea one afternoon before she leaves."

"That would be delightful. Don't you forget to tell her."

"No, ma'am. I won't."

"Goodnight, Lieutenant Jefferson!" Docia went back inside and extinguished her porch light.

"Damn you, turn me loose!" Dothan whined.

Jefferson released his tie, and he slid down the hood onto the pavement. He held onto the bumper and stood up.

"You're dead, Jefferson!" he snarled as he stomped to the driver's side door. "YOU ARE DEAD!"

The Corvette engine roared to life, and Jeff jumped aside as Dothan raced off down Leckie Street. Rage overtook him and he snatched the rifle from the grass. The streetlights on either side of the boulevard cast a clear silhouette of Dothan's head he sped away. Jeff aligned the crosshairs of the scope, and his finger tensed on the trigger.

"Don't do it, Partner! He's not worth it!"

Defrange's voice ran through him like a soothing balm. He lowered the weapon and tuned toward her.

"You're right," he said calmly.

"Anyway," she went on, "how would it look for a descendant of the man from Charlottesville gunning down people in the street?"

Jefferson momentarily froze and looked at her.

"How do you know about that?"

She started to answer, but he shushed her.

"Never mind," he said. "I'm sure you divined it somehow."

They walked arm in arm back to 1500 Leckie Street where they found Palachi snoring in the porch swing.

Jeff chuckled. "Good old, Martin. His tactics are different, but he's always there in a pinch."

They roused him, and they all went back inside to make a pot of coffee. They discussed Dothan and the likelihood he was the Raptor. Defrange still disagreed, and they moved on to other things that were unsolvable at one in the morning. Palachi finally said goodnight and left.

"Whew!" Jeff exhaled as he leaned against the door. "It's been a hell of a Tuesday."

"Yes, it has," Defrange agreed. "And now I'm going to bed. Wanna join me?"

"Yes, I do, but I think I'll stay down here in case we have an unexpected visitor."

"Ok," she said as she started up the stairs.

"Partner? One question."

Defrange turned around. "Yes?"

"How do you know about my heritage?"

She laughed. "Let's just say that, many years ago, a moonstruck young woman started the Jefferson Fan Club and found out everything she could about you."

Jeff nodded. "It seems that you've wasted a lot of time on me."

She shook her head slowly. "Not at all Lieutenant."

He stared into her green velvet eyes for a moment. "I think I will go upstairs with you after all. Surely Dothan has had enough for one night."

"Well," she replied, raising one mischievous eyebrow, "that makes one of us."

Dothan exited the phone booth. He's been screaming a Saperstein for the better part of an hour until the man agreed to take action against Detective Jefferson.

"I've got that bastard now," Dothan mumbled as he got back into his Corvette.

As the engine roared to life, he thought of Almyra Defrange and how he would love to feel her cold, lifeless, magnificent body…and those eyes…. The fantasy aroused him, and he gunned the motor, racing off into the dark, warm Virginia morning.

CHAPTER 29

J EFF TURNED OFF the alarm before it rang. There was an ominous feeling about the morning, probably not owing exclusively to the rainy, dismal weather outside. He looked over at Defrange.

"Good morning," she said. She blinked a couple of times, her eyes flashing a deep malachite.

"Oh good," he said, kissing her. "I'm glad you're awake."

"I haven't slept much," she confessed. "My vision-maker is working overtime."

"Oh? Anything I should know?"

"Not specifically," she said, "but suffice it to say that today will be unusual. I'm not exactly sure how, but unusual."

He kissed her again and was headed for more when the phone rang.

"*Lieutenant Jefferson, this is Pherson, down at the Precinct.*"

"Good morning, Sergeant," Jeff greeted him. "Shouldn't you be getting off about now?"

"*About ten more minutes. Captain Chambers asked me to call you to request that you come in as soon as possible.*"

"What's up?"

"*I don't know, sir, but the Captain has been here for over an hour. Evidently the City Attorney called him at home, and he's been with folks from that office ever since he got here.*"

"Ok, Pherson. I'm already up, and I'll be rolling shortly. Thanks."

"*You're welcome, Lieutenant, and have a good day.*"

Jeff turned to Defrange, who'd heard one side of the conversation.

"Dothan?" she asked.

"That's my guess, or maybe his lawyer. The Captain has been down there for a while, and he wants me down there now."

"Sounds serious," she said as she got out of bed. "Gimme ten minutes."

They scrambled and dressed. By the time they left, the rain had stopped. The sun was bright and the heat stifling by the time they got to the Precinct. A rainbow arced over the Elizabeth River behind the Precinct Building.

Jeff pulled up to the main entrance.

"What's this?" Defrange asked.

"I thought you might want to go in while I park," he offered.

"Are we gonna play this every time we go somewhere?" she asked. "You're my partner, and if you're walking in from the parking garage, then I'm walking in from the parking garage."

Jefferson rolled his eyes in mock annoyance. "Typical. Give a girl a nice place to stay, buy her dinner, chase a serial killer, make love, and then they won't leave you alone."

Defrange took his hand.

"Don't count on that, my love," she said. "Under the right circumstances, I might have to leave you on a moment's notice—but I don't have to right now. Indulge me. I'd like to walk with you."

"Ok, Partner. Whatever you say."

The phone was already ringing when Jeff entered his office. It was Marsha. Chambers wanted to see him—*now*.

He hung up the phone. Defrange's eyes were ice.

"I'll get down there and get this over with. I think some people are really pissed off at me."

"That means *us*," she said.

He went down to the fourth floor. Marsha smiled nervously.

"Go on in, Lieutenant Jefferson," she said. "He's waiting for you."

Jeff walked into Chambers' office. The Captain sat with his back turned staring out the windows.

"What's up, Captain?" Jeff ventured.

Chambers slowly swiveled his chair around.

"Lieutenant Jefferson," he began in a voice much too formal, "did you brutalize a citizen last night?"

Before Jeff could answer, Chambers nodded to the chair across the desk from him.

"Not nearly as much as he deserved," Jeff replied as he sat down.

Chambers folded his hands on the desk.

"I see," he replied, "and was it necessary to kick him on the side of his head after you choked him at gunpoint?"

Jefferson carefully considered his answer.

"No sir," he said finally. "I don't suppose it was necessary, but it seemed like the right thing at the time. Anytime I find a citizen of questionable, criminal character lurking near my home with a high-power rifle with a night scope, especially a citizen who's threatened and assaulted police personnel all day, I tend to use whatever force is needed to stop that person."

Chambers turned his chair back around and stared toward the river. Jeff could sense his frustration. A minute later he spun around back around to face him.

Lieutenant, I'm afraid that I must ask you for your badge," he said.

Jefferson jumped to his feet, stunned.

"Jesus, Cap! Don't tell me they've gotten to you with their political b s?"

The Captain's eyes narrowed.

"That will do, Lieutenant Jefferson. No one has gotten to me with anything. Sit down!"

The older man leaned across the desk and made full eye contact. Jeff felt like a school boy in the principal's office. The Cap relaxed and leaned back. He flashed a curt grin.

"Please, Jefferson. Sit down, let's talk."

Chambers sat back, pulled a cigarette from a pack on the desk and lit it. It was something Jefferson had only seen him do once or twice in all the years he'd known him. He inhaled a log drag before the tamped it out in the ashtray. He was collecting his thoughts.

"Lieutenant," he began finally, "Dothan's attorney, David Saperstein, woke the City Attorney at three-thirty this morning. He said that he considered waiting, but he was so angry he couldn't sleep. I guess he decided that no one else should sleep either. He wants your badge, and in return he won't pursue action against the city for police brutality, undue process, defamation of character, et cetera, et cetera, et cetera. I've decided to comply with all of his demands, at least in appearance."

Jefferson sat back down and leaned forward in his chair.

"What do you mean 'in appearance'?"

The Captain was pensive.

"Donaldson, our fearless Commissioner, is a distant relative of Dothan's, and while he might not want to admit it, he wants Dothan left alone. If Dothan's kinship came out right now, it might blow his chances for re-election. You see, he's playing politics, and if you'll go along, we'll beat him at his own game. I'm very confident that you and Dr. Defrange can apprehend the Raptor, and I want you to continue on the case."

Jefferson had several questions, but the Captain wasn't finished. He took an envelope from his desk and handed it to Jefferson.

"That's an airline ticket," he said, "for Flight 946, and it's scheduled to leave Norfolk at 11:40 this morning."

Jeff pulled out the ticket and looked at. It was a one-way flight to Milwaukee.

"Make sure Defrange is on that flight," Chambers said.

Jefferson was on his feet again.

"But Captain, I thought you said—"

"Sit down and hear the rest!" he ordered.

The Captain's eyes had taken on their old sparkle.

"I want you to put Dr. Defrange on that plane. I've already laid the groundwork for a lot of press coverage for her departure, and I'll be holding a press conference this afternoon. I'm going to announce that, due to your mis-handling of Dothan's arrest, Defrange resigned and went back to Milwaukee."

Jeff was intrigued, and he leaned back.

"I'm also going to announce that you've been put on administrative leave until an investigation can be made into Saperstein's allegations. As far as the world is concerned, your last official act will be to put Defrange on that plane."

"Then what?" Jeff asked.

The Cap smiled. "Then I want you to run up to Richmond, and the two of you get back here as quick as possible. Just because she has a bona fide ticket to Milwaukee for the sake of deception doesn't mean that she has to go there in reality."

Jeff was smiling now.

"I know this is all unorthodox," the Captain continued, "but I'm going to get rid of this legal arm-twisting; and, I'm going to get rid of Donaldson. That piece of shit isn't fit for dog catcher, much less Police Commissioner, and I would be remiss in my duties to stand by and let him push people around for his own benefit. People like you and Defrange are too valuable to the common good to be mauled by the likes of his crew, and by God I'm not standing for it!"

Jeff felt like applauding, but he waited for the rest.

"You two get back here and continue your work. You'll just be out of sight. I've arranged with Dr. Palachi for the two of you to work out of his office until I can come out in the open with all of this."

"All of what?" Jeff asked.

"Bringing Donaldson down—and I have plenty of ammo. The City Attorney is actually in on this with me, and he'll help cover you and Defrange. There's going to be chaos around here for the next few days, so you two keep doing what you do and keep your heads down."

"You can count on us, sir."

Chambers stood. "Gimme your badge."

Jeff, confused, fished it out and handed it over. Chambers took it, and then he returned it immediately.

He smiled. "I can honestly say I took your badge. I don't think anyone will ask if I gave it right back to you."

They had a good laugh, and Chambers walked around the desk. A signal that the conversation was over. He extended his hand.

"You get Dr. Defrange to the airport, and then you get her back here from Richmond as soon as you can."

"We're on the way."

Jeff left the office with a sense of foreboding. He wondered if Donaldson knew that Chambers was on to him, and he wondered how far the Commissioner would go to keep his job. Jeff decided that the best thing he could do was to do what he'd always done: trust Captain Chambers emphatically.

He went back to his office and updated Defrange on the Captain's plan.

She checked her watch. "It's nine-thirty. What time do we need to leave for the airport?"

"If we leave by ten, we can be there in forty-five minutes. That will give the press ample time to hound us."

"Ok," she replied. "I'm concerned about Captain Chambers."

"Me too. He seemed more than a little uptight about it all."

Her eyes darkened.

"The danger to him could be more than he can know. Some men, as you know, will do anything to seize and hold power."

They headed for the airport, where the press was waiting en masse for any information the detectives would share.

"Lieutenant Jefferson," one reporter asked, "is it true that you've been relieved of duty?"

"No comment," Jeff replied.

"Detective Defrange," another called, "is it true that you were instrumental in erroneously identifying Clifton Dothan as the Raptor?"

"I can't speak to that," she replied, "but Captain Chambers will be holding a press conference this afternoon, and he will answer all of your questions."

"Jefferson. Is it true that you attacked Mr. Dothan while he was in custody? Did you beat a confession out of him?"

"No comment."

They pushed their way to the boarding gates, and the press hounded them all the way. The call came for Flight 946, and Defrange made a display of shaking Jeff's hand before she escaped to the safety of the plane.

"No more questions!" Jeff declared to the waiting pack of reporters, but in Defrange's absence they tried to push him even harder for answers.

"Lieutenant! Tell us, are you fired or not?"

He shook his head, and he raised his hands for silence.

"I'm afraid you're on to me," he said. "I can honestly tell you that Captain Chambers took my badge this morning, and I'm on administrative leave for an unspecified time. My last official act was to put Dr. Defrange on that plane."

"Will Clifton Dothan just go free?"

Jefferson raised his hands again to silence the crowd.

"Look, I've told you all I know, and since I've more or less become a private citizen, I'd appreciate it if you don't ask me any more questions."

The reporters seemed to respect that, and they began to drift away. A couple of them stopped to shake Jeff's hand and to wish him luck. Little did they suspect that in less than ten minutes he'd have his car headed for I-64 to go pick up Defrange. His gut was tight with both relief and apprehension.

Dothan fumed as he watched the live coverage of Defrange's departure. He considered what he might do to close the distance between them now that Jefferson was out of the picture.

He picked up the phone and dialed Saperstein's office. His attorney needed to know that the media was associating Clifton Dothan's name to the Raptor again, and that it might be worth some money—maybe several million dollars in a defamation lawsuit.

His aunt was caterwauling in the basement, and the TV was blaring: he almost missed the sound of the doorbell. He hung up the phone before Saperstein's secretary could answer, closing the basement door on the way to the front foyer.

"I'm coming!" he yelled as he jerked open the front door.

"Oh!" he exclaimed and partially raised his hands. "This is unexpected! What are you doing way out here?"

CHAPTER 30

J EFFERSON DROVE STRAIGHT to the airport in Richmond and found Defrange. He hugged her as though they hadn't seen each other in years.

"I'm starving," she said. "Is it lunchtime yet?"

Jeff looked at his watch.

"It's after one, actually. I know just the place."

They drove to East Grove Street and found a parking space. Leon's was the most popular Italian restaurant in town – there was a line out front.

"Is this place worth the wait?" Defrange asked as they fell in at the back of the line.

"I'll let you decide for yourself," he replied. "What the hell, we're non-existent back in Portsmouth, so we might as well take time to eat. I don't think the captain meant for us to go hungry."

Leon, the owner, came out to reassure his waiting patrons and broke into a wide, toothy grin when he spied Jefferson.

"There you are, Mr. Jefferson!" he called out as he bustled over to them. "You must not have heard me call your name for your reservation. Come right in! Your table is ready."

He winked and indicated that they should follow him past the other waiting diners. When they were inside, out of the crowd's view, Leon turned to embrace Jefferson.

"My old friend! "Why were you waiting in line? You should never have to wait!"

"Well, my friend," Jeff replied warmly, it's good to see you too, but I didn't think we should barge ahead of these people who were here first."

"Nonsense!" Leon fussed. "You wouldn't stand in line to enter your own home, would you?"

"No, I guess not."

Leon looked at Almyra.

"Oh," Jeff bumbled, "forgive my manners. Mr. Leon De Poma, allow me to introduce you to Almyra Defrange from Milwaukee."

Leon clasped his chest in theatrical acknowledgement of Defrange's beauty as she extended her hand. Leon bowed, took her hand, and lightly kissed it.

"Jefferson, it's no wonder I haven't seen you for such a long time. This one keeps you busy, no?"

"Actually, no," Jeff replied. "She's a fellow police officer, and we're working on the Raptor case. We only met last Friday—for the second time. We'd met once before, at a bad time in my life."

Leon reluctantly released Defrange's hand and arched his bushy eyebrows. His eyes were beacons of pleasure, and his dark mustache made his teeth appear to be even whiter as a smile spread across his face like syrup over hot pancakes.

"Old friend," he said, "I recognize Dr. Defrange from magazines and newspapers, and regardless of the Raptor, even two great sleuths cannot hide *amore* from Leon. But, please, come in and sit down—your table is ready."

They followed him into the dining room; just as he had promised, there was a vacant table beside the fireplace.

"How can this table be ready when we just got here?" Jeff asked.

Leon held Almyra's chair.

"Simply because I never allow anyone else to sit here. This table will always be ready for you."

"Leon," Jeff said, "I appreciate this, I really do, but you must need this table during peak times."

"No matter," he insisted. "No one sits here but you and yours."

He asked Almyra to fold the tablecloth back at her end of the table. When she did, it revealed a small, brass plaque.

"In loving memory of Carolita," she read aloud, "and with special thanks to my friend Philip Jefferson. October 1982."

She looked up quizzically, and Leon took one of her hands and one of Jeff's into his.

"*No one* sits here," he reiterated, "except for Jefferson and his guest."

Jeff felt a lump swell in his throat. "Thank you," he said.

Leon released their hands and dabbed the corners of his eyes with his apron.

"Enough of this," he said. "I'll send your waiter over, and my friends I will have no arguments. Lunch for the two of you is on Leon!"

Jefferson tried to protest, but Leon bowed and disappeared into the kitchen.

Almyra took his hand and squeezed it gently.

"What a charming man," she noted. "My Grandfather would have said he's of 'the old country'."

"Yes," Jeff agreed. "He is a good and gentle man, and his heart is as big as Italy."

She looked at him for a moment.

"Obviously, you're family around here," Defrange ventured. "Wanna share some history?"

Jeff's mind raced back to 1982 when he was coming to Richmond three nights a week to work on his Masters in Criminology. It was a painful memory, and his hands began to tremble. She took them both into hers.

"I feel your distress," she said, "and you know you don't have to talk about it."

"I know," he said, "but since you asked, it might help me to say it out loud to someone who understands."

He took a sip of water.

"I discovered this place totally by chance," he began, "and I started coming in after class almost every time I was up here. The de Pomas befriended me. Leon and his wife, Carolita, and I would sit at this table and visit. Frankly, our hours of conversation were a way for me to decompress. They were good listeners."

Jeff stopped to collect his thoughts.

"It was an outlet for me," he continued, "since my wife Jean wasn't interested in conversing with me. Hell, she didn't even want me to come up here for classes. It think she saw it as some sort of declaration of independence."

Almyra smiled. "Well," she said, "at least one member of the Jefferson family has been in on writing one of those before."

"I didn't mean to make a pun," he said.

"What happened to your wife? Almyra asked. "I've obviously wondered, but I didn't want to pry."

"It's ok. "I should have told you, except for the fact that we haven't had time to talk about anything very much. I guess I thought you knew, she died of breast cancer nearly six years ago."

"I'm sorry," Defrange replied. "I knew it was a bad question, but since I feel the way I do about you, I guess I had to ask."

"Oh, Jean hadn't cared about me for years, and she had told me as much."

"Why on earth would she not care for you?"

"I've thought about that for a long time," he replied, "and even aside from my other bad qualities, it all really boiled down to the fact that I was a cop. I tried to do other jobs, but I always came back to the force. As you well know, being in law enforcement is a calling—it's more than a job."

"How well I know," she agreed. "Any kids?"

"No. She wanted them, but she didn't think a policeman's life was conducive to the family atmosphere she had always dreamed of. She blamed that one on me too. It was like my armor was rusty, and my white steed was only good for fertilizer."

"But you were a cop when you got married, weren't you?"

"Yeah. It's all I've ever really done in one way or another. I guess she thought she could change all of that, and I honestly tried to change until I realized that she had made up her mind to be unhappy, no matter what I did. The simple fact was that she didn't really love me. She loved the idea of what she thought she could make of me."

"A common mistake," Defrange asserted.

"Yeah, and it's too bad," Jeff replied. "I don't know too many happily married couples. Most stay together for the kids, or convenience, or whatever, and eventually it all just leads to a lot of hate and resentment. Jean was having an affair with a minister, but I didn't care. If we could have just been honest enough to admit our human frailties, we both would have been better off. It was all so pointless. But, way too much about me. What about you? Ever get married?"

No," she said. "It seems that all of my Mr. Rights could never share me with what I do, or why I do it, so I decided years ago just to do what I do and skip the romance." She paused a moment. "Also, I've always known… since Duke…that…that someday, somehow, you and I would find each other again."

Jeff looked into the depths of those beautiful eyes and felt the passion and sincerity of her words. He swallowed hard.

"I'm glad you're here now, for real…not just a dream in my head," he said.

The waiter suddenly appeared to take their order. He looked at the two of them and excused himself. "Just let me know when you're ready, sir," he said as he made a quick exit.

"Look," Defrange said, "I have no right to blow into your life after all these years and drop this on you. You're probably still vulnerable, and to paraphrase you, let's play this by ear, with no strings."

"Let's," he agreed.

Jeff summoned to waiter to come back, and they ordered. Defrange resumed their conversation.

"So, 1982? What happened? I mean, only if you want to talk about it."

"It was Columbus Day," Jeff resumed, "and I came in after class. The crowd was thin, so the de Pomas and I sat down for our usual visit. It wasn't long before the stragglers left, and the cashier went home. It was just the three of us, but, unfortunately, no one thought to lock the front door."

Almyra tensed, and Jefferson sensed that she saw clearly what had happened.

"Anyway," he said, "four creeps came in, and *they* locked the door behind them. They pulled the blinds, and one of them checked the kitchen. Carolita, in her naïve way, thought they'd just come in as late diners, and she went over to tell them that the restaurant was closed. One of them grabbed her and put a knife to her throat.

Defrange's eyes turned to jade. She saw his memories.

"And," she said, "since you hate bullies, and since you don't push well, I can see what happened."

"Right, but maybe I should have been a little more push-able that night. I took down two of them, but the third one, the one who had checked out the kitchen, bolted for the cash register and emptied it. He started for the door, and he told his pal to kill Carolita if we moved."

The waiter appeared with their food and a bottle of Chianti. He served them quickly and left them to their privacy.

"You wanna eat?" Jeff asked.

"Not yet," she said. "Tell me what happened."

"Well," he continued, "since our criminal geniuses never dreamed that I was a cop, or that I might be armed, they were surprised when I pulled my weapon and demanded that the one holding Carolita let her go."

"*Déjà vu,*" Defrange said. "I think I was there yesterday."

"Exactly," Jeff replied. "But that night I didn't have Winetraub show up and get the drop on the attacker. The one with the money ran, and his accomplice started to back out the door with Carolita in tow."

Jeff paused.

"And?"

"And," he said, his voice shaking, "I shot him right between the eyes, but Carolita, in her haste to get the money back, ran into the street and… the bad guy who was running away shot her."

He stopped to dab his eyes with his napkin.

"I've always felt it was my fault, that maybe for once I shouldn't have acted like a cop. Leon's always remained my devoted friend, but, I'm not sure why."

"You *know* why," Defrange said, giving his hand a reassuring squeeze. "You know exactly why. You did what you had to do, and Leon recognizes that no matter how it turned out, you were willing to risk yourself to protect his family and property. That's the stuff real friendships are made of."

Jeff forced a weak smile. "Thanks, Partner," he ventured. "I've never told that to anyone. You're probably the only one who would care enough to listen." He shook it off. "Let's eat!"

When they had finished, Jeff thought about ordering some more wine. He wanted this meal to go on forever.

She waved her hand. "No more wine. I'm afraid I'll go to sleep on you. I not a very good traveling companion when I'm so full and relaxed."

"I'm wide awake," he said, "and I'd rather be traveling with you when you're asleep than anyone else I know who was wide awake."

She smiled just as Leon approached the table.

"Lunch was delicious," Jeff said. "Thank you."

"Yes," Defrange added. "You are a gracious and charming host, and the food is indescribable."

Leon beamed. "Think nothing of it. It's always a pleasure to see you, Jefferson, and of course this time I got to meet this enchanting lady. Why don't you two stay with me for a coupla days? We can enjoy Richmond together?"

"We'd love to my friend, but we're under strict orders to get back down to Portsmouth as soon as possible. How about a rain check?"

Leon nodded. "Of course, anytime. But before you go, I must tell you something." He again took Defrange's hand and then Jeff's and pressed them together in his.

"Children," he began, "I know that there are Raptors in the world, and I know that the two of you feel a personal responsibility to get rid of them; but, while you're at it, don't forget to stop every day to enjoy each other. There will always be Raptors, but this is the only chance the two of you will have. If you waste it, well then, you will have missed the opportunity to have something meaningful on this earth. I often wish that Carolita could come back for a little while, and believe me, if she could, I wouldn't waste time making pasta dishes for other people. I can see it in both of you, and you need to understand this precious gift is not guaranteed forever—not even for one more day."

Defrange's eyes welled, and Jeff looked down at the table.

"Thank you, my friend," Jeff said in as much voice as he could muster.

Leon released their hands. "I wish Carolita was here to see you. She would be so glad to see the happiness in Jefferson's eyes."

"Thank you, Leon," Defrange replied.

"Now, you two go. This table will be waiting for you when you return, which I hope will be soon."

"It will, Leon. I promise," Jeff said as he and Defrange rose from the table. They exchanged some tearful hugs, and then the detectives made their exit."

"After they got in the car, Defrange laughed and said, "I'm really having trouble getting used to this."

"What?" he asked.

"Having a man treat a woman like a lady instead of a sack of flour," she replied.

Jeff chuckled. "Why ma'am," he drawled, "you ah now in the Capital of the Ol' South, and ah would personally hoss whip any cad who treated y'all like a sack of flour."

"Well, suh," she drawled in turn, "since we ah heah, my we please ride down Monument Avenue so I might see that li'l ol statue of Arthur Ashe standing there amongst all those Confederate Generals?"

Jeff laughed out loud. "I see you've done your homework," he said as he drove toward Monument Avenue.

After some brief sightseeing, they headed back to Portsmouth. Defrange napped as Jeff drove. When they reached the city limits, she awoke with a start and began jerking her shoulder harness. Her eyes were wild and distant as Jeff pulled to the curb.

"Partner! What is it? Defrange!"

She was trembling and blindly looking around. He put his hand on her arm.

"Are you alright?"

"Jefferson," she gasped. "It's the Raptor. Get Palachi on the radio!"

Without hesitation he picked up the microphone.

"Digger one, this is Virginia Creeper, do you copy?"

There was a momentary silence and then Palachi's voice broke across space.

"This is Digger one, go ahead Virginia Creeper."

"Palachi, what's going on? Where are you?"

"I can't relay that over the radio, but if you head to your home base, you'll run into me. What's you ETA?"

Jeff looked around until he saw some familiar landmarks.

"About ten minutes," he replied.

"Roger. Ten minutes! Digger one, out."

Jefferson put the mic back in the holder and looked over at Defrange.

"Can you tell me?" he asked gently.

"The Raptor has been to Leckie Street—he's killed one of you neighbors."

Jeff drew a sharp breath. "Whom did he kill" Do you know?"

"A white-haired lady with a shrill voice," she replied, her eyes darting back and forth. "She lives in the corner house down toward the Naval Hospital—where you got the drop on Dothan."

Jeff put the blue light on the dash and accelerated from the curb. He quickly pushed his speed to seventy-five.

"It's Mrs. Treadway. Dothan saw her the other night, and now the son of a bitch killed her!"

They slid around the corner from High Street onto Crawford Parkway. Jeff killed the blue light just as they passed the Naval Hospital and took the back streets until they got to the lower end of Butler, where he turned and headed toward Leckie. Jeff immediately spotted the Mobile Crime Van behind the Treadway house and pulled in behind it. Palachi appeared out of nowhere, motioning for Jeff to roll down his window. His tone was solemn.

"Hi ya, kids. Sorry about the homecoming."

"Was it him?" Jeff asked.

"No doubt about it," the ME replied. "Listen, there are a lot of people hanging around up front, so why don't you meet me at the morgue in about twenty minutes? It'd be a shame for somebody to see Defrange since we spent so much effort making her disappear."

"Right," Jeff said. He pulled away and headed back in the direction of the Naval Hospital.

CHAPTER 31

JEFFERSON STRUGGLED TO control the car as he sped around Crawford Parkway. A barrage of emotions overwhelmed him.

"I'm gonna call Captain Chambers," he announced. "I'm bringing Dothan in again!"

Defrange put her hand on his knee.

"Easy, Partner," she soothed him. "You're wasting your time. Dothan didn't do it."

Jeff slid around the corner onto High Street and locked the brakes. They came to a stop right in front of Clyde's Barber Shop, causing several pedestrians to scatter as they caromed off the curb.

"Damn it, Defrange! That's enough! How can you take up for that guy? Not only has he threatened us, he's surfaced at every turn since you got here." Jeff's frustration got the best of him and he began to shout. "Say something to me that makes sense! I know who you are and what you are, and I respect your abilities, but, my being in love with you aside, this time you're flat-ass wrong. That slimy mortician has made a fool of us already, and this time I'm bringing him in for good!"

He thought she would argue. Instead, she took her hand from his knee and sat back.

"Okay, Lieutenant," she said calmly.

Jefferson glared at her. "Is that all you have to say?"

"Yes," she said quietly, "that's all I have to say. You're convinced that you have your killer, and until you see for yourself that you're wrong, you might as well go ahead and chase him."

"Partner, don't you see?" he pleaded. "Dothan is the closest thing we've had as a suspect since this whole thing started, and even if I didn't think he was our killer, which I do, I don't have any choice but to arrest him on suspicion if nothing else."

Her silence was oppressive as he pulled back on to High Street. He parked in the Morgue lot next to Palachi's vehicle. The ME was waiting for them at the back door, anxiously waving them inside.

"I wonder what that's all about?" Jeff whispered aloud.

"I think he wants to show us our new office," Defrange ventured.

"Oh, yeah," Jeff admitted, "I'd forgotten that we live here now. You're probably right."

"So, you believe me about this?"

Jeff killed the engine.

"Partner, I always believe you. It's just that my instinct tells me that Dothan is our killer, and until we have a better suspect, that's what I have to believe. We just have a difference in professional opinions."

"I understand, and I hope it's not long until we find the *better suspect*."

Her demeanor told him that his outburst on High Street hadn't insulted her, but he didn't like the way she was patronizing him.

"C'mon," Palachi called when they got out of the car. "C'mon, hurry up! I have something to show you."

"Partner," Jeff added wearily, "you're definitely right about Palachi, even if you're wrong about Dothan."

Palachi scampered ahead of them like a sea lion chasing a beach ball until he disappeared into a room at the darkest, most distant end of the hallway. He peeked back around the door to make sure they were still following him. When they got to the room, Jeff craned his neck around the doorframe: he was looking into an old autopsy room that probably hadn't been used since the nineteenth century. In the center, decorated with a desk lamp, a blotter, and a telephone was a steel table that Jefferson was sure had been used for things he didn't want to know about. Two folding chairs from Palachi's office were side by side.

Palachi smile proudly. "Ain't it great?"

Defrange was trying, without success, to stifle her laughter, which was either at Palachi's child-like enthusiasm or Jeff's mortification—he wasn't certain.

"Just look over here!" Palachi said as he excitedly opened a dilapidated, rusty, hinged door. "You've got your own private john."

Jeff joined in Defrange's laughter when Palachi winced at the sight of a skeleton on a stand adjacent to the ancient commode.

"Damn it!" he cursed. "They were supposed to hide this. Anyway, aside from the skeleton, ain't this great?"

Defrange gave in to wild laughter as Jeff deadpanned.

"Yeah, Martin, this is wonderful," Jeff said. "I love the retro plumbing, and hell, you should leave Mr. Bones in there. He can hold my coat while I'm using the toilet."

Palachi began to pout in disappointment. It was too much for Jeff.

"C'mon, buddy. You know how I feel about this place. It'll just take time to adjust. Otherwise, it's wonderful. Honest!"

The ME looked at them both for a minute. Defrange had managed to stop laughing and put on a sincere expression of appreciation. "Ok then," Palachi said finally. "If you say so. Now, let's go down to my office and go over this latest murder."

They followed him out. "Goodnight, Mr. Bones," Defrange quipped as she killed the light.

When they got to the office, the detectives cleared some piles of magazines and boxes from the two chairs that were left and sat down. Palachi took his seat at the desk.

"Ok," he said, glancing at the file in front of him," from what I observed from the gross examination of Mrs. Treadway, she died either last night or early this morning. I'll be able to narrow that down after the postmortem. The whole scene over there was classic Raptor – and he left another poem.

"Do you have it?" Defrange asked.

Palachi handed her a plastic folder with a piece of notebook paper inside. She began to read aloud.

> *"jefferson and defrange so hard you labor*
> *so, i decided to call on your nosy neighbor,*
> *she saw me, but i saw you,*
> *and i knew exactly what i would do…*
> *i helped her over to that silent place*
> *even sang a verse of amazing grace*
> *she went in peace so I forgive her*
> *so much that I took her aging liver…but*
> *roses are red and palachi is dumb*
> *but you'll never find it, alas it's all gone…*
> *baked in a pie i ate alone…*
> *a pie, yum delicious, i enjoyed the flavor, but*
> *it's defrange's eyes i'll soon savor.*
> *a matter of time, my dear, you'll see*
> *she's gone…she's gone…no*
> *she's now part of me…*
> *Xoxo raptor"*

Defrange swallowed as she dropped the note in her lap.

"C'mon, Partner," Jefferson said. "He's not gonna have you in any way. I'll just call Captain Chambers."

"For what?" she asked.

"For what?" he repeated, a little terser than he intended. "I'm gonna arrest Dothan, that's 'for what'. Look at that poem where he says 'she saw me'. It's Dothan she saw. She saw him the other night when she turned on her porch light. How can it be anyone else?"

"Pretty strong argument," Palachi agreed, "since we know that Dothan saw her the other night. It's psychological warfare. He might not be able to get the two of you, but by God he can get your friends and neighbors. I wonder who's next?"

Jeff stood up. "*Nobody*, if I can help it," he replied adamantly. "May I use your phone to call the Captain?"

Defrange put her hand on his arm. "Wait, Lieutenant. I know you think, and maybe with good reason, that the evidence on Dothan is conclusive, but he still doesn't feel right to me. Can we review the evidence before you call?"

Jefferson sat down. "Ok Partner, but every minute we spend screwing around is just one more minute that Dothan has to kill someone else."

"Let's look," she said quietly, "and afterward you can call the Captain with my blessing."

Palachi eyed them both for a moment before removing a notebook from his desk drawer. "Here's what we know absolutely. From the angle of the slash marks, and the angle of the amputations, we know that our killer is right-handed. These stats include Dan Hinson's murder, by the way."

Jeff looked at Defrange. "Dothan is right-handed," he reminded her.

"We know," Palachi continued, "from the measurements of the bite marks, that each victim was bitten, well, *most likely bitten* by the same person."

"What do you mean 'most likely'?" Jeff asked.

"What I mean," Palachi explained, "is that the law of averages would suggest that there might be several million people with the same bite pattern, but the consistent thing here is that there wouldn't be that many people in this immediate area who, number one: are killing people, and number two: have the same bite pattern. It's the same pattern on every victim, and I don't believe there are two people in this area that have the same bite."

Jeff nodded, and he looked at Defrange.

"Unfortunately, we weren't able to hold on to Dothan long enough to get a sample of his bite pattern," he said.

Defrange shook her head, but she didn't say anything.

"Ok, Martin, what else do we know?" Jeff asked.

Palachi flipped a few pages.

"Oh, yeah," he said, "and this might be important. Whoever our killer is knows human anatomy, and he knows how to use a scalpel, or something like a scalpel."

Jeff threw his hands in the air. "It's Dothan. Maybe we can pick him up and question him. I'm going to call Captain Chambers."

Jefferson got up and reached for the phone.

"Partner, hold it!" Defrange pleaded. "Look. Try this. We haven't thought of this because it's new. Can we bring Dothan in long enough to get a blood sample? Palachi can do that new DNA test, and if Dothan's DNA is the same as samples from the murders, we'll know we have the right man."

"I already know!" Jeff declared.

"Maybe you do, Partner," she replied, "but follow this scenario. Saperstein and these younger attorneys know about DNA. It we arrest Dothan, and they order the test, if it turns out not to match the evidence, who is in trouble for a false arrest. You'll never get a judge to order a warrant or anything else on him again, ever! That means he might walk on everything—even Erica Merriweather."

"I see what you mean," Jeff agreed. "Palachi?"

"Yeah. She's absolutely right. I should have thought of it, but I guess I was so sure that he was our man, I wasn't thinking."

Jefferson did call the Captain and explained their suspicions and doubts based solely on the note and the fact that Dothan saw Mrs. Treadway when he was stalking him and Defrange. He asked for a warrant to collect a blood sample, not to arrest Dothan for murder.

The Captain agreed but with stipulations.

"*Absolutely no arrest unless you have some concrete evidence or probable cause.*"

"Yes, sir. Our plan is to get a sample of Dothan's blood, and Palachi can check the DNA with the evidence from all the murders. Defrange thought of this one."

"*Tell her it was good thinking—but I wouldn't have expected any less. I'll check this all with legal, and while I'm at it I'll get a warrant to search Dothan's premises. Maybe there's something there that will give us a lead. But, be careful. If he is guilty, and if we can prove it with this DNA test, we don't want to blow it because of a sketchy search. Do it all by the book.*"

"Right, Captain," Jeff agreed. "And, I've just thought of something else. Since Defrange and I are officially missing, Palachi will have to come pick up the warrants."

"*I'll take care of the warrants right now, and I'll get them over to Pherson. Palachi can pick them up from him in the PreCom center. I should have them over there in thirty minutes or so.*"

"Ok, Captain." Jeff hung up.

"Ok, Martin. Pherson will have the warrants in PreCom in about thirty minutes. You can pick them up so Defrange and I can remain anonymous."

"Gladly. I guess you two will wait here for me?" Martin asked.

"I hadn't thought about it," Jefferson confessed, "but I suppose we will since we don't have Dothan's address until you get the paperwork. I don't know where he lives."

"I can take you to Dothan's," Defrange spoke up.

Jeff started to question her but gave up. She'd been right at every juncture.

"Martin, if you can get the warrants, we'll go ahead to Dothan's place, and we'll be ready when you get there."

"Just be sure not to go in before I get there!" Palachi warned.

"Don't worry," Jeff said. "I don't want anything to screw this up."

CHAPTER 32

"WHERE TO?" JEFFERSON asked when they got in the car.

Defrange closed her eyes, and, after a moment, she began speaking.

"Take 164 west and head toward Newport News."

"How far?"

"I don't know yet," she replied, "but it's beyond the James River Bridge. Don't worry—I'll know when we get there."

She opened her eyes and looked at him.

"Ever heard of Ed Gein?" she asked.

"Yeah, the name is familiar, but I don't remember why."

"Plainfield, Wisconsin," she added. "A book and movie called *Psycho*. Does that help?"

"Oh, yeah," he recalled, "he was the little guy who dug up graves, wasn't he? Some sort of fixation with his mother, right?"

"Partially, but if you remember, after a while, the grave robbing didn't do it for him anymore and—"

"And he started *killing women* for...why was he doing all of that? I can't remember the details."

Defrange leaned her head back and put her feet up on the seat.

"There's a whole plethora of psychological theories about that," she said, "but what I want you to consider is how did he get away with it for so long?"

"Police incompetency?" he ventured. "I don't know what you're getting at."

"Consider this," she offered. "Ed Gein was a mentally slow man who was transparent in his community. He was helpful to his neighbors, but largely kept to himself and never did anything to draw attention. Dahmer was the same, just in a different environment. He lived in Milwaukee with his grandmother before moving out on his own. A large metropolitan area lends itself to anonymity just as much as a rural setting. Do see what I'm getting at here?"

"Sure, I follow that. Those men were so obvious that no one noticed them."

"Exactly right."

"So," Jeff reasoned, "that supports my suspicions of Dothan."

Defrange sighed. "Right and wrong. Follow this: while you've been chasing this killer, have you ever considered that the person who was robbing graves here a couple of years ago might be the same person?"

"Not really," he admitted. "We just thought our grave robber was a transient who either moved on or died."

"Right. You never considered a personality like Ed Gein. Someone who couldn't meet his needs, whatever they were, by just robbing graves anymore. You never looked at it as a macabre, natural progression."

"No, we never considered that."

"Well, think about it," she pushed. "If you were an embalmer, a successful funeral director, would you rob graves? Of course, you wouldn't. You'd have all the bodies you'd ever want right there at work every day."

"I follow you, but Dothan's sick. Maybe he couldn't help it."

"I agree that he's sick, but he isn't stupid. Far from it. He's acutely aware of public opinion and reputation. If he were going to do the things the Raptor has done, he wouldn't do it here—I mean, in the community where he lives and works. You saw his embarrassment when we apprehended him and held him for a while. No, Dothan doesn't have the nerve to do what the Raptor does. Oh, he loves being a dirty little boy but he'd be mortified if the public knew that he'd been making mud pies."

"All right," Jeff conceded, "but if it isn't Dothan, and I'm still not sure that it isn't, who the hell can it be?"

Defrange looked out the window. "Someone even more transparent," was her ominous reply.

"Well, if it isn't Dothan, should I radio Palachi and have him skip the warrants?"

"No. We need to be at Dothan's tonight, and the search warrant will be helpful."

"Why are we discussing all of this now?" Jeff asked. "Are you trying to tell me something that I'm missing?"

Defrange smiled. "No, Lieutenant. I've learned. I know how you feel about me, but you're not ready to do anything based on somebody else's say-so. That's actually good. Your gut instincts have probably saved your life more than once over the years, and I'm very thankful for that. If I'm trying to tell you anything, it's that we're not dealing with the average, dumb street killer who does predictable things—if you accept that, I want you to consider that some of your hypotheses might be wrong. And, as far as I'm concerned, my love, who's right or wrong makes no difference. I just want you to be careful."

"Fair enough," Jeff agreed. "And, if I'm wrong about Dothan, I'll be the first to admit it."

"Partner!" she whispered.

"What is it?"

"In about a mile, give or take," she said, "we'll cross a drawbridge. Take the road to the right immediately after we cross it."

"Got it."

He wasn't surprised when the bridge and the turn-off appeared just as Defrange had said. He turned right onto Freestone Ferry Road, and after about two miles they came to an exclusive development that bordered the James River.

"Third driveway," she said, her eyes still closed. "Pull in there and stop. It's another quarter-of-a-mile down to the house, so we can wait up here for Palachi without being seen."

Again, Jefferson wasn't surprised when the sign over the mailbox at the third driveway proclaimed the estate of "Clifton Ramon Dothan, 28 Freestone Ferry Road". He turned in and switched off the headlights.

Jeff looked over at Defrange. Her eyes were open and glazed. The was a pale blue aura around her, and if she had been anyone else, he would have abandoned the car and gone for help. They sat in total silence for about twenty minutes.

The night sounds were deafening, and they seemed to get louder as they waited. When one lives in the city, it's easy to forget how loud thousands of crickets and cicadas can be.

Jeff hadn't smoked in years, but he suddenly had a craving for a cigarette. Defrange fumbled around in her tote bag, and much to his total lack of surprise, produced a pack of Winstons. She took out a gold lighter, lit two, and handed one to him.

"I didn't know you smoked," he said, taking the cigarette.

She French-inhaled and blew a perfect smoke ring.

"Ordinarily, I don't—just sometimes. Like when I'm sitting in a car on a stakeout."

Pleasantly astonished, Jeff took a deep drag. "Damn! This is disgustingly good." He exhaled and took another puff.

Defrange nodded. "Sometimes there's nothing like a good smoke to clear the head."

They smoked in the darkness, their cigarettes tiny, floating pinpoints in the middle of the tall pines.

"Jefferson," she said as she extinguished her cigarette, "we're going to learn some things tonight, but you should know that it's not what you expect to learn."

"What do you mean?"

"Your primary suspect won't be your primary suspect anymore."

Jeff nodded. "Well, like I said, when I find out that Dothan isn't our killer, I'll be the first to admit it but, until then, I'm ready to lock him up." He looked at his watch: they had been there for almost an hour.

"This is going to be horrible," Defrange said.

"Nonsense," Jeff replied. "Palachi will be here soon, and we'll just go in and look around."

"That's what I mean. We're going to discover something horrible."

"Yep," he teased, "we're gonna find out that Dothan is the Raptor. I wonder if ghouls like him have to wander at night, or if they just stay home?"

Defrange shuddered so hard Jeff thought she might be having a seizure.

"Partner!" he whispered, grabbing her hand.

"I'm alright," she reassured him. "And don't worry. Dothan is at home."

"How do you know?"

"I've seen him."

Fifteen minutes later Palachi pulled up behind them.

"Sorry," he said as he walked to the car, waving some papers. "I missed the road after I crossed the drawbridge. Anyway, I got the warrants."

"Ok," Jeff replied. "We'll lead, and you follow us in— slowly!"

They pulled around the circular drive and saw that Dothan's Corvette was parked at the side of the house.

It turned out that Defrange was right. Dothan was at home – as a matter of fact, he was all over the house.

CHAPTER 33

"**M**Y GOD!" PALACHI said under his breath as the three of them peered through the window of a side door leading from a screened porch into Dothan's kitchen. Defrange, after looking on the horrific scene momentarily, quietly took a seat in a porch swing.

The curtains above the sink were soaked with what appeared to be blood, and the freezer compartment of the refrigerator was open with a crimson substance dripping onto the floor. Jeff tried the door, but it was locked.

"Wait, Lieutenant!" Palachi urged. "I'm going to call my Crime Unit. Let's stay outside until they get here."

Jeff reluctantly hesitated—but, of course Palachi was right. He looked over at Defrange for any recommendations, but she was staring off into space.

"Partner?" he called to her.

Her green stare was fixed. It occurred to Jeff that she didn't want to look further because she's already seen it all in her mind.

Palachi crossed the porch. "I'm going to use my radio and have Pherson call Dixon for me," he said hurriedly. "Try to resist going in there. This will the only time in the Raptor investigation where the Crime Unit goes into a scene before anyone else."

The spring on the screen door squeaked as the ME exited the porch, letting the door slam behind him. Jeff sat down in a chair opposite Defrange.

She would speak when she was ready. She was pumping the swing back and forth, her eyes closed. Palachi returned from his call and nodded toward her.

"I think she's seeing what happened here," Jeff whispered.

Martin sat down. The heat and the drone of the insects made ten minutes seem endless until Defrange suddenly stopped swinging

"The Raptor killed Dothan," she said without opening her eyes.

Palachi and Jefferson leaned forward.

"The Raptor killed everyone in the house," she added.

Everyone?

Defrange answered as if Jeff had asked her the question out loud.

"There is an elderly woman," she went on, "and I see Cleopatra—"

Palachi looked incredulous. "*Cleo—?*"

"Shhhh," Jeff said, waving him off.

"They're both dead," Defrange went on. "There are viscera in the freezer, and the remains of Dothan's fingers are in the garbage disposal. He was tortured most of the day. The old woman in the basement is whole."

Defrange leaned toward them. Palachi opened his mouth to say something, but Jefferson raised a finger.

"Dothan's arms are in the umbrella stand in the foyer," she continued, "and his feet and legs are affixed to a pair of skis in the basement. His head is in the toilet on the second floor, and his torso is—"

Her eyes popped open: they were electric. She was suddenly up and moving so fast that she nearly knocked Palachi off the ottoman where he sat. It was useless to try to stop her—when she bolted out of the screen door. Jeff just hoped that he could keep up with her.

"Partner! Defrange!" he called out, but she was racing down the sloping yard toward a lighted pier where a small cabin cruiser was tied.

As they ran, Jeff could make out mooring lines being tossed over to the pier. A moment later the engine started and the cruiser began backing into the river, turning a' port and heading south toward Portsmouth. Defrange dropped to one knee, taking aim at the boat with her Glock.

"Don't shoot, Defrange!" was drowned out by the explosion of the pistol. There was the sound of glass shattering as the boat finished turning and sped away.

Jeff dropped down on the grass beside Defrange, panting.

"Sounded like you got the cabin window," he said.

"Yes, I got the window—but I also got the Raptor."

Her eyes told him that she was back from her psychic realm.

Jeff helped her up and waited while she reloaded and holstered her weapon.

"You alright?" he asked.

"Yeah, I'm fine. We need to call the Coast Guard and ask them in intercept that cabin cruiser."

Palachi had stopped half-way from the house.

"Call the Coast Guard!" Jefferson yelled. "Tell them to stop that cabin cruiser headed downriver!"

Palachi waved and raced back toward his vehicle.

When they got up the slope, Palachi was in the driveway on the radio. The Mobile Crime Team had arrived and were awaiting instructions from the ME. He spoke to them briefly and headed back toward Defrange and Jefferson.

"Did you raise the Coast Guard?" Jeff asked.

"Yeah. I talked to the radio room at Base Portsmouth. The *Avenger* is on routine patrol, and they're on the lookout for the cruiser. Did I hear a gunshot?"

"Just getting in some target practice," came Defrange's dry comment.

"Hit anything?"

"Oh, yes," she replied with an impish grin.

Palachi looked to Jeff as if he needed clarification, but Jeff ignored him. "Let's go, Partner," he said. "We'll take the car and head back toward Portsmouth. Maybe we can spot the cruiser from the road somewhere."

Defrange headed for the car, and Jeff followed. He was bracing for the "I told you so" about Dothan not being the Raptor.

They raced onto 164 E, and Jefferson put the blue light on the dash. He picked up the mic and turned the radio to Marine Band.

"Coast Guard Cutter *Avenger*," he called. "This is Virginia Creeper. Do you copy?"

There was a moment of static.

"This is the Avenger. Go ahead Virginia Creeper."

"This is Lieutenant Philip Jefferson of Portsmouth Homicide, and I'm in a land barge headed east on Highway 164. Have you seen the cabin cruiser that was reported a few minutes ago? Over."

"That's affirmative, Lieutenant. She's dead in the water off Geezer's Point. We're working a tow. Do you want us to board her?"

"Affirmative," Jefferson replied. He shot Defrange a quick glance, and her smirk was approaching a smile. "Be advised, there may be a killer aboard, and he's wounded. Consider the entire boat as a crime scene. Over."

"Your transmission is understood, Lieutenant, and we will comply. We'll let you know what we find. USCGC Avenger clear."

Geezer's Point was just ahead. Jeff pulled onto a gravel road and headed for the overlook parking lot. The lights on the river were a pleasant diversion—it would have been easy to forget under other circumstances.

"Beautiful," Defrange observed. "You wouldn't be kidnapping a girl to love's lane, now would you?"

"That's a wonderful idea, but we should save that for another night."

"Too bad," she teased as the kissed his earlobe.

"Hold that thought," Jeff said as the radio came to life.

"Virginia Creeper this is the Avenger. We boarded the cruiser. There are human remains aboard, but there is no fugitive. Over."

"Copy," Jeff replied. "Are you towing the subject boat to Base Portsmouth? Over."

"Affirmative. ETA forty-five minutes."

"I'll see you there. This is Virginia Creeper out and clear."

"Roger. This is USCGC Avenger out and clear."

Jeff turned down the squelch and looked at Defrange.

"I admit I was wrong," he said.

She grinned. "Ok."

"Do you think you killed the Raptor, or is he alive somewhere?"

"I didn't kill him, and he's very close. Defrange stared out at the river. "He wounded—and he's angry."

Just across the river in a dank, dark basement, the Raptor was cleaning the wound to his left arm.

"That bitch, that bitch, that *bitch!*" he repeated as he poured kerosene into his wound. Fortunately for him, the bullet had exited the bicep muscle without hitting the humerus.

"This will suffice until I can do better," he whispered. He stumbled up the stairs into the darkened house. By the grace of God, the owners were away.

"*Amazing Grace, how sweet the sound,*" poured out into the night—the notes wafted on the air and rolled along with the quiet flow of the James.

CHAPTER 34

JEFFERSON DECIDED TO go back for the Medical Examiner before proceeding to the Coast Guard Base. Defrange agreed that Palachi would want to see the boat for himself. Mason Dixon came out of the house just when they arrived.

"Good evening, Detectives," he greeted.

"How's it going in there?" Jeff asked.

"A huge mess," he replied, holding up a specimen jar. "Fingers!" he declared.

"Oh, that's just great," Jeff carped. "I knew I should have been a shoe salesman!"

"Really?" Defrange replied with skepticism. "Is it the shoes or the feet that turn you on?"

Jefferson gave her a dismissive look.

They entered the foyer just as Palachi bounded down the steps.

"Did they find the boat?" he asked.

"Yep," Jeff answered, "but nobody was aboard except a part of Dothan. At least Defrange *says* it's Dothan. They're towing it to Base Portsmouth. Wanna go?"

"Sure!" Palachi replied. "And from what I've already seen here, I can tell you which part of Dothan is on the boat. I would like to see how it all fits together, so to speak."

"Let's go," Jeff said.

"In a minute," Palachi said. "First, you have got to see this. He put a new twist on his old theme."

He led them upstairs. To Jeff's dismay, he directed them to the bathroom. The ME opened the door and stepped aside. The room, unlike any other room in the house, was spotless.

"This is just the way I found it," Palachi said. "Neat and tidy."

Jefferson looked into the tub – except for a slight trace of blood in the drain, it was clean.

"The photographer's downstairs," Palachi added. "He's working his way up, and I'm leaving everything as is until he's finished."

"Is Dothan's head in there?" Jeff asked, nodding toward the toilet.

Palachi lifted the lid: the head was there. Sticking to the crown of the pate was a large nail driven into the skull—with a note attached. Jeff took his reading glasses from his jacket, leaned down toward the toilet and read aloud:

"i'm so disappointed as you can see
you actually thought this fool was me
and now you know he's not the one, but
we don't need him to have our fun…
before he went, he made a stand, and
said he killed mortician dan…
so now I've told you all in all
the bigger they are the harder they fall
xoxo raptor"

Jeff lifted the note up by one corner. "Oh God! Martin! What's in his mouth?"

Palachi snorted. "Without disturbing the evidence," he replied, "I can only make an educated guess that what you see in his mouth is the head of one of the smaller species of African reticulated pythons."

Sweat popped out on Jeff's forehead.

"Cleo," Defrange offered.

Quigley, the photographer suddenly appeared, and the detectives had to evacuate the room.

"Same as usual, Doc?" he said.

"Yeah," Palachi agreed. "But try to get some pictures of the snake's head in Dothan's mouth before they remove it from the commode."

"Will do, Dr. P," Quigley said as he started snapping.

"Let's go to Portsmouth," Palachi said.

"I thought you'd never ask," Jefferson replied.

They went downstairs, and Palachi asked Dixon to drive the ME's SUV back to the morgue.

On the way to town, Jeff and Defrange briefed Martin on what the Coast Guard had relayed, with Defrange asserting that the man who escaped the boat was the Raptor.

"Maybe he just got in a car somewhere and drove away," Palachi offered, "is there anything to indicate that he's still in the area?"

"He's here," Defrange stated quietly. "I don't know where, but he hasn't left."

Martin didn't challenge her.

They pulled into the Coast Guard Base and were greeted by their old friend.

"Good morning, Detectives, Dr. Palachi," he said when Jeff stopped. "You know what to do with your weapons."

"Thanks, Guns," Jefferson replied, returning the man's salute. "We'll put them in the trunk."

"Thanks, Lieutenant," he said, and handed Jeff the usual visitor pass for the windshield.

Jeff parked in a space across from where the *Avenger* was being tied up with the cabin cruiser secured to her stern. Palachi got out and headed for the brawl which was just being secured to the dock. Defrange and Jefferson secured their weapons and followed him.

"We'll wait on the dock," Jefferson called to Palachi. "The fewer people stirring the evidence, the better."

"Right!" Palachi replied as he was greeted by Commander Pitillo.

They moved down the port air castle to the fantail, and Palachi lowered himself down to the cabin cruiser. He disappeared into the cabin while the detectives waited anxiously. It was a short wait. Palachi was back in less than ten minutes telling them that in fact there was a human torso aboard the boat. He informed them that he was going to leave it there until daylight hours.

"I'll come back with the Crime Team, and we'll go over the remains and the boat," he explained. "Commander Pitillo has already gotten permission to tie the cruiser up to the dock."

The ME fished into the upper pocket of his lab coat.

"Here's one piece of evidence I removed," he said. He tossed a small plastic bag over to Defrange.

"Yours, I believe," he said with a smile.

Jeff looked over her shoulder to the item in the bag. It was a damaged bullet.

"Looks like a .9 millimeter to me," Jeff said with a chuckle. "Good shooting, Partner."

"That's not all," Palachi went on. "There was blood on the bulkhead where I dug this out. It looks like you really did hit him."

Defrange grinned and looked to Jeff. "I told you so!"

Jeff was just glad that she hadn't said that on all the other occasions when she could have.

"C'mon, Dr. Palachi," Jeff offered. "If you're done, we'll give you a lift."

"I'm quite done for now," the ME replied.

It was a quarter past midnight when they got in the car.

"I don't want your excuses!" he growled. "Stop crying and just clean this wound."

"You need to go to the emergency room," she sniveled.

"You know I can't do that! Gunshot wounds are reportable to the police, and I don't believe, even as stupid as they are, they'd believe I accidently shot myself in the upper arm."

"But—"

He slapped her. "Hurry up! I have something else for you to do before daylight!"

"What is it?"

His face contorted, and an old woman's voice emerged. "This stupid, stupid, ass dropped something on the boat, and if you don't find it before the ME does, there's going to be a lot of explaining and trouble."

The face changed again, and the woman stepped back.

"And, they'll catch you!" the child said, "and they'll lock you up forever."

"They can't catch me!" the old woman cackled. "I'm like the gingerbread man. They can't catch me!"

His face relaxed.

"You have to go—*now*," he said. "And you can't screw this up."

CHAPTER 35

A T 1:23 A.M., a phantom dressed in black climbed over the back fence of the Coast Guard Base. The figure dropped silently to the ground and ran to the cover of a large buoy that had been placed on the dock for repair. Satisfied that no one was in sight, the shadow scampered across the dock toward the cabin cruiser which was bobbing up and down in the wake of a Navy destroyer that had just passed on the way up river. Silent as a mist, the intruder dropped from the dock to the deck of the cruiser and then crawled toward the cabin door. The shadow stood up to enter the door.

"Halt!" a voice rang across the slip. The phantom reached for his hip at almost the same time the M-14 barked, its blast echoing off the surrounding steel and concrete structures. The dark figure went overboard, and the roving security guard grabbed his radio.

"Gate! Security! There's an intruder on base, slip Four. I need lights."

Spotlights flashed on over the guard's head.

"*Security this is the OD,*" came the radio call. "*What's going on?*"

"Sir, there's an intruder on base. One shot fired!"

"*Who the hell fired it?*" the Officer of the Day demanded.

"I did, sir. The intruder is overboard in Slip Four."

"*I'm on the way!*"

Lieutenant Ed Lawing, Officer of the Day, met Petty Officer Mozalewski coming from the guard house and they ran together to the security guard's position. The deck watch on the *Avenger* had activated spot lights on the ship, and the messenger of the watch awakened Commander Pitillo. The entire area was now lighted, but no one could locate a body.

"We have to find him!" Lawing called to Pitillo. "Dead or alive, we've got to find him."

Pitillo waved and turned to the messenger of the watch.

"Get the swimmer!" he ordered.

An hour of searching the slip between the two docks was futile, and after a search of the buildings, Lawing made his decision.

"Let's go upstairs to the office," he told Pitillo. When they got there, Lawing divulged his plan.

"I think the current pulled the body out into the river," he said, "and we need to find it before some tourist walking along the boardwalk finds it. I'm going to call the Medical Examiner and see if he wants to go along, since he has such an interest in the cabin cruiser. Meanwhile, perhaps you could make the *Avenger* ready to get underway."

"I agree," Pitillo replied, walking out of the Base Administration Office. Lawing got Palachi on the phone. It was 2:45 A.M. when Palachi called Jefferson.

Jefferson related what Palachi had heard from the Coast Guard while he and Defrange got dressed. When they arrived at the base, Palachi was there. He made introductions and Lawing told them what he knew. The detectives also interviewed the guard who had fired the shot before they headed to the *Avenger*. Lawing walked with them, expressing his concerns.

"If my man shot a civilian," he said, "I need to know, and we need to find out what that person was doing on base."

"I understand what you mean," Jefferson said, "but if it's the murderer we've been chasing, your security guard deserves a medal."

"I just hope a Board of Inquiry sees it that way," Lawing said with concern in his voice.

Jefferson, Defrange, and Palachi went aboard the cutter, and Pitillo invited them to the bridge.

"You can see better from up here," he said. He gave the order to reverse the ship's engines in order to back into the river, where the headed slightly northeast towards downtown Portsmouth.

Jefferson and Palachi joined Pitillo on the flying bridge, but Defrange wandered out to the port wing. She worked her way down to the air castle and went aft toward the stern.

She seems to need to be alone, Jeff thought.

The Chief bosun and the diver were waiting on the fantail in case they needed to go in after a body, and as the ship made the turn down river, Defrange headed in their direction. The Chief doffed his cap.

"Good mornin', ma'am."

Defrange smiled graciously. "Good morning, Chief."

"Is there something we might do for you, Detective?"

"I hope so," she replied. "Do you know of an area not too far down the river where there are lots of pilings, and maybe some debris left over from some sort of construction?"

The Chief considered for a moment.

"There's a place like that on the port side, behind the new post office. We've been after the construction company to clean up their mess, but so far they haven't done anything."

"Thanks, Chief. That's a great help." Defrange wandered back toward the bridge, and her eyes were green infernos. Jefferson saw her coming.

She knows where the body is.

"Mr. Pitillo!" she called out. "We'll find the body behind the new post office, caught in construction debris. She's trapped in some sort of steel reinforcement rods and pilings."

"She?" Palachi and Jefferson echoed in unison.

"She," Defrange repeated. "The person we're trying to recover is a woman."

"Lawing won't like that," Pitillo commented. "He was worried enough that we shot a civilian, but a woman civilian! I'm sure he never considered that."

Defrange walked back out to the port wing of the bridge, and Jeff followed.

"Have you seen her?" he asked.

"Yes, or at least her energy," Defrange replied. "It's definitely a woman."

Palachi joined them.

"The Raptor's a *woman?*" he asked in disbelief.

"No," Defrange replied. "But she's very close to him. She was on an errand."

"An errand for the Raptor?" Jeff asked.

"Yes—he's left something important on the cabin cruiser, and he sent her to get it."

"What is it?" Palachi asked.

"I don't know," Defrange confessed, "but it must be something incriminating if it was important enough to send her to get it."

Their course changed, and they were moving toward the left bank—toward a seawall where there was a lot of junk sticking out of the water.

"Post office?" Defrange asked.

'Yep," Jeff answered. At that moment they heard the lookout shouting above them.

"Body in the water!" he called, and he switched on a powerful search light.

Palachi crowded to the rail, "Where? I don't see anything," he groused impatiently.

Pitillo joined them, pointing to the base of the seawall.

"There," he said, "you see those pilings? The body is fowled between them and the wall."

"I still can't see," Palachi complained.

The engines slowed, and the swimmer went overboard. The Chief engaged the winch and skillfully hoisted the dive platform into the river.

"Watch the swimmer," Jefferson said to Palachi. "He's swimming right toward the body."

"Oh, yeah!" Palachi replied excitedly. "I see it now!"

In ten minutes, the diver was back to the platform, and the Chief hoisted platform, diver and body onto the fantail. The officers, civilian and military ran to see.

"This guy sure is light!" the diver said as they approached.

Palachi knelt and removed the ski mask from the victim. A profusion of blonde hair spilled onto the platform. He stood up, his eyes glued to the body at his feet.

"It's a woman all right," he said solemnly, "and we know her. Sally Brevet."

Jefferson looked at Defrange, who nodded.

"I felt it," she said, "but I was never quite sure."

"Mr. Pitillo," Palachi asked, "may we go back to the base?"

"Absolutely!" he replied and headed for the bridge.

In a moment the engines revved back to life, and they were underway. Pitillo radioed Lawing, and he was on the dock when they pulled into the slip.

"Dr. Palachi!" he called out. "What's the word?"

Palachi held his comments until he joined Lawing on the dock.

"Mr. Lawing, from gross examination of the body, this person jumped overboard and hit her head. The fact is that she drowned, and there's no evidence of a gunshot wound. I'll know more after the autopsy."

"Thank God," Lawing replied. "Does anyone have any clue as to why she was on Base?"

"We're not sure," Defrange replied, "but we hope to find out."

Lawing took in a long breath. "Well, when you find out, will you please let me know. I'll be pressured to write a report as soon as possible."

Defrange nodded. "Of course. We'll call as soon as Palachi's done."

Palachi accepted the offer of man power from Commander Pitillo, and he directed his men to move the body from the ship to the ME's van.

"I'm gonna do the post, now," Palachi announced. "Lawing needs everything he can get for his report. This is the kind of thing that potentially gets senators' bowels in an uproar."

"Ok," Jeff replied. "We're going to try and get some sleep—at least for a while."

Palachi eyed the two of them for a moment, smiled and walked toward his van.

Defrange yawned, "I'm for that," she said. "I wonder if Martin will call Dr. Winetraub. He'll be lost without Sally."

"I'm sure Palachi will call Winetraub," Jeff replied.

Lieutenant Lawing sat down at his desk and tried to start organizing a report. A noise in the hall interrupted his thoughts, and he glanced up at the seaman standing just outside his office door.

"Whatcha need, sailor?" he asked, motioning for the young man to enter.

"Lieutenant, I'm sorry to bother you—it's probably nothing. The other guys told me to forget about it, but I just didn't feel right."

"Yeah, okay," Lawing said. "What is it? What's bothering you?"

The man laid a gold fountain pen on the edge of the desk.

"I was assigned to watch the cabin cruiser," he said, "you know, after the intruder fell overboard, and I found this. Like I said, some of the other guys told me to keep it, but I couldn't do that, so I'm turning it in to you."

Lawing took note of the man's name tag.

"That's commendable, son. I'll take care of it. You get some sleep, and for your trouble, I'm going to put a commendation in your personnel record. Good going."

"Aye, sir," the sailor said, and with a look of satisfaction, saluted and left the office.

Lawing glanced at the pen, and he returned to organizing his report.

CHAPTER 36

JEFFERSON HAD JUST dozed off but hadn't quite started dreaming when Defrange sat bolt upright. She turned on the light, and Jeff roused.

"Partner! What is it?"

Her eyes looked as if she'd gone mad.

"We have to go!" she said.

"Go where?"

"To the morgue. It's the Raptor, and Palachi's in pain."

That was all Jeff needed to hear. He dressed quickly, but she beat him to the car; and the blue light was on before they peeled out of the garage. Jeff was on the mic as they turned down Leckie Street.

"This is Virginia Creeper: Code One. There's an emergency at the City-County Morgue, and I need all patrols in the vicinity to converge there ASAP. Approach with caution and detain anyone found there other than the Medical Examiner. Any person apprehended may be armed and extremely dangerous. Acknowledge."

"*Virginia Creeper, this is High Street Patrol We're rolling. ETA three minutes.*"

"Roger High Street. Use extreme caution. You may find the Raptor at the morgue."

"*Roger, Virginia Creeper.*"

Jefferson slid the car sideways into the parking lot, and he and Defrange jumped out with their weapons drawn. The High Street patrol car roared in right behind them and followed their lead.

"Cover the exits!" Jeff called out. One of the patrolmen raised his pistol to indicate that he understood, and he started toward the back door while his partner went toward the front.

Jefferson and Defrange went in the rear entrance to the morgue. When they were satisfied it was clear, they used a leap frog advance to move from doorway to doorway down the darkened hall toward the lighted embalming room.

"Stay here!" he whispered to Defrange as she crouched in to doorway across from him.

He took a deep breath, leveled his pistol, and dodged around the doorframe in a low stance. The only illumination was from the operating room light situated over the embalming table: there was no one in sight, other than whoever lay on the table. Jefferson circled, staying just outside the pool of light so that he could clearly see without being seen. Palachi lay there, dressed in his scrubs, a pool of blood around his head. There was the stench of death and chemicals. Jefferson lunged forward.

"Palachi!"

No answer.

"Palachi!" he repeated. There was a moan, and the ME moved his head.

"Palachi!" Can you hear me?"

There was another moan, and his friend moved his arms. Jeff circled to the foot of the table—he caught the odor of bourbon.

"Palachi!" Jeff repeated, shaking his friend's foot. "Wake up!"

Without warning, Palachi sat up.

"Jefferweferson," he belched. "Where have you been?"

The overhead lights came on, and Defrange walked over to the table.

"Martin," Jeff said, "are you alright?"

"Suuuuure, I'm good. Are you good?" he slurred.

Defrange looked at their drunken friend in amusement. Jeff was all confusion.

"Martin, are you intoxicated?" he asked.

Martin held up his thumb and forefinger. "Well, maybe just a little. My head hurts!"

"Nasty gash," Defrange said. She grabbed some gauze from a prep tray, and held it to the back of Palachi's head. The blood had clotted but was beginning to ooze when he sat up.

"Palachi," Jeff asked, "what happened?"

The ME offered a goofy grin. "Well, I was here, and you two were God knows where, and somebody hit me. When I came to, my head hurt so bad I decided to have a little drink, so I finished the Wild Turkey we cracked on Monday. Shit! My head hurts!"

Jeff looked at Defrange, and she winked.

"Well, old pal, we're glad to see you're alive."

"I'm glad to see you too, Jefferweferson. Ya know, I've always liked you"—his head swiveled toward Defrange—"and I like you too, Almyra."

Jeff rolled his eyes. "And we like you too, pal, but what happened to Sally Brevet's body?"

Palachi winced and looked up at the ceiling. "Hmmm. Somebody hit me, and when I woke up, she was gone."

"Who took her?" Jeff asked.

"I don't know," the ME replied, brushing Jeff away. "Whoever hit me, I guess! Is there any of the Wild Turkey left?" he glanced weakly around the room.

Defrange eyes appeared to be glazed. "The Raptor," she said. "He's taken her to the Precinct."

"The Precinct?" Jeff echoed. "Why there?"

"I don't know yet, but that's where she is," Defrange answered."

"Stay here!" Jeff said. "I'm going to the Precinct."

"Alright," Defrange replied. "But be careful."

"Jefferweferson," Palachi groaned, "my head hurts, and now you're leaving again."

"It's ok," Jeff reassured him. "Almyra is going to stay with you."

Palachi looked at her and grinned.

"That's good. I've always liked you, Almyra."

"I've always liked you too, Martin."

Jeff started for the door, and Defrange grabbed his arm.

"Be careful, Partner," she said. "He's in sickbay, and he has her body. That's all I can tell you."

"That's enough for now," Jeff replied. He brushed her lips with his. Her eyes were mint green.

"I'll go check this out if you'll just take care of Palachi."

"Of course," she smiled. "Just remember I love you."

Jeff paused to form the words. They'd never really said it before. "And I love you," he said finally.

He pulled away while he still could.

It was a little before five a.m. when he pulled into the lower parking lot at the Precinct. He entered the building on the basement level. Sickbay and Wintraub's office were at the far end of the building, and Jefferson was headed that way when he ran into a uniformed officer.

"Morning, Lieutenant," the officer greeted him. "You working early or late?"

"Both, I suppose. Anyway, I'm on administrative leave."

"Yeah, I heard about that bullshit," the older man said.

"Can I help you with anything?"

"Yeah, come to think of it. I don't have my work keys on me. Do you have your master key?"

"Yes sir," he replied, waving his keyring.

Jeff studied the man's face for a moment, and what he saw was years of freezing stakeouts, bloody auto accidents, missed birthdays, and too many funerals. He was a veteran, and Jeff could count on him.

"I'm gonna level with you, sir," Jeff said. "I have reason to believe that the Raptor is hiding in sickbay."

The man looked at Jefferson to see if he was joking. Jeff didn't smile.

"You're serious?" he said as his hand dropped to the butt of his pistol.

Jeff glanced at the name tag.

"Yes, sir, Mr. Spires. I am. I want you to come with me, but only if you're willing. This could be deadly."

Spires looked at Jefferson, ignoring the last comment.

"Let's go!" he said.

They walked down the corridor to the door of sickbay and paused to listen: all quiet. Jeff tried the door, but it was locked. Spires handed him the master key which turned easily in the lock, but the click of the tumbler sounded like an explosion down the deserted hallway. Jefferson turned the knob and slowly opened the door.

The only light was from an exam room at the back of the small medical office, and Jeff entered with his pistol drawn. Spires followed with his pistol drawn also. They side-stepped the registration desk and moved toward the lighted exam room.

When they got to the door, Jeff motioned for Spires to stand by as he reached for the privacy curtain that separated the exam area. The metal rings sliding across the curtain rod were like nails on a chalkboard as Jeff jerked the curtain back and dropped to one knee.

"Oh God!" Spires exclaimed.

On the exam table lay the remains of Sally Brevet. Her chest was open, her eyes were gone, and it only took a moment to see that other things were missing. Jeff backed toward the waiting area.

"That's what I was afraid of," he said.

Jefferson and Spires were moving back to the registration area just as the bank of overhead fluorescent lights flickered on. Jeff stepped into the area to face a man he'd never seen before. He was wearing a three-piece suit, and his hands went up when he saw Jefferson's gun pointed at him.

"L-Lieutenant Jefferson," the man stuttered. "Wait! Don't shoot!"

"You'd better freeze," Jeff ordered as the man's hand started toward his chest area.

"Who the hell are you?" Jeff demanded.

"I'm Inspector Rosenthal from the Virginia SBI. I was just reaching for my ID."

"Put your hand back up!" Jeff ordered. He gestured for Spires to check the man's inside coat pocket.

Spires laid his own gun on the desk, well out of reach, and frisked the intruder. He retrieved a .45 identical to Jefferson's, a pair of handcuffs, and a leather ID case. Jeff opened it and compared the picture to the man himself.

"Inspector Nick Rosenthal," he read. "Virginia State Bureau of Investigation."

Jefferson holstered his weapon.

"Inspector, it seems that I owe you an apology, but I've had one hell of a week around here."

Rosenthal lowered his hands.

"I know you have," he said, "and an apology isn't necessary. That's why I'm here. I was just doing some snooping on my own. I didn't know you were in here, or I might have introduced myself a little differently than sneaking up on you in the dark."

"Well, still, I apologize," Jeff said. "We've got a body in the back that was autopsied but since has been mutilated. I was just about to go find whoever put it here."

The Inspector nodded. "You go ahead, Lieutenant. I'm to meet with you and Captain Chambers later today. I think you'll find it all quite interesting."

The phone rang, startling everyone. Jeff grabbed the receiver.

"Jefferson!"

"Hey, buddy. I hoped you'd answer."

"Palachi?"

"Yeah. Look, Defrange took a call right after you left, and I got worried about the two of you."

"Who called?"

"Dr. Winetraub. He told her that the Raptor was holding him hostage on the Lightship, and if she didn't come right away, he'd be killed."

Jeff's heart went to his throat. "Listen carefully Martin! Sally Brevet's body is here in sickbay. Winetraub must have stumbled in at the wrong time, or maybe the Raptor lured him in here. Either way, it sounds like the Raptor has him. How long ago was the call?"

"At least thirty-five…forty minutes. She's had time to get to the Lightship"

"Right. Look, I've got to believe that bastard has the Doc and Defrange— I'm going to the Lightship. Call Pherson and get me some backup!"

"Will do. And then I'm on my way!"

"Do you feel up to that?"

"You're damned right I do—this wound is superficial, and I'm sober as a judge."

Jeff hung up.

"Inspector—"

"Go to it, Lieutenant," Rosenthal said. "I'm not here to interfere, but," and he picked up his .45, "this body will be safe here until somebody comes to pick it up."

"Thanks, yeah, Spires here can see to that. Jeff looked to the older officer. "One more favor?"

"Name it, LT."

"Please call Pherson, and make sure he's heard from Palachi. From his condition the last time I saw him, he might not remember or be able to call."

"You got it, Jefferson."

Jeff ran to the loading dock entrance on the side of the building closest to the Lightship. He opened the door: the hundred-yard distance to the ship looked like a hundred miles. He covered it in about twelve seconds, and stopped at the foot of the gangway to catch his breath. He checked his .45. Satisfied, he eased up the gangway and stepped onto the main deck. All at once his head exploded, and he fell face-first onto the cold, steel deck.

CHAPTER 37

WHEN JEFFERSON CAME to, he was upright on the top of the pilot house, and his hands were tied above his head to the mainmast of the Lightship. He's couldn't know how long he'd been out, but the pain in his shoulders was excruciating. He tried to focus his eyes, and as he did, he saw Defrange up on the bow. She was on her back, spread eagle with her wrists lashed to the forward railing and here ankles tied to the devil's paws from the port and starboard anchor chains. He thought he saw her move.

"Partner!" he called. "Defrange! Can you hear me?"

She looked in his direction: he imagined her eyes were ablaze.

She raised her head. "*Shh!*" she warned.

"Are you okay?" he called in a loud whisper.

"Yes, for the moment," she replied in the same manner.

"Is the Doc alright?"

"Yes and no," she replied.

Jeff began to tug at his bindings. "Does the Raptor have him?"

"Partner," she answered almost aloud. "They're the same person!"

Her words were a blow far worse than the physical one he'd received earlier. What did she mean? Then, after a moment or two, things started to make sense. The Raptor…*Winetraub!* He was a medical person and knew anatomy. He always knew police movements and investigation status. He has a police ID—no forced entry. Hell, they let him in. All according to Defrange's profile. Down to the mousey woman—Sally Brevet. Many mysteries began to dissipate. Winetraub was too obvious to be a suspect, even when Sally was found in the river, no one even considered that the Doc could be involved. *And, he was instrumental in getting Defrange to Portsmouth in the first place. She was his greatest challenge—his greatest fear!*

Suddenly, Jeff heard what sounded like singing in the distance. It was a woman's voice, and it was growing louder.

"Defrange! Where is he?"

"Below deck somewhere. I'm not sure."

"Whistle if he shows up," Jeff said as he tried to loosen his bonds.

While his hands were bound tightly together, he found that he could move them vertically up and down the mast pole. He remembered his knife, hoping that Winetraub hadn't found it. He pulled his hands down as far as he could and twisted his wrists around the steel mast far enough to feel under his collar with his thumbs.

"Thank God!" he whispered as he felt the upper edge of the hilt of the knife.

His efforts were interrupted by louder singing, and the sound of leather soles scraping a steel ladder.

"He's coming!" Defrange warned.

Jefferson strained around so that he could see Winetraub as he emerged from the hatch. When he did see him, his face was so distorted that if he hadn't known him, he'd never have recognized him. Winetraub looked toward Defrange before turning his attention to Jefferson.

"Lieutenant Jefferson," an unfamiliar voice said. "How nice of you to accommodate me. I was so afraid you might miss my, and please excuse the term, intercourse with Detective Defrange."

Jeff shook his head in disbelief. "Doc! What are you doing?"

Winetraub climbed the ladder to the top of the pilot house, walked over to Jefferson and gave him a brain-rattling, Bette Davis slap.

"Oh, don't worry. I plan for you to see it all," the crone's voice announced. And, then I'll take care of you."

Defrange was struggling with her bindings. Jeff *had* to divert Winetraub's attention.

"Who the hell are you?" Jeff asked.

"Me? Why, you silly!" Winetraub cackled. "I'm Constance Dahlgren Cassidy, lately of Morning Glory, Mississippi. I'm here in Portsmouth visiting my grandson! He lacks social graces, I'm sorry to report, and I've had my hands full trying to keep him out of mischief! He's such a little whoremonger I've decided that I must stay here indefinitely."

"I understand," Jeff replied in an effort to keep the man engaged.

"You do *not* understand!" Winetraub shrieked. Jeff saw stars with yet another slap. "If you understood, you wouldn't associate with the likes of her!" He pointed toward Defrange.

"What's wrong with her?"

"What's *wrong?*" Winetraub's crone persona repeated. "Why, that trollop lives in sin with you, and she has visions that can only be attributed to the work of *Satan!* How can you be so stupid? I know she wants my Tad too, and if I don't stop her, she will have him."

The Doc's face contorted, and his eyes grew wide.

"You see, sir," came the voice of a child, "Grammy thinks you're like my daddy, like all other men. She loves me and wants to protect me. Sometimes, she does bad things because she loves me so much."

Defrange was struggling without success, and Jeff tried for more time.

"So, you're Tad, but are you Dr. Winetraub too?"

Winetraub grimaced. "Of course not!" the old woman snapped. "Tad is a little boy, and Milton, unfortunately, is a man who acts like a little boy."

Jeff kept his eyes on Defrange as he addressed Winetraub's freak show. "Well, Grammy, I know some of the people you did bad things to. Why did you kill Mrs. Treadway?"

Winetraub giggled in falsetto. "Because the nosy old bitch saw me, so I really had no choice."

"Saw you when?"

"The night that stupid mortician was going to kill you on Leckie Street. You see, I was following him while he was stalking you."

Jeff heard commotion on the dock. *Pherson with backup.* He hoped everyone would stay calm for just a few more minutes while he continued his conversation.

"I see," Jeff said. "You had no choice about Mrs. Treadway, but what do you know about the Merriweather girl?"

The old woman cackled, and then suddenly it was the Doc's voice.

"Help me, Jefferson!" he begged "Dothan sat that girl out on my dock of all places! My house is just down the river from his, and before I could stop it—"

"I killed her!" The old woman had returned. "And now I'm going to get rid of that whore from Milwaukee!"

Jeff watched in helpless horror as Winetraub started down the ladder toward Defrange—he caught the glint of what appeared to be a scalpel in his hand. He pulled at his knife: he could pull it up far enough to expose the blade. He held it between his thumbs and moved the blade up and down against his bindings until he felt the rope starting to give. He moved faster and faster while he watched the Raptor lean over Defrange and extend the scalpel blade toward her face. Jeff pressed the knife as hard as he could against the ropes, and, suddenly, they gave way.

Defrange started to evade her attacker.

"Oh, bitch!" the old woman assailed her, "it's so good to see you struggle! Don't worry, though. You'll be dead by the time I have those lovely grapes in my pouch!"

He bent closer to Defrange, and Jeff quickly untied his feet while he tried to calculate the distance between himself and the Doc: he would never make it in time.

"Winetraub!" Jefferson screamed, throwing his knife as hard as he could.

Winetraub turned, and the force of the knife hitting him in the chest hilt-first caused him to lose his grip on the scalpel. He fell against the railing just as Jefferson heard the distinct crack of a rifle.

The shot ricocheted harmlessly off the steel rail.

"Bastard!" Winetraub screamed as he and Jefferson dove toward the scalpel and the knife.

Winetraub prevailed, pinning Jeff to the deck and sitting on his chest, wielding the scalpel. Jeff shoved him off and stood up as Winetraub lunged toward him. The detective managed to grab his wrist and kick him in the solar plexus. Winetraub dropped the blade, and Jeff tried to gain ground by running to the ladder that led to the top of the wheelhouse. On the second rung, Winetraub brought him down with a belaying pin. He landed on the deck, winded and groggy as Winetraub approached Defrange again.

"Now, you slut!" the shrill voice proclaimed. "I'll just have those pretty whore's eyes."

Jefferson struggled to his knees and watched in horror as the Raptor put his face to Defrange's. He imagined that the killer was going to kiss her before he killed her, but Winetraub suddenly jerked back with a horrifying scream. Blood spurted from his face. Defrange had bitten off the end of his nose.

"Atta' girl, Partner!" Jeff yelled. He felt a weight at his left ankle. *The Derringer....*

"You bitch!" Winetraub screamed as he regained his balance. "I'm going to kill you first and I'll eat you later, piece by piece!"

He started toward her again with the scalpel. Jeff had time to clear the anchor chains and shove him hard against the forward railing. The Doc gasped, the breath knocked out of him.

"Doc, Doc! It's me! Jefferson! We can help you! Come back!"

There was a moment of recognition, but the return of the Doc's contorted grimace let Jeff know he had lost him. He tried to slash at Jeff with the scalpel as Jeff shoved the Derringer into his chest.

"Doc, please! Doc, it's me! It's Jefferson!"

Winetraub's face contorted again: it was somewhere between an old woman and a wild animal. Jeff nearly shoved him over the railing, pulling both triggers on the Derringer.

The explosion and Winetraub's scream echoed off the Precinct Building and back across the parking lot, yet reverberating as Winetraub hit the water. His body was quickly pulled out into the river by the undertow created by an aircraft carrier on its way to the open sea.

"Partner!" Defrange cried.

Jeff ran over, loosened her hands, and embraced her.

Palachi, Pherson, Spires, the SWAT team and Inspector Rosenthal were standing at the top of the gangway. They had all rushed aboard when the Derringer went off. Palachi ran over to them.

"Are you alright?" he asked.

Defrange gave him an impish look.

"We're fine," she said, "now that Jefferson has stopped screwing around."

Palachi laughed as he untied Defrange's feet while Jeff put his jacket around her shoulders.

"Excuse me, gangway!" came Captain Chambers' voice as he pushed his way through the crowd.

"*Now*, do you believe that you got the Raptor?" he asked.

"I do," Jefferson replied, and Defrange and Palachi nodded in agreement.

"I want you two to get some rest," the Cap smiled. "Come in tomorrow around one, and we'll meet with Inspector Rosenthal. He has some news to share with all of us."

Jeff took Almyra's arm.

"You ready to go, Partner?" he asked, "I guess there's nothing left to do at this moment."

"Hold it!" a familiar voice called out from behind them. "There's one thing left." Jeff turned to a uniformed officer approaching from the crowd.

Jeff grinned. "Oh, yes. As a matter of fact, there is one more thing I had promised to do. Detective Almyra Defrange, I am pleased to introduce you to Sergeant Stanley Pherson, from the Precinct, Portsmouth PD."

Pherson fairly beamed as he gently took Defrange's hand.

"I finally get to meet you. After all this, I finally get to meet you."

"Ohh, Sergeant," Defrange cooed, "we shouldn't be so formal."

Defrange gave him a long, lingering hug, and a light kiss on the lips. Pherson reeled back, his face red and his eyes wide.

"Thank you, m-ma'am," he stuttered. "I'll never forget this."

"Nor I, Sergeant Pherson," Defrange assured him.

Everyone said goodnight, and as the detectives headed for the parking lot, they were joined by the ME. He was full of plans to drag the river and find Winetraub. Jeff looked out to see the first pink rays of daybreak over the Elizabeth.

"Ok, pal," Jeff said when they finally reached the car. We gotta get some sleep. We'll see you later today."

"Sure thing," Palachi said. "What day is it anyhow?"

Jeff checked the date on his watch. "It's June nineteenth, Thursday. Tomorrow's Defrange's birthday. You and Annie got dinner plans?"

"Not that I know of," Palachi replied. "Hey, you two don't' want to come by the Morgue for a nightcap, do you?"

"No!" they answered in stern unison.

CHAPTER 38

THE DETECTIVES MADE it to the Precinct just before one, and they went straight to the Captain's office. They were greeted, as usual, by Marsha.

"Come in!" she welcomed them. "What an exciting night you had!"

"Oh, it was exciting," Defrange said, her tone acknowledging the understatement.

Marsha opened the door to the inner office where Captain Chambers and Inspector Rosenthal were looking out the widows chatting about the view.

"Please, come in," Chambers said as he turned around. "Sit down and be comfortable. Marsha a round of refreshments and then join us if you would."

Marsha disappeared and the four law enforcers discussed the events of the evening before. When she returned, she had a carafe of coffee and several soft drinks or varying varieties.

When everyone was settled with a beverage, the Captain began. "Marsha has something to tell Defrange and Jefferson, and then Inspector Rosenthal will take the floor."

Marsha sat her drink aside and stood up. "Well," she began self-consciously, "about two months ago, the Precinct mainframe computer went down. That in itself is not unusual. I called the service man, and he told me a series of commands to use to regain my bootstrap. I swear, I followed his instructions to the letter, and, as promised, my terminal came back online."

She paused.

"Go ahead!" Chambers urged, pouring himself a cup of coffee. Jeff nearly laughed out loud at the Captain's boyish excitement.

"Well," she continued, "when my terminal came back, I was in an area of the mainframe I'd never seen. The menus and options were totally different from mine, but I found that I was able to look at the different files. That's when I accidentally discovered all this financial information."

"What was it?" Jeff asked eagerly.

Masha smiled.

"It was spreadsheets and financial statements, and deposit slips for the Precinct budget into Commissioner Donaldson's personal bank account. I didn't think that this was standard operating procedure, so I showed it to the Captain, and he said that he would take care of it."

Chambers sat his coffee on the table.

"What I found," he said, "was that Donaldson was embezzling hundreds of thousands of dollars from the City of Portsmouth Police Department. That's when I called the SBI. You're on Inspector?"

Rosenthal cleared his throat.

"What Marsha and the Captain discovered was the tip of an iceberg. Review of the hidden files by our forensic accountants showed that Donaldson had not only diverted money from the police budget, but he's skimmed from other city accounts too. It totals a couple of million dollars so far. I arrested him this morning."

Jefferson and Defrange looked at each other in disbelief.

"This is too good!" Jeff observed. "The Raptor, Dothan, and Donaldson all at the same time."

"That's all true," the Captain agreed, "but now that we have those problems out of the way, we have others to take their place."

"Sir?" Jeff asked.

Chambers smiled. "The City Council had an emergency meeting this morning shortly after Donaldson's arrest, and I've been appointed Police Commissioner."

Jeff stood and grabbed the Captain's hand.

"That's great, Cap. Nobody deserves it more than you. Congratulations!"

"Thank you, Lieutenant, but please sit down. That's just the beginning of it."

"Sir?" Jeff said as he sat back down.

"Jefferson, by a unanimous decision of the City Council, you have been appointed interim Police Captain."

Jefferson was stunned. "No…."

"Yes," the Captain countered.

"Just a minute, sir," Jeff begged. "There are lots of people who deserve this more than I do."

The Captain shook his head, "Not according to a vote by your fellow police officers and the City Council."

Defrange reached over and took Jefferson's hand.

"Can I think it over?" Jeff asked.

The Cap broke into uproarious laughter. "You see, Rosenthal," he said, "I told you. I told you that's what he'd say. Of course, the answer is 'yes you can think it over', and you're officially off until Monday morning. I trust we can have your answer by then."

"Fair enough," Jefferson agreed. "But I won't know what to do with myself until Monday."

Chambers winked at Defrange.

"C'mon, Lieutenant," he said. "I have every confidence that you'll find *something* to do."

Marsha giggled and blushed as everyone stood.

"All right, Capt—I mean, Commissioner," Jeff said. I'll be to work Monday morning with your answer."

The Coast Guard buoy tender *Evergreen* had just pulled in her drag nets for the twentieth time since early morning.

"Fuckin' Medical Examiner!" one seaman complained as he sorted through the debris on the deck. "This is a big river, and I don't think we're gonna find a body. It's probably washed out to the Chesapeake Bay by now."

Another seaman echoed his comrade's sentiments until something in the net caught his eye. He waded over to retrieve it.

"Hey, Chief! Look at this!"

Chief McBains, who looked like he'd just come from central casting, shut off the noisy crane engine.

"Bring in over here, squid! The Chief hollered. "Lemme see what you got."

The man obeyed, slipping through the slime toward his superior.

"Looks like one of the vests we use in riot training," the seaman commented.

The Chief took the bullet-proof vest and turned it over to see the reverse side.

"Yeah, it does," he agreed. He walked over to the bulkhead and took the mic for the ship's PA system.

"Now hear this," he called. "Duty Gunner's Mate lay to the focsle."

"You men take a break!" he called out. The soaked seamen didn't wait for a second invitation. *"But,"* McBains added. "You be on the mess deck when I need you!"

A First-Class Gunner's Mate appeared from below.

"Yeah, Chief," he said. "Whatcha need?"

McBains handed him the vest.

"Is this one of ours?"

The man looked carefully at the exterior of the vest, turning it inside-out.

"Well," he said, "it *is* Kevlar, but it's *not* military issue."

"Then whose is it?" the Chief asked.

The Gunny checked the seams and studied the vest for a minute.

"Worse guess," he said, "some militia group. Best guess is that it belongs to the cops, but look at these burns, here. They're right over the left chest. Whoever was wearing this got hit, and I mean *got hit hard!*"

"Ok, Guns. Thanks," the Chief replied. He took the vest to the bridge.

"Sir," he addressed the Ensign in charge of the *Evergreen*. *"I think* we've found something important."

"Really? What is it?" the impervious officer asked.

"It's a bullet-proof Kevlar vest," McBains explained, "and the gunner's mate doesn't think it's military."

"What's your point, Chief?" the Ensign asked impatiently.

"Well, sir, it may be nothing, but whoever was wearing this may be injured. I'd like permission to send a message to the Portsmouth Police to see if it means anything to them."

The newly graduated officer was unimpressed.

"Chief McBains," he said dismissively, "just put that with the other junk we've found. If you want to call the Police when we get back to base, you have my permission."

"Aye, sir."

"And get those men off break!"

"Aye sir," the Chief repeated, and he left the bridge.

"Marlowe!" he called to Second-class bosun's mate on the main deck.

"Yeah, Chief. What can I do for you?"

"Go get the lads off the mess deck and have them stand by on the fantail. I'll be out there in a few minutes."

"Will do, Chief," Marlowe replied as he headed for the mess deck.

McBains went to the radio control room.

"Sparky," he said to the radioman.

"What can I do for you, Chief?"

"I need to send a little unauthorized communication."

"Sure, Chief. Your girl waiting for you?" he asked jovially.

McBains smiled. "No, but I wish! I need for you to radio the Portsmouth Police and let them know that we've found a Kevlar vest. It's got number 49832 stamped on it, and I think it belongs to them. These things are expensive, and I think they may want it back. I just need for this to be blind to the bridge. It seems that our new Commanding Officer is the result of too much formal education. He doesn't seem the understand the subtleties of the real world."

"I understand, Chief," Sparky said. "Consider it sent."

"Thanks, Sparky. You can count on a pitcher of beer on me tonight."

The message *was sent*, and it *was* received, and it was put in a pending file where it stayed for nearly a week.

CHAPTER 39

FOR THE DETECTIVES, the rest of Thursday was a passionate blur followed by dinner of soup and grilled cheese sandwiches. Since Friday was Defrange's birthday, Jeff asked her if she's like to go out and celebrate early. He asked what she might like to do.

"Stay home."

"But tomorrow's your birthday—don't you want to do something special?"

Defrange smiled. "Staying home with you is the most special thing we could do. Maybe dinner tomorrow night, but for now, I just want to be here with you."

Jeff looked at her. She was serious, and that suited him.

They did laundry together like some old married couple. Defrange fell asleep during the evening news while he read...for a while. He awoke around midnight, and Defrange was still sound asleep on the sofa.

He nudged her. "Partner," he whispered, "you wanna go to bed?"

She opened her eyes and stretched before she raised up and kissed him.

"Sure," she said, "as long as you're going with me."

"I wouldn't miss it," he said.

They struggled up the stairs and fell into bed. Jefferson was asleep immediately, and he dreamed...

Their wedding was in the Lee Chapel in Lexington, Virginia. Almyra was beautiful in her nineteenth century wedding gown. Jeff wore the dress uniform of a Confederate Lieutenant. The short ceremony was surrounded by friends and family.

As they left the Chapel, they were attended by a Confederate honor guard. Jeff laughed when the Captain of the Guard, in the order of tradition, swatted Almyra on the butt with the flat side of his saber. She squealed delightfully.

They started for their carriage and Jeff looked up and saw him: General Lee was a'mount Traveler, who reared impatiently. The General removed his hat.

"Congratulations, Lieutenant, and best wishes to you Madam!"

Jefferson saluted, and Almyra curtsied.

"Thank you, General," Jeff said.

"I know you two were intended for each other," he said, "and I wish you both a long and happy life together."

"Thank you, Sir," Jeff repeated, and he helped Almyra into the carriage.

They moved slowly through the streets of Lexington. People lined the boulevards to wish them well. Suddenly, there was a scream – a Yankee attack!

Jeff shot up in bed. The screams were coming from Defrange. He turned on the lamp on the bedside table.

"Partner?"

Her green eyes were ablaze as she stood looking out the window. He put his arms around her.

"It's horrible!" she gasped.

"What is it?"

"I have to go now," she replied.

"Go where? It's the middle of the night."

"Milwaukee!" she said.

"C'mon, Partner. You're having a bad dream. "Let's go back to bed."

She pulled away from him. "No, I can't," she insisted. "I have to go."

Jeff knew that until her eyes returned to normal, there was no need to argue with her. The phone rang loudly, and Jefferson grabbed it from the nightstand.

"This is Jefferson," he growled.

"Lieutenant Jefferson, this is Pherson, down at the Precinct. I have a call from Police Chief Polanski in Milwaukee, and I need Detective Defrange's number."

Jeff's newfound world began to disintegrate.

"Patch it, Pherson," he said. "She's here with me."

"Ok, Lieutenant. Hold on."

He handed the phone to Defrange.

"It's for you."

"This is Defrange," she said. She listened for a moment or two. "Yes sir, I understand. Flight 1036, Norfolk International."

Jeff couldn't believe what he was hearing. He pounced as soon as he hung up.

"Partner, do you wanna tell me what's going on?"

She looked at him with her sad, green pools.

"I just dreamed a murder in Milwaukee," she said. "A young woman was being killed close to my home in New Berlin, and now Chief Polanski has confirmed that it actually happened. It's real, and I have to go. The brutality of the whole thing is beyond the usual homicide. It's more …it's like—"

"Like what?" Jeff demanded to know.

Defrange sighed. "It's like the Raptor, and the Chief wants me back immediately. He's afraid we have a copycat killer."

Jeff started to protest, but then he suddenly remembered his speech about how being a cop is not just a job but a calling. He remembered that all of her Mr. Rights had never been able to understand what she did or why she did it, and he knew what *he* had to do.

"When do you have to be there?"

"Flight 1036 leaves at 4:55 A.M., and they've already booked me. I have to pick up my ticket at the airline desk."

He looked at the clock. It was 3:36.

"All right," he ceded, "we'll have to hurry. If you wanna get a shower, I'll get your things out of the dryer."

As Jeff listened to the sound of the shower, he couldn't help but remember the joyous place it had been a short time ago. He went downstairs, retrieved Defrange's clothes and packed them.

The conversation on the way to the airport was little more than small talk. Jeff parked, and they scrambled to the desk. It was 4:40, and the first call for the flight came as they headed for the boarding area. Jefferson was numb.

They showed their badges to the officer at the metal detector, and he allowed them to pass around behind the machine. They reached the boarding area just as the clerk announced the final call for 1036. Defrange took charge.

"Sir," she said, "I'm Detective Almyra Defrange, and I need for you to hold 1036 for a couple of minutes."

He was initially unimpressed.

"Sure, you do," he sneered. "Who do you think you are?"

Defrange produced her badge, and she turned cop.

"Young man, you get on that microphone, and you have them hold that goddamned bird, or I'll arrest you for obstruction of justice."

His attention level immediately changed.

"Ten-thirty-six," he called, "this is the terminal, and I have a request form the police the you hold your departure for a few minutes. Detective Almyra Defrange will be boarding momentarily."

"*Roger terminal, will do, but ask her to hurry, please.*"

Almyra turned to Jefferson. His heart was breaking.

"Happy birthday," he offered.

She smiled. "It was," she replied, hugging him.

"I guess this is it," he said.

Tears welled in her eyes. "No," she said, "this is not 'it'."

"It sure feels like *it* to me," he said.

They kissed deeply until the clerk's radio broke into their bliss.

"*Terminal this is ten-thirty-six. Would you please tell the detective that my time's up. I have a hundred and sixteen souls out here, and they all need to be somewhere else as soon as I can get them there.*"

Defrange pulled away, the color of her eyes darkened by four shades. She picked up her tote.

"Tell 'em I'm on the way," she growled.

"I love you," she whispered to Jeff, brushing her lips with his once more.

"You too," he smiled weakly.

With that, she turned and strutted across the tarmac.

The clerk watched her as she approached the boarding ramp.

"Wow!" he said. "What a woman!"

"Sir," Jefferson replied, "you have no idea."

He rushed up to the observation deck where they had arrested Dothan just a few days before. He watched helplessly as Flight 1036 backed away and taxied to the far end of the runway. Fire blasted from the tail as the nose lifted and the 737 charged down the runway, making its rendezvous with the sky. He kept his eye on the jet as it veered north, pulling his heart right along with it.

Back in his car, he sped along the Virginia Beach Expressway. He was almost to the Downtown Tunnel when his radio squawked.

"*Virginia Creeper, this is Digger one, over.*"

Jeff picked up the mic.

"Hey, Palachi. What's up?"

"*Jefferson! Where have you been? I've been calling you at home and there was no answer. I got worried since you're supposed to be off 'til Monday. Where are you?*"

"Just on the Norfolk side of the Downtown Tunnel. What's up with you?"

"*I had a call about 2:00 this morning. A couple of sailors got into it: one of them ended up dead. I was just wondering if you and Defrange wanted to meet me at the Merrimack for breakfast.*"

"Sure. I'll meet you. When?"

"*I'll be done with my dictation in five minutes, and I'll have to shower so, say forty minutes?*"

"I'll be there."

"*This is Digger one, out.*"

"This is Virginia Creeper. I'm out and clear."

EPILOGUE

He peered cautiously over the edge of the roof. The flashing blue and red lights—and the appearance of the Medical Examiner's van—had rekindled his erection.

"*Ohhh*," he moaned as he masturbated and ejaculated into space.

With a feeling of sheer delight, he reached into his special, leather treasure pouch and took out a treat. After all, tonight had been perfect.

He slowly and deliberately chewed as he watched the excitement across the street. The sight of the policemen, the men in white lab coats, and the general dread in the chaos below sent him into a trembling fit that went beyond arousal.

"They're going in to see Sharon," he whispered aloud, "but she's in the bathtub, so they'll have to let themselves in."

With one final look, he ran across the roof and descended the fire escape on the back side of the building. The sound of the busy harbor tugs signaling to each other on Lake Michigan drowned out the clicking of his footsteps and his low laughter as he disappeared into the cool Wisconsin night.

"Defrange will be home soon."

Printed in the United States
By Bookmasters